RED SKY
AT NOON

Also by Simon Sebag Montefiore

FICTION
The Moscow Trilogy
Sashenka
One Night in Winter

CHILDREN'S FICTION
The Royal Rabbits of London
(with Santa Montefiore)

NON-FICTION
Jerusalem: The Biography
Catherine the Great and Potemkin
Stalin: The Court of the Red Tsar
Young Stalin
Titans of History
The Romanovs: 1613–1918

RED SKY
AT NOON

SIMON SEBAG MONTEFIORE

PEGASUS BOOKS
NEW YORK LONDON

RED SKY AT NOON

Pegasus Books, Ltd.
148 West 37th Street, 13th Floor
New York, NY 10018

ISBN: 978-1-68177-673-6

10 9 8 7 6 5 4 3 2 1

Printed in the United States of America
Distributed by W. W. Norton & Company, Inc.

TO MY SON,
SASHA

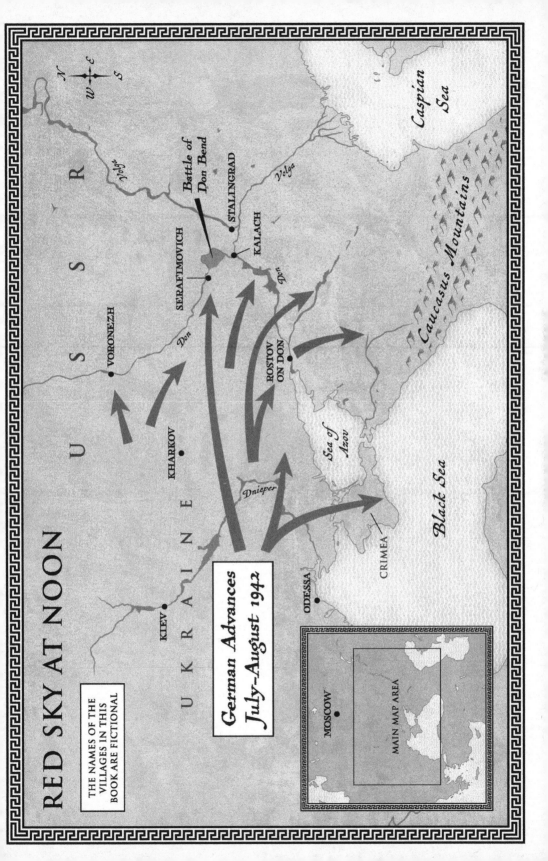

RED SKY AT NOON

THE NAMES OF THE
VILLAGES IN THIS
BOOK ARE FICTIONAL

German Advances
July–August 1942

Caspian
Sea

U S S R

Volga

Volga

Battle of
Don Bend

STALINGRAD

SERAFIMOVICH

KALACH

Don

VORONEZH

Don

Caucasus Mountains

U
S
S

ROSTOV
ON DON

KHARKOV

U K R A I N E

Dnieper

Sea of
Azov

CRIMEA

Black Sea

KIEV

ODESSA

MOSCOW

MAIN MAP AREA

On 22 June 1941, Adolf Hitler launched Operation Barbarossa, his invasion of the Soviet Union, which was ruled by its dictator Josef Stalin. It was to be the most savage war of annihilation ever fought. Taken totally by surprise, the Russians lost vast numbers of men, tanks, planes and territory in the early months as the Germans fought their way towards Moscow. But the Germans were thrown back.

Early in 1942, Hitler planned a new knockout blow. Stalin expected another attack on Moscow but instead Hitler launched Case Blue, an offensive across Ukraine, and then the vast flat grasslands of southern Russia, towards the Don and Volga Rivers, and southwards to seize the oil fields of the Caucasus. The Nazis were aided by their allies: the Italian Fascist dictator, Benito Mussolini, sent an army of 235,000 Italians to help in the assault.

That summer, Soviet forces collapsed and tens of thousands of soldiers were surrounded while hosts of Russian or Cossack anti-Communists turned traitor and collaborated with the Nazis. If the Germans broke into the Caucasus, there was a real danger they could link up with their forces in the Middle East — and the war would be lost.

Soon the mighty Don River was all that stood between defeat and survival. Beyond the Don was a city on the Volga River, now known as Stalin City.

Stalingrad.

This was the desperate, uncertain moment that the characters in this novel joined the war . . .

'My name is Nothing, my surname is Nobody.'

Order 227

'It is time to finish retreating. Not one step back! ...
Panic-mongers and cowards must be exterminated on the
spot ... These are the orders of our Motherland ...
Military councils of the fronts and front commanders
should: Form within each front one to three penal battalions (800 persons) where officers and soldiers who have
been guilty of a breach of discipline due to cowardice or
panic will be assigned, and placed at the most difficult
sectors of the front to give them an opportunity to redeem
their sins by blood ...'

Josef Stalin, People's Commissar of Defence
Moscow, 28 July 1942

A Cossack rode to a distant land;
Riding his horse over the steppe.
His home village he left forever.
He'll never come back again.

Cossack song

RED SKY
AT NOON

Prologue

The red earth was already baking and the sun was just rising when they mounted their horses and rode across the grasslands towards a horizon that was on fire. There are times in a life when you live breath by breath, jolt by jolt, looking neither forward nor backwards, living with a peculiar intensity, and this was one of those times.

They had come out of the clump of poplar trees where they had spent the night, sleeping on their horse blankets, their heads on their saddlebags, fingers curled around their pistols, saddles and rifles lying beside them. Their horses stood over them, soft muzzles savouring the air, deep brown eyes watching the masters whom they knew so well.

The captain awoke them one by one. They saddled the horses, tightening the girths under their bellies, inspecting hooves and fetlocks, stroking withers or neck, talking to them in lullaby voices. The horses tossed their heads at the horseflies that tormented them, their chests shivering, tails swishing, rolling their eyes at what lay just beyond the trees.

The horsemen scanned the plains fretfully, each knowing that their future was as ominous as the land was boundless. Their struggle under the burning sun made no sense – they were hunted as well as hunters – yet their thoughts were not hopeless, not at all, for each of them had known hopelessness before, and this was far better. Here they could be redeemed by the blood of their mission: they believed this with a baleful conviction, and for some of them it was the first decent thing they had ever done . . .

They turned to their horses, whom they loved above all things, giving them some fodder and hay that they carried in a net on the saddles. The horses needed calming, but the grooming, the loving care, the routine of so many mornings, reassured the animals.

The swab of sun had turned the sky a pinkened yellow yet the horizon behind them was jet black with a slow-billowing plume of smoke so solid in appearance that it resembled the domes of a dark cathedral. In the distance the crump of battle. It was already hot, burning hot, and there were jewel-drops of sweat on every man's nose and upper lip. There was a wind but it too was burning, a swirl of blackened straws of stubble and the chaff of wheat. The grass had turned blond with the slanting golden rays of invincible summer.

Pantaleimon, the oldest of the band, extinguished the night's campfire, treading the ashes into the earth, and packed the coffee pot into his saddlebags, which were a sort of movable shop of food and tools and supplies. 'Never throw anything away,' he would say. 'Everything has its moment, brother, everything's useful in the end.'

The Cossacks called each other 'brother' just like the Communist Party members called each other 'comrade'. Pantaleimon, always known as 'Panka', pressed Benya Golden on the shoulder. 'Be cheerful, Golden,' he said. 'It's always sunny on the steppe.' Then they checked the sabres were in their scabbards, the guns over their shoulders, the zinc ammunition boxes packed into the leather pouches, the dried meat, bread and sugar and rolled-up horse blankets in the bags behind the saddles. They had left nothing behind . . . nothing, that is, except the body that lay down the slope from them, with the blood blackening like a ridge of tar on its throat. Benya glanced at it but only for a moment; he had become accustomed to the dead.

'I don't think he's going to miss us, do you?' said Mametka in his high-pitched voice. He was tiny – he claimed to be five foot – with the rosebud lips of a faun and a voice so girlish and eyes so childishly tameless that the Criminals in the Camps had nicknamed him 'Bette Davis'.

They were lost behind enemy lines and Benya Golden sometimes felt they were the last men left alive in the world. But their little squad wasn't a typical Red Army unit. These were sentenced men, and the rest of the army called them the Smertniki, the Dead Ones. Yet these men would never die in Benya's mind. Later, he found they were always with him, lifelike, in his dreams – just as they were that day. Some had been in prison for murder or bank robbery, some for stealing a husk of maize, many merely for the misfortune of being surrounded by German forces. Only he, Benya, was a Political and this meant he had to be even more careful: 'My name is Nothing, my surname is Nobody,' was his motto. This discretion had once been a challenge for him; now they were all beyond the control of the Organs or even the military.

It was July 1942 and the Red Army was falling apart, Stalin's Russia was on the verge of destruction, and the distrust and paranoia of the Camps still gnawed at each of them. Having broken through enemy lines at a terrible cost, adrift on the endless blond sea of the grasslands, they had one more mission to pull off.

Benya tested the girth of his horse, Silver Socks: 'Better to forget your pants and ride naked than forget your girth,' the older man, Panka, had taught him. 'A loose girth means a ride with the angels!'

They were ready. Their captain, Zhurko, gestured with a small motion of his head: 'Mount your horses. Time to ride out.'

Prishchepa, his spiky hair gilded into a metallic sheen by the sun, had lost none of his easy, feral joy. Spurs chinking, he vaulted into the saddle, laughing, and his horse, Esperanza, as playful a daredevil as he, tossed her head with the game. Benya wondered at Prishchepa's capacity for happiness, even here: wasn't that the greatest gift on earth? To be happy anywhere.

He watched as Panka, who must have been at least sixty, laid a light hand on his mount's withers and mounted Almaz without bothering with the stirrups. He had a slight paunch but he was sinuous, strong, effortless. Not all of them were so gentle with the horses and it showed. When Garanzha approached Beauty, she flattened her ears and rolled her eyes. All the horses were scared of 'Spider' Garanzha and no wonder; Benya was scared of him too. His lumpy, shapeless head looked as if it had been hewn out of wood by a wild blind man with an axe; his mouth was a tiny-teethed scarlet gash and he was covered from head to foot in long, straight black hair. He never rushed but moved with a hulking slowness that always stored the energy of concentrated menace. And then there was 'Smiley', the Chechen, who from a distance was lean with noble features and that prematurely grey hair which makes Caucasian men so handsome – until he was happy enough or angry enough, and then, thought Benya Golden, you knew . . .

Benya was last, always last. Agonizingly stiff, his thighs were chafed and arse bruised by so long in the saddle. He had only learned to ride properly during his short spell of training, and now he placed his booted left foot in the stirrup and huffed as he pulled himself up and into the saddle.

'Careful, Granpa!' Young Prishchepa caught him by the shoulder and held him with an iron grip until Benya was steady.

Panka, whose white whiskers and topknot placed his youth before the first war, chewed a spod of tobacco and sucked on his moustache vigorously, usually a sign of amusement.

Men rode as differently as they walked and their horses each had life stories, charges and retreats, crises and triumphs on this frontier that their riders knew and understood, as if they were their children. And as they moved off, each whispered their own salutations. '*Klop, klop*, graceful lad,' said Panka to Almaz, his roan stallion, while Prishchepa leaned close to blow over Esperanza's white-tipped ears, which perked forward and then flattened with pleasure. Benya, a Muscovite who had spent some of his life in Spanish cafés and Italian villas, chanted catechismic praise like a rabbi's haunting prayers to Silver Socks, his high-handed dark chestnut Don mare with the white blaze on her forehead and white front legs that earned her the name. Silver Socks turned her gleaming neck round towards Benya, and he stretched forward, slipping his arms around her. He loved this horse as much as he had ever loved a person. Besides, he reflected, he had never needed anyone as much as he needed Socks now.

Captain Zhurko raised his hand, his shirt already stained with sweat, his peaked summer cap low over his spectacles. 'If you're scared, don't do it,' he called to his men. 'If you do it, don't be scared!'

For a moment the seven men looked out over the scorched steppe. Their faces were already coated with dust: dust was in their eyes, in their mouths and nostrils, in their clothes. Pungent eye-watering dust hung in the air as they rode over clover and lavender and meadow grass.

Captain Zhurko wiped his spectacles and stared out. 'I was thinking about my son,' he said to Benya, the member of the unit with whom he had most in common. 'His mother tells him he doesn't have to work at his studies. I blame her . . .' How quaint it sounded to Benya to hear a man grumble about normal things amidst this pandemonium.

Now Benya started thinking about the body. They had all seen it, understood what it meant and nobody said a word, no surprise, no questions. They had known him well, after all. But they knew death well too. In the Camps, death came fast as a breath. Bodies loomed dark out of the snow as the ice thawed — where they had fallen or been shot in the back of the head by a guard. Sometimes men walked with death on their shoulder for days: there was something about the glassiness of their eyes, the beakiness of their noses, the sunkenness of their cheeks, and they were dead in the morning lying in their bunks in the barracks with their mouths wide open. Benya knew they would not let the body with its tracks of brown-black blood spoil their concentration or distract them from their mission.

Zhurko was still talking about his son's laziness — his refusal to study, heavy smoking, and his seemingly indefatigable self-abuse. Benya looked around him. His fellow mavericks might never be as at home in a family as they were in this unit. All across the steppe, on both sides, strange misfits had found a place in the hierarchies of this cruel chaos. Benya wondered if there had ever been a more terrible moment on earth than this one. Zhurko was the one straight man in this posse, the only one who, if he lived, could return to a normal job in civilian life, an accountant or manager, someone wearing a suit, the sort of guy you might see on the Moscow Metro swinging a briefcase. He was fair to the men and imperturbable under fire and it was a measure of his coolness that he did not bother to comment on what he had seen.

The plains were almost flat, broken up with bowers of willows and poplars but mostly they stretched forth, a wilderness of high grass sometimes swaying and rich with yellow-headed, black-faced sunflowers, the horizon interminable, the sky fast-changing from scarlet to yellow to lilac: a hazy, dusty, grainy luminosity. The sheer beauty of this vastness gave Benya a sense of floating helplessness that allowed him to live in the present and not try to understand anything other than his intimation that he was a weary man longing to stay alive for one more bewildering day.

In the distance, squadrons of tanks like steel cockroaches ploughed up the coffee-brown dust. They were heading towards the Don, and sixty miles beyond it lay Stalingrad.

In the ripped-open sky above, planes swooped through the haze, Yaks duelling with Messerschmitts. Close to them, a German Storch, watching the Russian forces, resembled a clumsy pterodactyl, Benya thought. The Nazi advance over the last few weeks had been so fast that the steppes were now chaotic. Whole Russian armies had been captured in German encirclements; many traitors had defected to the German side, others left behind on the steppes. Out there in the cauldron of blood it was not just German vs Russian, Nazi vs Communist but also Russian vs Russian, Cossack vs Cossack, Ukrainians against everyone, and everyone against the Jews . . .

On the roads and the open steppe, peasants with carts stacked with their paltry belongings trekked back or tramped forward, weary and stoical, confused by the advances and retreats of the soldiers. And in villages, woods and high grass, Jews were hiding, lost people who claimed to have witnessed things that sounded incredible in their maleficence. Far from their shabby Bessarabian villages or great Russian cities of Odessa and Dnieperpetrovsk, they fled alone, just darting from haystack to barn, seeking sanctuary.

'All right, squadron forward,' said Captain Zhurko as if there was a full squadron, as if so many of them had not died, as if there were not just seven of them – and the eighth member wasn't seething with flies just behind the copse. 'Let's lope and cover some distance before the heat. Ride on, bandits!'

They walked at first, Captain Zhurko followed by Little Mametka on his tiny pony that Benya thought was not much taller than a big dog, then Panka on Almaz followed by Spider Garanzha with the rest of them bringing up the rear.

They loped through a sunflower field, divebombed by sparrows. Prishchepa leaned over and grabbed the wide, happy heads of the flowers and shook out the seeds, pouring them into his mouth as if this was a day out with his pals. And as the flat land dipped slightly in tribute to the stream that ran before them like a trickle of mercury in the sun, they spotted the mirror flash in the village far ahead, and through the binoculars Zhurko saw horses and field-grey men and khaki metal.

They checked and rechecked their weapons. Panka rode alongside Benya now. Chewing on his whiskers, he put a huge hand, dark as teak, on his arm. 'This is big country,' he said. 'You've got to stretch yourself just to keep up with it.'

Benya looked into Panka's narrow eyes, not much more than glinting wrinkles in that weather-beaten, foxy face, but blessed with almost miraculously sharp sight. Panka never ceased scanning the steppes, listening for the sounds of birds, the bark of deer, the grumble of engines. 'That's a swallow,' he might say. Or: 'That's the grunt of a buck on the rut.' He might point ahead. 'Watch out! A gopher's burrow there.' Then there were the planes: 'It's one of ours, a tank-killer.' Or a gun: 'That's an eighty-eight millimetre.' He always knew.

The adrenalin pumped into Benya's throat, making his palms slimy, his belly churn and, for a moment, the heat made him dizzy. His parents were somewhere out there. Sometimes he knew they were dead and he wanted to join them, but today hope surged and he was sure he would find them. For a moment, he recalled the woman he had loved in Moscow. He smelled the skin on Sashenka's throat, admired her grey eyes, the sinews in her neck straining as they made love – it was all so vivid that it made him ache. Life after her was truly an afterlife, ground down to its essentials: trial and the Camps. He had been at war for months now but somehow this simple life, this lethal struggle, the company of Cossacks and their horses in the realm of sunflowers and grass, this empire of dust and horse sweat and gun oil, made him feel more alive than he could remember. If you had asked him later if he had been afraid, he would have said, 'Afraid? More terrified than you can ever know.' And yet beyond fear too. 'We are singing a song,' wrote Maxim Gorky, the great writer who had once been so kind to Benya, 'about the madness of the brave.' Benya was riding to kill a man, perhaps many men, and, struck with a presentiment of catastrophe, he was unlikely to survive. But he still believed in his own luck. He had to. They all had to.

We in this country were raised with death, tutored in killing. Death was the booted, belted joker whose heels we heard clicking up our stairs, stomping through our woods, visiting our neighbors for a shot of vodka in the night. Killing is the one thing Russia does well, smiled Benya. Yes, really well.

As she headed through the sunflowers, Silver Socks turned her head to the right, ears pricked, and Benya Golden felt her shorten her stride. She was telling him something. Panka and Prishchepa were already dismounting, guns cocked. Benya rested his hand on the PPSh sub-machine gun hanging over his shoulder.

If you die now, he told himself, you died long before . . .

Day One

I

'Stand up, Prisoner Golden!'

Benya stood, his knees buckling. It was two years earlier, the winter of 1940, and the three judges were filing into the plain room in the Sukhanovka Special Prison. In front of him were two fat grey men in uniform and boots, and the third he knew, not just from the newspapers, but in person. Slim and lean in his Stalinka tunic and high boots, his nose aquiline, grey-black hair *en brosse*, Comrade Hercules Satinov, a favourite of Stalin and member of the Politburo, took the right-hand chair. Once Benya had been excited to know such potentates, proud that Stalin knew who he was. Such sickening folly in his younger, restless self! Now he wished they had never even known of his existence.

Benya also recognized the man in charge, a shaven-haired bulldog in uniform with a patch of moustache under a puce nose that was the texture of pumice stone. Vasily Ulrikh, Stalin's hanging judge.

'I, V.S. Ulrikh,' he droned, 'presiding, declare this sitting of the Military Tribunal to be in session here in Special Object 110.' He meant Sukhanovka Prison. 'It is four thirty a.m. on the twenty-first of January 1940. Considering the case of Golden, Beniamin.'

13

It was the middle of the night? Benya looked at Ulrikh's scar-puckered face first, still not quite believing that they could possibly find him guilty when his only mistakes were childish curiosity – and falling in love with the wrong woman. But in Ulrikh's boozy, watery eyes he saw only a bored disgust and Benya recalled with a shudder that the judge was said not only to attend executions but sometimes do the job himself.

Benya savoured the strong smell of cigarettes, vodka, coffee, pickles emanating from the judges – the fug of grown men without sleep in airless offices. It was familiar, reminding him of long happy nights when writers sat up till dawn in Muscovite kitchens to bicker about that bestselling poet, or the best movie, or the latest scandal . . . A life gone forever.

Glancing down at the papers in front of him, wiping his fuchsia-tinged eyelids, Ulrikh read: 'Golden, Beniamin has signed a confession admitting to his crimes and he is hereby found guilty of terrorism, of conspiracy to murder Comrades Stalin, Molotov, Kaganovich and Satinov (who is present on this tribunal), and of membership of a counter-revolutionary Trotskyite group, connected to White Guardists, controlled by Japanese and French secret services, under Article 58.8.'

'No, no!' Benya heard his own voice, high-pitched, from somewhere far away.

Ulrikh pivoted to the right. 'Comrade Judge Satinov, would you read the sentence?'

Satinov did not reveal the slightest emotion but then Stalin's grandees were masters of sangfroid. They had to be.

He coolly raised his eyes to Benya: 'In the name of the Union of Soviet Socialist Republics, the Military Tribunal of the Supreme Court has examined your case and you are hereby

sentenced by the Military Tribunal to *Vishnaya Mera Naka-
zaniya*, to be shot.'

The words – the Highest Measure of Punishment – hit
Benya in a hot rush, winding him. Suddenly he couldn't breathe
and he gulped frantically for air. He was close enough to see
Ulrikh scrawl the fatal initials: 'V. M. N.' – known as the
'Vishka'; everything in Russia, every department, every job,
even killing, had its sinisterly neat acronym. But this was a
mistake, a terrible mistake! The words bounced around his head.
He knew how the Vishka worked because, ever the curious
writer, he had once asked a top Chekist how they killed their
prisoners, a question he had asked in the naive certainty that he
himself would never face this moment. We take them to a cell
deep under the streets, he was told. Two guards hold their arms
while, quickly, before the prisoner can think, a third fires Eight
Grammes from his Nagant pistol into the spot where your neck
meets your head. Finally there is the 'control shot' to the
temple.

'I didn't confess. Never! I didn't . . .'

Ulrikh sighed, whispered to Satinov and showed him a wad
of papers.

'I have in front of me your signed confession, Prisoner
Golden,' said Ulrikh.

'It's false! I'm not guilty of anything!'

'Quiet, prisoner!' shouted Ulrikh, banging the table.

'Did you or did you *not* sign this?' asked Satinov in his
Georgian accent.

'No!' Benya replied. 'You see, I had no choice – I was beaten.
My confession was forced out of me. I deny everything, I was
tortured . . .'

Ulrikh wiped his flat face with a liver-spotted hand. It had been a long vodka-fuelled night of Vishkas – prisoners condemned and executions attended – and Benya could see he wanted to send his report to Comrade Stalin and get to bed.

'A signed confession carries the full force of the law,' said Ulrikh, sounding both furious and indifferent. 'The sentence stands, the verdict is final and to be effected without delay . . .'

Benya started to hyperventilate. A drop in the belly like the trapdoor of a gallows and then a drenchingly fearsome nausea; he thought he would die then and there. The guards caught him and held him up like a broken mannequin.

Then Satinov leaned sideways and whispered to Ulrikh. Satinov was the top man present, he was Stalin's comrade-in-arms, and he was not a judge. He was there for a special reason. Stalin had nominated him to be the 'curator' of the trial because Satinov had been friends with the people whom he was going to have to sentence to death. That was a test set by Stalin.

Ulrikh shrugged, and Satinov cleared his throat. 'Prisoner Golden, your death sentence is reprieved. Instead, you are sentenced to ten years . . .' And the rest was lost in the roar of relief in Benya's ears. Did he really hear it? Yes. There it was. Ten years! The joy of life – all thanks to Satinov!

'Thank you,' Benya whispered to the judges but they were no longer paying him any attention. They were standing up, collecting their papers. He rushed forward but the guards caught him, shook him and held him back: 'God bless you!' he shouted.

'No talking!' A rifle butt in the side. 'Silence, prisoner!'

A man who has heard his own capital sentence has lived

more profoundly than any other, and for Benya Golden, nothing would ever be quite the same again. Now he could live, passionately, expansively. He could love again. Oh, how he loved life. He barely noticed the judges filing out of the room.

Then there was the march through the corridors and the ride in the Black Maria back to his cell, where he understood it all better. He was condemned to a realm beyond mere death, his entire life up to his arrest was over. He was almost dead, a death without instant decay, trapped while he still breathed, in the hell of the eternal now. He recalled the slaves who rowed the Roman galleys: now he was to be a galley slave, toiling to death in the Camps known as the Gulags. But then he thought: ten years! It is not forever. I can survive ten years and come back to life, can't I?

Weeks and months of 1940 passed in that cell. He became accustomed to the routine but he knew that would soon end and every prisoner hates the change of rhythm. Change is dangerous. But he knew what was coming: the transfer, known as the *etap*, the journey to the east, to the Gulags.

And then it came. Four a.m. reveille. The guards burst into his cell. 'Wake up! Get your things. *Davay! Davay!* Let's go!'

Benya didn't know where he was going, just that he was heading east in cattle cars, chugging slowly across the endless spaces of the Urals, Siberia and onwards. The trains were packed with filthy, lice-infested prisoners (many Poles, Benya learned, victims of Stalin's new conquests), the stinking bucket overflowing with urine and dysentery. Sometimes Benya and his companions talked about Stalin's astonishing alliance with Hitler, how they'd split Poland between them. Paris had just fallen to the Nazis. How long would Britain hold out? But mostly Benya just lay in his corner, saving his energy, trying to stay alive, learning to listen and not talk. Being a 'Political', he was the lowest in the hierarchy of the prisoners. Even murderers and thieves were higher than him, and the highest of all were the Criminals who ran the cattle car, received the best food and took whatever else they wanted. A quick shuffling amongst the huddling prisoners and a man was killed for his new boots in the gloom of Benya's cattle car, quickly stripped for his clothes, coat, hat, ration. There was a sudden glare as the door was slid open; and Benya glimpsed the broken-ragdoll dance of arms and legs as a naked body was tossed out, filling the roaring frame of the open door for a second before the door slid shut again, and Benya wondered whether he had seen it at all. From then on, in this life, the death of a man, once an event remarkable and unforgettable, something you might tell your family or read about in the newspaper or discuss with a friend, was often merely an occurrence in a succession of occurrences for Benya, quickly forgotten in the drone of the day. The seething of lice on his body drove him crazy but he spent his days catching them and crushing them, feeling the pop of their bodies, a rare satisfaction, a lesson that small unlikely pleasures could make life almost tolerable. Sometimes he felt he had become the master of the enjoyment of minuscule things, and that that was the art of living.

He spent weeks at each transit prison – each one a world of its own, with its own rules of survival – until his next *etap* was called, and the next. A succession of cities. Petropavlovsk. Novosibirsk. Irkutsk. Everywhere his fellow prisoners said, 'Pray you're not going to Kolyma . . .' But by the time he saw the blue waters of Lake Baikal, Benya knew that was *exactly* where he was going.

Still dazed after the horrors of the voyage in the hell ship across the Sea of Okhotsk, they arrived at Magadan, where a new world of snow-capped mountains, bracing air and the lunar landscape of the gold mines awaited them. Benya imagined the gold-rush towns he had read about in his beloved Jack London's White Fang, the frontier of Fenimore Cooper's *The Last of the Mohicans*. It was still September, the last weeks before the Sea of Okhotsk froze, and Kolyma was about to be cut off from the mainland for many months.

The guards marched them up the hill in groups along a muddy lane called the Kolyma Highway and into a compound where Benya and his fellow prisoners were stripped, washed, shaved and their clothes steamed and deloused. In the showers, Benya saw men feast on each other, some on their knees, others bending over, coupling frantically, seizing white-knuckled fistfuls of gratification. Next day he stood naked in front of the medical examination board, a doctor and a Chekist, trying to look as weak and old as possible. But the doctor, a prisoner himself, stamped his file: 'KOLYMA-TFT. Fit for Hard Physical Labour.'

'But I'm not strong enough,' protested Benya.

'Shut the fuck up, cocksucker,' said the guard. 'The sentence for falsifying illness is Eight Grammes in the nut. For complaining you face the Isolator. Get a move on!'

Next day, he was woken at 4 a.m. '*Davay! Davay!* Let's go! Grab your belongings!'

Riding in a truck, fuelled not by petrol but by a furnace fired with wood, Benya travelled up the Highway into a mountain wilderness of rushing streams, reindeer herds and precipitous canyons. Then he saw first the barbed wire and watchtowers; next the wooden barracks and finally they entered the gate of their Camp: Madyak-7.

A giant sign declared:

GLORY TO STALIN THE GENIUS
GLORY TO STALIN OUR BELOVED LEADER
GLORY TO STALIN, FRIEND OF THE WORKING
CLASS, FATHER OF SOVIET CHILDREN

And finally at the bottom:

MORE GOLD FOR OUR SOCIALIST PARADISE!

Early next morning, the first roll call, hundreds of men standing to attention in the mist: pairs of favoured prisoners – known as Camp Trusties – waved whips and bully sticks to herd them into work brigades. The brigadiers reported to the Commandant. 'There are twenty-seven in this brigade,' called out Benya's brigadier, a Criminal called Shurik. 'One died at the mine yesterday; one executed for insubordination. One dead this morning in barracks; two sick in barracks; one self-injured in the Isolator. Five new prisoners. Total: twenty-seven!' He marched them up to the mine. 'You work, you eat,' Shurik warned Benya and his fellow Zeks – that was the Camp nickname for prisoners. 'You don't work, Zeks, you die.' Facing Benya was a capacious and gigantic scoop of mud and rock carved out of the mountainside, an ants' nest of teeming workers and armed guards, all creeping along plank walkways or excavating deep gulches, tiny figures in a landscape that the Zeks already called the Dark Side of the Moon.

II

'Bandits, today your training is over,' announced Penal-Colonel Melishko, the battalion commander. How Benya had survived his time in Kolyma he never knew, and here he was eighteen months later, in July 1942, in southern Russia, not far from the city of Stalingrad.

At sundown on that broiling summer night, they stood in a half-circle around Melishko in the manège of the Marshal Budyonny Stud Farm Number 9, very close to the Don River. It was horse country, land of the Don Cossacks. They had been training for seven months.

'You are ready to be assigned your first mission – and you will be needed faster than any of us thought. The Motherland is in peril!' roared Melishko.

Benya caught the eye of his friend Prishchepa next to him. Prishchepa smiled flashily, but Melishko's gruff confidence did not hide the panic of the other officers. When Benya had started his training in December 1941, the front was far away and the Germans had been defeated outside Moscow. Now the war had come to them; since yesterday, they could even hear the belch of artillery as the Germans approached the Don.

'You bandits have a special reason to fight hard for the Motherland! I found you as scum. Now you're as battle-ready as regulars, good soldiers, fine horsemen' – Melishko's eyes, under his crescent-shaped eyebrows that looked like wings, glanced at Benya with a bolt of warmth – 'and even the most unlikely of you can at least keep your seat.'

Prishchepa wiped away the tears that ran down his young cheeks. He wept and laughed easily; he went through life as happy as a swallow; nothing disturbed his geniality, not his sentence to the Camps, nor this parade today, nor tomorrow's battle. 'Life is easy for a simple soul like mine,' he said cheerfully. 'You just have to live it.' Benya enjoyed studying Prishchepa; he'd never lost his interest in human nature, and there was no laboratory so fascinating as the Gulags and this battalion of vicious criminals and court-martialled soldiers.

Benya and Melishko had been in the same Camp in Kolyma. After his arrest, General Melishko had been so severely tortured that he had no teeth or fingernails left; only his moustache, thick, white and stiff as a painter's old brush, was the same. Nevertheless when the war started, he had been one of the first officers recalled to fight but instead of being assigned a division or corps, he had been made a colonel and given this rabble. He was, however, still called 'the General' by everyone and Benya loved the fact that Melishko was unchanging, whether waiting for soup in the dining block in Kolyma or how addressing the men as their commander.

In the barn-like manège, its sandy ground designed for training horses, Melishko stood alone at the front. Behind him: Captain Ganakovich, their *Politruk*, the Political Officer, and Pavel Mogilchuk, head of their secret police Special Unit.

Benya did not know the details – the truth was always '*Top Secret*' – but he did know the Russians were retreating fast and now there must have been some new debacle. Ganakovich was fritzing with nerves, Mogilchuk visibly shaking. At each crump of the guns, the fear slithered another degree up Benya's belly.

'Remember what I always say,' bellowed Melishko, his false teeth breaking the vowels. 'You can't get me!' It was a line borrowed from his favourite movie and the men loved it.

'Urrah!' they cried but then there was the sound of footsteps and Benya peered round as Captain Zhurko ran into the manège and handed Melishko a piece of paper.

'As you are,' said Melishko. 'We're awaiting an important order from Stavka.' 'Stavka' was headquarters in Moscow. Benya and Prishchepa looked at each other, and Prishchepa started to sing under his breath: *'Don't circle over me, black raven . . .'*

III

Far to the north, in Moscow, a small, tired old man, wearing a military tunic and baggy grey trousers tucked into soft calf-skin boots, sat at a huge desk in a long office. His face was seared with exhaustion, bleached a sallow pockmarked grey.

Outside, the Kremlin was draped in camouflage netting, and air balloons floated above the city to disorientate German bombers. Inside, the long table, the desk with the T-shaped extension and the chunky row of Bakelite telephones, the dreary drapes over the windows and the illuminated death mask of Lenin on the wall were unchanged, but now the founder of Soviet Russia was joined on the walls by oil paintings of Tsarist paladins, Suvorov and Kutuzov. This office known to regulars as the Little Corner was the headquarters of the Soviet armies, and the phone lines and telegraph wires in the communications room next door linked the man in this office to a boundless and often unpredictable and uncontrollable world of savage struggle between millions of men.

'We were tricked,' said Stalin quietly. 'The whole south is collapsing. Our commanders are fools and yes-men. We lack good men. We still await the main offensive against Moscow.'

At the nearest end of the long table sat three men. Molotov, a squat blockhouse with a round head and pince-nez, nodded. The only one in civilian clothes, he wore a grey suit, grey tie and stiff white collar. He had the clammy pallor of the bureaucrat who never saw the sun, a condition known to Stalin's familiars as 'the Kremlin tan'.

'You're right, Comrade Stalin,' said Lavrenti Beria, the People's Commissar of Internal Affairs, chief of the secret police. Wearing his blue-tabbed NKVD uniform, he was broad-spanned and grey-faced but bristling with ingenuity, vigilance, ferocity.

The third of them, Hercules Satinov, dressed as an army colonel general, spoke up: 'Comrade Stalin, I believe *this* is the main German offensive. They are throwing everything against the Don and the Caucasus. We made the wrong judgement. There is no Moscow offensive. I myself was mistaken and I wish to take responsibility, and if you believe it necessary, stand trial. We were tricked . . .'

Stalin stared witheringly at Satinov for a long moment. Until today, he might have called him a fool, a traitor, perhaps even ordered his arrest. But Satinov, his favourite and, like him, another Georgian, had always told him the truth. And now he needed the truth. Six weeks earlier, on 19 June, a German Storch plane had crashed behind Soviet lines near Kharkov.

Inside was a staff officer, Major Reichel, with a briefcase that contained the plans for Hitler's southern offensive, Case Blue. Hours later, those plans were reviewed in this very room by Stalin, accompanied by the same Greek chorus of Molotov, Beria and Satinov.

'It's a trick,' Stalin had said. 'It's classic disinformation. The bastards expect us to fall for this? The southern offensive will be a diversion. The big offensive will be against Moscow.' The three Politburo members had agreed – as they always did. But now it was clear they had called it wrong and Hitler's panzers were charging across the southern plains towards Stalingrad. Russia was about to be cut in half.

Stalin looked down the table at the only other man in the huge room, General Alexander Vasilevsky, his Chief of Staff, who was leaning over a map of the southern theatre, marked with arrows and symbols. 'Comrade Vasilevsky?'

Vasilevsky, who had the professional air of an old-fashioned Tsarist officer, stood up straight. 'He's right, Comrade Stalin. This *is* the main offensive.'

Stalin nodded, rubbing his face with his hands. Ripples of exhaustion seemed to emanate from him. Satinov could only admire Stalin's self-control, the steely, intelligent coldness that he radiated despite his egregious mistakes. But he had aged in this past year of war; his clothes hung off him.

The padded door opened silently and a dwarfish figure, Alexander Poskrebyshev, also in boots and uniform, looked in: 'They're here, Comrade Stalin,' he announced.

Stalin beckoned, and two old cavalrymen entered and stood at attention before him. Both had just flown in from the front and been driven straight to the Kremlin. The dust of battle was still on their faces, and Satinov could smell their sweat, and their despair.

'Report, Comrade Budyonny,' commanded Stalin in his light tenor voice.

'German Army Group A has broken through the North Caucasus Front,' said Marshal Budyonny, his barrel chest, his rider's bow legs in boots and red-striped britches, even his magnificently waxed moustaches, diminished in defeat. 'Our troops are in retreat. They've reached the Don, and are breaking into the Caucasus, targeting the oil fields. We are struggling to regroup. Rostov has fallen.'

'Rostov?' repeated Stalin.

'A lie! You're spreading panic,' cried Beria. 'Report properly!'

But Budyonny ignored him. In 1937, when they had tried to arrest him during the Terror, Budyonny had drawn his pistol and threatened to kill them and shoot himself, shouting, 'Get Stalin on the line!' Stalin had cancelled the arrest order.

'Our forces fell back from Rostov,' said Budyonny. 'They turned and fled. Just ran! I admit there was cowardice and incompetence. I take full responsibility.'

'And you, Marshal Timoshenko?' Stalin turned to the other cavalryman. 'What good news have you got for us?'

Timoshenko shook his gleaming bald head. 'The Stalingrad Front is in disarray. German forces have reached the Don and the only thing holding them back are two armies defending the bend in the river. And we can't hold Voronezh. I would say . . .' He struggled to speak.

'Tell Comrade Stalin the truth!' said Beria.

'I think Stalingrad itself in danger.'

Stalingrad! Stalin's own city where he made his name in the Civil War. Satinov felt breathless suddenly with disbelief.

'That's a lie! Stalingrad will never fall,' said Beria in his clotted Mingrelian accent. 'Panic-mongers should be shot! The Germans are hundreds of miles from Stalingrad.'

Stalin's hazel eyes flicked towards Vasilevsky, who was plotting the new information on the maps spread on the table. He trusted Vasilevsky. 'Well?'

Vasilevsky appeared to consider his answer unhurriedly.

'We will halt the German forces on the Don Bend but the defence and fortification of Stalingrad must be urgently prepared along with evacuation plans for the tank factories. I propose a radical reconstruction of the southern fronts and I've informed them to expect new orders from Stavka.'

Stalin thought for a moment and lit a Herzegovina Flor cigarette. In the silent room, with the two marshals standing to attention, with Vasilevsky again perusing the maps, the three henchmen waiting, the wheeze of every breath of smoke seemed laden with fearsome concentration.

'Timoshenko, Budyonny, wait outside,' said Stalin.

The two men saluted and left the room.

'Of course Stalingrad is not threatened. Not yet. But I will not tolerate a single step back. Not one step back . . .' He allowed this phrase to sink in.

'Comrade Stalin,' said Satinov after a pause. 'The Hitlerites have very successfully used penal battalions in battle made up of court-martialled soldiers and criminal elements. We have punishment units of cowards and criminals already being trained, some recruited in the Gulags, but I propose we formalize this structure, and create penal battalions on every front and throw them into battle . . .'

'Desperate men fight like devils,' said Stalin. 'Very well.' He lifted one of the many Bakelite phones on his desk, 'Get in here.'

Poskrebyshev appeared at the door, notebook and pencil already in hand. 'Take this down,' Stalin ordered. 'Order 227 from the People's Commissar of Defence.' He stood and started to pace up and down, his hands shaking as he inhaled his cigarette. 'Telegraph this to all fronts. To be read to all units urgently on this very night . . . The enemy throws new forces against us . . . The German invaders penetrate towards Stalingrad . . . they've already captured Novocherkask, Rostov-on-Don, half Voronezh . . . Our soldiers, encouraged by panic-mongers, shamefully abandoned Rostov . . . I order: Not One Step Back . . .'

IV

'Not One Step Back! That is our slogan!'

In the sultry heat of the manège's arena, Melishko was reading out Stalin's orders which had just arrived, smoking off the telegraph from Moscow. Benya felt the hair rising on his neck. His life was entering a new and daunting stage.

'Stavka orders: "Every army must form well-armed blocking squads (two hundred men) and place them behind any unstable divisions. In the case of any retreat, they are to shoot panic-mongers and cowards on the spot . . . Not One Step

Back . . . We are already training punishment units of prisoners.' Benya and his comrades concentrated; Stalin himself was addressing them and their destiny. 'Now I order the formation of penal battalions — *shtrafnoi batalioni* — of eight hundred persons on every front made up of men guilty of crimes, breaches of discipline due to cowardice or confusion. They are to be placed in the most difficult sectors of the battle to give them the chance to redeem their sins against the Motherland by the shedding of their own blood . . . These are the orders of our Motherland. People's Commissar of Defence. J Stalin." '

Melishko folded the paper and peered grimly at his 'bandits'. 'Comrade Stalin has spoken and—'

'Permission to speak!' a voice called out. Melishko nodded.

'What does "redeeming sins by shedding blood" mean?' said Prishchepa. Only he would have dared ask such a thing.

Melishko wiped the sweat from his forehead into the wisps of his meagre rust-coloured hair. The men waited; Benya could feel them craning forward.

'Comrade Stalin means that there are only two ways to earn your freedom. Death or by being wounded in battle.'

The men held their breath for a moment as they, like Benya, absorbed the primitive simplicity of their fates.

'See, my bandits?' said Melishko. 'You have the chance to free yourselves in battle. Your deployment is imminent. Get some rest tonight . . . Yes, comrade?'

Ganakovich whispered in Melishko's ear.

'Right,' said Melishko. 'Comrade Ganakovich will tell you more.'

Captain Ganakovich swaggered to the front. 'Lads, comrades, muckers, Shtrafniki,' he started in a deep voice of rasp and raunch that he adopted for momentous occasions. 'You bear the taint of alien elements, bourgeois illiterates, counter-revolutionary delinquents, murderous degenerates, but you've been re-educated and retrained and now you have the honour to fight for the Socialist Motherland and the Great Genius Stalin – and I'll be right there with you, shoulder to shoulder!' Ganakovich he drew his pistol and held it above his head. 'As convicts and cowards, you have no rights as soldiers. You will not even be informed of the name of your front, and there'll be no maps for you. You will gratefully receive your mission and you will fulfil it. If I or the Special Unit notice the slightest hesitation, deviation, insubordination, a word, a look, yes, even a thought, you'll get the Eight Grammes: instant execution!' He gulped – he had a tendency when excited to forget to swallow his saliva, which then built up in his mouth until it had to be consumed in one phlegmy wad.

Melishko looked embarrassed but the ex-prisoners were unmoved. The things they had seen in the Gulags, or in the great retreats of 1941, had accustomed them to the malignant buffoonery of Soviet bureaucrats.

'Thank you, very useful, Comrade Ganakovich,' Melishko said, stepping forward again. The men could feel his disdain for the Party hack – and they shared his disgust. 'Good luck, bandits! I will be there with you! Long live Stalin!'

'Excuse me, penal-colonel,' the secret policeman Mogilchuk interjected. 'There's one more thing. Captain Ganakovich will enlighten the men.'

30

'They need to rest and tend the horses. Haven't my bandits listened to us enough?' objected Melishko.

'Not quite,' said Mogilchuk. 'Proceed! Bring out the prisoner!'

A hush fell over the Shtrafbat as the NKVD men, machine guns sloping ready, pushed a figure in front of them. Benya saw at once it was young Polyak and he was sobbing. God, prayed Benya, give the boy strength! But there was no God there to help him now.

When Polyak reached the cluster of officers in the middle of the manège, Mogilchuk made a gesture and they brusquely stopped him. Polyak swayed but the guards held him up.

'Lads, pals, if the generosity of the Great Stalin is abused with trickery, there can only be one result,' declared Ganakovich portentously. A creature of the Communist Party, Ganakovich liked to present himself as a leader with the popular touch. Benya knew that if they were dancing the *kalinka*, Ganakovich would jump into the centre of the circle and make his fancy leaps. If the men were taking a drink, Ganakovich, slapping backs and massaging arms, would buy shots and tell stories of his dubious exploits – his heroics in the grain campaign of '32, the time he met Molotov, the day he defeated a Trotskyite cell in his factory, and of course the girls whom he had conquered. Only his upturned snout and piggy eyes hinted at his self-glorification. He swallowed loudly. 'I hand you over to our Chekist knights of the Revolution.'

Flanked by his NKVD soldiers, Mogilchuk stepped forward. 'Anyone who deliberately wounds themselves to avoid battle or win redemption will receive the Eight Grammes. Penal-Sergeant Polyak was sentenced to serve in this penal battalion for retreating without orders during the battle of Kiev. Last night, hearing our deployment was imminent, this coward went to elaborate lengths to fake sickness, by cutting himself.'

'It was a real cut!' Polyak wailed.

'Silence, prisoner!' snapped Mogilchuk. 'He was denounced by one of the medical team. After an investigation, following this order from Stavka, he is hereby condemned to the Vishka, the sentence to be carried out immediately and in front of the battalion.'

An intake of breath.

'Shtrafniki, my lads, my muckers!' cried Ganakovich, making no effort to conceal his excitement. 'Volunteers from the ranks to execute the prisoner?'

Melishko stared at his boots. It was so hot that Benya found it hard to breathe. He remembered how he had once heard his own death sentence. He stared at the boy: Mitka Polyak, we talked often; if you were so afraid, why didn't you come to me?

The men swayed slowly, shifting foot to foot, flies buzzing.

'I repeat,' cried out Ganakovich. 'Volunteers to execute the prisoner!'

Silence.

Ganakovich raised his pistol again. 'Or must I do it myself?'

Benya and Prishchepa glanced at each other. They lived in a Russia dominated by Ganakoviches but it was ironic that in a regiment of murderers, no one wanted to kill.

'I will shoot the boy!' said a voice. Spider Garanzha had raised his hand.

'Step forward, Penal-Private Garanzha,' said Ganakovich.

Moving with his customary slowness, relishing the strength of his cyclopean limbs and the terrifying effect of his face, Garanzha stepped up to the front of the battalion and crossed his hairy arms. A giant swollen spider, a birdeater perhaps; Benya could see how he got his nickname.

'Who else? We need one more. Come on, men. Who's it to be?'

'Count me in!' It was Smiley, a Chechen gangster whom Benya had met on the atrocious sea voyage to Kolyma.

'Come forward Penal-Private Ulibnush,' blared Ganakovich, using Smiley's real name.

'Proceed to your positions,' said Mogilchuk, who believed that saying 'proceed' frequently granted him a patina of authority. 'Or you'll face the tribunal yourself.'

Smiley moved sideways with the loose, dancing gait of one who has lived beyond the law all his life, who has never slept without remaining half awake, never crossed a road without watching his back, who was always running from one heinous thing towards another.

Polyak cast a glance at these two cutthroats and started to shake.

'Please get this over,' whispered Benya.

Prishchepa was praying, touching his icon necklace. When Benya looked around, he saw that many of the Cossacks in the battalion were also moving their lips silently.

Ganakovich handed out the Nagants. Both executioners took the pistols as if born with guns in their hands.

'On your knees, prisoner!' cried Ganakovich with a gulp.

The guards turned Polyak away from the men and then let him drop to his knees. Benya saw his lowered freckly neck flush bright red. Sometimes you can learn as much in a man's neck as in his face, Benya thought. Polyak started to breathe greedily, tossing his head back, gulping air. He was no longer a human, just an animal seconds from death, like a cow in the abattoir, straining at the hands of his captors.

Garanzha and Smiley cocked their pistols. First Garanzha and then Smiley fired into Polyak's neck, the shots merging into one. When Benya opened his eyes Polyak lay on his side. Mogilchuk drew his own pistol and, wincing with the strain – no gunman he – fired the control shot into Polyak's temple. Benya noticed that Melishko had never looked up.

'Good work! Medics,' called Ganakovich.

Two nurses rushed forward with a stretcher and rolled the body on to it. Then the battalion medic, whom Benya knew well from the Camps as Dr Kapto, knelt beside Polyak, touched his neck, and nodded at Ganakovich.

'Prisoner deceased,' he said.

'Thank you, doctor,' Ganakovich replied, glaring at the men. 'Lesson learned, lesson learned, eh lads?'

V

Benya walked alone out to the training arena and leaned on the white railing. The night was rosy and soft, a true *soomerki*, one of those perfect summer nights when it was so hot that no one could sleep and the air had the texture of creamy velvet; it was a night, thought Benya, for a boulevardier to walk a girl he hopes to kiss. The horizon flashed; the guns boomed, seemingly ever closer; sometimes he heard the roar of engines as tanks detrained at the station and moved towards the front. Somewhere, across the Don, thousands of Russians were fighting for survival; and somewhere very close, Polyak's body was being dumped into an unmarked grave, dug in this rich black earth. Had they shot the boy *pour encourager les autres*, to instil discipline in this unreliable crew, Benya wondered, or had the imminent transfer to the front simply terrified Polyak into wounding himself?

The solitude was a tonic to Benya. One of the torments of the Camps and of the army was the loss of personal space. He craved the luxury of loneliness. That is why he adored the space of the steppes. He often walked out here at night, to smoke, to dream, and often he remembered his daughter who lived with her mother, Benya's estranged wife. Were they safe in Brussels or Paris or had they made it to Madrid or London? His daughter must be a young woman now — he had not seen her for years ... Then there were his parents. Odessa had fallen to Hitler's allies, the Romanians, who were said to have unleashed such havoc that most of the Jews of the city had been slaughtered in the streets. Could such a thing have happened to them? Or had they escaped eastwards?

And then he looked up at the stars and Sashenka came to him. Was she even alive? He was overcome with a wave of love; he craved her lips, the stretch of the tendons behind her knees when her legs were around him. If she was reachable out there somewhere, he sent her kisses: 'I love you!' he whispered. But though he strained to hear something back, there was no sound, not even an echo. Of all the people in the world whom he loved, he did not know if a single one of them was alive ...

The fear of tomorrow loomed over him. In the meadows beyond, the horses whinnied. There were thousands of them in the paddocks here, Budyonny horses bred by Russia's first cavalryman, Marshal Budyonny. Silver Socks was there. He peered out towards where she might be and thought he saw the white blaze on her forehead and her white shanks. He walked out further into the darkness and stood at the fence, clopping his tongue, the way the Cossacks did, and the horses came to him. First amongst them was Silver Socks and he felt he was not so alone any more. She put her soft muzzle in his hand and, as he leaned towards her long face, his eyes so close to hers, he found he was weeping: for others, for Polyak, for himself perhaps more. Silver Socks slowly rocked her head and her breath smelled of sweet grass.

Then he heard a click and he turned, leaving one hand on Silver Socks's neck. It was Prishchepa lighting a cigarette.

When it was lit, he offered it to Benya. 'One for you; now I'll roll my own.'

The *makhorka* was so strong it made Benya cough but he was grateful. He could see the doctor and one of his nurses standing behind Prishchepa; his friends from the Camps at Kolyma. Dr Kapto looked at Benya. 'Are you OK, dear friend?' he said, placing his hand on Benya's arm. 'We're all a little unsteady. Easy, now, easy! You'll be fine.'

'Thank God you'll be with us,' said Benya.

'And you, Prishchepa, how are you feeling?' Kapto asked the Cossack.

'I never think about tomorrow,' replied Prishchepa sunnily. He had forgotten about Polyak already.

'Tonya, will you be with us?' Benya asked the nurse, who had worked for Kapto in the clinic in Kolyma.

'Of course, I ride with you,' she said.

Tonya always said little. She was, thought Benya, like a light without a bulb, and was overshadowed by the brown skin and long legs of Nyushka, Kapto's other nurse. 'We saw them bury him,' was all Tonya said, and Benya knew she meant Polyak.

Together they had undergone their training here, far behind the front lines in Russia's vastness. Gun training, how to fire the basic weaponry, the Moisin–Nagant rifles and the light Degtiarev machine guns . . . Captain Zhurko had held competitions to assemble and disassemble them in record time. The greatest skill was learning to load a PPSh machine gun at night, taking the lid off the drum, tightening the spring and pushing in the cartridges. Then there were the pistols, Nagants and German Parabellums to master and Degtiarev–Shpagin heavy machine guns. They had nicknames for everything: the PPShs were Papashas, the Degtiarev–Shpagins were Dashkas, and the new missiles fired from trucks Katyushas.

They had been quartered at this army base designed for cavalry and there were so many Cossacks in the penal unit that Melishko, an old cavalryman himself, decided they should be trained as cavalry.

'Even in the age of the tank,' Melishko told them on their first day, 'our Red Army theory, developed by Marshal Budyonny under the guidance of the Great Stalin, states cavalry is a powerful strike force, of peerless speed and flexibility,

37

suitable for frontal assaults, screening manoeuvres, reconnaissance, and deep raids behind enemy lines. In ideal conditions such as the Don steppe, cavalry can achieve averages of seven or even ten miles an hour . . .'

After that pep talk, their instructor, Sergeant Pantaleimon Churelko, stepped forward. This Don Cossack whom everyone called Panka had a head of thick grey hair worn in a topknot, and a handlebar moustache and whiskers so extravagant and broad that they seemed almost to be a piece of equipment in their own right. Leading them into the paddock, he swished his quirt and looked into the faces of the gathered hundred or so Shtrafniki. Benya stood out. He was one of the oldest – and probably the most delicate.

Pantaleimon pointed at him. 'You! Step forward! Has this Zhid ever seen a horse?'

Benya took a breath; Cossacks were known for their attitude to Jews. 'Yes, I've ridden,' he replied. 'But a long time ago . . .'

'We'll see about that,' said Panka. 'First, walk into the meadow and choose a horse. Remember, this is the most important choice of your life. More important than choosing a wife!'

The moment Benya stepped into the paddock, a horse with a white flash and white feet walked right up to him.

'That's Silver Socks! She chose you. She's a smart one. That speaks well for you. Now you'll learn to ride properly and then to fight,' Panka said. Benya's acquaintances, Smiley and Little Mametka, sniggered but Panka spat out his tobacco wad and simply observed: 'You laugh at the Jew learning to ride? Apart from we Cossacks, no one knows anything. Your tongues have tails but rein them in. Lesson one: your horse is your son and daughter, wife and mistress, priest and commissar. Listen to your horse! Tend her like a wife! Respect her like a mother! Feed her like a daughter! Ever made love to a beautiful woman, Jew? I doubt it.'

'He's too slight to handle a woman!' teased 'Fats' Strizkaz, a pink barrel of a man who never lost weight, even in Kolyma.

'Or too old,' chortled another man, Ivanov, who Benya recalled was nicknamed 'Cut and Run'.

'Enough,' said Panka. 'Next one who says such a thing, I'll thrash him myself.'

'Really?' sneered Ivanov. 'You wouldn't dare!'

'Who spoke?'

Panka stepped towards Smiley's gang of Criminals and Benya noticed them slink back an imperceptible inch.

'Don't cross us,' piped up Little Mametka in his usual soprano. Benya recognized the tone of the Gulag where the Criminals ruled. 'Get off our backs, old man.'

'I am not going *anywhere*,' Panka replied affably and calmly. 'Now listen to me or the Germans will get you before you're even in the saddle. You there, Ivanov, mount your horse. Now!'

Ivanov hesitated.

'Go on! Let's see you do it,' cried Mametka. 'Anyone can ride a horse!'

Ivanov put his boot in the stirrup, swung his other leg around and climbed up on to the horse with a triumphant leer.

'Very good,' said Panka, hands on his hips. The horse reared up and bucked Ivanov off and he landed on his back with a thump. His gang snickered as Panka offered a hand and pulled him up. 'Mount your horse.'

'Not again!' said Ivanov.

'That's an order.'

'He's frightened,' piped Mametka.

'All right.' Ivanov heaved himself up again and sat white-faced on the horse.

'Try to hold on this time,' said Panka, who made a soft kissing noise – and the horse bucked off Ivanov once more.

The Criminals whooped as Ivanov thwacked on to the sand where he lay groaning.

'Not so easy, is it?' said Panka. 'No wonder they call you Cut and Run!'

Afterwards Benya realized that Panka could get any horse to throw its rider. He spoke horse language – amongst many others. 'Who's next? You' – and he pointed to Fats Strizkaz.

'Fats Strizkaz was once a Chekist torturer,' gabbed a voice next to Benya. It was Koshka – 'the Cat' – bilious, scurfy and rail-thin, an Uzbek thief who liked telling tales about prisoners. 'Just saying.'

'Keep your stories to yourself,' said Benya, who knew that stories were dangerous, that gossip could kill you. Best to say nothing and hear nothing.

'Ivanov once killed a whole family in their beds,' said Koshka. 'Just saying.'

The training was exhausting: reveille at 4 a.m., first duty to groom the horses, then exercises, day after day, loping, cantering, trotting, galloping, learning to charge, ride in squadron. How to saddle and feed the horses, check their fetlocks and hooves. Each man was issued with a Red Army sabre and they were taught how to sharpen it, how to slash and pierce sacks on posts – to simulate human bodies – how to stab on the charge. Benya was a 'townie' but he had learned to ride when he'd covered the civil war in Spain and he'd spent many hours on horseback. But this was real riding. He learned quickly, or, as Panka put it, 'Benya Golden can ride. Perhaps he is a Zhid with a Cossack mother!'

The horses made their long hours of training a joy, and Benya's companions, most of whom were Cossacks, who had lived on horseback since childhood, took every chance to show off their skills. As they rode they sang songs of the Don under their breath. Panka arranged contests and soon the Cossacks were vaulting on to their mounts, slipping on to the side of their horses to shoot over their backs, picking up a glove at the gallop, ordering their horses to lie on their sides so that they could rest their rifles on their flanks. 'Speedy' Prishchepa could run up, mount his horse, gallop and shoot a bullseye. Benya came to love the smell of leather, the jingle of spurs and snaffles, and the sweat of the horses, which enveloped their clothes. Before long, it seemed to him that he had almost become an extension of Silver Socks. At night they played accordions and sang the songs of the Don and Kuban and talked about horses with a mixture of love and cruelty, like men talking about their wives.

'Spend a quarter of your day grooming and loving your mount,' Panka told Benya as he groomed Silver Socks one evening. 'Look after your Socks and she'll look after you. Make her your heroine and she'll be your saviour. Do you know how to caress a woman?'

'I think I do,' said Benya.

'Do you know how to beat a woman?'

'No.'

'Ha, you townies treat your women far too soft. Well, with a horse you need to do both. That's why we Cossacks are so

41

good with horses and women. But when you want to reassure Socks, don't pat her on the neck like most fools. She won't understand that. These horses' mothers nuzzle their necks right here at the withers when they are foals, so when you're in the saddle, you roll back the blanket under the saddle and caress her there. That does the trick. And never take Socks for granted or she'll bring you down to size!'

'Sergeant, you've fought in many wars?'

'A few. The Great War against the Kaiser, the Civil War, now this; yes, a few.'

'Are you afraid of war?'

'No! What's there to be afraid of? When your ride is done, 'tis done. And that's up to God and your horse.' Panka chewed on his moustaches, his eyes so small they were almost invisible. 'Until then it's always sunny on the Don,' he said as he walked off, bandy-legged, moulded by the saddle.

Benya took a growing pride in the beauty of Silver Socks. If her hooves seemed worn or ill-shod or sore, he called in 'Tufty' Grishchuk, the farrier with a patchy, crusty face. If she was not herself, he consulted Lampadnik, the battalion vet. He spent hours grooming her chestnut coat till it gleamed, and polishing her accoutrements – the pommel of her saddle and the handle of his sabre. There is, he thought, no tonic for being a ruined man, like the love of a horse. Sometimes he just sat in her stable and let her nuzzle him.

In the evenings, Melishko allowed them into the village and once the local girls heard they were Shtrafniki, they were even more impressed: 'You're bad boys,' said the girls. Prishchepa, with his face like a cherub and shaven hair growing back like a harvest of gold, was their darling. But when they saw Benya, they giggled. 'Who's your *dedushka*, your granpa?' they'd ask Prishchepa.

'But I'm only forty-two!' Benya protested.

Prishchepa chuckled. 'He's a bookworm, he knows nothing about girls!'

'But he can at least perform,' said Fats Strizkaz, 'unlike Little Mametka, who's a girl in disguise. In the Camps, we called him Bette Davis. Like the film star. Big eyes, nasty face – and a bitch!'

Now, as Benya, Prishchepa, Dr Kapto and Tonya stood at the railings of the paddock, they were joined by a few others, come to stroke their horses before sleep.

Prishchepa started to sing:

> '*Fly away, black swallow,*
> *Fly along the Alazani river,*
> *Bring us back the news,*
> *Of the brothers gone to war . . .*'

'Dr Kapto?' It was the colonel's adjutant. 'Colonel Melishko wishes to talk to you. Says it's about his bunions and piles!'

Kapto smiled. 'I'm coming.'

They looked back towards the buildings. The lights were shining brightly, and the staff would be working into the early hours. A Willys jeep, a Lend-Lease gift from the American allies, drove up and Benya saw senior officers getting out.

As Kapto walked back to the office, Benya wondered if their mission was settled, because somewhere, he knew, someone was deciding their fate.

VI

It was midnight in Moscow but Stalin was still presiding over the meeting in the Little Corner of the Kremlin.

'We must counter-attack on all the southern fronts – relieve the pressure!' said Stalin, standing at the table with the Chief of Staff General Vasilevsky, looking at the small flags on the map that marked the positions of his armies from the Finnish front in the north to the foothills of the Caucasus in the south – two thousand miles and ten million men. 'We launch Operation Mercury in forty-eight hours with Operation Pluto launched in twenty-four hours.' He looked back at the little T-shaped table attached to his desk where Beria, Satinov and Molotov were still sitting, like expectant – if ageing – school boys.

'Operation Mercury is being prepared but there are few divisions available,' replied Vasilevsky. 'We've formed the available units into the 62nd and 64th Armies, thereby reconstituting the intact forces of the sector into a new Stalingrad Front.'

'That's all? Bring more forces across the Don to support the 62nd and 64th holding out there. We must exert pressure there right now. Attack in force. When can we launch these counter-attacks?'

'We're rushing in reinforcements to stop the retreat,' said Vasilevsky patiently. 'But we are short of tanks, artillery, men.' Stalin's constant demands for counter-attacks before adequate preparation had already brought many disasters, but that was the nature of the man. He was relentlessly aggressive.

'There must be more forces in the sector,' said Stalin. 'Find them! Who's available now? Tonight?'

An aide brought Vasilevsky more papers which he swiftly perused and then reported in his level tone: 'A moment please.'

Only he and General Zhukov could say this to Stalin, who had shot so many of his generals in '37 that the survivors were now understandably cautious and jumpy.

When Vasilevsky was ready, he cleared his throat: 'Cashiered troops and criminal volunteers have been training for the last six months on the Don and are ready for combat. Now you have formally created the Shtrafbats, the staff are working at this very minute to deploy them at the front according to your precise orders.'

'They're already on the Don?' Stalin sounded surprised.

'They've been training at the Budyonny Stud Nine at Vennovsk close to the bridgeheads at the Don Bend.'

'How many men?'

'Five thousand.'

'Better than nothing,' interjected Satinov. 'And convicts will fight to the death.'

Stalin nodded. 'Can they launch a counter-attack? How quickly can they be deployed and with what units? They have artillery and machine-gun battalions? What strength do we have in tanks?'

Vasilevsky looked troubled. 'We will deploy artillery and machine-gun battalions but we are grossly short of tanks, Comrade Stalin. We have only a hundred T-34s in reserve for the entire sector and—'

'No tanks? That is treason.' Stalin's voice rose an octave,

but when he started again, he was his controlled, soft-spoken self. 'Then throw these criminals into the fray without tanks. Let them give their lives for the Motherland.'

'We have a few old Betushka tanks for them. We are driving new T-34s straight to the front off the assembly line at Stalingrad,' said Vasilevsky, 'but . . .'

'I wouldn't waste new T-34s on these jailbirds,' advised Beria.

Stalin padded to his chair, sat down, closed his eyes. 'What to do?' he said.

'May I speak?' It was Satinov, still sitting further down the table. 'I believe there is another possibility. I recently spent some time down on the Don with Marshal Budyonny. May we call the marshals back in?'

A nod. Satinov sprang up and opened the door, returning with the two marshals. He could tell they both expected punishment. Instead Stalin looked at Satinov: 'Well, what's the idea?'

'Marshal Budyonny, you're aware that penal forces are training at Stud Nine? How many horses do you have there?'

'Twenty thousand of my new Budyonny breed,' replied Budyonny. 'But these horses are our future. Beauties, trained and bred for the finest cavalry.'

'The prisoners there have been training as cavalry,' said Satinov.

'Correct,' said Vasilevsky. 'Since many were Cossack prisoners from the Gulags and the horses were on site, I approved cavalry training. And, since we are now so short of tanks, Comrade Stalin has ordered the formation of new cavalry regiments on all fronts.'

'I knew the tanks would be a passing craze,' boomed Budyonny, and Satinov could almost see the vodka oozing out of him. 'This new-fangled technology never works. They just run out of diesel – unlike my horses.'

Satinov looked at Stalin, who cocked his head as if to say: Tell me more. So Budyonny did. 'Cavalry is the future, the heart of any army. But my horses are bred and trained to perform as the world's best. Please, Koba,' he appealed to Stalin, using his old nickname, 'they shouldn't be thrown away on ill-trained prisoners.'

'How dare you speak such shit to Comrade Stalin!' hissed Beria.

Everyone waited for Stalin's reaction.

'Pah!' Stalin waved his hand. 'What a typical Cossack. Comrade Budyonny prefers horses to men. Perhaps one of your horses would have commanded your front better than you? Well, fuck that, now we need your beloved horses!'

'Yes, Comrade Stalin,' said Budyonny, bowing his head.

Stalin stood up and paced the long room in his soft calf-leather boots. 'I propose the following: Stavka has lost confidence in Timoshenko's ability to manage his front. Timoshenko is dismissed.'

Timoshenko saluted and left the office. Stalin kept talking. 'Gordov will take command of the Stalingrad Front and you, Comrade Satinov, will fly down to Stalingrad and take control. Budyonny, you will fly back to the North Caucasus Front accompanied by Comrade Beria who will shoot anyone who takes one step back. You all leave tonight!'

Budyonny saluted.

'General Vasilevsky, form your criminals into cavalry

battalions for immediate deployment. Who's in command of these prisoners?'

'A certain Melishko.'

'General Melishko?' Stalin glanced at Beria. 'He's still alive? Wasn't he with you, Lavrenti?'

'He was,' replied Beria, who had tortured Melishko personally. He had smashed all his teeth out and still no confession. Very stubborn man, old school. Admirable really.

'Maybe God preserved him to serve,' said Stalin thoughtfully. 'He must have been a good man all along. That's decided then. Melishko's First and Second Cavalry Penal Battalions to launch Operation Pluto on the Stalingrad Front.'

'Orders are already being telegraphed to Penal-Colonel Melishko – that's his present rank,' Vasilevsky said.

Stalin stopped pacing and sat behind his desk. 'Beria, stay behind; the rest of you have your orders; go straight from here to the airport.'

'Right, Comrade Stalin!' Satinov and all the others left.

'Lavrenti,' said Stalin to Beria, now speaking their native Georgian. 'Isn't this the ideal moment for our game of daggers and mirrors?'

'Yes. Our special operative is ready. His key task is in order, and it's essential he's delivered behind enemy lines – even if the Shtrafniki achieve nothing else and not one of them is left alive,' said Beria.

'Make sure that happens.'

Stalin stood up and walked out of his office through the antechamber where his bodyguards jumped to their feet, brandishing PPSh sub-machine guns. Four moved in front of him, four followed. It would be so easy for one of them to shoot me in the back of the head, thought Stalin, so easy!

Lighting a cigarette, head down, thinking, he walked through the long deserted corridors of the Kremlin palaces, along a pathway of red carpets over shining parquet, until he reached his apartment. Leaving the guards outside, he closed the door and entered the kitchen where a small but curvaceous teenage girl in a plain blue skirt and white blouse sat alone. She was holding a pencil over an open book.

Svetlana Stalina, red-haired and freckly, jumped to her feet. 'Papa, you look exhausted!' She threw herself into his arms and he kissed her forehead.

'Why aren't you in bed, girl? It's after midnight.'

'I am sixteen, Papa, and I have to do my homework.'

'It's good you are working,' he said. 'Everyone must work for the Motherland . . .'

'Can I feed you, Papa?'

'My little sparrow can cook! But I've eaten.'

'I heard the Germans are nearing Stalingrad. Can this be true?'

'Pah! What's with the questions, Sveta? Who are these panic-mongers you talk to? Papa's girl doesn't listen to foolish chatter! Kiss your old peasant papa goodnight and finish your homework.'

After he had gone to his study at the back of the apartment, Svetlana sat down again, and for a moment, she dreamed of the things that all teenage girls dream of. She had never had a boyfriend; no one would touch her. She was Stalin's child and none of them wanted her. 'Your friends will want to worm their way into the family because you're Stalin's daughter,' her father had warned. But, on the contrary, all the boys she knew were afraid of her. She was the princess in the Kremlin fortress; the girl in the tower. At the Josef Stalin Communal School 801, she saw her friends meeting boys after lessons, walking around the Patriarchy Pool, even kissing in the Alexandrovsky Gardens right outside the Kremlin. Not her, never her . . . If only she could fall in love and someone could love her back.

She threw aside her book and started to read an article in *Krasnaya Zvezda* – or *Red Star* – the Red Army newspaper. It was by a correspondent called Lev Shapiro who reported from the Stalingrad Front. A few writers stood out: the novelist Ehrenburg with his murderous bombast, a younger writer called Grossman – and this Shapiro whose tales of the carnage in the south hid none of the tragedy of war. Yet he saw the world through such romantic eyes. Who was he? His words reached her, even here in her tower.

In his study along the corridor, Stalin shut the door and, taking off just his boots and tunic, lay down on the long divan, pulled a counterpane over himself, and closed his eyes. Svetlana, my little dove, he thought. You look just like my mother. There was a picture of his late wife, Nadya, Svetlana's mother, on the table next to his couch. He looked at her round, pouchy face, her dark eyes. Pah, he thought. She let me down. But it's hard to be Stalin's wife, Stalin's daughter. And it's hardest of all to be Stalin.

And then he thought of the crisis in the south, the direst of the war, and the punishment battalion on the Don. The only way they can redeem themselves is by shedding their own blood, he mused, pleased with his idea, which seemed to belong in Ancient Rome. My reading of history helps me, soothes me, he told himself. But he was too tired to read now. He tried to sleep but he was still shaking. Russia was close to the edge – but this was his destiny in history. To command Russia, and ultimately to triumph, whatever the cost. That was the meaning of the word 'Stalin'. It was the name he had invented just for this.

He slept spikily in fragments, then awoke again, thinking of that wild, boneheaded, horse-worshipping fool Budyonny and his stallions, and the mission of the Shtrafniki. He half remembered three years earlier ordering Beria: 'Beat Melishko — he might be a bastard; don't treat him with silk gloves; he's mixed up with enemies in Spain; he knows something.' But he had been a good man all along. And now he was right where he, Stalin, needed him.

He got out of bed in his vest and britches and lifted one of the phones. 'Get me Melishko,' he said. 'Now.'

VII

At the Budyonny Stud Farm Nine, Melishko had finished talking to the General Staff in Moscow and had organized his bandits into the new units ordered by Stavka. Wearing only his underwear, he was now asleep on his mattress on the floor, snoring deeply, when the phone started to ring in his command centre in the farm manager's house.

51

His adjutant, fast asleep in a chair in the room, picked up the phone. 'I'm listening,' he said.

'Is this the command of Colonel Melishko at the Budyonny Stud Nine?'

'It is,' replied the adjutant.

'Comrade Stalin on the line for Melishko,' said the voice impassively.

The sergeant's first thought was this was a joke. 'Who?' He paused and the words stuck in his throat. 'I'll get him,' he said, and ran in his underwear to Melishko's room in the outhouse.

'They say Stalin's on the line,' he stuttered.

'Fuckers! Taking the piss, are they?' But Melishko got up and staggered in his bare feet across the yard to the house, his exposed paunch shaking. He tripped up on a bucket, swore, got up again and ran into the headquarters where he picked up the phone.

'Melishko on the line,' he panted. He'd forgotten to put in his false teeth. Hell, I'll sound like a simpleton, he thought.

He heard the operator connect the call and then the echo of breathing. He stiffened to attention.

'Melishko.' The Georgian accent reverberated down the line. 'How are you feeling?'

'I am well, Comrade Stalin.'

'They gave you a hard time in prison. There are too many yes-men in this country who harm innocent people. That's over now, isn't it?'

'It is, Comrade Stalin.'

'The Motherland needs you. You have your orders? After this attack, you will have your rank back.'

'Thank you, Comrade Stalin.'

'And, Melishko?'

'I hear you, Comrade Stalin.'

'Your criminals are now Soviet cavalry and you must attack the Germans at full charge. Give no quarter. If you run out of bullets, use your sabres, and if you run out of sabres, kill them with your bare hands . . . Even if none are left, your men will redeem themselves by shedding their own blood.'

The phone line went dead. Melishko still held the phone. 'Even if none are left . . .' Then he shook his head and called for his adjutant. 'Get the men on parade,' he roared. 'We move out at dawn.'

Day Two

I

It was early morning, the cavalry was massing on the ridge, looking out over the endless plains. In the half-light, Benya could see the flash of hundreds of equine eyes, the gleam of stirrups, hear the stretch of girth straps, the clink of spurs, the jolt of rifle bolts being cleaned and checked, the thump of hooves – and, over it all, the drumming of his own terrified breaths. They were walking forward into squadron, so tight, Benya felt he could hear the heartbeat of the nearest rider. Right next to him, Speedy Prishchepa was drawing and redrawing his sword from its scabbard making a sound like a sharpened cymbal.

He grinned at Benya and leaned over to whisper: 'Did I ever tell you I was married back in the old country? She was such a sweet one, a real apple pie, a bun with currants! The Cossack girls have such style, not like Russian peasant women – they're mules dressed in sacks – but a Cossack girl, phew, she knows how to walk. Who knows where she is now? Maybe I'll meet her today,' and he started to sing under his breath.

On the other side sat Spider Garanzha, his large soft hand on his curved Cossack sword. 'This *shashka* can cleave a man from neck to hip with one blow,' he said, spitting. 'The human body's soft as a watermelon. With a sword like this, bones are like

57

butter. Do you know how to do the Splitter? They don't teach it at your Jew schools? No worries! I'll teach you. Once when I was in the old country, I met a farrier who . . .' They were packed so close, their boots were rubbing against each other, their stirrups almost entangled, but Benya was not listening. The suspense was intensifying. Garanzha went quiet but Prishchepa was talking incessantly. Smiley swivelled his steel teeth, his eyes hooded, and Little Mametka beside him, on his little horse, peeped ahead, looking, thought Benya, like a scared marmoset. It was always a relief to find someone more afraid than he was.

'How long until . . . ?' stammered Benya.

'Till what? Till Christmas?' joked Prishchepa. 'Till you get kissed again?'

Spider shrugged and spat out a sunflower seed.

Benya was trying frantically to remember his instructions: how would he fire his weapons? His Mosin–Nagant M38 carbine was slung over his back. Training seemed ages ago. He fingered the sabre, remembered its weight in his palm, but could he swing it? On to a man? His hands were shaking violently, the energy dripping out of him. He knew with a sudden certainty that he would die out there.

They had crossed the Don several hours previously. The majesty of the great river had astounded him. Hundreds of men and horses were wrangled on to creaking old ferries, hooves thudding, guns clanking, the men quiet and breathless once they felt the rise and fall of the water. The German guns had, for some reason, eased, and as they had pushed off, there was, for a moment, a collective intake of breath, followed by an eerie stillness, a stillness more still than any he had ever felt. Crickets chirruped and bitterns boomed and he even heard the frogs croaking and the lap of the river breathing, wide and shimmering under a red sky, its waves green and foamy, and although the near bank was high, the far one was low. It was indeed the sacred river he had read about, the one the Cossacks sang about.

'This is home,' said Prishchepa and he started to sing and the others joined in:

'*Our dear gentle Don is adorned with youthful widows;*
Our dear gentle Father Don is blossomed with orphans;
The waves of the Don are rich with tears.'

An ungodly whistling put them on edge and then his comrade's voice vanished as German shells exploded on the water, sending fountains into the air. Benya gripped the edge of the boat, knuckles white. I am going to die!

'Be calm, men,' said Zhurko. 'These aren't targeted yet. They haven't got any Storches over us.'

That's all very well, thought Benya, but suppose the shells hit us even so? He was about to say this when he recalled he could be shot for panic-mongering.

They had claimed their horses off the ferries as soon as they landed. It had been utter chaos in the grey-lilac light, horses bumping into each other, their snaffles and stirrups snagged. Finally Benya found Socks and rode up the riverbank with Prishchepa and the Uzbek thief, Koshka.

'Cigarette?' Captain Zhurko offered a Belomorkanal to the men. Only officers got Belomorkanals. Benya took one, just to do something. 'There's a lot of waiting around in war. We stand here; no one moves till I say,' he told them. 'We just have time for a cigarette.'

When Benya took it, his hand was shaking so badly that he almost dropped it. Prishchepa lit it for him; his own hands were still. 'You're quite calm,' said Benya.

'I am too simple a soul to fear death,' Prishchepa said. 'Besides, I am younger. The more you know, the harder it is. I might die now. But I prefer to live.' On the other side of Prishchepa sat Koshka, who appeared to be rigid with fear, and then Mametka, who wiped his brow over and over, eyes as big and empty as sinkholes.

'This is going to be a beauty of a day. We might get a tan. Do you know I had a girl in that village over there?' chattered Prishchepa.

'Shut up, magpie,' said Spider Garanzha.

'Are you Cossacks? I'm writing about the battle. For the newspaper *Red Star*. I got on the last ferry. I know you're Shtrafniki but I want the public to know . . .' They looked down at a gentle-faced man in uniform with a shock of black hair who was walking along the line between the horses, holding his notebook and pencil. Benya could see the men liked him, even the roughest of them: he could hear him interviewing 'Lover-boy' Cherkashkin, the youthful Party Secretary from Belgorod who had murdered his mistress's husband out of passionate jealousy; even 'Cannibal' Delibash was answering his questions; then he was questioning the swarthy Shundenko.

'Time's up, scribbler. Get out of here. Advance is imminent,' Mogilchuk shouted.

Benya's hands and legs were thrumming; sweat spread across his shirt, and a socket of fear pulsated in his belly. He stayed close to the men of his squadron but he had no idea where they were going, what they were meant to do. He recalled something about advancing under cover of the tanks, then going into a charge and, if successful, a raid behind enemy lines.

'Right, lads, you'll be entering a sector where many Soviet troops, some lost, some traitors and cowards, will be at large,' Captain Ganakovich was bellowing. 'Stavka orders all forces on southern fronts to be given this information: You will cooperate with our brave Soviet partisans. But there are bands of traitors fighting for the Hitlerites, and particularly in this sector, a special unit under the traitor and collaborator Mandryka. These you will annihilate on sight. Instant redemption awaits the man who kills Mandryka or any collaborationist leaders . . .'

Benya had never killed a man, making him something of a novelty in a battalion where even those who hadn't murdered anyone, like Koshka, liked to imply that they had. He knew neither how to kill nor how to die, and he told himself now that it was the not knowing that made them both frightening.

'When you shoot, please at least aim at something,' said Captain Zhurko. 'Seventy per cent of shots fired in battle are totally unaimed . . .'

They had all laughed then; now Benya had forgotten how to shoot, how to breathe . . .

Zhurko rode up and down. 'Remember, fellows,' he said, repeating his catchphrase to each squadron. 'If you're scared, don't do it. If you do it, don't be scared!'

Benya's panic boiled a hot broth in his gorge. The crump of shells – for a moment flying high over them from the German side – was shaking the earth as if a giant was stomping towards them. A boom, then another, made Benya jump, his ears almost bursting, the afterblasts buffering the air. The

61

regimental artillery, 76-mm howitzers, were positioned right behind the horsemen and now they began to fire over them; then the 122-mms . . .

Now came the revving of engines, and nimble BT-7 tanks – Betushkas – motored past them; Benya knew they were out of date and he could see them rumbling, stalling, grunting and pumping out black smoke. It was starting.

Panka was riding up the ranks, ladling out their hundred grammes of vodka into the metal mugs that hung from their saddlebags. He handed one to Benya and watched him drink it: 'It's always sunny in the saddle,' said the old Cossack as Benya knocked it back, still sure he was going to die.

'Squadrons. In file formation: forward!'

Oh God, this was it! Benya thought of his mother, just his mother, and he actually said 'Mama', and he wished he was anywhere but here. He didn't even believe in God, hadn't prayed since he was a boy, but now he was reciting the *Shema* in Hebrew. The fear of death was so visceral that Benya looked behind him, the muscles in his thighs tensing so he could dismount and just run, run, run down to the Don. He could swim to safety. He was not made for this! But then he saw Mogilchuk standing behind the NKVD blocking squads, their machine guns set up right behind the artillery. They were ready to shoot down any cowards, the entire brigade if necessary . . .

'Squadrons!' cried Melishko, riding in front of them on his twenty-hand horse, Elephant, a steed big enough to carry a knight in full armour. 'Prepare to advance at the walk. Wait . . . !' The artillery tossed another volley over their heads. Benya saw the shells explode far ahead of them, smoke rising, debris in the air – could they be real? Melishko's words were lost but Zhurko repeated the orders; as did the sergeants all along the line: 'Wait for agreed signals to lope then on the order: charge!'

Benya's skin was squeezing him like a shell, and he knew he could not fight. But Prishchepa, humming a song, was riding forward, and so was Spider and the entire line. Between the thuds of shells he could hear the Cossacks were all singing together.

'Squadrons! Draw sabres!' There was a flash of blue steel along the line as eight hundred blades were drawn. The sight, accompanied by the haunting Cossack harmonies, was so rousing that for an instant wild optimism overcame Benya's fear. He thought of Borodino and Waterloo and found that he had drawn his own blade and that the *shashka* was heavy in his hand. Just yards ahead, Melishko thudded forward on Elephant, those plough-horse hooves tossing clods of turf into the air, gaining speed.

Zhurko was behind him, his sword raised.

'Prepare to gallop, bandits!' Melishko shouted and Zhurko, twisting round to face them, called out:

'Not yet! Hold it, hold it!'

Sliver Sock's three-beat gait was making Benya bounce around in the saddle. In vain, he tried to steady himself as he held his sabre over his head but it was too heavy. He felt himself falling, until a hand steadied him and Prishchepa was right beside him, laughing in the wind, head back. Benya just had time to think that a single German machine gun could finish them all in one minute before they overtook the Betushka tanks (two had stalled already), and he heard the cry: 'Charge, men! To the gallop!'

'Forward, you motherfuckers, or I'll shoot you down! *Za Rodina, za Stalina!* For Stalin, for the Motherland!' cried Ganakovich, waving his pistol unconvincingly.

'For the fucking Prosecutors!' shouted the Shtrafniki as one.

Keeping pace with the horses on either side of her, Silver Socks lengthened her stride and began to gallop, the surge of muscular power sending Benya bouncing around in the saddle once more. 'Stay on, fucker, stay on!' he grunted, holding on to the reins and Silver Socks's mane for all he was worth.

Melishko turned in his saddle: 'Enemy sighted!'

And Benya saw them. A compact mass of riders, maybe thirty of them, shirtsleeves rolled up, red caps, and swords flashing, riding straight at him. He could see their faces: all wore uniforms with red ties. A dark-skinned man on a limber grey, black eyes and low brows, nostrils flared, was concentrating hard on him, no one else, just him, riding at him, sword raised – Benya understood the brutal simplicity of war; this man wants to kill <u>me</u> – but then he galloped right past. Benya hung on to Socks. Around him was the clash of steel on steel as another rider in a red cap came at him, but he swerved past him too. A third flew at him, shouting – Benya could see the blackheads on his nose, that was how close he was, he had black eyelashes – and this time Prishchepa spun round in his saddle and brought his sword down on the man, missing the top of his head but slicing off his ear. Benya thanked God that no one had reached him yet. He tried to stay close to his Cossack friends but this time a bulky rider, smiling under a black moustache, was right in front of him, his bay horse foaming, and before Benya could pull on Socks's reins to avoid him, he had drawn a pistol and was raising it.

There was a loud thump as Spider Garanzha rode his horse right into him, knocking him to the ground. Benya did not see what happened next, because a blow hit him so hard on the chest that he almost fell off Socks and surely he was wounded, even dead? Someone had struck him with a sabre but it must have been the flat side for he was unharmed; the sword had hit the pommel of his saddle and glanced off, grazing Silver Socks on the neck. He saw blood, and it was this that outraged him. This man had wounded his Silver Socks, his beloved Budyonny chestnut.

'You bastard!' Benya shouted, swinging his sword at his opponent. He was thin-faced, sunburned, perhaps Benya's age, and now Benya saw fear in an enemy's eyes and he feasted on it as he swung the sword just as he had been trained: parry, withdraw and strike. The sword smashed into the man's face, slicing right through his cheekbone, tearing his face in half. There was a sound like the fracturing of an eggshell and the slurp of the yolk and Benya saw his opponent's teeth flying up to scatter like a broken pearl necklace. By the time he realized that he had wounded him, even perhaps killed him, the man was on the ground, his riderless horse galloping into the distance, and Benya was charging on with Prishchepa, Smiley and Little Mametka, all using their quirts on their mounts.

Seconds later, he and Prishchepa faced two enemies, riding at them together; one was unhorsed and Benya brought his sword down on the man on the ground with unrealized strength, cutting deep into him. Blood sprayed up at him, red heat cooling on his face, a coppery taste in his mouth. How delicate a thing is a man, he thought, how much softness there is to spoil. He heard singing and he realized it was his own voice, joining in with the Cossacks. He was changing; a switch clicked within him, as if he was a new animal who bore little resemblance to his usual self: a crimson-sprayed Jew on a Russian Pegasus riding the hot wind and killing with profilgate efficiency, and a sort of ecstasy.

Silver Socks pricked her ears and slowed suddenly, turning her head to the left. Once again, Benya saw the crimson on her neck but then she rallied, leaped forward, her gallop stronger than before. A squadron of four riders was heading towards him, wearing field-grey tunics – German uniforms – but they weren't Germans. One or two had raised their sabres, the others held up their carbines like Red Indians. 'Brother Cossacks, join us,' one of them called over. 'The war's lost, brothers! It's not our war!'

Cossacks fighting on the German side. And then, dropping their reins, they started firing at them. Benya managed to swerve behind his comrades. By hesitating for an instant, Silver Socks had saved his life.

'Motherfuckers! Traitors!' Prishchepa turned his mount and slid over to one side, behind his saddle, as the shots rang out; then, holding his pommel, he swung back into the saddle and raising a pistol, shot one of them right in the face.

The horses were suddenly packed against each other and Benya and the others were fighting with everything, hands, swords, everyone terrified and angry, the horses foaming in the heat. Benya drove his sword into a man until he felt it hit the spine, not so soft after all, and the man started to slip backwards off his horse, hands flailing for the reins, mane, finally tail, anything. In panic, with the man's blood running down his sabre on to his hands, Benya spurred Silver Socks and she reared up and jumped out of the tangle with Benya just keeping his seat.

'Onwards! We've surprised them!' Captain Zhurko was still riding ahead of them, now shooting with his Papasha submachine gun. Cannons opened up on each side. Shells whined and landed to their left and right, and starbursts of earth, flame and turf exploded over him. Benya looked back. The Betushka tanks were burning, and men were jumping out of the turrets which vomited jet-black smoke. Benya had the impression of torn horses on their sides, legs still treading the air with men staggering around them, but his squadron galloped on, untouched somehow. They were approaching an enemy position, but the soldiers there saw them and turned and ran; so did those at the next enemy position and suddenly they were riding alongside running men.

Benya came up behind one, a man in a helmet with a cockerel-feather plume who was running like a mechanical doll, and he brought down the sabre on his head, splitting it right open like a melon. He heard singing and it was him singing again loudly, at the top of his voice. Riderless horses joined him galloping forward; they were Russian horses, Budyonnys and little Kalmyk ponies – and one dragged the body of a Shtrafnik by the boot; it was his comrade Skakun with his hands bouncing above his head. Benya passed abandoned tanks: one was a Betushka, but two belonged to the enemy – although the markings weren't German. He saw his Uzbek comrade Koshka overtaking him, out of control, holding on to his horse's mane, reins flying, google-eyed with panic. Silver Socks's hoof crashed down with a crunching pop on to the head of a fallen man but Benya didn't look back.

More men were running before him; the Cossacks were yahooing and ululating like banshees; yet more enemies appeared out of trenches and golden fields and ran for their lives. One turned to point a rifle at him but Silver Socks leaped forward and Benya brought down his sword, hitting his enemy's neck, cutting deep; this killing had its own queer wantonness that made him thirst for more. Two boys wearing helmets with feathers raised their hands to him. As Benya was about to slash one of them, he fell to his knees and cried out: 'Mama, Mama!' The other boy was young, much younger than Benya, with a long nose and big teeth and sheepish eyes and he remembered thinking their voices were beautiful, their faces were tanned and dark, and their uniforms were baroque. Feathers and red ties and fezes. Fancy dress! The boy stopped crying 'Mama!' and was pointing a pistol at Benya until, in a swish, the arm was gone, his torso cloven from shoulder to ribs in a throb of blood. Spider Garanzha raised his dripping blade and waved it wildly at Benya as if to say: You see, the Splitter!

They were still riding forward but they were cantering now. The horses were foaming, their coats dripping sweat. They came to a stream, the horses stopped to drink and some of the men jumped into the water.

'Get on your horses – no dismounting. Now! Keep advancing, keep moving,' Zhurko yelled at them.

Now they loped more easily, crossing cornfields, riding through sunflowers. What time was it? They had charged in the early morning but now it seemed much later. The sun burned high. Each field they came to there was an enemy position but, at the sight of them, the men, wearing feathers in their hats, jumped up shouting and ran away. Benya and Garanzha galloped after them, Benya swinging the sabre. What damage cold steel could do, he thought. Enemies still fled, dropping helmets, mugs, boots, pans, until riven by steel they fell and didn't rise again.

The guns were quieter behind them, Benya noticed. Still fritzing with adrenalin, he was almost jumping out of his skin. 'This is how victory feels!' said Prishchepa, whirling his *shashka* over his head, flicking out a spray of sweat. The sky seemed to Benya to reflect his blast of gaudy fierceness. It was as blue as the sea, a sea upside down.

They rode on and on, under the scorching sun, over fields full of broken young men lying amongst the ripened wheat.

The words those fleeing boys were shouting sounded so graceful. It was not German, or Hungarian; could it be Romanian? No, you idiot, realized Benya, it was Italian. They had been chasing Italians.

'Halt!' Zhurko pulled his reins and held up his hand. The squadron managed to stop on a slight spur, though Koshka went straight over his horse's head on to the ground and lay there whimpering.

'Look!' Sergeant Panka rode up to Zhurko. 'A church tower, captain. A village ahead.'

'Form into two squadrons, sergeant,' said Zhurko. 'You take Squadron One to the east. Squadron Two, come with me. Let's go!'

They rode down the street feeling as light as a pack of wolves on the hunt.

II

An old Cossack woman is cooking a goose for a hundred men in the house by the church, a pot meant for the Italian soldiers who had been occupying the village until hours earlier. The old man beside her sleeps in an alcove with its scarlet rugs and tassels; her children are packed together like puppies in a basket. She's toothless with sunken cheeks and she sucks her gums as she watches the men who've just ridden in, her eyes as murderous as sickles. If the riders expected a warm welcome for liberating the village, they do not find one here. Benya understands there is no welcome amongst broken people.

It's early afternoon. It's too hot to move yet everyone is moving. To Benya the village seems bright and rich. After years of a life in black and white, in prisons, Camps, military training, every moment in this village will be imprinted on Benya's mind forever, like the first film you ever see in colour. They clop down the street, standing high in their stirrups, yahooing loudly, singing songs, brandishing swords still streaked with blood and grass. Ahead of them, a dead horse, then a man with rosy cheeks and open eyes but missing the top of his head, a dome of creamy matter still immaculate and quivering in its fragility: these are just some of the sights that overwhelm him. The village radiates freedom with its colourfully painted cottages, eggshell blues and fiesta reds, and some of the girls have dressed up in white blouses and skirts in red and green, woven with white hems hung with bells. The horsemen follow the swing of the girls' hips with their eyes. They smell the food, hear the ringing water of the stream. It is a time that will live in the men's memory in the perpetual present, a time of wonder divided into jagged but discrete scenes.

The Shtrafniki find olive oil and chocolate and even eggs.

There's wine and vodka and the men start drinking immediately. These Italians have things Benya hasn't seen since he was in Madrid. The place is fragrant from the cooking. The Italians left in a hurry when the Shtrafniki galloped right into the village, that's for sure. There's coffee ground in a helmet, real coffee, and plates of polenta and vermicelli that are still warm. There is a dead man in the yard and Smiley is pulling off his boots and trying them on. 'These'll do,' he says.

Someone has already tossed his pockets, spilling love letters in playful italic writing and sepia photographs of a beautiful woman posing with a chocolate-box-ish background in a studio in some small Italian town. The letters are spread into a fan-shaped collage that reduces the story of an entire life to its pathetic essentials: a body, an ID card, a photo of a family. *Finis.* We killed them without even bothering to find out who they were, thinks Benya.

After swigging some water and swallowing a piece of cheese, Benya walks his horse to a stable where the vet Lampadnik and the farrier Tufty Grishchuk are checking the hooves. He hands Silver Socks to Lampadnik, worried about her neck. 'Oh dear. Doesn't look good. Sorry, Benya,' Lampadnik says.

'What do you mean?' says Benya, suddenly worried.

'What do you think?' asks Lampadnik, turning to Panka.

The old Cossack touches the neck carefully, checks his finger. 'She is still bleeding.'

'What do we do?' Lampadnik is cautious and shy. Doubt is sketched on his long face with horsey teeth, and Benya knows he has been tentative since he was sentenced to ten years in the Camps in 1937 for 'Trotskyite wrecking' after two horses died of croup.

'Golden, be calm. Let me do this,' says Panka, his teak-coloured face grave. 'I have some old twine in my saddlebag and, Lampadnik, you scald some tree bark. Ask the woman for some honey.'

Benya holds Silver Socks, who is pouring sweat, and talks to her while Panka finds the twine in his saddlebags and quickly binds Socks's upper lip to distract her and then washes the wound in water, then with the juice of scalded bark. He threads the twine through the eye of a knitting needle and sews up the gash in Socks's neck with lightning dexterity, pulling it tight, applying more of the scalded bark and painting on the honey. 'A poultice, you see?' and then he releases the horse's mouth. Socks is still shivering but her eyes are different, relieved somehow.

'There,' says Panka, stroking her muzzle. 'You're going to be fine. I'll watch her. Golden, go and get some grub and sleep. It's always sunny on the steppe, eh?'

Outside the Cossacks in the squadron cheer Benya and rub his shaven head with its spiky grey-blondness. 'I saw him swing his sabre,' they tease him.

'I thought he could only lift a pen,' says Spider Garanzha.

'The Jew has it,' says Panka.

'That's a compliment from Panka. He might even call you "brother",' jokes Fats Strizkaz, embracing him, kind suddenly and Benya loves him with the love of men who kill and die together.

Panka shrugs and spits, busy with the other horses. He is too experienced to share the exhilaration of the hopped-up Criminals but he has a shot of vodka or two and is cheerful in his level way.

Benya looks around him. His companions are scarlet-cheeked and shiny-eyed with butchery. There's madness in the air, and they swagger giddily with the strange aura of rare men who've ladled out death and know the secrets of the world. Benya wonders if they are about to slip the reins and go berserk in the village. Socks is going to live though; he has been through a battle – and he feels eerily powerful, hungry for more war, more savagery.

There's singing from the millhouse where the rest of the squadron are swimming in the stream, stark naked. Benya looks at their tanned faces and necks with a 'V' down their chests; their bodies are as white as snow. He throws off his clothes, so hot suddenly that the cold seems to scald him.

Wearing damp clothes that dry fast, Benya lies on a mattress in the shade of a house behind a wattle fence. The house smells of *kvass* and sausage. There's the pungent fug of closely packed, sweaty bodies, which he recognizes as one of the pervasive smells of war and prison. A peasant woman in an embroidered hat and skirts sits and stares at him. She gives Benya a glass of milk but she has a sly look. It's hospitality – or a dagger in the back. Ruined people are cruel people.

Exhausted, Benya fights to stay awake. He hasn't slept for twenty-four hours or more, but he is still scudding from the revelation of his newly discovered other self. His sword arm aches and burns: he can hardly lift it; his thighs are agony, and he can barely walk. Yet he is alive. More than alive. He is trembling and transfigured. Through the blade he felt the softness of his fellow humans. He has killed several men, men whose eyes he looked into, not Germans but Italians, his favourite nation on earth. He thought he was killing German Nazis. Instead they were the people of Michelangelo, Raffaello and Tiziano and, as if to make the point, someone has found an Italian gramophone. The aria of *Rigoletto* soars into the still afternoon air. He falls asleep, dreaming . . .

The music stops abruptly, and Benya sits up. It's as if he has awoken in another dimension. The atmosphere is quite different, a swerve of mood, a darkening under the blinding sun. Perhaps it was something to do with the drink? Or just the flesh-eating instinct of born killers who have no other way of expressing themselves, or of feeling free and alive? He goes outside and sees those cutthroats he knows so well, Smiley, and Cut and Run, staggering into cottages.

The goose is ready. It's been cooked so long the flesh melts on his tongue. Plates of eggs and pork and kasha and the meat of a dead camel are put before him. For dessert: cherries and peaches. This is a rich, black-earthed land, and Benya eats like an animal, even the chewy camel meat, virtually licking the plate clean. He hasn't enjoyed such plenty since before his arrest, and the men trough almost silently, quaffing wine and *cha-cha*, getting sunburnt and soused, like lords of creation. Afterwards, Benya checks on Silver Socks, who is lying down outside in the shade, her legs folded under her. She is not feverish, she's eaten, and her neck looks clean.

When Benya went to sleep, there had been laughter and splashing and flirting, a sense of triumph, a glaze of evervescence. They had pulled it off. They had broken the enemy, taken this village. Haven't they earned their redemption? But now the milk is soured, the sun is so hot that Benya feels its pulse throbbing, and there's shouting behind the stables. In the yard of the priest's house, the Political Officer, Ganakovich, is interrogating a collaborator, a Kalmyk scout with wild sweat-pleated hair and grey German britches. The traitor is tied to a chair, bleeding from the eyes, and there are teeth scattered around like jewels. There's a fat Italian there too, just a boy, sitting against a wicker fence, watching as if this has nothing to do with him.

When he sees Benya, he asks in Italian: 'When will we go home? Will we ever eat spaghetti and wine again?'

'*Si, si, ragazzo, presto!*' Benya knows some Italian and he understands and is suddenly overcome with the urge to weep, to hug the boy.

Ganakovich is nervous. He looks around and sees Zhurko in the doorway. 'Where's the support? Where's the artillery?' he blurts out. 'Where's Melishko?'

'They should be on their way,' Zhurko opines. 'But I'll take a look,' and he heads towards the stables.

'What about Mogilchuk? We need the Special Unit here, don't we?' No one answers this and no one but Ganakovich misses those hyenas. Then he shouts at the scout, 'Where are the rest of you traitors? Where's Mandryka and his auxiliary police?' He is waving his pistol around in a way that proves he has never seen battle. Ganakovich, Benya knows, is a blowhard in the Russian tradition: a tyrant to those below, a slave to his masters.

Garanzha approaches softly and then suddenly his steps are as light as a ballerina's and the spasm of violence so quick Benya doesn't see it; and the scout starts to talk. With his round, leathery face and almond-shaped eyes, he's a descendant of Genghis

Khan perhaps. The Kalmyk scout is a tough customer, but he has betrayed Russia, and knows there will be no quarter given.

'Mandryka's Hiwis?' he asks. Benya doesn't know what he's talking about but he does know that 'Hiwi' is short for *Hilfswilliger*, 'willing to help', the name for all Russian traitors, such as the Schuma auxiliary police, who have thrown in their lot with the Germans. 'Yes, they're at that village, Shepilovka.'

'Where's that?' Even Ganakovich has no idea where they are.

'Ten miles west from here.' The scout speaks in a toothless monotone, no effort necessary now, death imminent, in an accent that mixes Russia with the Mongol East.

'Where are German forces massed?' Ganakovich asks.

'All around you. See the dust rising.'

Ganakovich peers around and sure enough, in the distance, clouds of dust roll forward like a giant wave.

'The offensive is about to start again soon. You got lucky, Cossacks,' the scout says.

'Lucky? What do you mean?'

'You're Shtrafniki, aren't you?' replies the scout. 'There's no backup coming behind you. The Italian Colonel Malamore was here with the traitor Mandryka and some Germans. Just a few hours ago. They know you're here . . . But as for you – you're on your own.'

Ganakovich is stunned. Unsure what to do, he tells Spider to send the prisoners back to headquarters, and reels out on to the street.

Garanzha has an ominous ticking stillness about him. 'What are you looking at?' he asks.

'What are you going to do?' says Benya.

Spider looks right at Benya and, surprisingly in that sharkish face, he has the milkiest goo-goo eyes that could loll a baby to sleep – even as he draws his dagger.

'Garanzha's got his butcher's grin! Like it's a holiday and he's about to slaughter a sheep.' It's Prishchepa, cheerful as a chaffinch. 'Put it away, brother,' he says.

Garanzha sheathes the dagger, and the Kalmyk nods gratefully but without much conviction.

'What's going on?' asks Prishchepa. 'The girls in this village are beauties. Mine's called Aksinya, fresh as a punnet of strawberries . . .' He beams carelessly at the prisoners and the Shtrafniki – as if both are equally his pals. 'Must go. Aksinya's waiting,' and as he leaves, it happens so fast: Garanzha is giving his goo-goo eyes to Benya, never even looking at the scout, as his steps go all quick and balletic and somehow, in that instant, the blade has done its work. The scout twitches slightly as if falling asleep, and the blood pumps out in fast and then shorter and shorter spouts.

'Ahh! Mama!' It is the Italian boy, staring at the dead scout. Something clicks as he realizes that gentle routines of the Venetian slums, licking *gelato* in the *campo* with his mama, coffee with his papa at his usual table, catching the *vaporetto* to his grandmother's, all the things he knew and took for granted that he would see again, are gone.

'*Ciao, ragazzo*, where are you from?' Benya distracts him in Italian.

'Venice. Alpini. The Tridentine Division.'

'What's your father do?'

'Cheesemaker. I work with him.'

Benya longs to grab the boy and run away with him to safety. 'I was in Venice once.'

The hope rises in the boy's lamb eyes. 'I could make you polenta, spaghetti,' he says. 'I'll cook for you. I was just cooking it up for my unit when——' He feels Garanzha's gaze.

'I'll take care of him, Garanzha,' says Benya.

'No,' says Garanzha in his gentle, detached voice. 'Ganakovich gave me my orders. I'll escort him back to our lines.' He gestures to the boy, who gets to his feet. They walk through the graveyard and out into fields. Benya watches them as they get smaller. He feels numb; he wants to get a grip but everything is slippery and runs through his fingers. He knows he won't see the boy again.

There's howling from a nearby house. Benya looks sideways and Smiley comes out through the garden, chuckling and wiping his hands on his trousers. There is more weeping as Fats Strizkaz looms in the doorway, pig-drunk and lairy, and barrerls in while just outside Little Mametka, poky-faced except for luxuriant lips, lingers like a randy schoolboy outside a cathouse.

Benya is afraid of Smiley though grateful to him for many things. 'How could you?' he asks now.

'Fancy swimming in my milk?' Smiley stands in front of Benya, who notices his maddened red eyes set in his strangely handsome face. 'Be my guest, Jewboy.'

'You . . . forced her?'

'Are you a priest? Never.' Smiley shakes his head. 'A dog doesn't harass an unwilling bitch. What about you, Mametka? Keen to lose your cherry?'

'I've had women,' pipes up Mametka.

Fats Strizkaz snorts as he slams the door of the house behind him – the weeping is now quieter – and stamps up the garden path. 'No, you haven't, you lying little eunuch. Your voice hasn't even broken. You've never touched a woman, have you, Bette Davis!' Strizkaz was a Chekist interrogator – until arrested himself. A Trusty in Kolyma, he has kept his connections to the secret police so the men humour him. But no one forgets what he was.

Smiley pokes Mametka in the side. 'You going to put up with that, Mametka?'

'Ignore him,' says Benya. 'Come on, let's go and see the horses.'

'Horses? Riding horses is all Mametka can do with his little woodpecker; he couldn't do a woman if he wanted, could you, Bette Davis?' leers Strizkaz.

'Not funny. Not funny,' says Mametka timidly. 'I won't put up with it.'

'What's that? You'll put up with it if I say you fucking put up with it,' replies Strizkaz. 'Won't you, Bette Davis?'

'You should apologize, Fats,' says Smiley in what Benya thinks is a statesmanlike, League of Nations-peacekeeping manner. 'I think you've gone a little far, eh?'

Strizkaz smirks but takes no notice.

'Ignore him, Mametka,' says Benya, concerned that Smiley and Strizkaz will come to blows. 'Look!'

On the village street, Captain Zhurko rides in. Ganakovich, clearly in despair, rushes out to meet him. 'Where are supply carts? Where's the guns? Where are the communications people?' he shouts, waving his arms.

'I don't know! How can I know?' This is the sensible voice of Zhurko. 'No one followed us.'

'And where's the rest of the battalion?'

79

'I rode back towards our lines. There are Fritzes everywhere, tanks and guns, and none of ours.'

'The Kalmyk said we got lucky. We found the Italians. But now we're on our own.' Ganakovich gulps. 'Where's Melishko?'

A silence.

'We need Melishko.'

Benya feels sick. Surely these two fools can't be right?

'Melishko will come,' says Zhurko decisively. 'Melishko will know what to do.'

Afterwards Koshka joins Benya. He has been listening too.

'Maybe this wasn't a victory after all,' he whispers hoarsely. 'Maybe we're lost!'

III

In Stalin's apartment in Moscow, Svetlana was alone and miserable. She could tell by the looks the teachers gave her at school that she was an outcast, albeit a much revered, almost sacred one. Although her father was the greatest man alive, her teachers were afraid of her; many of the boys and girls avoided her and she knew their parents told them to have nothing to do with her.

Her father sometimes stayed with her in the Kremlin apartment, especially when the war was in crisis, but more often he visited her after his meetings and then drove out to his real home, the Nearby Dacha at Kuntsevo, twenty minutes outside the city. In the apartment, she lived with her devoted nanny, her cook, and Mikhail Klimov, her bodyguard from the secret police. Her father was so busy with the war that he had little time for her, but Svetlana still worried about him. The stress, she knew, was almost unbearable. No other man could take it. Her elder brother Vasya – Colonel Vasily Stalin – certainly couldn't. He had just been cashiered for his outrageous and drunken behaviour. He had taken some of his men fishing but instead of fishing rods, Vasya had thrown grenades into the river and one of his men had been killed. Her father had been furious.

She sighed and looked at the newspapers as she always did in the evening and there it was in the *Red Star*. Another article by her favourite correspondent Lev Shapiro.

Sometimes even the lowest can perform like heroes. In the early hours, I caught a lift on the ferry across the Don and saw one of the new Shtrafbats go into action to defend our positions holding the Don Bend. They were outfitted on horseback with Marshal Budyonny's Cossack mounts and I saw them gallop into battle in squadrons. As Shtrafniki, they were criminals, cowards, officers cashiered for retreating without orders, rightly sentenced for crimes, but thanks to the ingenuity of our Great Stalin in Order 227, they have been given this new chance to redeem their sins and serve our Motherland. They were a mixed crew of misfits and criminals and there was even one writer. But their spirit showed the genius of Comrade Stalin in giving them this opportunity to bleed and be rehabilitated, for they were patriots long-ing to serve.

81

In a scene that would quicken every heart, the squadrons of eight hundred horsemen recalled some of the finest moments in our great Russian history, fighting against vicious invaders – the Teutonic Knights, the Swedes, the French and now the Hitlerites. They file into position. 'It's always sunny in the saddle,' says an old Cossack, a veteran of Budyonny's Red Cavalry; and then their commander, a Colonel Melishko, says, 'You can't get me!' and his men cheer. Then he shouts: 'Draw your sabres,' and I see the blades flash; then: 'Forward! Charge!' and, with their sabres held at an oblique angle, the curved steel glinting above their heads, I hear them shout, 'For Stalin! For the Motherland!' and, under brutal cannonfire, they charge the Nazis and fall in their droves – but some break through to terrorize the invaders . . . It's a sight that brings tears to my eyes: how can any Russian reading this not weep at such courage?

Tears ran down Svetlana's cheeks too. She had to write to this man to tell him that she adored his work. She reached for a pen and paper and wrote in a rounded girlish hand:

Dear Lev Shapiro,
    Forgive me for writing to you. I know you are busy. But I just wished to express to you that for this reader at least your writing is truly a service to our Motherland and is read keenly here.
    Best wishes,
    Svetlana Stalina
    The Kremlin, Moscow

IV

It is late afternoon as Benya walks through the village. Each house has its gated wattle fence at the front, and a back yard leading to a garden festooned with vines and cherries.

'Hey, Golden, look!' They've found more Italian bodies in one of the cottages. There is a dead Italian officer on the doorstep, a splendid-looking fellow, tanned and immaculately dressed – shot neatly through the heart. Everyone stares at him – before the Criminals start stripping him of accoutrements. Smiley, Cut and Run, Cannibal Delibash and Koshka are working their way through the houses, looking for food, weapons, girls. At the moment of impact: screams and smashed glass; afterwards; a light symphony of sobbing. It is not the liberation the villagers deserved.

Spider Garanzha appears suddenly, wiping his sabre on the grass, his guess-what-I-just-did smile on his gaping shark mouth, and they join the men lazing in the churchyard, which now resembles a macabre gypsy banquet with food, bottles and bits of uniform scattered amidst the gravestones. Some of the men are still drinking in the sun and a few have passed out. Lying on his back, his bell-shaped head sunburnt to a fluorescent puce, propped up on a doubled-up mattress, his belly a swollen winesack (the only man ever to emerge with a paunch from the Camps), Fats Strizkaz gives his opinions on all matters. Did you see Koshka in the charge? What a coward! How Ganakovich is scared of war – don't you notice when his voice goes high? Fats has a bottle of Italian wine which he happily

83

shares with Smiley and Garanzha. Then he scopes Little Mametka, who has stolen the Italian officer's gleaming boots, holster and dagger scabbard engraved with his initials.

'Hey, Mametka, those boots are too big for you!'

Smiley raises a warning hand but Strizkaz won't be restrained.

'Hey! What? We all called him Bette Davis in Kolyma! Jaba made it up.' That was true, thought Benya, but Mametka could take anything from Jaba, his Boss; he was younger then; and besides, Jaba had an affectionate way of saying it.

'I apologized,' Strizkaz drawls. 'I apologized and you accepted it, right?'

Mametka looks twitchy. He nods gingerly.

'It's OK,' Strizkaz tells Smiley and Garanzha. 'I apologized and he accepted it . . .' Then his face with its patch of moustache turns vicious again. 'Didn't you?'

'Yes I did,' said Mametka.

'Yes you did,' he bellows. 'Bette Davis, you little fucking girl!'

And that is it. Like watching a reel of film that suddenly trips and jumps a few frames, Benya misses the first moves, and then he sees Mametka has grabbed one of the shovels and, twisting its blade in the air, is thrusting it again and again into Strizkaz's throat with such power that his neck is virtually obliterated. Blood spatters all over him — a trip of the reel — before Benya and everyone else can even get to their feet to stop him . . . or join in. Then another jump in the reel and Smiley, Garanzha and a suddenly awakened Cut and Run Ivanov are beating Strizkaz with anything to hand: a rifle butt, another shovel and a slab of rock. Everyone else just looks on. When they are finished, they lug the unrecognizable Strizkaz into one of the half-dug graves and drop a tombstone down on top of him.

'What the hell's going on here?' Ganakovich is coming up through the graveyard, gawping at Mametka and drawing his Nagant, but Smiley and Garanzha take no notice of him. 'Lads, you need to tell me.'

'I don't think so,' says Spider Garanzha.

'Leave this to us!' adds Smiley.

Ganakovich looks them up and down, replaces his pistol and heads back down to the priest's house. The state has officially lost control of the Shtrafbat.

Smiley's forehead is pointed, temple veins swollen and charged, and he has come into himself with that strain of pure forthrightness he was born with, the killer's easiness — and there are moments that Benya envies it. But now not. He is desperate to get away from the graveyard. He hurries past Mametka, who is so besmeared that the blood looks like stage make-up — even his hair is congealed — and staggers down the lane to the Italian Red Cross tent, which is pitched on the far edge of the village.

'What's going on?' asks Dr Kapto, who is still patching up some of the wounded Shtrafniki. 'Something happened in the graveyard?'

'Nothing . . . it can wait till you're finished. Can I sit here?' Benya is just happy to be in the wholesome peace of the tent of serene healing — away from the others. He should be shaking after what he has seen — but he isn't. He prays Melishko will return soon and tell them the plan; there has to be a plan.

He watches the nurses Tonya and Nyushka working hard,

sewing up wounds and dressing them. 'I have no doubt we'll advance soon,' chatters the dimpled Nyushka. 'The Great Stalin knows what he's doing. He'll have a plan for us.' She's always been a fanatical Stalinist despite being arrested and sent to Kolyma. He notices how well she looks. Even though the doctor and nurses have ridden with the squadrons for many hours, she still has a bruised ripeness about her, her cheeks a little sunburnt, her auburn hair streaked gold. 'Comrade Ganakovich will know,' she says innocently. 'He always knows Stalin's orders.'

'Of course, he does,' agrees Benya, remembering that she is now Ganakovich's girl, his 'front wife'.

He turns to Tonya: she and Kapto seem to communicate without words. When he cuts, she is already there with the cotton wool to dab the wound, predicting his moves with smudged, half-closed eyes set in a flat, expressionless face. Does she love Kapto or isn't it like that? Is it her destiny to attend the doctor but never have him?

They sew up the last of the wounded. Breezy and direct, Kapto pats each patient on the side when he finishes: 'There! All done! Easy, now, easy!' Benya spots his uniform now boasts a captain's pips and he has a leather satchel which he always wears over his shoulder and across his chest.

'You got promoted, doctor? I hadn't noticed.'

'Looking after Melishko's piles has its rewards,' he says.

'And the satchel?'

'The morphine of course. Do you need some? How was the charge, Benya?'

'Terrifying . . .'

'I saw you. You were like a devil possessed. Since you gave

86

up writing, you might have found your new metier but . . .' He sighs. 'A sabre can do terrible damage – as you now know.' Benya feels guilty and yet somehow pleased with this new reputation for brutality. It is so unlikely. 'Cigarette? I have Italian ones. Africas. Shall we get out of the village?' Kapto says, stepping outside the tent and lighting up.

'We need to avoid the churchyard,' says Benya, 'but it seems quiet in the fields. They just killed Fats.'

'Revenge for what he was in the Camps. Only Melishko can control them,' muses the doctor. 'Is he back? Where on earth are we going next?'

Benya takes his rifle and Kapto draws his new sidearm, a handsome German Parabellum he has found in the village, and they stroll into the countryside where the fields have been harvested. Ahead of them, there's a combine harvester burnt out on the field. Benya looks back at the village and it might be a summer afternoon in peacetime. A magpie stutters; a skylark dances. But on the horizon, the dust broils densely, tainting the cornflower-blue sky a dirty burgundy, and the crump of the artillery is constant. To the west, there's the crackle of shooting quickfire and then single shots.

Kapto cocks his head: 'Doesn't sound like fighting.' Smoke rises, not fuel black, perhaps burning stubble.

'Think what we've been through,' says Benya. 'We've seen so many people gone . . .'

'Don't look back; don't look forward,' Kapto replies. 'Like in the Camps. Just live through today. Everything is out of our control, but even here a man can still save a man.'

They walk amongst the sheaves towards a haystack at the end of the field. Benya longs to throw himself into it; on impulse, he hands the doctor his rifle and runs and jumps and lies back kicking his legs in the air. The hay is sweet, prickly, bright yellow. But something twitches beside him. A rabbit maybe. Or a bird.

'Careful,' calls Kapto, coolly raising the rifle as Benya, spooked, jumps up.

'What the hell? It's something big,' Benya says, drawing his pistol.

'Come out!' says Kapto. 'We won't hurt you!' He pokes at the hay with his rifle. The hay slides off it and a child stands up, a little girl in a ripped floral dress, very frightened, black eyes, long auburn hair with a side parting held in a clip. She is matted in mud.

Benya kneels down and puts out his hand, coaxing her forward. 'It's all right,' he says. 'We're Russians. Where do you come from?'

She points to the west, towards the smoke and the occasional shots.

'Where's home?'

'Dnieperpetrovsk.'

'That's a long way away.'

She nods.

'How old are you?'

'Five.'

'Where are your parents?'

'They took them.'

'Who?'

'Schuma and Germans. Are you——?' She starts to shake.

'No, no, we're Red Army, not Schuma. Where are your parents now?'

She looks behind her and starts to cry. Benya notices that her legs are scratched, her little dress is in shreds, and her knee is bleeding. 'They left. We were all in the hole. I waited. When it was dark I crawled out and ran away.'

Dr Kapto goes on one knee beside Benya and takes over the conversation. 'You've been running all night and all day?'

She nods.

'You haven't eaten?'

She shakes her head.

'You're bleeding. May I see?'

'He's a doctor,' explains Benya. She relaxes and Kapto examines her knee.

'You ran through wire and cut yourself, quite deeply. I need to stitch you up. Will you come with us? I can carry you?' He opens his arms to her and, slowly, she comes towards him and he hugs her and she sobs. Kapto is so tender with her that Benya fights the urge to cry too as they walk back together to the village.

In the Red Cross tent, Tonya's smudged face lights up for an instant. She and the doctor have saved many children together. Perhaps children are the one part of her job that pleases her, Benya thinks. He watches the child eat; then Kapto stitches her leg with Tonya assisting.

Eventually, she falls asleep, and Benya and Kapto light up Africas and stroll into the village.

Outside, the orange sun has sunk so low that Benya feels he can look right into its bloodshot face and feel the red heat through his eyelids.

'What do we do with her?' asks Benya.

'Well, she can't go back and we can't leave her here,' says Kapto.

They hear the heavy clip of hooves down the tiny street ahead of them.

'Melishko is back, Melishko is back!' Benya hears his comrades shouting. He feels a surge of relief. Thank God for Melishko; thank God for Kapto.

Each man had saved his life.

In another world.

V

In the Camps, Benya was too old for Hard Labour. He was over forty, and although there were lots of other older men there, most of them died in the first weeks. The gold they were mining out of the mountain lay in the iron ore fifteen metres underground. After the earlier shift dynamited the rock, Benya's job was to heap the loose boulders on to his wheelbarrow and, balancing precariously up and down along the twisting wooden walkways high above the mine, push it to the conveyor belt in the steamshack. It was back-breaking hard work. If the wheelbarrow tipped over, neither he nor his fellow Zeks would be fed and he would be beaten. If prisoners were too exhausted to move, the guards simply shot them. His quota was seven cubic metres of soil and rock per day.

Then suddenly, after just a week, the light dwindled and the snow came. It was winter, grinding Kolyma winter, and the snow was so deep, the wind so strong, the blizzards so blinding that even around the Camp there were ropes to hold on to to get to the dining block. Winter clothing was issued – boots, padded coats and mittens – but the clothing was too thin, and the prisoners were always freezing. At roll call each morning, shoved into lines by Fats Strizkaz and his Trusties brandishing truncheons, the prisoners beat their own bodies with their hands to stay warm, and friends spotted the whiteness that warned of icebite. That's when Benya first met Melishko, who'd lost his teeth and fingertips to Beria's torturers.

'Rub your nose,' he said to Benya one day, 'or you'll lose it.'

It was night-time for nine hours a day, with the temperature sinking to minus forty. Men lost noses, fingers, toes; one man who urinated outdoors lost his penis when his urine froze; those with dysentery sometimes didn't get up again, glued to glacial faeces. Yet Benya learned to find gems and sparks of joy even in this hell – a delicious piece of bread, the chance to rest an extra few minutes – and the smile of a new friend, Shishkov, another Political who worked with him. Politicals were cautious, never talking of their cases unless they really trusted someone. 'My name is Nothing, my surname is Nobody' – '*Zvat nikto, familiya nikak*' – was what they said. But Shishkov immediately knew who Benya was. 'I was one of your readers,' he whispered one morning. Benya came to trust Shishkov, who was one of those prisoners known as 'Jokers' – sentenced under Clause 159.10 for 'counter-revolutionary agitation', usually for telling a joke about Stalin: 'Quite a funny one,' said Shishkov.

'Please don't share it,' retorted Benya.

'I have another about Beria!'

They managed to laugh.

Shishkov had once been very important; he'd been Second Secretary of the Kherson Party until denounced by his brother-in-law for his one-liners on Georgian geniuses, and was one of those owlish, bespectacled, sensible people who always looked older than his years. He was kind to Benya and taught him how to work the wheelbarrow, how high to pile the rocks, how to avoid a crash, and how to inflate the quota: the entire Camp was engaged in inflating their quotas, a science of mendacity known as *tufta*.

'Remember,' said Shishkov, 'love is life, love is what put your stars in the sky. Look at the moon. The moon shines everywhere and if you love someone, they can see the same moon! I call it Moon Magic. Loving will keep you alive.' Benya knew that he thought constantly of his wife and his two daughters.

The prisoners rarely cried or gurned, realized Benya; the faces of those in the deepest pain were set in brittle, expression-less masks – even as the suffering tore them to pieces within.

If Benya had not been chiselling away at the rock and carry-ing stones he would have died of cold, yet the work itself was so punishing that even during the first day he staggered rather than walked. If the brigade's quota of rock was not shifted each day, the prisoners received less food. Even so, the watery swill with its scraps of whale fat and herring bones daily ladled out from the Cauldron, plus the *paika*, the bread ration, was not enough for any of them.

Just a week into winter, Benya noticed his Political friend, Shishkov, was deteriorating. His face was touched with death, his skin yellow, his nose jutting out; it seemed to Benya he was just gristle, bone and parchment. Benya begged his older friend to eat more, to find the will.

'I realize that I will never see my children again,' replied

Shishkov, tears running down his face. 'I am dying of hunger.'

That evening Benya saw Shishkov sitting in the frozen garbage heap behind the dining block sucking on a herring bone.

'He's a goner, a *dokhodayaga*,' said Smiley, Benya's friend who had saved his life on the voyage to Kolyma, and who now resided in the most comfortable barracks with some of his Criminal brethren. The 'garbage-eaters' were not long for the world of the living.

Two weeks into winter, Shishkov fainted while pushing the wheelbarrow, spilling the rocks.

'Pick up those fucking rocks, cocksucker,' cried one guard, a Mongolian like many of them. 'Get working or we'll shoot you,' called another guard from the rim of the great hole.

Benya pulled him up, and collected his spilled rocks. 'Come on,' he said. 'They'll shoot you! I'll do your work today.' It was snowing heavily. The rocks, the wheelbarrow: everything was frozen.

A couple of hours later, Shishkov again lost his balance and fell off the planks into the muddy hole. Benya climbed down but the guards shouted: 'Get working! Leave the goner down there!'

He could see Shishkov was dying. 'When you get out,' he gasped, 'go see my wife and children. Tell them . . .'

Benya had memorized their address and understood. He was just leaning over his friend to tell him this when he was struck on the shoulder: 'Get to work or it'll be the Isolator for you!' shouted one of the Mongolian guards.

Benya took his wheelbarrow up to the conveyor hut but when he wheeled it back, the Zeks were down with Shishkov, stripping him of coat, hat, boots, trousers – everything, until there was nothing else to steal. 'Man is wolf to man' echoed in Benya's ears. Never was this truer than in the Gulags.

Shishkov lay there with his eyes open, stark naked, angular and sunken, less like a man than an old ironing-board, already covered by a delicate sprinkling of snow. Twice he blinked.

'He's alive,' cried Benya but the Zek next to him stopped him.

'No, he's gone,' said Melishko. Respected by all in the Zone, Melishko was known as the General, and was one of the soldiers arrested in 1937. 'And you mustn't join him. How can we survive? Live just in the present, not the past, not the future, live minute by minute.'

No one picked up Shishkov. The next day, he was just a shape in the snow, frozen solid in his crusty tomb. By the following day, he'd vanished into the polar landscape. Could men just vanish like this? Benya learned the answer in the first days of spring. When the thaw came, and the streams were seething with fresh water which rushed through new tunnels under the muddy carapace of winter, the ice revealed its first flowers, the 'snowdrops', of spring – and amazingly while all the Zeks in the brigades looked ten years older, these corpses were the same age they had been when they fell.

Benya had survived almost the entire winter but in its last days of almost eternal darkness, just when veterans said spring was coming at any moment, he began to weaken. Melishko, who was older than him but much tougher, was now his partner on the wheelbarrow. As the days became longer, Benya ached with hunger. He felt his legs get heavier, and he knew he was sinking. He experienced a strange weightlessness, like a speck of dust in the wind. Would he last the next day? Or the next? he wondered. Then came a day he could barely move.

'That's enough,' said Melishko. 'I'll talk to the brigadier. You need to stay in barracks for a day.'

But by the following day, Benya was too ill to get out of bed. His temperature was raging, and he was hallucinating, images darting at him. There was his father, in his three-piece suit and watch chain, seeing patients in the waiting room of the surgery that was the basement of their house.

Then he was with Sashenka again; she was right there with him, her Greek profile so noble it took his breath away every time. He saw the slant of her cheekbones, could even smell her scent, touch her skin. Tears ran down his face. 'Darling,' he said. 'I knew you were alive.'

Floating back to his parents, to his childhood home in Lemberg when that city was part of Habsburg Galicia, long before the Revolution, and he was in school uniform and his father was saying, 'Work harder at school or if you're not careful, Benochka, you'll turn into a true Galitzianer skirt-chaser . . .'

'I think that's enough, Zakhary.' His mother was at the door. 'I think Benochka's got the message. Come on, you two, we've got a feast! It's supper!' It was always a feast in the Golden house. He longed to hug his parents before he died – which was when he knew he was dying . . .

When Benya awoke, he realized there was no God but there was a doctor, who had a stethoscope around his neck, a white coat, a notebook, a doctor who was smiling down at him.

'There you are!' said the doctor as if he had been waiting a long time. 'You must drink. We'll feed you very carefully. Temperature normal this morning. You're very weak but you'll be all right.'

Benya looked around at what he assumed to be a hospital ward. The sheets were white, and there was the smell of disinfectant but without its antidotes, sweat and faeces. The wooden floor was clean. Was this Moscow? Had he escaped the Zone?

'Where am I?'

'You're still in Madyak, I'm afraid. You're in my so-called clinic. I'm visiting from the hospital at Magadan. It's simple, just this little room in a hut . . . We do our best. And you were lucky I was visiting this week.'

'Are you . . . ?'

'Yes, I am Dr Kapto.'

'So you're the Baby Doctor,' murmured Benya.

Dr Kapto was the hero of the Zone, beloved by the prisoners, the last evidence that humanity itself had not died on earth. A Zek himself of course, a veteran of many years serving a long sentence (he was surely a Political, Benya surmised), his acts of kindness were recited by the prisoners almost in nursery rhymes: how he had saved the lives of so many women who were pregnant or had been impregnated by gang-rapists or the guards; how he had delivered their babies and protected the women, refusing to let them return to work until they were strong, and how he tried to find them easy jobs thereafter. He was also rumoured to raise the children in the Zone's own orphanage at Elgen, playing father, teacher and doctor to them. Benya thought he had never loved anyone more than this doctor at this moment. So here he was: the Baby Doctor.

'You're safe here, Golden,' he said. 'I am looking after you.'

Benya looked up into his heart-shaped face and his wonderfully light eyes, and sobs of gratitude overcame him, and he reached up to Kapto to try and hold his hands.

'Easy, now, easy,' Kapto said with an all-encompassing breeziness. 'You're depleted. We've got soup for you and bread. We're going to feed you up. Ahh . . . you see?'

As if by magic, a short peasant girl with a flat face and heavy-lidded eyes wheeled in a trolley. The smell of food was dizzying. Benya gulped down the beet soup, the oatmeal with shredded whalemeat, the bread, the tea. He ate the butter on its own, rubbing it into his gums. He saved up the two sugar lumps and crunched them between his teeth, then let them melt on his tongue, the sensation making him shiver.

Kapto stayed with him, delighted by the sight of Benya's recovery.

'Who brought me in?'

'Melishko checked on you in your barracks and dragged you over here. A few more days here and you'll be strong.' He stood up. 'Now I must see to the other patients . . .'

Benya suddenly noticed that he was in a full ward. Other patients, some little more than living corpses of indeterminate age, were staring into the space, toothless mouths agape. As Kapto turned away, the fear returned. The nightmare was not over. They were restoring him just to kill him. He was going back to the work brigades. He could not do that. He would die out there! He leaned forward and grabbed Kapto's coat.

'But what happens when I'm better? I can't go back to the mine . . . I'll die . . .'

Kapto sat on the edge of the bed, rested his hands on Benya's

97

hands, and Benya could not believe that someone could be so kind to him. Kapto smelled sweet, soapy, not of compacted sweat and disinfectant and death like everyone else. He smelled like a human.

'Easy, easy now! You're lucky, Benya Golden. You're not going back,' he whispered. 'Everyone else has to go back to the mine. But not you. Aren't you a medical orderly? A *feldsher*? Don't you have nursing experience?'

'What?' Benya was confused.

'Don't you remember, Golden, in your *Spanish Stories*, when you spent a week with the medics and their ambulance at the Ebro front? You had medical training? Now you understand?'

'Yes, of course! I'm a nurse!' Benya nodded like a child.

'You see, I've read your book — and all your short stories too. You'll be joining the two nurses here in our little clinic. The most important thing is your kindness to the patients. Many are fading away but we must make them feel loved. We'll train you up. For us doctors, our duties don't end with just saving a life: those we heal we must also cherish.'

Benya tried to speak but he was so moved that he wept instead.

'Easy now,' said Kapto. 'You're a lucky man, Golden. And tomorrow you'll find out the very meaning of luck.'

VI

General Melishko is covered in dust; even his starched-white moustache and winged eyebrows are reddened with earth.

Thank God he's back! He hands the reins of Elephant to his adjutant and joins Zhurko and Ganakovich outside the priest's house near the church.

Benya listens as Zhurko and Ganakovich bombard Melishko with questions. When are reinforcements coming? Where are the supplies? Ganakovich is shrill, no longer the legendary friend of Politburo members and seducer of ballerinas.

'How are we to provision the horses? We need support,' says Zhurko, voice tight, calm, dry.

'How do we rendezvous with the others?' cries Ganakovich. 'What do we do now? We don't even have full maps.'

'We are where we are,' says Melishko.

'And *where* is that?' demands Ganakovich, gulping back a wad of saliva. 'Where are we? Should we go back to our lines . . . ?'

Melishko laughs huskily, rolling his false teeth. 'Really, Ganakovich?'

'No, I didn't mean that,' Ganakovich corrects himself. 'Not One Step Back! We know Stalin's order. Retreat means death.'

'Yes,' says Melishko quite jovially, poking him in the ribs. 'You almost had to execute yourself just then.'

'Forgive me! Please don't inform the Special Unit, I just meant—'

'Calm down, boy.' Melishko waves a bluff hand. 'We don't tell, do we, Zhurko?'

'Of course not,' said Zhurko, cleaning his spectacles with his shirt tail.

There is a strange stillness. Benya realizes the shooting has stopped.

'Thank you, comrades . . .'

'We're not comrades, remember, Ganakovich? We're bandits,' replies Melishko heartily. 'How many sabres are we here?'

'Three hundred, give or take,' reports Zhurko.

'Wounded?'

'Riding wounded included.'

'So with our three hundred, how do we rendezvous with the rest of the battalion, the rest of the division?' Ganakovich is almost weeping.

'Ganakovich, let me spell it out. We're alone. There are no reinforcements,' Melishko explains. He speaks slowly and deliberately. 'The other squadrons were wiped out when they charged the German tanks and machine guns. They redeemed themselves all right. I only just got through myself. Thanks to Elephant. That scout was right: our squadron got lucky. No one knew there were Italians in this sector. And because the Italians worry too much about their uniforms and pasta, we broke right through.'

'So what do we do now?' whispers Ganakovich.

Melishko lights a cigarette, taking his time about it, with a lot of puffing and chewing of false teeth. He talks when he is good and ready. 'We can only advance. And we have a mission of sorts, remember? If we break through, they said, we must hunt down and destroy all traitors. And the chief traitor in this sector is Colonel Mandryka. The Germans have given him his own little kingdom here with his own security police, the Schuma, who are working on special tasks with the SS. He's encouraging Soviet soldiers to surrender and defect. Moscow wants him eliminated, and the unit that kills him will be redeemed. That's what we're going to do. Tell Panka to saddle the horses, and gather all provisions. We move out at dawn.'

'But won't the Germans know we're here?' whines Ganakovich.

'Yes, but they'll be expecting us to retreat towards the Don. Instead we're going in the other direction, further into enemy territory. And we'll be moving fast and light as only cavalrymen can.'

'Forward's the only way back,' agrees Zhurko.

'But don't you realize?' says Ganakovich, and the fear in his voice echoes the fear in Benya's belly. 'We'll never come back.'

Day Three

I

An hour out of the village, the dawn sky began to lighten into lilac and then pink, and they saw a dead horse lying on its back, its hooves sticking up towards the sky. 'Eaten itself to death,' commented Panka wryly.

A few minutes later, they rode past a dead Russian run over by a tank. The body was shapeless, totally flat, just green fabric and pink flesh woven like a carpet. There was a smell of burning and Benya remembered the smoke of battle the day before. As they rode on, the stench grew stronger, the men grew quieter, three hundred riders, horses' tails swishing, the bits clonking between teeth, the creak of leather, clink of spurs.

'If you're scared, don't do it,' Zhurko had said as they moved off. 'If you do it, don't be scared!'

And Benya found he was not as scared as he had been before. He was more afraid of capture. Death seemed easier now; it was merely the agony in between that he feared. He rode in his place between Spider Garanzha and Prishchepa, noticing that Dr Kapto had the little girl, all cleaned up now, riding on his horse in front of him. Melishko loped up and down the squadrons, a word here, encouragement there, to make sure the men understood that this was the way they would win their freedom. But the men were muttering. They had heard something back in the village, the poison spread by Mandryka's traitors, that the war was lost, and that their fellow Cossacks had joined the Germans. 'Join our brothers!' a few of the soldiers were whispering.

Panka shook his head when he heard this: 'Careful, brothers, I saw the German promises last time. Hear me say this,' he said emphatically. 'I'm not going *anywhere*!'

The scouts rode back: 'Village ahead. Clear!'

They approached, walking slowly into the village's only street. Every house in it was a blackened shell, and the barn was still smoking.

Suddenly a voice cried out, '*Klop, klop!*' as an old-fashioned tarantass, a buggy pulled by an aged horse, trotted right into them. Benya and his comrades raised their guns at the old peasant holding the reins. He wore a Tsarist braided tunic with shoulderboards and a medal on it; an old hunting rifle lay across his knees. Seeing them, the old man jumped down and tried to run but Smiley shot him in the ankle and they brought him back.

Melishko dismounted and looked inside the smoking barn. Inside were the blackened forms of men and women, roasted with their hands raised and white teeth showing through wide-open mouths, wizened as small as children.

He looked back at Prishchepa and Benya, still on horseback in the little street.

'What happened here?' Melishko said as the peasant was brought to him. 'What happened, Cossack?'

Smiley gave the peasant a shove and he groaned, clutching at his ruined ankle. 'Mandryka's Schuma police came here,' he said.

'Where's the rest of the village?'

106

Smiley hit him with his rifle butt and the peasant whimpered, 'Don't hurt me again. Don't hurt me.'

Melishko ordered a half-burnt chair to be brought out so the peasant could sit.

'Are you working with the traitor Mandryka?' Melishko asked.

'No, but we're doing some spring cleaning for him.'

'What's that uniform?'

'His Majesty's Ataman Lifeguards Regiment. I served the Tsar in the Great War.'

'And fought for the Whites against the Communists?'

The peasant nodded.

'Where's everyone else?'

The peasant looked side to side as if playing the fool, like a child in a play. 'Some have joined Mandryka.'

'Why are you here?'

'To check the field. To tidy the barn. To see the sights.'

'What sights? What field?'

'The sown field. I'm also looking after the guests in the barn.' The rosy-cheeked old peasant grinned, opening his gaping well of a mouth. Benya noticed just the black stumps of teeth.

Melishko looked over the man's shoulder at Panka who made a 'he's insane' gesture.

'Who are the guests?'

'They were the strangers amongst us. They came from the cities . . .'

'And what do you do to them?'

The peasant looked right into Benya's eyes. 'You're one of them,' he said, pointing at him. 'That's one of them! A Christ-killer. Right amongst you!'

Benya felt the primitive impudence of evil, and shivered.

'Answer me,' insisted Melishko, still puffing on his cigarette. The smell of burning and of something infinitely more terrible was becoming unbearable and the men tied kerchiefs around their faces.

The peasant licked his lips and opened his mouth in what passed for a smile. 'We make them welcome,' he said.

To Benya this mouth was the sinkhole of death.

'A devil,' Panka murmured. 'Possessed by the midsummer moon.'

'One more thing,' asked the general. 'What's the traitor Mandryka's next task?'

'It's special work. Those strangers are running from the west, Odessa and Kishnev, and seeking sanctuary in the villages. That's where he picks them up. So we can welcome them in our special way.' Again the open gape.

Melishko nodded, rubbing his moustache with his hand. 'So this is Mandryka's work. See this, Cossacks! Here is our mission. Here is how we win our freedom back!' He turned and mounted Elephant. 'We ride on.'

Ganakovich still stood over the peasant.

'Shall we . . . ?' said Smiley.

Benya rode on, waiting for the shot, not flinching when it came.

The field outside the village had been ploughed with rags but when they got closer, Benya saw a white hand first, a perfect white hand, and then a bare foot and then a collage of gabardine and linen and then more flesh, a complete face. Silver Socks reared at the sight, snorting, spooked. The rich black earth had been freshly turned but now they were close Benya could see that it scarcely covered the bodies that lay in rows, intertwined, half-naked, indecently twisted. He and the men stared; their horses champed, their ears flattened back, the whites of their eyes showing – and a host of black wings beat the air before the birds returned and hopped closer and closer.

Melishko dismounted again, sighing with the effort, and gestured to Benya to do the same. 'I was in Spain, like you, and we saw things there. They shot the priests and nuns in the village square. But nothing like this. You must live to witness this, you before all the others,' he said gruffly.

'Why me?'

'You're our only writer. Who are they? Can't you see? Look more closely at these people.' Melishko knelt down and pushed aside the soil. The field seemed to emanate a sugary miasma even though the bodies were so fresh and Benya realized that death smelled of sweet blackberries gone bad. Vultures leaned their crooked necks from the closest boughs and the crows cawed, eyes glittering sharp and yellow as citrines. Benya's companions had dismounted and were kneeling, brushing aside the earth so they could see the bodies.

Each person had been shot in the back of the head: here was a girl with clear eyes, here a man's face where a leg should be, here a child as if asleep, all mixed up together with a horrible negligence. Melishko picked up a Soviet identity card, then another. 'They're not all from here. Look! They're all Jews, your people.'

Benya knelt down too, looking at the ID cards and seeing the Jewish names and their home towns: Paltrovich of Nikolaev, Greenbaum of Kherson, Jaffe of Mogilev. They were Jewish refugees, overtaken by the German advance. Frantic suddenly, he threw aside those and picked up more, tossed carelessly around the field. And then he found one – a family from Odessa . . .

'My parents lived in Odessa after leaving Galicia,' he said, his voice cracking. 'They could be . . .'

'Come on, lad,' said Melishko, hefting him up and steadying him. Benya saw Melishko's face was exhausted, noticed the dust in the crow's feet around his eyes. 'I'll wager your family are safe somewhere. But wherever they are, the best we can do is meet Mandryka with our sabres drawn.'

Benya wanted to weep as he looked at this field, this Jewish field, sown with Jews, scarcely buried. He'd often wondered – what was life for? For joy – and for this just war. How could he have done anything else but fight these monsters? He felt his own frailty beside these Nazi fanatics who were winning the war, but he could still do his bit. Today. That was what this mission was all about.

He heard shrieking and turned. The little girl on Kapto's horse was crying and pointing and the doctor was covering her eyes. Maybe this was where her parents were, whence she had escaped out of the earth – or somewhere like this. The Cossacks were crossing themselves. None of them had ever seen anything like this before.

Panka shook his head and rubbed his whiskers. 'The wolves have gone mad.'

II

When the normal order of life is shattered, thought Benya as he rode on, no one can predict where those fragments will fly, whose life will be spared, whose throat they will cut. There was only one certainty: the old world can never be put together again.

They had been riding since 4 a.m., and Mandryka's village was right ahead of them. The sky was a brightening lavender with white contrails, Benya noticed, and just a smudge of sun so far; this was going to be another beautiful day. The men were drawn up in two companies: orders were whispered; cigarettes put out.

At one point in the early morning, Benya had fallen asleep in the saddle, and when he awoke he had found himself alone with Silver Socks cropping grass at the roadside. He'd turned and just behind him were two strange horsemen. For a moment, he'd panicked and reached for his PPSh. 'You want a Daddy?' Panka had asked, handing over the weapon just after the first charge. My 'Pe-pe-sh', the soldiers called it, my Papasha – Daddy! Now he levelled it at the riders, ready to shoot.

Then he saw the fluorescent moons of the little girl's eyes. She was riding in front of Dr Kapto, his arm around her belly, so she would not fall, his heart-shaped face close to her hair. Tonya rode next to him, and perhaps Benya had scared them because Kapto was pointing his Parabellum right back at him.

'What are you doing? It's me,' Benya said. 'Put down the pistol. Are you lost too?'

'Easy, now, Golden, easy. Yes, we're lost,' said Kapto, not holstering the pistol, just holding it.

'How is she?' Benya looked at the child.

'She's going to be fine. No amount of care is too much for

111

her. A doctor's duty doesn't just end with saving a life, we must nurture, we must tend—'

'Ah yes: those we heal we must also cherish,' Benya quoted Kapto's motto back to him.

Kapto gave a lineless smile.

'I fell asleep in the saddle,' said Benya. 'Stupid of me. But the unit must be just across this field. Are you coming?'

'Good luck, friend,' said Kapto. 'Ours is another way . . .' And he nodded at Benya, and rode on.

Ten minutes later, Benya met up with Prishchepa and took his place. Melishko rode out in front to meet the scouts coming back from reconnaissance, headed by Panka.

'How many men in the village?' asked Melishko. Ganakovich and Zhurko were beside him.

'A few hundred,' replied Panka, saluting.

'Mandryka?'

'He's there, ruling his men like a Tartar khan.'

'Are there Germans there too?'

'We saw SS special task groups,' Panka said.

'Why are you alone, sergeant? What happened to the Cossacks I sent with you? Where are Delibash and Grishchuk?'

Panka looked awkward and said nothing.

'Speak up, sergeant.'

Panka patted his horse.

'They defected?'

He nodded.

'Ah. Well, they won't be the last,' said Zhurko.

Benya turned in his saddle, looking for Kapto with the queerest feeling in his belly.

'Where's the doctor?' he asked Prishchepa.

'Don't you know? He defected with the nurse, Tonya.'

Abruptly Benya understood their encounter. 'Good luck, friend,' Kapto had said. Was he mocking him? Tonya's stare had been contemptuous, he now realized. Benya was bewildered. Simple Cossacks and boneheaded villagers might join the Nazis – but the Baby Doctor, his friend? How could he join the Nazis after seeing the massacre? And what would happen to the child? For some men, war was an unshakling that liscenced them to become whomsoever they wanted, to play out extravagent fantasies and unspeakable passions, Benya thought. Men without nerves would enjoy short reigns of glory before the world tilted back but quite long enough to destroy many lives . . . Yet Kapto had never uttered a word about politics. So who was he really? There was something else. If Kapto and the others had defected to the Nazis, Mandryka would be expecting them . . .

Ganakovich drew his Nagant and turned to the men: 'Any traitors will be hunted down and executed! Their families arrested. Ride, motherfuckers, or I shoot . . .'

'Not now.' Melishko put his hand on Ganakovich's arm, and summoned Panka. 'Sergeant, do we have any Product Sixty-One?'

'Yes sir. The usual hundred grammes?'

'No, distribute it *all* right away.' At a nod from Melishko, Panka rode through the ranks, ladling out the vodka in a steel thimble hanging from his belt. Benya downed three of them, feeling the molten lurch as the alcohol kicked in. Then Melishko himself rode down the line on Elephant.

'Remember,' he told the men. 'The war's not lost. Russia is vast, and Hitler's a madman if he thinks he can defeat us. Napoleon took Moscow but Tsar Alexander rode his Cossacks all the way to Paris. Yes, to Paris! This offensive is Hitler's last gamble. You've already beaten the odds. We broke through, didn't we? This is our mission against the men who killed those people – and if we succeed, I will recommend every one of you for redemption, I promise. We give no quarter to traitors, and we ride to kill Mandryka. We'll make it, bandits. YOU CAN'T GET ME!'

In this scruffy, brusque growl of a man, Benya sensed the noble and fathomless depths of Mother Russia.

'Bandits!' Melishko drew his sabre and raised it. 'Squadrons, forward at the trot! Draw sabres! Forward . . .'

The Cossacks were standing high in their stirrups; Benya raised his sabre and felt his blood changing, almost frothing in his veins with anger, with exhilaration. For a man who often couldn't decide whether to order absinthe or cognac, and even sometimes which girl to choose, war granted simplicity: advance, retreat; live, die. Around him was the rhythmic thud of hooves as they changed from trot to lope to canter to gallop. He recited Gorky to himself: 'Those who are born to crawl cannot fly.' Now he was flying!

Then all of it was drowned out by something cruder and louder and for a second Benya could not understand what it was – and then he felt the force of it and heard the chugging as the belts worked their way through the heavy machine guns in the nests hidden in the rye of the fields. Next to Benya, Lover-boy Cherkashkin was trying to hold on to his horse's mane but, as the animal fell, he came out of his saddle, catapulted high into the air and over the rump, his sabre flying, his rifle tangled round his neck, his mouth a perfect 'O' of surprise. Men were falling all around him. Shundenko was being dragged by his foot behind his horse. He saw Cut and Run Ivanov riding on but with a chunk taken out of his face. Clinging on to Silver Socks, one foot out of his stirrups, he noticed that many of the horses around him were riderless. Amid the machine-gun fire, Socks reared up and tried to turn and Benya, having lost both his stirrups now, somersaulted right over the horse's head.

It was a relief to lie there in the sweet rye and imagine that he was about to die and that all this striving and gunfire was almost finished. Weariness like warm water rose within him, a benumbed heaviness. He feared Silver Socks was hurt and wished he could find her but she was gone. He knew he had been hit, and was surprised he wasn't in more pain as the deep metallic crack of the guns kept raking over him, and blood ran down his forehead into his eyes.

In front of him, he could hear voices in German and Russian talking between bursts of the big guns. Soon the men would come out and walk through the field, mopping up, and these irregulars were notoriously cruel. It was unlikely they would leave anyone alive.

Benya lay back and looked up at the long teal sky, but unlike earlier that morning, the blueness seemed utterly bleak and stark. He passed out, and when he awoke, he was being half pulled, half lifted backwards. The process was agonizingly slow. There was a burst of machine-gun fire, lighter this time, and the man pulling Benya gasped for a second, shook then went on. Soon they were in higher steppe grass beyond this blood harvest, and someone was giving Benya water. He sat up and wiped his face, but he saw they were tending another man right beside him, the man who had saved him, who had dragged him to safety. They were working on him, opening his shirt, but Prishchepa shook his head.

'He's gone,' he said and they laid him down. It was Ganakovich.

'Him . . . ?' Benya was confounded: the *Politruk* who had executed an innocent boy was the same man who had sacrificed his own life to save Benya?

'Sometimes a crow flies as an eagle,' said Prishchepa, looking at Benya now.

Benya felt fireworks exploding behind his eyes, silver hammers beating in his temple and he fell sideways.

'You have a bang on your head, and a cut on your forehead. You'll be OK in a minute,' said Zhurko.

'We have to go right now,' Spider Garanzha told them. 'I have horses for all of us and a surprise for you, Golden.' Spider was holding Socks by the reins. 'She found us. She's unscathed. Even her stitches are almost healed.'

Getting to his feet, Benya took Socks's reins and kissed her neck, burying his face in the mane. Never had he been more relieved to see anyone. Then they heard a voice from out on the field, a voice they all knew.

'Don't leave me! Give me some water, for God's sake!'

'It's Melishko.' Benya would recognize that voice in his dreams.

'Dear bandits, some water please! Or finish me off! I can't reach my gun. I don't want these bastards near me . . .'

'We just can't leave him,' said Benya. 'He's our father-commander!'

'We help him – we all die,' Garanzha muttered.

'He's right,' said Zhurko sadly. He too loved Melishko.

'But we've got to help him,' insisted Benya.

Zhurko rubbed his chin, thinking, then looked towards Panka.

Panka, showing nothing on his face, shook his head.

Zhurko sighed heavily. 'You're right. He'd be the first to tell us that.'

Zhurko and Panka crawled forward, and Benya watched Zhurko raise the binoculars in the direction of Melishko's voice.

'I see him,' said Zhurko when they were back. 'He's out there. His legs are crushed under Elephant and he's wounded in the gut. Elephant's done for too. We're not going to get him out of there.'

'Finish me off, if any of you motherfucker bandits are still out there!' came the voice again across the field. 'Don't forget! YOU CAN'T GET ME!' They smiled a little at this; even Panka.

'I can do it,' said Panka after a while. 'As to a wounded mare, beloved after many seasons.'

'I'll do it properly,' Spider Garanzha said, taking the Simonov sniper rifle. 'He's not far away.'

Panka patted his shoulder but could not speak.

'You set off,' said Garanzha, 'and I'll join you when you're away. One shot, I promise. And one for Elephant. Two shots, no more. I'll see you at the' – he was going to say the barn but no one could go there again – 'at the millhouse.'

They mounted the horses amongst the high steppe grass and rode back the way they had come. When they reached the mill in the burnt village, they watered the horses in the stream and waited for Spider. In the distance, they had heard one shot, then the second for Elephant. Panka crossed himself and looked away, very still for a moment.

Now in the safety of the mill, Benya lowered his head, then he cleaned his face in the cool stream.

III

It was lunchtime in the Kremlin and Stalin, who had just woken up, was hearing the first reports from the fronts. He had been up until 6 a.m. trying to organize the defence of the Don River, and Russian forces were just hanging on to the western bank. If the Nazis managed to cross the Don, then they would be just sixty miles from Stalingrad, Stalin's city on the Volga River. Meanwhile, further south, they were rifling towards the oil fields of the Caucasus.

Molotov, sitting stolidly at the table, flanked by an overweight younger comrade, Malenkov, and the rangy and dark-eyed Armenian, Mikoyan, listened to Chief of Staff Vasilevsky's report.

'And Operation Pluto?' Stalin asked.

'The Shtrafniki charged German positions,' Vasilevsky said.

'They were wiped out,' stated Stalin, his voice entirely neutral.

'Yes. They were charging heavily fortified German positions. The First Cavalry Shtrafbat has ceased to exist as a unit.'

Stalin broke a cigarette in half, took out the tobacco and stuffed it into the bowl of his Dunhill pipe (a gift from the British). 'Totally annihilated.' He lit the pipe, sucking the flame of the match into its bowl. 'But did the Shtrafniki distract the Germans sufficiently to ensure the success of Operation Pluto?'

'Operation Pluto failed to drive back the German advance though there is a slight weakening as they now regroup.'

'So the Shtrafniki did their duty. They died. But they fought. The idea works.'

'Yes, Comrade Stalin. Shtrafbats are being formed and trained on all fronts. These convicts fight to the last man in the hope of redemption.'

'Were any redeemed?'

'No. As far as we know there were few survivors. Now, moving on to Stalingrad itself, Gordov reports the Germans are bombing the city . . .'

'I know about that. I was just talking to Satinov by phone.' Stalin seemed distracted. 'But the Shtrafniki – that Melishko is a good officer. I remember him from the thirties.'

'Ah, yes, Comrade Stalin, I hadn't mentioned the Second Battalion.'

'Report.'

'Well, this is a very minor engagement. We have a lot to get through . . . The Stalingrad, Southern, Don Fronts and the Leningrad Front, not to mention the Central—'

'Report on Melishko's Shtrafbat.'

'They were not totally wiped out. The Germans are deploying Italians in these sectors to free up their resources for the offensives, and the Second Cavalry Shtrafbat, the one under Melishko, faced mixed Italian units of the Alpine Tridentine, Bersaglieri and Blackshirts, and two squadrons actually broke through into the Hitlerite rear.'

Stalin was silent. He tapped the pipe on the desk, relit it, and then sucked flame through once again. The general and the three civilians watched the match flare, the tobacco take light and heard the wheeze as Stalin inhaled. Then he raised his hazel eyes. 'Where are they now?'

'We're not sure.' Vasilevsky checked his notes. He was accustomed to Stalin taking an interest in small engagements and kept all the reports with him. 'Ah yes, we believe they drove the Italians out of the village of Little Yablako where they called for backup. They were given no logistical support – but all units are ordered, during their briefings, to destroy the traitor Mandryka and his units if they break through. If they still exist as a unit, they may be pursuing this mission.'

'Did Melishko survive?'

'Apparently yes.'

'If he returns, he is to be reinstated as a general.'

'I'll make a note of that.'

'Did any of Melishko's bandits win their freedom?'

'One Shtrafnik was executed by their Special Unit before the entire regiment right before deployment according to Order 227. Another five were shot by the Blocking Unit on the battlefield. But since there was no logistical backup, it was impossible to remove the wounded. We do not know if any earned redemption by the shedding of blood. They were also told if they managed to liquidate traitor Mandryka, they would be redeemed.'

Stalin rested the pipe in the ashtray, lit a cigarette – a sign of intense focus – and smiled for a moment, or at least the muscles of his face creased like an old tiger, and the men in the room smiled grimly back at him. 'I have a question about Melishko's bandits. Shall we help them?'

IV

Dr Kapto was sitting under a canopy at the priest's house in the pretty village of Shepilovka. Beside him was a neat, red-faced man in German *feldgrau* uniform and boots, and with his head shaven on the sides. The glare of the sun was almost blinding even in the shade.

Kapto had crossed the lines a few hours earlier and been welcomed like the other defectors. 'Surrender your arms, dismount and lead your horse!' You could read the fortunes of war in the number of defectors. Nine overnight, the pickets were saying, and more coming, all signs that the Germans were winning. But this one had a child on his saddle and a nurse with him. He was different, obviously educated, a doctor, he said. And he told them he knew their commander from their schooldays. 'Take me to Mandryka,' he'd said. They weren't going to fall for that one. Mandryka was protected. 'All right,' said the doctor. 'Tell Mandryka this: A friend from Briansk has come to visit with Sleepy Tonya. Say that the Soviets will attack in a few hours at first light. Be ready!'

'Why should we believe you?'

'Tell him now, fast, or you'll be sorry.'

So they took the doctor, the nurse and the child to Major Shavykin, and when Shavykin told Mandryka, their commander did a dance: 'It's him! I thought he was dead. It's my best friend from Briansk. The Bolshevik bastards sent him to the Camps. But here he is.'

'And what about the nurse, and the child?' asked Shavykin, who had a bullet scar on his face that looked as if a red worm was tunnelling under his cheek.

'He cares for children,' said Mandryka, buttoning his tunic and putting on a Wehrmacht forage cap and round dark glasses. 'That's it. From now on, Kapto joins us! Give him a uniform and a captain's pips. Tonya will be his lieutenant. She gets anything she wants. Bring Kapto to me. Meanwhile, prepare the men for the attack.'

'Right, chief.'

Now Mandryka poured a cup of ersatz coffee and another shot of Armenian cognac for his friend from Briansk, and they started to catch up on many years apart.

'One thing,' said Kapto after they had exchanged their experiences in Soviet jails. 'I have something for our allies.'

'The Germans?' Mandryka asked.

'Yes.' Kapto took the satchel off his shoulder and spread out a map. 'This will be useful to them.'

'Always resourceful.' Mandryka smiled. 'Shall I look?' But the maps were marked with complex symbols and signs that meant nothing to him – he wasn't a soldier; he had been a dentist in Briansk.

Kapto lit up a cigarette and leaned in to Mandryka, speaking confidentially. 'This isn't for any of the special task forces or police battalions. It's for the Wehrmacht. I need to give this to the staff of the army – the Sixth, isn't it? – further north, who are preparing to cross the Don and maybe push towards Stalingrad? It will come from you and me, Mandryka. It will help you. They'll be impressed.'

Mandryka nodded slowly.

'Obviously it's urgent,' added Kapto. 'It could really help our side.'

'We'll get it to them as soon as we can,' said Mandryka. 'Now tell me about the little girl?'

V

'Have you ever met Shapiro?' Svetlana asked. Her best friend Martha Peshkova had come to the Kremlin apartment for *chai*.

'Well, no, but I have seen him.'

'What's he like?'

'He's very tall. He has black hair with grey streaks, big dark eyes and he looks very . . .'

'Very what?'

'Turbulent – passionate!'

'Oh my God.' Svetlana fanned her face with her hands.

'But, Sveta?'

'Yes?'

'He's forty and he's married.'

'Oh,' said Svetlana. Dammit! Married, she thought, I have no chance. But she was Stalin's daughter. Anything was possible to her. She knew how to give orders.

'He's quite famous, you know,' Martha went on. 'His scripts have been filmed. He's a certain sort of Jewish intellectual. He's talented.' Martha knew about writers. Her grandfather was Maxim Gorky, the greatest Soviet writer. 'But, Sveta, he's *forty*. That's ancient! He's an antique. And he's a playboy. I've heard he's a notorious skirt-chaser!'

'Oh no,' said Svetlana very primly, but she was really thinking, Thank God. If he's a playboy I have some chance. If only I was as beautiful as Martha. She can have anyone she wants . . . She felt despondent suddenly.

'He's a *married* playboy!' Martha giggled. She was getting more amused by the minute. She savoured the smell of pipesmoke in the apartment. Then she looked serious, grabbed Svetlana's shoulders and whispered, 'What would your father say? Think about it!'

'Ugh, he's busy with the war, I hardly see him,' Svetlana replied. 'Besides, I have to live too.'

'I must go home,' said Martha, kissing Svetlana and going to the door. There, she hesitated. 'Oh, wait – I'll tell you who knows Shapiro.'

'*Who?*' cried Svetlana, running at her and hugging her. 'Tell me!'

'You're serious about this man, aren't you, dear?'

'Yes! As serious as you can be without actually knowing someone at all. But yes, I've written to him.'

'And you signed it?'

'Yes, from Stalina of the Kremlin!'

Martha's laughter pealed through the gloomy apartment. 'That will give him a shock. But he's arrogant. There are writers who think they are God's gift to women and he's one of them. He'll think it's his due and he deserves your favour.'

'Cut to the chase, Marthochka: who knows him?'

'Your brother Vasily, silly. He knows all the movie people. I saw Lev Shapiro at one of Vasily's parties at Zubalovo . . .'

It's going to be so easy, thought Svetlana. Alone in the apartment once again, she sat down and started to scan the pages of today's *Red Star*, looking for his name – and there it was: the latest article by Lev Shapiro. Where was he? She longed to know. Had he yet received her letter? Surely not, and even if he had, he was much too busy to read her silly note. From his articles, she could tell he was a man of the world. A playboy! A skirt-chaser! But it was just possible he had got the letter because she had given it to her bodyguard Klimov yesterday and he had managed to send it down on the Stavka plane to Stalingrad. If Shapiro was in the city, he could have read it. She blushed at the thought. Then another anxiety: had she made a fool of herself? Suppose he told his friends and mocked her? What would her father say if he heard of this?

The door opened.

She hid the paper, and jumped up: 'Papa, have you eaten?'

'Hello, my little sparrow. How's *moia khoʒianka*, my little housekeeper,' said Stalin and kissed her forehead. 'Just wanted to see you. I'm working the rest of the night out at Kuntsevo.'

'Goodnight, Papa. Get some rest!'

He turned and left, calling for his driver outside the front door. She was alone again.

VI

While they waited for Garanzha, old Panka knelt beside Benya and probed his head wound.

'If it's a sabre cut, swords are dirty; if it's shrapnel, cleaner; if a stone, cleaner still, but you can take no chances with a head wound. We need a poultice.' He was treating Benya just as he had treated Silver Socks.

He took out one of the cartridges and carefully broke it, taking out the black gunpowder. Then, as Benya lay on the ground in the shade, he walked to the nearest tree, scanning its branches until he reached for something. 'A spider's web,' he said, gathering it with surprising delicacy in his huge hands. He took his dagger and cut into the bark of the tree, collecting some resin; next he dug up some earth with his knife, mixed it around, and then popped it all into his mouth. Finally he leaned over Benya, placing his mouth close to his forehead, and regurgitated this sticky mess right on to the wound, plastering it down so it was level.

'Shame we have no honey but this makes a poultice that will heal you fast,' Panka said, taking a bandage out of one of his saddlebags and deftly wrapping it round Benya's head before fastening it in place with a pin. 'Always sunny on the steppe,' he said, smiling again.

He moved on to the next task: 'Everyone drink water. Eat one tack biscuit. Water the horses,' he ordered. 'Garanzha and Prishchepa, you take on guard duty. Golden, shut your eyes.'

The men were talking around the fire they'd made, mostly about Kapto. Had he always been a traitor? What about Tonya? Who else had gone with them? Nyushka – had anyone seen her? Koshka was another one who'd vanished. But no one would be surprised if Koshka was a snivelling traitor, and it would be no loss either because Uzbeks were the worst soldiers in the Red Army. But they kept coming back to Kapto – and so did Benya.

He remembered a morning back in Kolyma, recuperating in Kapto's clinic when his bed had shaken abruptly. He'd opened his eyes to find a man with a heavily tattooed face and head – a green bullseye encircling his skull and making his cranium look like some sort of instrument – standing over him. 'Get up,' said the man, clearly a Criminal. 'The Boss is waiting for his first lesson.'

The blizzard, perhaps the last of winter, ripped into the Camp with such blasting force that Benya, wrapped up in a felt hood, padded coat and felt boots, and trying to follow the Criminal along the walkways, had to hold on to the ropes to find his way. The Criminal, shrouded in furs, walked stiffly with his legs and arms straight like a mechanized Golem. The wind drove the snow at such a slant that it tore into his hood and almost blinded him and the temperature was something extreme, minus thirty or more.

Benya just thanked God and Dr Kapto that he was not working that day: he knew his brigade, which would have been up at the mine since 4 a.m., would lose men today. His guide disappeared inside the barracks next to the dining block, and Benya followed him.

Once inside, he was amazed by the light and the warmth. This barracks was quite unlike any of the others. The men who slept in these wooden bunks were lucky: this was the best-kept dormitory in the Camp. It still stank of sweat and bodies and disinfectant but also something resinous and heavenly. Perhaps it was the smoke of a woodburner mixed with stale, overcooked vegetables – what luxury! Most of the bunks were empty as the brigades were working but as he followed the Criminal up the central aisle, he saw the brazier up ahead and it got warmer as he approached.

'Here he is! That's him. The storyteller,' said Smiley, looking at him with his red eyes beneath his slightly pointed brow. Benya had guessed that 'the Boss' would be Smiley but he was wrong.

'Benya Golden? Is it really you?' said a much older man, who was sitting in reindeer fur boots, military britches and no shirt, in a half-gutted leather chair, right next to the brazier. The accent was Georgian, more particularly Svanetian, the remotest and most ungovernable province of Georgia. He was holding a dumb-bell and doing curls with one bicep while a girl, a young nurse from the clinic, was rolling a bandage around his shoulder. 'I strained it,' he said. 'It happens at my age.'

He handed the dumb-bell to Smiley who bore it away into the shadows. The girl finished her bandaging.

'All right, Bunny, go,' the older man said. The nurse, Nyushka, had a soft, bruised Russian beauty, and Benya noticed her feathery auburn hair, tied loosely back, and her peachy skin. But such beauty was a curse in here, and he realized she must need a strong protector in order to survive.

The muscular older man turned his attention to Benya. 'I've read everything you ever wrote. I have a proposal for you.'

Benya was so surprised that he didn't reply.

'Hey, Deathless, give him a pew,' said the older man to the thug who had escorted Benya to the barracks. Deathless, who moved as if wrapped in bandages like an Egyptian mummy, pulled up a chair and Benya sat down. A pot of soup bubbled behind them.

'Cigarette?'

'Yes please.'

'Smiley, roll him a *makhorka*, will you? He still looks frail. Mamekta, give him some soup.' Smiley lit his cigarette;

128

a tiny ratty boy with oversized lips, was stirring the soup. He ladled out a bowlful and gave it to Benya, who gulped it from the bowl without a moment's hesitation, licking it clean.

'Better?' said the Boss. 'Now . . . do you know who I am?'

Benya spluttered at the pungent tobacco but the cigarette, expertly wrapped in *Pravda* newspaper, warmed him as did a tot of vodka. He had an idea who this was but he was not foolish enough to risk a guess.

'I am Jaba,' said the Georgian, leaning forward to examine Benya closely. He was perhaps the only prisoner in the entire Camp who had hair, grey, thick and spiky, and it was clear that even here, somehow, he was clean and groomed. His Roman good looks were only spoiled by the tattoo that lapped up his neck like a sinister tide. His bare shoulders were inked with eagles' wings, his nipples eyes within stars, shoulder blades bleeding crucifixes on which a nude woman was nailed, a voluptuous female Jesus complete with stigmata. On Jaba's stomach, which was muscled and creased like that of a retired boxer, a tumescent penis thrust towards his sternum emblazoned with the words RUSSIAN GIRLS WORSHIP MY GEORGIAN COCK.

'You have heard of me,' Jaba stated as if checking an unimpeachable truth.

'Yes I have, of course.' Benya knew that Jaba Leonadze was one of the leading Criminals of the Kolyma Zone, a Mafia boss, a Brigand-in-Power who was entrusted by the Commandant with making the mines achieve their quotas.

Jaba beamed at this. 'Most people have. As for you, Smiley told me how you entertained him with your stories all the way

129

across the Sea of Okhotsk and I've read your *Spanish Stories*. Am I a surprise for an old bandit?'

Benya admitted he was indeed a surprising bandit.

'You see, Golden, life is like a plate of *lobio* beans. I missed school but now I want to write. You will teach me to write like Shakespeare, Pushkin, Balzac. Every day for an hour. And then there's something else. Prishchepa!'

A young man, blue-eyed and baby-faced and startlingly pretty, appeared from the back of the barracks, where he had apparently been manning a kettle, bearing a pile of papers which he handed to Jaba.

'Can you guess what this is, Benya? It's my play, based on my life. Entitled *Bank Robbery '37*.' Benya knew that Jaba's most outrageous exploit had been his Kharkov bank robbery in 1937. As Stalin purged the Communist Party, this bank robber had dared to defy him and steal his money. That was courage! He pulled off three or four of these heists, stealing the entire payroll of bureaucrats in Tashkent, Odessa, Baku. For years, he'd lived in luxury, bribing the *militsia* to turn a blind eye – until a shootout at the State Bank in Kharkov when he'd been captured. 'Ah, Benya, I put my heart into this work.'

Benya took the manuscript, noting that the script was typed. One of the Commandant's typists in the office must have typed it up, he thought. Jaba's influence was usually defined in violence and the availability of food but this typed play was a rare demonstration of pure power.

'You are to read it and criticize it.' Jaba took a shirt from Mametka and pulled it on, doing up the buttons as he gave Benya his orders. 'Didn't Gorky read your stories? Well, you're going to be my Gorky. In return, you get to work in the clinic and when we get out of this hell and back to Magadan, you'll come with me. Now, don't be afraid to tell me the truth; I can take criticism. You see, professor, it's a masterpiece and no one but me could have written it. Now, do we have a deal?'

VII

'Horseman approaching!' Spider Garanzha called out quietly. They grabbed their guns while Zhurko looked through his fieldglasses. 'At ease. That's the Cat. Koshka's back.'

'I thought he——' started Little Mametka.

'Perhaps the Germans didn't want him,' said Benya. The Cossacks snickered at this.

'The Germans always say: Can we swap our Romanians for your Uzbeks?' Little Mametka agreed.

'Shall we question him?' asked Garanzha.

Zhurko raised a hand. 'We are now only seven, eight with Koshka. We don't have the luxury to launch a witch-hunt. No, we welcome him and watch him.'

Koshka rode in. He was, Benya knew, one of those tedious men who thought it was his duty to tell others the truth about their lives such as whether their wife was secretly unfaithful or how they should become better at their jobs. 'Just saying,' he usually concluded.

The men gathered round him.

'I was thrown from my horse and then lost her for a while . . .' Koshka said. No one looked particularly convinced

131

but they let the twitchy Uzbek sit with them and share the food they had gathered in the Italian village.

'What do we do now?' Garanzha said after they had eaten.

Captain Zhurko cleared his throat. 'I was waiting for others but . . . it seems no more of us are coming in,' he said in his plain way. 'We need to make a plan.'

'You're our officer,' said Benya.

'If you wish me to command you, I shall,' replied Zhurko, stroking his strong chin. 'But I think our circumstances are a little unusual.'

Panka spoke up: 'I propose we form ourselves into a circle in the old Cossack tradition,' he said, 'and that we elect Zhurko as our *ataman*, our chieftain. What say you, brothers?'

Everyone agreed.

'What are our options?' asked Spider Garanzha.

'Well, I think we have five options,' said Captain Zhurko. 'One, fight our way back to our lines. Travel at night. Find a quiet sector, preferably Italian or even better Romanian . . .'

'What? After we've offered them Koshka as a present?' joked Mametka in his high voice. The men chuckled.

'They'd prefer you, Bette Davis,' replied Koshka.

'Not funny,' said Mametka. Benya remembered what had happened to Fats Strizkaz and held his breath.

'Enough,' said Zhurko. 'Cut it out. Mametka, you asked for that. Koshka, you have my protection.'

'Carry on,' said Smiley.

'Then we'd report back to our forces at the last strongholds in the bend of the Don or ford it somewhere and rejoin the Stalingrad Front. Find our units.'

'What unit? We're Smertniki – the Dead Ones – and we're damned whatever we do,' said Koshka.

'We all know what would happen,' Smiley agreed, gravely.

'We can't go back,' said Benya. 'We'd receive the Eight Grammes before we'd even given our names.'

'True,' Zhurko said. 'As a Russian patriot and a good Communist, death, for me, is better than defection and I propose surrender is out of the question. That's our second option.'

'We're stranded behind enemy lines. Our army has collapsed. Come on, fellows. Be honest. Is anything out of the question?' said Koshka. 'Just saying.'

'Surrender is impossible for me,' replied Benya. 'You've seen the things the Germans are doing here.'

'You say that because you're a Jew, right?' said Koshka. 'We can't listen to you.'

'Permission to shut him up?' said Smiley, those hornlets rising on his forehead.

'Wait,' said Benya. 'I am a Jew, it's true: I can't surrender. But I've heard too the Germans simply starve their Russian prisoners to death.'

'Some Russians surrendered to the soft-hearted Italians,' Koshka pointed out. 'Or we could defect to Mandryka and join the Schuma. They get good food. And girls, lots of girls.'

'If you wanted to join them, why didn't you?' asked Little Mametka softly.

'I don't want to. If I did want to, I wouldn't be here,' protested Koshka.

Sergeant Panka stood up. 'We've heard enough now, and I can tell you this, boys: I am not going *anywhere*! Captain, what are our orders?'

133

'I think there is a right thing to do,' opined Zhurko earnestly, looking at them through his steel-rimmed spectacles and lighting up a cigarette. 'But we could also hide out here and hope to be liberated.'

'But that might never happen,' said Koshka. 'Right now, we've got to face the possibility that we're going to lose the war. Just saying.'

'No, Koshka, we will win the war,' answered Zhurko. 'I am certain. I was an economist at Gosplan. That was my job in Moscow. We did the Five-Year Plans.'

'A great success!' said Benya.

'Is that Odessan humour?' asked Zhurko.

'If you're that clever, captain,' asked Smiley, 'how did you end up here?'

Zhurko grinned, cleaning his spectacles. 'I predicted a recession, but a recession is impossible in our Socialist Paradise. Anyway we, on our own, will out-produce the Germans this year. With the Americans, we are unbeatable. If Hitler didn't win in the first year, he can't win the war.'

'So he's gonna lose?' piped up Mametka.

'Exactly. All the laws of science confirm it but it will take years and we don't have the luxury of time. Next option, we find our Soviet partisans, who are fighting the Germans behind their lines, and join them.'

'But where are they?' asked Koshka.

'Honestly? We don't know and the steppe has been so swiftly overrun, it is possible there aren't any partisans here.'

'So far, these are not tempting options,' Koshka observed.

'Who are you to judge anything?' Garanzha glared at the little Uzbek. 'Where did you suddenly arrive from, Koshka?'

'I got lost, I told you. I looked for you. Finally I found you.'

'Got lost, found us? Hmm. It stinks,' said Spider Garanzha. 'Just saying!'

'Enough, both of you,' said Panka, suddenly drawing his sword. Panka never fooled around. He was straight as a lance. The two Shtrafniki stopped arguing.

'The last option is this,' said Zhurko, even-toned and sensible. 'We were told to eliminate the traitor Mandryka. If we kill him we are redeemed. If we are wounded, we are redeemed. We know where Mandryka is. That's our mission.'

'You're suggesting a few horsemen ride into his stronghold?' said Koshka. 'We tried that earlier and it was madness. Think of all the men we lost.'

'We're on a suicide mission after all.' Benya smiled as he spoke.

'More Odessan irony?' said Zhurko. 'We're still alive and I plan to stay alive. We don't attack the village of Shepilovka, which is crawling with Mandryka's men and a unit of Germans. We know though that he rides out each day with German colleagues to organize anti-partisan *aktions*. Let us ambush him when he ventures out of his stronghold. If we die in the attempt, so be it.'

'I agree,' said Panka. 'We have our horses; we are still Cossacks. I am not going *anywhere*! You'll see: it's always sunny on the steppe.' He got up, slid his sword back into its scabbard and started to build a fire.

'That was a cheerful talk.' Prishchepa chuckled. 'Who's gonna sing me my lullaby? I know. I'll sing my own.' As Prishchepa sang, Garanzha, half-lit by the orange flames, danced slowly around the fire swinging his meaty limbs in giant arcs, rising and falling, mouth wide open, eyes closed, yet finding a sort of grim, grinding rhythm all of his own.

Prishchepa sang in an angelic tenor:

> '*A Cossack rode to a distant land;*
> *Riding his horse over the steppe . . .*'

And then Panka replied in a baritone: '*His home village he left forever.*'

And they all supplied the chorus:

> '*He'll never come back again;*
> *He'll never come back again.*'

When Benya lay with his head on his saddlebag and observed Panka's long foxy nose and little eyes as he sang, he was amazed to see that tears ran down his face. They had chosen the most dangerous mission. How many of them would be alive to sing their songs when the sun went down tomorrow?

Day Four

'Where's Koshka?' asked Zhurko the next morning, but they all knew the answer.

It was dawn. The night had been sweltering. The men were sweating even though the sun was not up. Garanzha and Little Mametka stood near the horses, smoking Italian cigarettes. Beyond them, down the slope a little, lay Koshka, curled up like a child, hands stiffening already. The men followed Zhurko and stood around Koshka, looking down at him. Blackened blood ridged across his neck. Just saying, thought Benya, just saying.

Garanzha was calm, calmer than any of them. 'I like to know who I ride with,' was all he said, and he walked back to the campfire, now little more than ashes.

Benya wondered if Zhurko would say something, but he was arranging Koshka's belongings: PPSh, dagger, mess-tin, spurs, boots and quirt were all laid out in a neat row. 'Choose a gift,' said Little Mametka, and Benya got a second Papasha.

The fear was gathering like a bundle of wire in Benya's belly. He had slept deeply under the stars, without a thought, utterly exhausted, but when he awoke, he was sickened by what they had to do this day, and he felt the flickering of terror in every joint, as if his very bones were resetting and tightening inside him.

Sergeant Panka boiled the coffee and shared out the dried

meats from the village and the ration of biscuit. No one mentioned Koshka again. Ten minutes later the seven rode out, guinea fowls and partridges scattering before them. The woodpecker tapped; skylarks swooped; howitzers boomed on the Don.

They moved cross-country towards the village of Novi Petroshevo, keeping to the fields of sunflower and maize, riding to the lane that led from Shepilovka, Mandryka's headquarters. As they loped, they could hear music and shouting. The Schuma were celebrating, Zhurko told them, and Mandryka was unlikely to wake up early so the plan was to be in position when he headed out. If they missed him, they would catch him on the way back. Benya had started the day on edge, shaking with nerves, but as they rode through the heat, he began to daydream, to let Silver Socks find her way behind the others.

Just as they were riding through a defile of poplar trees, Socks's ears went forward and she tensed. Benya was suddenly awake and he put his hand on the round drumlike magazine of his Papasha just as the Cossack voice said: 'Who's that? Stop right there!' Around Benya, the men were reaching for their guns.

'Too late! Don't move! Keep your hands up or we'll kill you all!'

Zhurko turned to his unit: 'He's right.'

In front of them, men emerged out of the maize. Behind them, the black snouts of guns were raised.

'Who are you?' said a man, wearing Russian fatigues but holding a German Schmeisser. Benya guessed he was the commander but were these Mandryka's thugs? The seven Shtrafniki froze but kept their guns levelled.

'We're Red Army,' said Zhurko.

'What unit?'

'Second Cavalry Shtrafbat.'

'I see your pips,' said the man. 'Identify yourself.'

'Leonid Zhurko. Captain, penal rank.'

Just then a lanky young man pushed forward. 'Major Elmor, it's them,' he said. 'I can vouch for them.'

It was 'Grasshopper' Geft, a youngster who had vanished a day earlier from the Shtrafbat along with the vet Lampadnik and a couple of others Benya recognized.

'You're sure?' said the man they called Elmor.

'Sure.'

'All right. Dismount, Zhurko. Slowly!'

Zhurko stayed put, and gestured to his unit to do the same. 'I need to know who you are.'

'Partisans, Second Don Brigade.'

'I didn't know there was a First Brigade.'

'There isn't. We're the remnants of the Kharkov encirclement a month ago. We have orders to intercept you; Stavka sends regards to Melishko with reference to your last order concerning Operation Pluto.'

Benya felt Zhurko's relief. They were who they said they were: Soviet partisans in contact with Stavka in Moscow.

'Is Melishko with you?'

Zhurko just shook his head and Elmor understood.

'Where's the rest of your battalion?'

'We're it, but we're alive.' Zhurko dismounted and shook Elmor's hand. The partisan officer was built like a low-slung cooking pot, Benya thought, with a bald head topped with tousled strands of blonde-grey hair that flapped like the

141

earmuffs of a shapka hat. He and the others dismounted and they hugged the skinny Geft with real joy.

Elmor crouched down on his haunches like a Kazakh and Zhurko sat cross-legged. Benya noticed Elmor wore five grenades around his belt.

'What are your orders concerning my unit?' Zhurko asked.

'Moscow radioed us. Stavka informed us you were alive and needed support, and we had a message for Melishko, restoring him to his rank of general but . . . Well, anyway, we've been looking for you.'

'If I'm honest,' replied Zhurko, 'there are just seven of us and we're all that's left of an offensive close to the Don.'

'We would invite you for *pirozhki*, *shchi* and vodka; take you sightseeing; introduce you to the local girls,' said Elmor without smiling, 'but this area is crawling with hostile forces of every stripe. You had a mission here?'

'To eliminate Mandryka.'

'Us too. Headquarters has ordered his assassination, whatever the cost. I have men watching him and his people.' Elmor paused. 'You hear that shooting? That's a German unit engaged in what they call "anti-partisan *aktions*".'

'They're hunting you?'

'No. Their "anti-partisan measures" usually involve killing Jewish women and children or innocent peasants. And they are assisted by Romanian forces in the area. They're across this field and right beside the lane Mandryka will take, so we can't attack Mandryka with them in our rear, or shoot it out with them. A firefight would attract Mandryka and the Germans.' He looked around at Zhurko and his Cossacks. 'How are you with cold steel?'

Spider Garanzha drew his sabre. So did the others.

'Keen,' said Elmor. 'I'm impressed.'

II

Svetlana Stalina found the letter waiting for her when she got back from school. Even her nanny was excited.

'Could it be from *him*?' her nanny said, flush-cheeked with anticipation.

Svetlana opened it in the sitting room.

Dear Svetlana,

How kind of you to write. Your letter made my day and I have reread it several times. It arrived soon after the attack by the penal battalion that I described in my most recent article. They were so brave, these Criminals and mavericks, and I saw them charge the Fascists. I knew one of them, an old friend, a writer, but I didn't get a chance to talk to him. But I was happy to see him. Sadly they were almost wiped out and very few made it. I admit I was a little broken-hearted. I waited for them to come back but none came. I hoped to see my friend but no, nothing, and even though I am accustomed to the tragedies of this war, I was upset and moved. I admit I wept and then your letter arrived. It comforted me and restored my faith in life. It was so charming and right now, as I sit in the bunker here with the leaders and generals on the Stalingrad Front, I am thinking of you. You may be in

143

Moscow faraway, and I don't even know you, but I feel your passion and your love of writing and literature. I doubt we will ever meet but would I be crazy if I hoped that we can correspond? And maybe one day, we might talk about literature?

Write soon.

Lev Shapiro

Svetlana screamed with joy. Lev Shapiro had responded in such a warm fashion. He'd confided in her, shared his feelings and emotions with her, welcomed her letter.

'What do you think?' asked her nanny – but Svetlana was already writing back.

III

Five miles away from the grasslands where Benya and his comrades had met up with the Soviet partisans was the hamlet of Radzillovo, which had become a safe little corner of Italy, complete with its tastes and clothes and even its songs, right in the midst of the Russian steppe.

Sitting in the shade of a fruit-laden cherry tree behind a Russian cottage painted in the bright colours of these Cossack homesteads, Nurse Fabiana Bacigalupe closed her eyes and imagined she was home in Venice and had not just suffered a terrible loss.

The heat was soothing and out of the kitchen came the delicious aroma of garlic and coffee and the voice of the lieutenant singing his favourite Piedmontese song, 'In the shadow of a bush slept a pretty shepherdess', as he and others in the unit cooked up their polenta, chatting in their different Italian dialects about girls, love, pasta, wine and war. On pasta, it was simple: food was their first solace for being sent to fight in this war and the lieutenant's rye-grinding contraption allowed them to make perfect penne and sometimes polenta. Fabiana had shown them how to grind real coffee beans in a steel helmet – '*Perfetto!*' they cried – and this had made her even more alluring in their eyes – if that was possible. She could hear them loudly grumbling: why were they in Russia at all? Mussolini had sent 235,000 Italians to fight in Hitler's war and only the most fanatical Fascists, like their commander Colonel Malamore and his élite legions of Blackshirts, believed this crazy war was a good idea or embraced the Nazis' racial ideas. They had been inserted into Hitler's Army Group B for this summer offensive, and the Russians had collapsed so fast it had been a bit of a holiday. Fabiana's units had not lost a man until two days ago when a squadron of wild Russian Cossacks had suddenly fallen on them and driven them out of their village with the loss of several men including Ippolito Bacigalupe, Fabiana's husband.

'Do you think the *principessa* is OK? She seems quiet!'

Fabiana smiled as the men's voices dropped to stage whispers as they discussed her.

'Of course she's quiet! She lost her husband—'

'But he treated her badly. I heard him slap her once and she had a black eye next day.'

'Now she's sad; I saw her crying; she's a widow and we have to look after her.'

'Don't worry about her. Colonel Malamore will marry her if he can . . . but what would you give for a kiss from her?'

'A hundred lashes!' said one voice.

'Demotion. One rank for a kiss but for a full night, a long night, I'd happily go to the blockhouse for a year!'

'*Ottimo! Delizioso!*' She listened to them laughing, somewhat shocked by this, unsure if she was amused or not.

'Tell me what the *principessa* is going to do now? Shall we take her a taste of something? The polenta? Let's see!'

Fabiana was no princess — she was the daughter of a teacher — but she also wondered what on earth she was going to do now. Until two days ago, the war had been somewhat boring and everything had seemed simpler. She had married her husband, Major Ippolito Bacigalupe, back in Venice, and when he was sent to Russia, she had rashly volunteered to serve as a nurse at the front. She could have stayed in Venice and worked at the hospital but she had come to be with him and to see Russia — this was the sort of woman she was.

She soon became the favourite of her husband's entire unit. They were respectful to her — she was after all their major's wife — but they discussed (in those loud whispers) what on earth she was doing with this dapper but short-tempered popinjay (whom they nicknamed 'Il Duce' after Mussolini — not a compliment) and how to rescue her from his tempers.

The village they stayed in had been charming: blue and red cottages set in a sea of golden corn, black-faced sunflowers and high steppe grass. Then came the day of the charge. They had been cooking polenta and roast goose in the priest's house and they had seen the dust rising in the rosy dawn and had heard of a suicidal charge by a Russian penal battalion against their own Savoy Celere cavalry, but Fabiana's husband had been certain that the Germans had wiped them out – until they heard the drumming of charging cavalry, then the clatter of hooves on stone and the thwang of bullets. One of the Kalmyk scouts had ridden fast into the village and reined in his little horse so hard it fell to its knees, shouting that the Cossacks were coming. A pig had run squealing down the street; a camel had broken loose, nuzzling loudly; '*Pronti a fare fuoco!* Prepare to fire!' her husband had ordered the men, who pointed the Breda heavy machine guns out of the windows, trying to keep the Cossacks at bay just long enough to allow them to retreat. '*Madonna santa,*' he shouted. '*Muovetevi, ragazzi!* Move it, boys!' Fabiana had seen an officer of the Bersagalieri shot down in front of her, and two Savoy cavalrymen had been dragged through the village behind their horses. Then spikes of sunlight had glimmered through the cloud of dust, their swords just streaks of bedazzlement, and a horde of riders emerged out of the haze performing crazy acts of horsemanship – she had even observed some Cossacks slipping to their horses' side to fire; others had halted and then stood up, one boot in their stirrup and another on the saddle to shoot. And somehow in the chaos, as they were waiting in a doorway to jump into the Fiat and Bianchi trucks, one neat bullet in the chest had killed her husband . . . and they had had to leave his body in the village.

Much later, Benya Golden would ask Fabiana what she thought when she saw those Cossacks standing in their stirrups, sabres glinting above their heads, mouths open, yelling to hell, and she threw her head back and laughed: 'What did I think? Prepare to die! *Santissima madre di Dio!*'

Now she sat in the garden here and tried to collect herself. She loved to read and she had her books, Leopardi and Petrarca, and Fogazzaro. She was listening to the men in the house when she heard the brisk clip-clop of horses. She stood up and looked out down the lane: it was her commander, Malamore, with a thin German officer, his uniform bearing the lightning runes, and an escort of Cossack and Kalmyk collaborators, all in German uniforms.

Malamore dismounted stiffly from his magnificent sorrel stallion with a ching of spurs and, straightening up, he saluted her. She saluted back. He was their colonel, and he had always made it obvious that he was her admirer, even when her husband had been standing, seething with indignation, right beside her.

He came through the gate and stood looking at her, in no hurry to talk. Malamore was not afraid of silences and he was accustomed to death, and she was a little frightened of him.

'How are you feeling, Nurse Bacigalupe?' he asked, removing his fez.

'Still shocked, consul,' she replied with a salute and a twist in her ghost of a smile. The way she said *'console'* – using his Blackshirt rank, designed by Mussolini to evoke the Roman Empire – made her hauteur obvious.

'I am sorry for your loss,' he said, bowing. 'This is the message I bring from the Blackshirts.'

She showed him to the other chair in the garden. When he sat, his britches, his high boots, his very bones seemed to creak. In the light, his skin was scaly and rough, and she thought it was like magma that had dried centuries ago. The heat was suffocating and he ran his hand over his grey buzzcut; he offered her a cigarette and took one himself. He lit hers and then his.

Butchery and the African sun had hardened him into a sort of fossil.

'We'll get him back, nurse,' he said. 'I saw him just after he went down, hit right in the chest.'

'You were there, consul?' she asked.

He nodded. Her husband's death seemed surreal; she expected Ippolito to stride into this garden at any moment, with his Clark Gable moustache, and gleaming boots, dyed black hair, utterly immaculate as ever. She had loved him, she supposed, even with his faults – and what would become of her now? She blinked back her tears, priding herself on her control. She had cried before and she would again, but not now.

'You said, consul, that the Russians had been defeated and yet they drove us out of that village in a few minutes.'

She knew that Malamore blamed her husband for the incompetent Italian response but instead he replied, 'That's war. But that Bolshevik cavalry was annihilated yesterday.'

'That's reassuring,' she said, looking into those features gouged into a mask by the glare after years of fighting in Abyssinia, Spain, Greece and this second summer in Russia. There were, she thought, not many Italians like Malamore. Even though he wore Blackshirt uniform – the black fez with tassel, the black blouse with scarlet flames and fasces, the symbols of the Fascist Party – it was impossible to embellish this harsh man who, she thought, belonged to another time, a *condottiere* of the Renaissance perhaps, and whose eyes were like the slits of a castle in the sun. 'Then victory will be ours?'

'Our German allies are just finishing off Ivan's last bridgeheads on the Don. Then we push for the Volga and Stalingrad. Ivan will collapse. Victory.'

'*E poi . . . console?* Then what?'

There was a long silence punctuated by the hiss of the cigarette and the gravelling of his breathing. Between the cottages
she could see his Kalmyk scouts holding his stallion Borgia and
their horses. Then Malamore's hand was on her bare arm:
'Malamore is here for you.' Using the third person, she noted.

'Thank you, consul.'

'Not consul. Call me Cesare.'

As Malamore stood with his hand on her amber-skinned
arm, the boys in the house (unaware that the dread consul
was present) started singing again, achieving an operatic cre-
scendo of Italian passion that made Fabiana want to laugh
wildly.

'What is this unit, an opera?' he muttered. He took her hand,
kissed it abruptly, and replaced his fez; and she watched him
mount Borgia and ride out with the SS officer and the Kalmyk
scouts.

Looking back, he raised a hand to his fez, and was gone.

IV

Every few minutes, Benya heard another crackle of gunshots.
Then quiet. Then a few more gunshots. He knew by now what
story this morbid rhythm told.

He and his fellow partisans had taken up positions on either
side of the lane that led between Mandryka's headquarters in
Shepilovka and the scene of his latest murderous *aktion*. First,
they had dealt with the Romanians. It had been easy; they were

drunk. Now they were closer to Novi Petroshevo where Mandryka and his men were.

Benya and the others left the horses behind, hobbled and waiting, then crawled through the grass until they could see some of what was happening through their binoculars. Large pits had been dug amongst the trees. Under the orange sun, naked civilians stood together, guarded by Mandryka's Schuma, who were wearing German tunics marked with the nationalist insignia of the cross of St George. Benya noticed that the naked adults assumed that wincing pose of shyness, hands covering themselves, assumed by people in ordinary life when they were in a changing room at the swimming pool or waiting for a doctor — but now, amidst this barbarity, its gentility broke his heart.

'Recognize any of your former friends among the guards?' asked Elmor, who was lying next to Benya.

'At least five defectors from the Shtrafbat,' whispered Benya, amazed to see the traitors Delibash, Ogloblin and Tufty Grishchuk in German uniforms. And there were Germans there too, some with SD on the sleeves, some in police uniforms. As Benya and the partisans watched, Mandryka's men selected another ten people – including women and children: At gunpoint they walked them to the edge of the pits and then the shots rang out.

Three officers in German uniforms rode over on horseback to watch.

'That's Dirlewanger,' said Elmor, pointing at a stick-thin German officer with the SS lightning runes on his tunic. 'In the 1920s he was convicted of murder and rape, but when the Nazis came to power, he put together his own gang of cutthroats, the Poachers' Battalion. These Germans are soldiers in his *Sonderkommando*. He's said to burn people in barns.'

'Who's beside him? With the knout?' asked Zhurko.

'That's Mandryka himself,' said Elmor. Benya saw a small, red-faced man in German-style uniform, swishing a thick leather whip in his hand.

Dr Kapto rode right beside Mandryka. Wearing a German tunic with Russian markings, he was carrying on his saddle the girl, just like before. Benya remembered her wide moonlike eyes, but this time she seemed to be almost lost in a trance in a desolate land beyond hysteria.

'He was our doctor till two nights ago,' Benya said.

'Lyovka,' Elmor asked the man on his right, a scout who had managed to spend some time amongst Mandryka's men. 'Why is Kapto trusted by Mandryka?'

'His arrival was a big surprise,' Lyovka reported. 'He was greeted with honour and some amazement. Mandryka calls him his "best friend"!'

'And the child?'

'He rides everywhere with that little girl, even eats with her next to him.'

'He arrived with a nurse?' asked Zhurko.

'Tonya. She's taken to life with Mandryka's men. She carries a gun and she uses it.'

Another group of civilians lay down in the pit. The shots rang out. Can there be so much sadness in this world? Benya thought. Isn't there a measure to decree that this is enough?

'Can we stop this?' asked Benya.

'Not yet,' Elmor replied.

'We can't just do nothing!'

'Go back to the horses,' ordered Zhurko. 'If we fight and die now, we don't help anyone. Obey your orders, Golden.'

Benya felt Elmor's wintery glance, sensing he wouldn't hesitate to execute an insubordinate Shtrafnik.

Benya crawled back to the horses and he stroked Silver Socks and wept for what he had seen and heard. Over and over again, he could hear the volley of shots, then silence, then the scattered shots again. He covered his ears, longing for this to be over but inside he was raging. He longed to kill Mandryka himself – and Kapto.

His mind was whirring. Kapto had been a special case even in Kolyma. He had received the best rations; no doubt the 'Baby Doctor' looked after the Commandant's family as well as the illegitimate children of the guards. Benya remembered their final evening before they were thrown into the fighting, when Kapto had been called to see Melishko. 'Bunions and piles,' the men had joked but if it was just about the colonel's ailments, why was there a general there as well? And why did Kapto return with a new uniform? Benya recalled the Willys jeep parked outside the headquarters, and also that Melishko was receiving orders at the time. If the telegraph was faulty, he thought, the jeep might have brought the orders. All coincidence? Benya sighed. The Baby Doctor had deceived everyone, winning trust in the Camps so that he managed to get to the front. But what were the chances of him getting to a sector where Mandryka was serving? Such things could happen, he supposed. War was a river in flood that washed everything downstream, its rapid, throwing together unspeakable events and implausible people.

When the officers returned, Elmor placed the men on both sides of the road. Benya lay in the grass with Prishchepa and Little Mametka. A skylark dived and flipped over him;

higher still, the vultures circled. He prayed the horses wouldn't whinny, but as Panka liked to say: 'You can train horses to do anything except sing or be silent'. After a while, Lyovka, the scout, rode down to them fast – 'They're moving,' he hissed – and leaped the ditch, leaving his horse in a bower of poplars just back from the road. Mandryka was coming. Benya pulled the wooden butt of the Papasha into his shoulder and against his cheek and waited, heart scudding.

And there they were: the Schuma on horseback loping down the track and in the middle of them all Mandryka. Dirlewanger was not with them, neither was Kapto or the little girl. When they were just about level, Elmor opened fire with his Degtiarev, aiming right at Mandryka. Benya saw him jerk bolt upright and knew he had been hit even before he opened fire on Mandryka himself, but it was hard to get a clear shot after that. He hit two of the guards for sure but then they had closed in around their leader and they were galloping for the safety of the village, and just at that moment Lyovka went down; heavy machine guns scythed down a couple of others, including Geft. Benya tried to lie flat, panicking.

Where was the gunfire coming from? Then down the lane Benya saw German soldiers and Schuma jumping out of trucks and fanning out, their fire raking the partisans, ambushing the ambushers; and he knew he had to run back or they would trap him. He sprinted towards the horses, spluttering for air.

A punch in the shoulder threw him to the ground. He felt an intense burning feeling, and black water closed above him, and around him.

V

Kolyma on a hot summer's morning in June, a day Benya would never forget. Nor would Russia. Jaba's barracks was suffocatingly hot, buzzing with mosquitoes, gnats and obese bluebottles that drove the men to distraction. Benya, who by now had covered *Macbeth*, *Eugene Onegin*, *The Count of Monte Cristo* and much else, was reciting a sonnet of Shakespeare to his pupil, Jaba, the Boss, sitting in just a pair of khaki shorts. Smiley (who officially worked in the dining block, hence the supply of food) stirred the pot of beet soup; Deathless was getting out the dumb-bells (Jaba did his calisthenics after his literary lesson); and Prishchepa, the boyish Cossack, was carving a wooden horse, all of them just in their underwear.

'Beautiful lines,' Jaba said. 'Isn't Shakespeare really just saying "Life is like a plate of *lobio* beans"?' He stood up as a staccato twang rang from the loudspeakers and the rails started to sound. This was highly unusual. These were only used for reveille, or prisoner escapes, and were almost never rung in the middle of the day.

'What the fuck, Boss!' said Smiley.

The loudspeakers zonked tinnily and then out buzzed a familiar nasal voice: 'This is the Commandant. I have a news announcement. The traitorous Hitlerite Germans have betrayed Russia and invaded. Never has there been a more wicked infamy and we shall repay it. Under the command of Comrade Stalin, the Soviet forces have counter-attacked and are repelling the Hitlerite invaders on all fronts. Long live our brave Red Army! Long live our great Socialist Motherland! Long live our Great Stalin!'

'What does this mean, Boss?' asked Deathless.

The men glanced sulkily at each other. War would change things. Less food. More gold. Every Zek knew things would only get worse.

'Quiet,' said Jaba. 'Are we so uncultivated that we interrupt a sonnet for this shit? Say the last two lines again!'

But Benya couldn't concentrate.

Now the war was here: Hitler had attacked his Soviet ally, ending Stalin's diabolic compact with the Nazis. He was almost feverish with excitement. Everything at last was clear. This was his war, his moment . . .

'Hey, Golden!' said Jaba, squeezing his cheek till it hurt. 'Are you daydreaming? This is *not our war*. Governments fight wars; we don't recognize any state! Life is just a plate of *lobio* beans!'

But Benya had walked straight from the barracks to the Commandant's office escorted by a cloud of gnats, hovering in a column just above his head. Beyond the wire, the bleak mountains gleamed like jagged silver and, in the distance, a herd of reindeer grazed on a steep hillside. Outside the office, a prisoner was already repainting the slogans:

GLORY TO STALIN, BRILLIANT MILITARY
COMMANDER
UNDER STALIN'S LEADERSHIP, ONWARD TO
VICTORY
UNDER STALIN'S LEADERSHIP, WE WILL DEFEAT
THE NAZI HYDRA

DEATH TO HITLER AND HIS HENCHMEN
WATCH WHAT YOU SAY, SPIES ARE EVERYWHERE
DEATH TO SPIES
MORE GOLD FOR OUR VICTORY!
WELCOME TO MEDYAK-7

Outside the Commandant's office, a Mongolian guard shoved him so hard that he fell. But he persevered, and because the guard knew that Benya was protected by Jaba, he let him in to see the Commandant's assistant, a man whose eyes bulged so gloopily behind his bottle-thick spectacles that they resembled hard-boiled eggs.

'What can I do for you, Prisoner Golden?' asked Lieutenant Bobkin in a neutral drone. Now in a blue Chekist uniform, he was an ex-prisoner who had made the crossover from Zek to officer of the NKVD. 'What's your request?'

'I want to volunteer to fight the Nazis,' said Benya.

'State your code!'

'KRTD 58.8. Ten.' Every prisoner had a code; KRTD meant Benya was guilty of counter-revolutionary Trotskyite activity; 58.8 denoted the clause of the criminal code reserved for those guilty of terrorism; ten the years of his sentence.

'Ten?' said Bobkin. 'You've been misinformed. Your sentence is ten years for each indictment plus five for counter-revolutionary agitation, to be served consecutively.'

Benya staggered, so great was his shock. 'Wait, so how many is that?'

'Twenty-five in total.' Bobkin sighed. 'Put your request in writing, Prisoner Golden, and I will pass it on to the authorities. But I have to warn you, you'll die here in Kolyma.'

VI

The night was drenchingly hot in the village of Shepilovka and, when he awoke, Benya found himself a prisoner in one of the village stables that had been converted into makeshift cells. The bars to his cell were nailed crooked and he thought of escape, but he was afraid to move, too broken. His terrified mind jerked from thought to thought: his shoulder was hurting, his shirt sopping wet with blood, and it had been hours since he had eaten or drunk a thing.

He could see through the bars that the flags in the village were at half-mast and the bodies swayed on the makeshift gallows in the courtyard. He couldn't tell who they were. Death just wiped their personality as a rag wipes letters off a black-board. Perhaps they were the lucky ones, thought Benya.

But Mandryka was dead. They had got him! He had heard the music, a discordant village band, out-of-tune trumpets and balalaikas, playing a death march. This had been followed by volley after volley of gunfire as Mandryka's men let off their guns in salute for their fallen chieftain, and the beginnings of a drunken wake, accompanied by the breathy notes of an accordion. Benya listened to the songs — he knew some of them: 'Black Crow', 'Volga-Volga'. As speeches were made, and more volleys fired, he sensed a spasm of a grotesque and truly terrifying spirit abroad, made up of military ritual and peasant drunkenness and the lairy cruelty of this black-hearted time. He waited for what would happen next. He was bleeding from his shoulder; the pain made him sweat, the shivers came in gusts, and he guessed he would die. If it happens, at least be calm, he told himself, don't beg, don't shriek, don't wet yourself, but then he knew he would do all those things, and anything, *anything*, to survive, and the hysteria made him shudder. We killed Mandryka, he told himself, at least we achieved something – and he remembered Melishko saying, 'Maybe we'll do something to make our families proud – even if they never know it.'

But Melishko also had said, 'You can't get me,' and they *had* got him.

The party is over, and the shouting suddenly gets nearer. Mandryka's men are pouring into the courtyard and taking out the prisoners. They are now so close, Benya can hear their breath, the chink of keys, locks grinding, and the breathless panting of excited, drunk men. Benya waits his turn. Then the door is opening and they seize him under the arms and toss him out into the courtyard, Russians, Cossacks and Ukrainians, all babbling at once, hard men, peasants and farm-boys, villagers and flotsam. They are kicking him and beating him with whips. There's just a roil of bodies and Benya can't focus. The band has started up again, somewhere else in the village, and some of the men are dancing, weaving in and out, singing to themselves, and a shirtless old Cossack is playing an accordion. One group are trying to hang a man from the gallows but the rope keeps breaking and the man swings back and forth like a macabre pendulum. Some of Mandryka's men – yes, he can see his former comrade Ogloblin amongst them – have a man on the ground and others – he spots Bap and Delibash – are less focused, and are staggering from one scene to another, coming in for a kick. The orders are being barked out in a hoarse feminine voice that he recognizes and then he sees her: it is Tonya, in a German grey tunic with a Schmeisser on her shoulder: the long flat face with its smudged gaze, her almost invisible eyebrows and reddish eyelashes are the same but now her fat legs are clad in fancy stockings and riding boots. Everyone is sweating alcohol, he can smell it, and garlic and peppers.

Tonya wipes her forehead on her cuff. 'Cut the nettles!' she says to the men. 'Make them feel it.' They enjoy following her orders, these hard, angry men. They are joking about her: 'Smertina' – the Death Woman – 'cooks spicy dishes, the bitch!' they say, but they obey.

'Yes, nurse, if you say so, nurse!' cackles one, swinging his whip.

'We can't deny you, Mama,' gasps the shirtless Cossack, who drops the accordion, which gives out a few winded squeaks, and bends over a man who's lying on the sand.

'Are the horses well shod?' she says.

'I'm seeing to that, Mama!' It is the voice of Tufty Grishchuk, the farrier who's shod Silver Socks so many times. Drunk and husky, he wears his leather apron over a grey tunic.

Tonya sees Benya suddenly, and she darts at him, her quirt striking him across the face. The sting brings tears, but he stares right into her eyes, her sleepy eyes, always so bored. But now they shake him to his bones. Now her eyes are greedy with that freak lust he himself recognizes. Tonya has been recast and then unleashed.

She smiles as she never did all the months he knew her, a smile stained in the brightest pink lipstick, and before he knows

160

it, she's struck him again with the butt of her gun, so hard that he falls through the grip of his handlers and finds himself on the ground. From this boot-level vantage, he sees across the yard to where a crowd has gathered.

He can't fathom it at first. They're holding one of the Shtrafniki, young fair-haired Geft, who's lightly wounded, and Grishchuk, the farrier in his leather apron, is laying out his tools, asking his assistant, Delibash, for them one by one: 'Clinchers!' 'Hoof knife!' 'Nippers!' 'Shoe!' 'Nails!' and finally with relish: 'Hammer!'

The group leans over to see more, jostling each other but, at the same time, straining to hold someone still.

'He's not saying a word!'

'Now we'll hear him!' Benya has a sudden view of Grishchuk as he hammers in the nails. 'Giddy up, horsey!' he shouts. Inhuman shrieks of pain and intoxicated guffaws. And there is Geft on all fours, the horseshoes nailed to his hands and feet.

Benya is shaking his head over and over: such things can scarcely be absorbed.

He crawls away, the whip falling on his back, and finds Captain Zhurko right there, in his underwear, and he is bleeding from the face. Benya sees he has no eyelids. This is fine work for the nurse with the balletic fingers, and he knows instantly that it is Tonya's special gift to the captain who had never noticed her. Benya and Zhurko look at each other but can Zhurko see him without his spectacles? 'It's me, Golden,' says Benya.

'Golden, my wife, my son . . .' he starts. He wants Benya to tell his son something but his voice trails away.

'Yes, of course I will,' says Benya, thinking: Neither of us will get out of this. Then Zhurko is pulled out of his reach. The men are seizing the others, dragging them all up and standing them against the wall.

'I'll cut the nettles,' Tonya says, and Benya sees the sub-machine gun on her shoulder.

'Let's see how Mama cuts the nettles,' cries Delibash.

'Line 'em up,' she says. They pick up Benya. 'Not him. But him and him. Line them up!'

'Can nurses shoot? I'll wager not . . .' says one of the men, daring her.

This 'cutting of nettles' is the mantra of the night, it seems. Tonya lets rip with the gun. It's deafening. Burst after burst.

And then he sees they have Nyushka, Jaba's Bunny, the other nurse. Tonya's distracted by this girl whom she knew so well. 'Take the slut, she wants it, she's yours!' she calls to the men. Nyushka, whom Benya himself admired, the sweet-hearted one who slept with Jaba and Ganakovich – how Tonya must have hated her in their shared room. He hears the ripping of cloth, Nyushka's shrieks, the grunts of men, and Nyushka lets it happen, and afterwards she lies as they leave her, exhausted, her limbs awry.

'Look, it's the writer!' Benya is kicked again, hard. The boot catches his shoulder where he's already wounded and the pain is so overwhelming, he blacks out. Back in his stable, he hears the volleys of machine-gun fire. The presentiment of death is clear – and he welcomes it. Now let me die, he prays. He has done all he can. Mandryka is dead but Kapto . . .

He swears to himself that if he ever gets the chance, he will kill the doctor.

By the time the bolts screeched open, Benya could scarcely move. He recognized the voice speaking to him through the open door. It was Kapto, the Baby Doctor in a tunic of German field grey.

'How are you feeling?' It was Kapto's habitual question but he was whispering.

Benya opened his mouth but found he could not speak.

'Did you want to kill me today?'

Benya nodded. Oh yes! He was too desperate, too gone, to lie.

'I had to bring the child home for her rest. She's always falling asleep, little angel, poor mite. I've always despised the Bolsheviks, but what can I say? I believe in our nation. Nothing is achieved without force. Stalin taught us that if nothing else . . . I haven't come to talk, Golden . . .'

But Benya knew he had come to talk, and that he wanted to explain the reasons for his betrayal.

'Mandryka was my friend,' Kapto continued. 'To be sure, the lads went a bit crazed last night – it's partly the Pervitin tablets they insist on taking. But because you people have killed him, we will kill every local in the villages round here. In any case, the war is nearly won. Stalingrad will fall.' He smiled suddenly, that open guileless smile, the smile Benya used to love so well. 'You were my friend too; the only civilized person in Kolyma. I brought you back to life. In that way, you're like a baby I've brought into the world and you know I can't destroy something I've created – or saved. They

163

don't know you're a Jew, of course. . . . Here, let me help you up.'

Benya could scarcely stand. He tottered in the heat, red sparks rained like meteors behind his eyes, silver hammers beat in his temples and he held on to the doorpost of the stable. It was dark outside, and Benya could only sense the splayed shapes on the ground, the creaking of the gallows.

'Benya? Do you hear me?' Kapto shook him. 'Wake up! Listen!'

'Don't torment me now,' said Benya.

'No, listen, I mean it, friend. Ride away.'

'You're letting me go?' A glimpse of life, a rising sun, a tunnel with light.

'We've been through such things. Go down that road. The Italians are that way, and they're kinder than us, and yes . . . I want you to know that I'm a decent man.'

Benya raised his eyes to the bright eyes of the doctor, to his lineless heart-shaped face with the pointed chin and his tight-curled hair. 'What about the little girl?'

'A doctor must care for his patients, first heal and then cherish,' Kapto said and, for the first time, Benya saw there was something terribly wrong in his open smile and unblinking eyes. 'I have to keep her close every second. The others are monsters: you've seen them. If I let her out of my sight, they might take her—'

'What were you in the Gulags for? You weren't a Political, were you?'

'Easy, now, easy. Don't say another word, Golden.'

By now they were at the horse lines, and Benya saw Silver Socks waiting for him. He whispered her name and she turned her velvet neck towards him, and her soft muzzle explored his face and he loved that horse: darling Socks. He tried to mount her but he couldn't raise his leg. Kapto helped him put one foot in the stirrup and hefted him up into the saddle, where Benya stayed precariously swaying, hand on the pommel.

'Ride away now, just ride,' said Kapto. 'Don't look back. Are you trying to make me hang you in the morning?'

He gave the horse a smack, and Socks loped down the ghostly road.

VII

Late at night in the Kremlin, Svetlana was leafing through the magazines from the West, sent by Comrade Maisky of the London embassy. She was imagining what dresses she would wear when she met Shapiro. Her dresses were made by the special atelier run by the Service Bureau of the NKVD where all the Kremlin wives had their gowns copied from the magazines.

Recently she, Martha Peshkova and Molotov's daughter had gone there for the first time. All they had to do was rip out a page from the magazine and take it to the atelier in Kitaigorod, up the small staircase to the door marked: 'Service Bureau'. Abram Lerner was the last old-fashioned tailor in Moscow; he made all those tunics for Stalin himself, each one the same, in grey, sand, green and white. To Svetlana's delight, Lerner, a dapper Jewish man, balding and slight, had welcomed her, kissed her hand as though she was an emperor's daughter and introduced her to Cleopatra Fishman, a plump grey-haired Jewish lady, who had measured her for her dress.

A new consignment of magazines had just arrived. *Vogue* and *Bazaar* were the best for the dresses but Svetlana also enjoyed the *Illustrated London News* with its photographs of British aristocrats and even the royal family. She leafed through it and suddenly something caught her eye. It was a photograph that she knew intimately. She raised her eyes from the magazine to the photograph that stood in a frame on the table across the room. It was the same picture: her mother Nadya Alliluyeva Stalina.

Her mother had died almost ten years earlier and Svetlana missed her every day. Svetlana's English was perfect (she had read Scott Fitzgerald and Hemingway in the original and she had heard that the latter had written a new masterpiece, *For Whom the Bell Tolls*) so she started the article, and what she read made her heart palpitate.

'In November 1932, Nadya, Stalin's wife, committed suicide in the Soviet leader's apartment in the Kremlin . . .'

No! This was not possible. Capitalist lies! Her mother had died of kidney failure; everyone knew that. Her own father had told her this himself.

'It is said that Nadya shot herself in the heart with a pistol after a raucous dinner in the apartment of the People's Commissar for War Kliment Voroshilov to celebrate the anniversary of the Revolution . . .' the article stated, and Svetlana instinctively knew this was the truth. She had sensed her father's ambivalence towards her mother but could not understand it. But why had Nadya killed herself? Naturally her father was a difficult man; quite likely he was an impossible husband. He was certainly not attentive. He could be very harsh, and he sucked the oxygen out of every room, leaving no air for anyone else, anyone weaker – but he was also so affectionate to Svetlana. So why had Nadya ended it all? Wasn't her love for her daughter enough for her?

The door opened and her father came in.

He kissed her forehead. 'What is it?' he asked.

'Papa, there's something I've got to ask you,' Svetlana said, feeling sick with nerves suddenly.

'Ask.'

'Papa, did Mama . . . ?'

His hazel eyes looked right into her. 'Go on.'

'Did Mama . . . How did Mama die, Papa? Really. Please tell me.'

There was a long silence.

'Who's been talking to you?' said Stalin finally. 'Who's been blabbing? Tell me who!'

'I . . . read in an English magazine that . . . she . . . committed . . . Please tell me . . .'

But Stalin, standing before Svetlana in his military tunic and baggy trousers tucked into his boots, just looked at her.

'I loved her,' he said. 'But she was fragile. Yes, she killed herself with a little pistol she got from your stupid aunt who bought it in Berlin and gave it to your mother. Yes, I loved her and she let me down, let me down and you and your brother too. I had to bring you up on my own. She left me when I needed her most.' He hesitated; then he turned away from Svetlana: 'I'm driving out to Kuntsevo. Goodnight.'

And he was gone.

Day Five

I

'You have a patient, nurse,' Major Scipione di Montefalcone told Fabiana Bacigalupe, who was working in the village that was now battalion headquarters. 'We don't know what he is; he's wearing a mixture of uniforms. He was found by the patrol lying out on the ground, his horse standing over him. He might be one of the Schuma, I suppose. You better check if they're missing anyone but it's chaos over there today.'

The major was a count from Tuscany, the sort you would find only in the grandest cavalry regiments. His father had commanded the Savoy Celere and so, when the war came, Montefalcone chose the family regiment. Fabiana sometimes sensed that with every breath he took, Montefalcone was accompanied by the cardinals and princes in his bloodline, even though his grandfather had squandered all their castles and paintings. He and his wife lived in a house not much better than a turreted cottage, but he loved to hunt with his retrievers Pushkin and Potemkin. Yes, as he sometimes discussed with Fabiana, he'd always loved Russia, always wished to visit, but *not* in this way.

'You know the partisans got Mandryka yesterday?' he asked now.

Fabiana straightened up. Wearing her white nurse's uniform

with the big Red Cross on the right side, she stood beside the major in the street outside the peasant's house where she had been staying. 'I heard.'

'The man was an animal,' said Montefalcone, making no attempt to lower his voice in front of his effete batman. 'But it doesn't excuse the Soviet partisans, let me make that clear. But Mandryka was lower than a beast. Now there's a Russian woman lording it over them who's worse than all of them – she was once a nurse, they say.'

Fabiana nodded and looked up into Montefalcone's swarthy, oval face and the loose chins that wobbled as he wiped the sweat with a crested handkerchief.

'Oh, look who's here.' A skinny mongrel, not unlike a starved fox, trotted in confidently and poked Montefalcone with its nose. 'We've adopted this one,' he said as he stroked it lovingly with his soft hands. 'Jacopo, bring Anastasia some milk,' he called to his batman. What a kind man he was. For a moment, Fabiana longed to be treated like the fox-red dog. Her mother had dreamed of her marrying such a man, an aristocratic connoisseur with puppy's eyes. How different he was from her husband Ippolito – not to speak of Colonel Malamore.

Now she was on the Don steppe where the dust itself was thick with blood, not just of soldiers but of women and children. Her husband was dead. And Malamore visited each time he rode through, several times in the last couple of days. His intentions were clear, she thought, and shivered.

'Don't you want to go home?' Montefalcone asked her.

'*Si, signore*. But first I must bury my husband.'

'Of course, of course. We will find him. Then you must go

home. I can arrange it for you. Let me, my dear, let me. This is no place for a girl like you . . .'

Fabiana wondered what sort of woman he took her for. What did they all take her for? She guessed they all presumed there was some shady story, perhaps a father who was a Milanese industrialist, or a mother who was the mistress of some war profiteer. She did not realize that in her mid-thirties she had become beautiful, because in her teens she had been plain and awkward. Girls who are plain in their teens never believe they can be anything else. And there was no glamorous mystery: her father was the custodian of the Venetian State Archive just round the corner from their home, a fourth-floor apartment in Campo San Stin.

She sees herself running to the nearby Campo dei Frari to that shop with the big oil-painted signs of salami and cheese, or walking with her mother to the Rialto market. She has flashes of colours and crowds and the smell of incense while crossing the votive bridges of boats with her family during the Festa del Redentore and every Sunday her mother takes her to San Rocco church. She smiles at the thought of her mother, an elementary teacher at the school on the Vignole island. The old boatman rows them there every day.

Words form Fabiana's world. Love for her is expressed in things of beauty and shaped in words. She always checks the bookshop Tarantola on Campo San Luca for editions of Luigi Pirandello, her passion. She is fascinated by his characters for whom there is not an objective reality but only a subjective one that crumbles when in contact with the truths of others. The eccentric owner lays out Pirandellos which she can't afford, but she puts her hand on them, smells their paper. Her mother took her there first but now, daringly, she goes on her own everywhere, walking around the SS Giovanni e Paolo church to look at the tombs of the men who made the Republic of Venice into the Serenissima of cities, or the Palazzo Ducale where she admires the suits of armour, the cannons, the frescoes and the paintings of doges. She is proud of her Venetians: Florence has Michelangelo but Venice has Tiziano. She takes the *vaporetto* to the cemetery and lays flowers on the tombs of Stravinsky and Diaghilev: it was they who encouraged her to learn Russian – and to come to Russia.

'Fabiana?' Montefalcone asked her now.

She roused herself, remembering where she was. '*Si*, I want to go home. Soon. But while I'm here, I want to help.'

'Good, good. We are short of medical personnel. We lost a nurse in that Russian raid and we lost a good officer too – oh, of course you know . . . Excuse me, I . . . Oh! *Maremma maiala!*' He cursed his own tactlessness.

'It's all right, really. It is,' Fabiana said, not minding that he was referring to her husband. A fool, but a sweet one.

'*Bene!* Time to get back to work. Take your mind off everything. Are you ready?'

'I think so,' she said.

'The medical tent is just beside the stables. Take a horse and ride over there. Your patient needs you. There's no doctor here at the moment. You'll have to organize it all yourself. You're on your own. Can you do it?'

Fabiana stiffened her back and wiped the sweat from her eyes. 'Yes, yes I can.'

'I have no doubt you can. The new offensive is about to start again and I fear you'll have too much work to do then.

Listen, you can hear the guns on the Don and can you hear the engines? They're German panzers driving east.' Adopting the tone of one of the propaganda newsreels, he declaimed: '*On to the Volga! On to Stalingrad! TUTTE STRONZATE! IDIOTI!* All shit! Idiots!' He waved a hand. 'Oh, we have no business being here . . .' He stood up and bowed.

Fabiana saluted but, when she looked back, Montefalcone was further down the little street talking to some of the Kalmyk scouts. Once again, she was on her own.

As she passed the camels, two of them pulled back their lips and showed their yellow teeth and started to nuzz. Hideous beasts, she thought. They unsettled the horses. She took her palomino named Violante, her body gold, her tail and mane white, out of the stables and rode around the village to the edge of the steppe where they had put up the khaki Red Cross tent. She tied Violante outside and looked on to the plains. Although still morning, the sun was beating down, the horizon was long and stark, so deep an azure that it was almost like cold marble.

Planes, flying in perfect formation, crossed the sky – she saw the German crosses. Across one panel of sky in the east, over the Don, rose jet-black smoke like a dark curtain pulled across a window. The factories of Stalingrad perhaps? She heard the uproar of engines, suddenly close as dust enveloped the village. A column of German tanks, self-propelled guns, and trucks, too many to count, was approaching. The tanks, painted dark khaki, juddered and growled, black exhaust pumping out, their caterpillars crunching over the sandy road. Riding on their backs, German soldiers, sunburnt young men in Wehrmacht grey-green, some with rifles, others with anti-tank bazookas, grinned at her as they passed and blew kisses and made signs of devotion.

Fabiana stood in the sun until they had passed, closing her eyes as she felt the chaff settle on her, and when she opened them, the column had disappeared across the steppe, burnt straw and black fumes whirling above it like its own divine cloud.

She saw the horseman appearing, out of the dust, and she sighed. It could only be one man.

'Malamore inspecting,' he said, his sun-gouged face, almost chiselled, like rock, expressionless. 'Inspecting his favourite medical unit. Are you resting?'

She nodded up at him, shading her eyes with her arm, feeling vulnerable in her white pinafore. 'I have a patient,' she said.

'One of ours?'

'I think so. I must get on and examine him.'

'Right.' He saluted. 'I'll be back at nightfall.' And he rode on into the haze.

II

Inside the brown Red Cross tent made of canvas and burlap, Fabiana saw five bare camp beds with stained mattresses. Atop one of them lay a fully clothed man who had been unceremoniously placed there. He was still in his riding boots, and there was a dirty bandage round his head. His face was heavily bruised, and he bled from his nose, lip and right eye. He was very thin, and he was not young. Most of the boys Fabiana saw were between eighteen and twenty-five. This man was somewhere, she guessed, between forty-five and fifty, and he had been badly fed for some time. He seemed tiny and shrunken on the bed; his shirt was stained with blood, some of it black and crusty, and his trousers were filthy with compacted dust, sweat, gore. If he had lice she wouldn't be surprised. She was not sure what nationality he was, so she searched his pockets, but there were no papers. He was too old for a conscript and too ill-nourished for an officer so Fabiana guessed he was either one of Mandryka's Russians or one of Dirlewanger's German ex-convicts who were said to be killing Russians and Jews, women and children, in the villages. If he was a member of either of these special units, he was a degenerate. She remembered meeting Mandryka and Dirlewanger, when they were out riding with Malamore, and they had disgusted her. But she was just a nurse, and it was not her job to judge Italy's allies, and that, she thought, was the quiet crime of these times: if you made your conscience elastic enough, you could learn to tolerate anything and still find joy in the blossoming of flowers.

As Fabiana started to examine him, she realized with a shock that he had been shot, and that his shirt was wet. She wondered if he was going to die. Instantly she set to work, cutting his clothes off him and attending to the wound in the shoulder. She had no orderly so she had to do it all herself. She lifted his shoulder. There was no exit wound which meant the bullet was still within.

I am going to call him Patient Number One, Fabiana decided, Il Primo. 'Whoever you are, whatever you've done,' she said aloud to him, 'you're my new beginning, my rebirth, the first patient I have cared for on my own, and you are going to live.'

Benya was dreaming. He was in Kolyma on 22 June 1941, the day the Germans had invaded Russia. After he had finished work with Dr Kapto in the clinic, he found Deathless waiting for him.

'The Boss wants you,' said Deathless, who held his hands like trowels.

In Jaba's barracks, most of the prisoners were lying exhausted in their bunks, peering down the aisle of the dormitory towards Jaba's section where the Criminals held court, playing cards and boasting about heists and shootouts, girls and money. Benya noticed a new arrival on the bunk by the door, a dark boy smoking. Probably a transfer from a neighbouring Camp.

As usual, Jaba was shirtless, and playing cards with two females and another Criminal nicknamed 'Poxy' – for his scarred face. No wonder every man was almost falling off his bunk to watch this card game, thought Benya. Except for nurses, there were not meant to be women in a men's Camp.

Opposite Jaba sat a woman who resembled a black bird, radiating such an aura of darkness that it glowed. She did not look up when Benya arrived.

'Sit and watch,' said Jaba. Benya sat on the edge of a bunk. He couldn't take his eyes off the woman.

'You know who that is?' hissed Deathless in his ear. 'The Atamansha!'

Everyone knew that the Atamansha was the Cossack boss of the neighbouring women's Camp, which she ran just as Jaba

178

ran this one. *Ataman* was the title of a Cossack general – but, as far as Benya knew, this woman was the first female chieftain. He thought her gypsyish looks were quite beautiful, and all the more so when she put down the cigarette and absent-mindedly ran her hand through the hair of the nurse Nyushka, who was sitting next to her.

'She's here for a card game?' asked Benya.

'She's asking a favour,' said Deathless, 'and the Boss said he'd play for it.'

They were playing Camp poker with special rules. Twice they showed their cards and it seemed the Atamansha had won but Jaba, narrowing his eyes and ruffling his plumage of grey spiky hair, somehow raised the stakes and they played on.

'Is that your storyteller, Jaba?'

It took Benya a moment to realize the Atamansha was suddenly looking at him.

'He's my teacher,' said Jaba.

'You're the book-writer, the ink-shitter?' She addressed him directly in such a strong Don accent that it sounded absurdly quaint.

'Yes,' said Benya.

'Well then, storyteller, sit beside me,' said the Atamansha. 'Maybe your blue eyes will bring me luck.'

'A cunning gambit, Atamansha,' said Jaba, 'but those belong to me.'

'All right, throw in the peach,' said the Atamansha. Nyushka looked down.

'I didn't know you liked peaches,' said Jaba.

'I like everything,' replied the Atamansha.

Jaba gestured at Benya, who obediently sat next to her on

the chair. Without looking at him again, she showed him her cards. It had been two years since he had been this close to a woman. His leg was close to her leg and he could smell her skin and feel the spicy warmth radiating from her. He took in her britches in their tight boots, her blue Zek shirt open at the neck, her skin dark like baked earth, and he amazed himself by imagining what it might be like to make love to her. He was certain that he could handle her. She offered him a cigarette and he took it. Deathless lit it with a smirk. When she moved, she let her hands brush him; as she smoked, she blew the blue smoke into his face; and Benya started to imagine how this very scenario in the Boss's barracks could lead to his kissing her coarse lips, to his unclipping her britches and reaching for her thighs . . .

He was alive again, he realized suddenly. After his arrest and sentencing, he had no longer felt such things. He had been ground into Camp dust. I had become a eunuch, he thought, a neuter, a husk. He had lost all sexual desire. He had ceased to be Benya Golden. But now here it was again on the very day the war started.

'Show your cards,' said Jaba quietly. He did everything quietly and never raised his voice.

The Atamansha threw down her hand.

'You win,' Jaba said.

'I collect,' she said.

'All right,' replied Jaba, nodding at Deathless, who suddenly locked his arms around Poxy, who couldn't move. Smiley grabbed his hand and, quickly, wielding a pair of wire-clippers, sliced off Poxy's pinkie finger. Poxy howled and convulsed with the agony. Deathless released him and led him away.

180

Smiley tossed the finger on to the table in front of the Atamansha. Benya jumped up in horror.

'Finally,' she said. 'Now can I have what I came for?'

'In return for a diamond,' Jaba said.

'What do you want to know?'

Jaba's smile was dazzling when he wanted it to be. 'Something about your friend.'

'All right, Batono Jaba,' and, using the Georgian for 'Lord Jaba', she whispered in his ear for a while.

'Thank you Atamansha,' said Jaba.

She got up. Jaba rose too. She turned back to Benya.

'I have a feeling we'll meet again,' he said, surprising himself. The gangsters snorted at his impertinence.

'I doubt it,' replied the Atamansha, showing her teeth, one of them gold. 'We break fresh ponies where I come from. Go back to your books!'

Jaba stood up and bowed, every bit the mock Georgian nobleman. Deathless led the way out, followed by Jaba. The Atamansha looked at Nyushka, held out her arm and Nyushka took it, eyes cast down like a bashful bride. Finally the Atamansha and Nyushka proceeded slowly down the aisle as if they were at a gypsy wedding.

'You want to fuck the Atamansha?' sneered Smiley, husky breath on Benya's ear. 'Careful! She wanted to play for your blue eyes but had to make do with Poxy's finger.'

Benya swallowed hard, finally understanding what had been going on.

'You know how she killed her lovers in Rostov?' Smiley said. 'She cut them while they fucked her, throat to groin, like you gut a fish.'

'What was that she said about her friend and the diamond?'

'She's the mistress of Shpigelglas, the Zone Commandant, and a diamond is a priceless piece of information that can be used against someone.'

The Atamansha had reached the door – but she hesitated and then looked over at the young man on the last bunk. The new arrival.

'Is it you, Mikhail Cherkin?' she said.

The man looked up in surprise. 'Yes, but I don't think . . .'

'No, we haven't met,' she said cheerfully. 'But I hope you like your new home here?' Before he could agree, she added, 'Did you watch the game?'

'Yes.' He was sitting up now, nervously. 'What were you playing for?'

She gave a piratical smile, a flash of gold. 'You,' she said.

Cherkin's face was still swinging between uneasiness and bewilderment when Deathless lifted a board that was hanging on the wall by the door and in one unbroken movement of intense force smashed it on to the top of Cherkin's head and removed it with the same gusto, hanging it back where it came from. It happened so fast that Benya had scarcely processed the popping sound, but he knew there was a long nail in the middle of the board. Cherkin, without altering his uncertain expression, raised his hands to his temples as if trying on a hat that did not quite fit, then two neat lines of blood began to run like treacle down his forehead. The men in the bunks stared for a moment and then started to look away as, very slowly, Cherkin toppled sideways on his bunk and began to twitch in his death throes.

The Atamansha guided Nyushka out of the door and into

the night, which was when Benya realized she'd also won some time with Jaba's girl.

He felt Jaba's hand squeeze his neck. 'In case you're wondering, that man disobeyed an order from the Atamansha. We never forget that. Sit down.' Benya sat. 'I hear you volunteered for the army?' Jaba asked this as if nothing of any significance had occurred, as if a man's body was not being lunked out of the barracks by his men with much falsetto swearing from Little Mametka.

'You heard?'

'Why would you do such a crazy thing, Benya?'

'To fight the Fascists.'

'And you think the Red Army can't cope without your war-like ardour?'

'It's something I have to do. Boss, I am a Russian, a Jew. The Nazis are my enemies.'

Jaba shook his head. 'In our code of Brigands, we don't work for the state and we don't fight for the state. None of us will volunteer. Aren't you missing something, writer-in-residence?'

Benya hesitated. Smiley, Deathless and Mametka were back now, watching their master, like guard dogs waiting for a whistle. 'What?'

'To survive here a man needs two things. The spirit of life; you have it. But he also needs luck, not once but many times. Golden, I am your luck. Don't I look after you?' A pause. He was still grinning but the almond-shaped eyes were slate-cold.

'I apologize, Batono Jaba,' answered Benya, who sensed this was the moment for antique Georgian courtesy. 'I was ungrateful. I will never go to the war . . . Yes, you saved my life. I belong to you.'

III

'He's here, just back from the front,' said her brother, Vasily Stalin. 'Let's find him!' Wearing his air force uniform with a colonel's pips, he led Svetlana through the carousers in the white stucco dacha with its Grecian pillars. 'Zubalovo's made for parties, isn't it? Shame Papa never enjoyed it.'

Svetlana had almost not come. The revelation about her mother had so upset her. Why had her mother abandoned her? She had been tricked all these years only to discover the truth in a newspaper. She wanted to discuss it with Vasya but he was so frivolous and so soused that this was obviously not the moment. Instead she took a glass of champagne and downed it and felt a little better. If it hadn't been for the possibility of meeting Shapiro, she would have missed the party, but she sensed that this opportunity might not come again.

The rooms of the villa were filled with officers in boots and tunics and tall glamorous Russian Veronica Lakes and Ingrid Bergmans with curled hair, bare shoulders and vertiginous décolletage. Svetlana was wearing her first dress, copied from *Vogue* magazine, and flat shoes, and she felt awkward amongst so many of Moscow's beautiful women and dashing men, the *Stiliagi* – the Stylish Ones. She recognized many of them: there was the poet Simonov and his wife the film star Valentina Serova; over there, the movie director

Roman Carmen with his wife Nina, another actress. Svetlana knew all the gossip: her brother Vasily was in love with Nina; Vasily had moved Nina into his house, kicking out his wife Galina. Nina's husband was so furious that he'd written to Stalin to complain!

Vasily was pulling her by the hand, a sour-faced imp whispering horrible things to her: 'I fucked that one with her husband in the next-door room,' he was saying. 'And that one . . .'

'Stop telling me, or I'll block my ears,' said Svetlana – but he didn't. Making love couldn't be as ugly as he made it seem, she thought, surely it must be exquisite when you're in love? Women danced to the gramophone. The foxtrot was the new dance, so fast, so close – and Svetlana longed to be able to do it. Sometimes a girl wrapped herself around Vasily snickering and dancing and she was left standing apart.

'Oh, wait, Sveta, I'll be right back,' he'd say, and she had to wait like a fool. But soon he was back, and pulling her onwards. 'Why do you want to meet him?'

'Just to talk about his articles.'

'Ugh, don't bullshit your brother. You're in love with him!'

'No! You're wrong.'

'You're just a girl. It's a schoolgirl crush then. But do you want to kiss him, do you want to get naked—'

'Shut up, Vasya, don't be disgusting. Not everything's about that . . .'

'Isn't it? Yes it is! You want to fuck him!'

'Stop it, Vasya, or I'll leave. You coarsen everything! Really I should leave . . .'

'Go, leave then, you little prude . . .' Vasily turned nasty so quickly. His sallow face was tightening, his lips thinning. But then he changed again. 'Then you won't meet your fancy man!' he said.

'He's not my – Oh, please, Vasya.'

'Come on, little sister, we'll find him. And you can fuck him later!'

'Vasya—'

'Wait!' He grabbed her arm. 'He's right here. See! You can't leave now.'

And finally there he was.

'Lev!' cried Vasya, embracing him. 'Look who wants to meet you!'

A tall man in army uniform with a thick shock of grey-streaked black hair and intense dark eyes was talking to a group of women who were listening to him intently. Svetlana would always remember that his hand was raised in a fist with one finger pointing to make his point. He put his arm around Vasily.

'Lev Shapiro, this is my sister Svetlana,' Vasily said. 'I hope she doesn't bore you. She's very serious!'

Shapiro looked down at her, and in that moment Svetlana felt tiny and ugly and very young. The women turned to her with their scarlet lips, curled hair and black made-up eyes, and they seemed irresistible, carefree and sophisticated. But to her amazement Shapiro left them without a further word and led her aside.

'Your letter made my day,' he said. 'How daring of you to write like that! And I wrote back.'

'I know! How did you dare to reply?'

186

They laughed with mouths open as if they already knew each other.

'Aren't we lions?' he said.

'Yes,' she said. 'That's your name.'

'And it will be your name too. I am going to call you Lvitza. May I, Lioness?'

'Yes, oh yes.'

He looked very closely at her: 'You have something sad in your eyes. Do you want to tell me about it?'

It was the strangest thing, Svetlana thought later. He had just met her and he saw right into her heart. It was the greatest secret in her life and this man whom she had known for a minute seemed to know about it. So she told him about her mother and what she had learned. And he comforted her, told her it was unjust, analysed how she must be feeling, listened to her. What kindness there was in this man.

'Now we've talked are you feeling better?'

'So much better.'

'Would you like to dance a little with me?'

'The foxtrot?'

'Yes, the foxtrot. Have you tried it?'

'Yes, but only with my girlfriend Martha. She taught me.'

He took her hand and pulled her on to the dance floor and held her so close that she sensed his virility. Gradually she relaxed against him, trusting him, following his movements. Afterwards she said, 'I was useless. Sorry! My flat shoes are hideous!'

'What do you mean, Lioness? You were brilliant. I loved dancing with you. And that dress is so chic. Is it new?'

Then he took her hand again, just like that, without a

moment's hesitation, as if she was an ordinary girl. 'Tell me what you think of the coverage of the war. Are we getting it right?'

She did not remember her answers, but he listened carefully and discussed her opinion as if she was a literary critic, a scholar, not just a schoolgirl. He asked her about books and movies and history and not once did he mention her father or the Kremlin. She was accustomed to flattery of a Sultanic intensity. No one ever disagreed with the Tsar's daughter, but they always wanted something or they escaped from her fast, afraid of her name. But Shapiro did not flatter her once. He disagreed with her about an article of Ehrenburg, and treated her as an equal: 'You only say that because you didn't read the whole article,' he said. 'If you'd read the last sentence . . .' When finally she looked at her watch, it was past midnight and she caught Captain Klimov's eye and the policeman nodded.

'Oh, I must go home,' she said. 'I have—' She caught herself: she was about to say 'school'! Disaster!

'Must you go?' Shapiro said. 'I'm so enjoying our conversation.' He paused and smiled at her. 'Yes, you're so refreshing. Not like these jaded actresses. You're the only person here I can have a serious conversation with . . .'

'Don't mock me.'

'No, I mean it. Your views are purely intellectual, quite untainted with vanity or ambition. Can we meet again?'

'Yes, yes, of course. I have absolutely nothing to do every evening.'

'You see? No one here would say that. They'd claim to be busy. Play games. And they'd already be flirting with ten men and . . .' He looked at her very intensely. 'You're not like that at all, are you?'

She shook her head.

'I'm going back to the front the day after tomorrow. So tomorrow night? It'll be my last night in Moscow.'

On the way home in the back of her car, with Klimov and the driver in the front seats, she lay back and closed her eyes and gloried in what had happened. For the first time, she was absolutely happy, in her own right. Happy as a lioness with her lion.

IV

Stalin was alone in the Little Corner with General Vasilevsky. Even Molotov and the other leaders were away and running their commissariats, directing fronts or catching a few hours' sleep. Only the burly Chief of Staff with the big, plain face and the curl across his forehead remained.

Stalin went to the little room behind his desk and made himself tea, in a glass with a silver base and handle, then took the bottle of Armenian cognac and poured in a teaspoon of brandy, stirred and then sipped it.

The news from the south was dire. The Germans were massing vast forces to push further into the Caucasus and they were squeezing the last Soviet forces on the Don. Soon they could cross the river and charge across the steppe towards Stalingrad. Yet he knew he must hold his nerve, and seek the chance to attack; attack whatever the cost.

'Any more news of Melishko's Shtrafbat?' he asked Vasilevsky after he had heard the rest of the reports.

Vasilevsky understood that Melishko's Shtrafbat had become something of a distraction for the Supremo, almost a talisman.

'No news of Melishko himself,' Vasilevsky said, 'though one of his officers informed us that he always called the Shtrafniks "my bandits".'

Stalin blinked and Vasilevsky continued, 'On your orders, despatched by radio, the small Second Don Partisans Brigade under Major Elmor, made up of soldiers who had escaped from Kharkov encirclements and regrouped in the Don, successfully rendezvoused with them for a joint operation against the Schuma and Nazi elements under the traitor Mandryka.'

Stalin lit up his Herzegovina Flor and watched Vasilevsky talk through the veins of white smoke. 'And how did Melishko's bandits do?'

'I am waiting for confirmation of this, Comrade Stalin. I don't like to report until I know . . .'

'Tell me anyway. I won't hold you to it.'

'I've heard that at five p.m. yesterday, they assassinated the traitor Mandryka in an ambush. The partisans lost forty men. Mandryka's security police, now commanded by the traitor Bronislav Kaminsky, have joined forces with German Einsatzgruppe D along with special task forces under Dirlewanger. They are conducting savage reprisals against villages in the area.'

'But Mandryka is dead.'

'Yes.'

'How do we know this?'

'Our source? I assume there is an agent loyal to us, a source amongst Mandryka's Hiwi units.'

Stalin nodded, knowing more than Vasilevsky on intelligence matters: 'Darkness is as important in war as the daylight,' he said. 'So, a success for Melishko's bandits. Please radio Stavka's congratulations to General Melishko.'

'If that is all, Comrade Stalin, I should return to headquarters and review the latest reports.'

'Sit down, Alexander Mikhailovich.'

Vasilevsky did as he was told. This had never happened before.

'You know my son Yakov is a prisoner of the Germans?'

'If that is so, it must be hard for his father,' said Vasilevsky. Of course he knew that Stalin's eldest son from his first marriage, Yakov Djugashvili, whose gentle, self-deprecating nature irritated his father, had been captured. But with Stalin it was prudent to be extremely careful.

Stalin stared into the air, wilting visibly, haggard and grey-faced. 'I am just one father amongst the millions who has lost someone. I'm not special.'

'But they must wish to use him against you?'

'Of course,' replied Stalin. 'I expect it every day. His surrender was a crime and I treated him no differently from any other soldier who let himself fall into enemy hands. His wife is under arrest.'

Vasilevsky was in no hurry to commit himself. Where was this going? he wondered.

'He was always a spineless boy. I don't know if he was a coward or just unlucky.'

'I am sure he was unlucky, Comrade Stalin. We can't be responsible for our children.' Vasilevsky shrugged. 'They are born with characters and we can't always change them.'

'Perhaps you're right.' Stalin blew the blueish smoke towards the ceiling where it billowed and washed back. 'If he had betrayed us, they would have paraded him by now. Perhaps Stalin's son is braver than we all thought.'

'In this case, no news is good news.'

Stalin examined Vasilevsky searchingly: 'I hear your father was a priest.'

A bombshell! Vasilevsky took a breath, aware he was sweating suddenly. 'That is correct, though obviously such elements as clergy are class enemies. I broke off relations more than ten years ago and have had no contact since then. None at all, I promise.'

Stalin nodded. 'I was trained as a priest.'

'Yes, Comrade Stalin.' Vasilevsky answered this with rigid neutrality.

'It was a good training for politics. A training in how to judge men.'

'I can imagine that.'

'Alexander Mikhailovich, in a time of war, it seems a shame that a son does not contact his old father.'

'Yes, Comrade Stalin.'

'When you have time,' said Stalin, 'will you contact your father again? Don't let days or even hours pass. Death takes the old so easily. Call him from my anteroom and let him know his son cares for him. Make sure he has the right rations. Will you do that?'

'Yes . . . yes, I will do it.'

'Tonight?'

'Yes, tonight.'

'Goodnight, General Vasilevsky.' And Stalin stood up and walked out of the office towards his apartment.

He was filled with a sudden, and rather surprising, yearning to see Svetlana. But oddly, Svetlana was not home. He sat at the kitchen table for a moment. He was glad he had spoken to Vasilevsky. Beria had given him this information to use against Vasilevsky, but sometimes family was as essential as ideology. Perhaps this was something the seminary had taught him. Priests were sometimes more cunning than commissars. Yes, family had its place, he thought.

As if on cue, the door opened and Svetlana, her skin gleaming and eyes bright, burst in, wearing an evening gown with eyeshadow and lipstick and her hair curled. Stalin was momentarily shocked by how grown up she looked. His little girl was too young for this!

'Sveta, you look so . . .' He had the urge to shout at her: You're overdressed, you look ridiculous. What do you think you look like? A whore! Who gave you permission to dress like this? But after the chat with Vasilevsky, he was enjoying the mellow thought of family and love, and he quelled his fury.

'What do you think, Papa?' She did a twirl for him.

'You look so grown up, I hardly recognized you. You're only sixteen. You surprised me, darling.'

'But do you like it? Do I look good?'

She was radiating such glamour and joie de vivre that he did not know how to respond, something that didn't happen very often. 'My princess, my darling girl, has grown up,' he said awkwardly and stiffly.

'Oh, Papa,' she said, smiling.

He hugged her as he used to but her perfume made him feel sick. 'Good day at school? How's the homework?'

Svetlana gave him such a dazzling smile that he shook his head: some people lived entirely in their own little worlds. But a Bolshevik has no time for family, he thought. The Party is his family. Sentiment and love are bourgeois indulgences, and the Revolution is everything. He remembered his first wife, Kato, who'd died young. That had been innocent first love but he had loved his second wife in a mature way: Nadya, Svetlana's mother; Tatochka he called her. But she wasn't strong and she listened to his enemies, and let him down. Then there were his sisters-in-law and brothers-in-law who moved in to take care of him after Nadya's suicide. They chattered, they found out secrets, they interfered and got mixed up with enemies, and some were no longer amongst the living. He'd been forced to liquidate them. Yes, he'd sacrificed his own family too. Then there were his children. Yakov: he let me down, he told himself. Vasily too.

'Where have you been?' he asked Svetlana harshly.

She jumped. 'At Zubalovo with Vasily.'

A bolt of anger struck Stalin. 'That upstart behaves like a baron's son. They bring me reports of his antics. The husband of Vasily's mistress even wrote to me to complain. I don't have time to deal with his crew of crooks and whores. When every family is bleeding – even ours, yes, even ours – he's chasing actresses and playing the fool. Be careful, Svetlana, there's trash out there who would like to worm their way into our family. Be vigilant. And I suppose it's Vasya who got you all dolled up?' Like a chorus girl, he wanted to say but he didn't.

He looked up again at Svetlana. She was so young, all freckles and auburn hair, looking so like his mother Keke, smiling at him shyly even in the midst of this most terrible crisis. She'd been led astray by the runt Vasily, that's what had happened.

Calm again, he kissed her forehead, something he did so rarely, and then he did it again. Even though he was the great Stalin, he was still a man, just a father. Family, he thought, as he left the kitchen, having bid her goodnight. Family!

Day Six

I

Fabiana was in her hospital tent, reading a book of Foscolo's poetry while she waited for Patient Number One to wake up. It was early morning, and she had worked on her patient much of the night. After administering a light anaesthetic, she had removed the bullet from his shoulder that now lay on a tray, crumpled like a metallic bug. She had cleansed the wound and sewn it up again. Then she had undressed the man and washed him with a sponge. Now she sat watching him. She had worked alone, lifting him and turning him, and she was weary. Her patient would probably sleep for a while more.

She shook herself awake. The operation on her patient made her realize that she was herself, quite herself, in the way she had always been before she married. Sitting in the tent, she thought about her life: she remembered her school, run by the Nevers nuns, near her home in Venice, a school for rich girls and aristocrats. She had got a scholarship there, and a teacher had changed her life, a nun who'd been born in Russia and taught her history and Russian. After that, she'd trained as a nurse at the Hospital of SS Giovanni e Paolo with its monumental façade and shabby, poorly lit wards. Everything before Russia took place in that small part of Venice and yet it had all led here, to this moment in this war.

I am a widow, Fabiana thought, and if I go home, I will return to my parents' apartment with nothing. I'm not a young widow either; I'm in my thirties. I entered the marriage with nothing and I came out with nothing, and I am precisely the same. Ippolito did not change me an iota. I just have his name, the memory of his punches on my skin – and Russia. It's the things I have seen out here that have changed me.

She sighed, and had turned back to her poetry book, reading Foscolo's 'I Sepolcri' – on the subtle line beween life and death, and how out of this desolation can burst a hymn to life and love, and the sweetness of illusions – when Il Primo stirred. Rewarding herself with a handful of cherries and a slice of black Borodino bread, she reviewed her work. The operation had not been difficult. She was good at the suturing. She was strong too, and unembarrassed by his naked body. When a man was so ill, it was like caring for a child or a pet. The cut on his forehead was a scratch on which a native doctor had spread a sticky poultice that may have helped it seal itself. Perhaps Il Primo was a Cossack, yet the ankles and thighs were chafed from riding, suggesting he was new to life in the saddle. His face and body were black and blue with bruising, and he had been struck with whips and blunt objects. Perhaps he wasn't one of Mandryka's torturers but one of their prisoners? Either way he was lucky. His head wound had not fractured his skull; the bullet in his shoulder had missed all his major organs and muscle groups. He had been beaten but he had escaped, and he'd been just strong enough to ride away. Plus his horse had waited with him, instead of bolting and dragging him across the countryside, something that killed more men during cavalry engagements than the slash of sabres.

'*Chiunque tu sia, sei fortunato,*' she said aloud. 'Whoever you are, you are lucky.'

The man opened his eyes and looked right into her face. His eyes were an unusually bright blue with yellow speckles in the middle.

'No one . . . who knows me . . . would call me . . . lucky,' he said in a whistling wheeze in hesitant Italian.

'Don't try to talk,' she said strictly in Russian. 'Please rest. I don't want you to spoil my hard work.'

'Strict!' he said, falling asleep again. Italian words, he thought, Italy – what memories of happiness he had, of Maxim Gorky's villa in Sorrento. It had overlooked the Bay of Naples. He recalled one particular night when he and Gorky had sat out in the heat and talked past midnight. Plates of pasta were brought out and consumed, and more bottles of wine. They talked of politics, books and revolution, and love of course, making toasts. The old writer told him stories of his life on the road as a penniless tramp, of his first fame as a writer, of the fighting in Moscow in 1905, his respect and friendship for Lenin, and how he had been disappointed in his dictatorship and gone into exile. They had spoken of Russia as the cicadas chirped, and jazz played on the gramophone. Benya was still young then, in his twenties, learning his craft as a writer, and had been dazzled to know Gorky, to sit with Babel and others. He had learned Italian, drank espresso every morning, made love to Gorky's Sicilian maid every afternoon, and in the evenings joined the little commune of Russian writers and their mistresses. My God, the food, the mountains, and the beauty of the women! Then Stalin had persuaded Gorky to return to Moscow, tempting him with flattery, with a mansion and an endless allowance. Benya visited the house and there was Gorky, his mistress and his son, living in an art deco palace that had become a magnificent prison full of secret police spies. But Gorky still read Benya's stories, correcting them himself, and published them in his journals, and he had introduced him to the Party grandees in the Union of Writers. 'Write about war if you get the chance; war is all life distilled to its essentials,' Gorky had told him before he died. 'It's the grit in all of us.'

When the Spanish Civil War started, Benya, hungry for 'the grit in all of us', every writer's ideal material, rushed to Madrid. His despatches to *Pravda* recounted his adventures at the front, and the irony of being a frail Jewish writer amongst fanatical killers. Once, on the Madrid front, he had even seized a rifle and fired at the Fascists, just for the thrill of being alive and so close to death. During the fighting on the Ebro, he had learned to ride and galloped out with the soldiers, afraid and yet so thrilled that he was where it mattered, at the hot stope of war and life, where every man who cared about the struggle wanted to be.

And then the Terror started in Russia. There were show trials and famous Bolsheviks were being executed but Benya never seriously considered staying in the West; he was Russian and he was sure his soul would wither abroad. Besides, back in Moscow, the secret police would surely never touch him. But when he got home, he found they were arresting many of his friends: writers, officials, actors, and their wives and families, and they never came back. Eight Grammes in the head or the Camps, that's what they got. Benya wrote a few articles in praise of Stalin, just to be safe, but then, so sterile was the atmosphere, he dried up altogether, and couldn't write a word.

The Head of the Writers' Union called him into his office one morning and sat him at the T-shaped desk under the obligatory portrait of Stalin.

'So, Writer Golden, how is the book coming along?'

'I haven't started yet—'

'Listen carefully, Writer Golden. Last week Comrade Stalin said, "Why doesn't this Golden write anything on Spain? On our fighters there? Where's the book?"'

'Comrade Stalin said that? He knows I exist?' Benya didn't know whether to be flattered or terrified.

'Comrade Stalin reads everything, and that includes your articles. Comrade Stalin understands literature and, now Gorky is dead, he takes an interest in you. I don't need to tell you this is an honour, but that wasn't all Comrade Stalin said. "Is Golden on strike?" he asked. "Is he holding out on us?" When Comrade Stalin makes such a joke, he does so for a reason. Well, the Party demands that you produce some work now. So I'm sending you to the writers' resort at Sukhumi for three months. Don't come back without a book!'

Hailed by critics as 'vivid, grotesque and sensual', Benya's *Spanish Stories* had been a bestseller in Russia and beyond. The Head of the Writers' Union called him back: 'Comrade Stalin enjoyed the book but he noted it was more emotional than political.' He checked his notebook. 'He grinned and said: "This scribbling Casanova cares more for skirt than war . . ."'

Benya was confused: 'Is that praise or isn't it?'

The Head of the Writers' Union smiled lugubriously, relishing the power Stalin had delegated to him. 'Take Comrade Stalin's comments to heart, Citizen Writer.'

II

Benya awoke. He didn't know where he was. It was so humid that the drugs and heat anaesthetized him into a trance that was deeply pleasurable and he felt he could sleep forever. He saw a chair and a nurse sitting there, not looking at him but facing away, reading a book. It was a scene of exquisite langour. And then she reached up and took off her white nurse's cap and started to pull the clips out of her hair. It was copiously thick and when her dark brown locks fell around her ears and down her neck, he could almost smell its sleek sweetness.

He watched how her hands reached down and took a strand of hair and plaited it, and then reached for another . . . Hands, fingers stretching, gathering the thick tresses, holding them, weaving them through and starting again, time and again. He watched for a very long time and he thought it was the most beautiful thing. It was almost hypnotic, the rhythm of it, the delicacy, the repetition, the concentration, the thickness of the nurse's hair and yet its exquisite fineness, and the scent of skin and sweat; he was observing a delicious ritual that soothed and delighted him. He plunged in and out of sleep; sometimes he heard his own voice speaking and realized that he was delirious but always rapturous, and each time he opened his eyes, the nurse was still there, sometimes reading, other times combing through her hair, and each time it transfigured him into some- one else in another, kinder place.

He heard the whispering shift of the canvas flap, and his eyes opened a slit. An ominous figure was standing in the doorway, one moment in uniform, the next in a carapace of armoured, ridged skin like a dinosaur. Benya gasped in fright, but the nurse had turned. She evidently knew the man in the black shirt.

'*Buonasera,* Console Malamore.'

Malamore circled the bed, looking at Benya, inspecting the dressings on his wounds. Benya lay still.

'You did this yourself?' said Malamore, boots creaking.

'*Si, signore.*'

'Impressive.'

'For a woman, you mean?' she said, raising her chin in a defiant way.

'Killing things is easier, that's all.'

'That I can see,' she replied. 'No one finds that a problem out here.'

He took out a cigarette and struck a match.

'Not in here, consul' – and she blew it out. Benya almost laughed out loud with surprise and approval.

'Strict, eh?'

'You're not the first to say that. This is a medical facility.'

'It's a tent in a damned Russian village, that's what it is,' Malamore rasped.

'Well, in here, I do as I wish,' she said.

'Some men wouldn't take kindly to that . . .' Malamore said.

If this was his attempt at flirting, thought Benya, the old crocodile needs some lessons.

'How do you put a woman in her place, consul? Ippolito's way?'

Benya wondered who Ippolito was – her husband? It sounded

as if he was violent. He felt protective suddenly of this nurse with the braided hair.

'God bless his memory,' Malamore said, 'but I guess his way didn't get him anywhere, did it?'

The nurse crossed herself. He is dead, thought Benya. Thank goodness!

'He didn't suffer. You know I saw him. It was a single shot. Just plain bad luck.' Malamore coughed. 'I must go,' he said but at the flap he turned back. 'This is for you.' He put a bottle of wine on the table. 'It's Russian stuff from the Crimea. Massandra. I'm not good with words . . . but only a strong woman . . . can do this.' He gestured towards Benya. 'Well, my mother was an able woman. She could do something like this. She and you.'

The canvas flapped shut.

Fabiana dropped into her chair with a sigh.

'*Sti cazzi!*' exclaimed Benya. His temperature was still dangerously high, and it came out louder than he'd intended.

'What did you say?' said the nurse, sounding shocked.

'*Sti cazzi! Porca puttana!*'

'That's vile language.' She looked at him very strictly, her black eyebrows lowered, but Benya found he was smiling a little, and then so was she. It was the first time Benya had laughed for ages.

'You can swear in Italian too? Not bad but how do you even know that? Don't use Roman swear words with me: I am a Venetian. How long have you been awake?'

'A while,' said Benya. He was shivering again but quite lucid.

'So you heard all that?'

206

He nodded weakly. 'It was painful.'

'Your wounds, you mean?'

'No, hearing that old crocodile flirt with you . . . Are you tempted?'

'How about you mind your own problems?'

'Am I an impertinent patient?'

'The worst so far.'

'I'm just a *curioso*,' he said. He thought for a moment. 'I don't know your name?'

'Nurse Bacigalupe,' she said cooly. 'Are you thirsty?' She gave him water. 'Hungry?'

'Very. What do we have? *Carciofi alla romana? Fiori di zucca fritti? Spaghetti all'arrabbiata?*'

'You know some Italian? Maybe you've even been there?'

He nodded.

'Stop showing off now. You need to rest or I'll have to leave.'

'What? And send back that crocodile to finish me off? What about the food? Is that ever coming?'

Smiling and shaking her head, she brought him bread, cheese and tomatoes, cutting them up for him. She watched him eat: he so enjoyed it, he sighed and almost mewed aloud.

'This is as good a meal as I've ever had in my entire life,' he said when he finished.

'You've had a hard time.'

'You too,' he said, quoting: ' "I'm a widow. I entered the marriage with nothing and I came out with nothing." '

'*Cosa?* How did you . . .'

'You may not have been aware of it, but you've been talking to yourself. I heard it. I was awake.'

207

He had that high after surgery, before the anaesthetic wears off and the pain kicks in.

'You were beaten,' she said, changing the subject. 'What happened?'

But he'd fallen back into unconsciousness, swooping through a confusion of images, all terrible, all overwhelmingly immediate, everything that he had forgotten, or had tried to. How he'd been sentenced to death, then the gold mines, the Splitter in the cavalry charge, the hands he'd seen reaching out of the earth, Melishko trapped under Elephant, Tonya and the shod man, the child and Dr Kapto. He was talking wildly in Russian and Fabiana understood phrases of it, and she went to him and stroked his forehead, calming, speaking softly to him, wiping the sweat that poured from him. Suddenly he started to weep, and she sat and held his hand until, as the sun rose higher in the sky and the heat became intense, he fell asleep.

She leaned over him. 'Are you actually asleep now?' she whispered tenderly. There was no reply. 'I thought so.'

III

It was early evening and Klimov, Svetlana's bodyguard, sat nervously in the hall of the apartment in the House on the Embankment just across the Moskva from the Kremlin. He was nervous because he could not see his charge. He smoked and listened; he was so fond of Svetlana. Her life was hard; she had lost her mother, and as for her father, well, he had other duties — so he, Klimov, did not want to spoil her fun. Surely a girl could go on a date? But she was his responsibility and he had to answer to Stalin who was not just the Tsar but also a Georgian father. He looked at his watch and became even more uneasy. She had been in the apartment for almost an hour. What was he to do?

Svetlana was in the kitchen with Lev Shapiro. The table was between them but they stared at each other across the spread of *zakuski*, salted fish and little vodka glasses. At first they said little. He was in uniform; she wore a floral dress. It was a hot summer's evening in Moscow and she was so anxious that her palms were wet and she worried about the sweat under her arms: God forbid if it showed!

Lev Shapiro leaned across to her and took both of her hands in his big ones. 'I'm so glad we could see each other,' he said.

'It wasn't easy,' she said.

'Nothing priceless is easy,' he replied. 'And nothing easy is priceless.'

'You leave tomorrow?'

'Yes. To Stalingrad — before dawn. I have to be there . . .' and he started to talk in a stream about ideas and projects, articles, journeys, scripts, impressions, which Svetlana found quite intoxicating. Wait, she wanted to ask about the script — was that a film or a play, and which newspaper was that article for, and what did Ehrenburg say to Grossman about whom?

'But let's not talk about that,' he said suddenly.

'But I wanted to ask about—'

'We can't waste time on that. You can ask me anything anytime. By letter. But here, now, every minute is golden. I had to tell you, Sveta, I've been thinking of you every minute since we met, since you wrote. It's a strange and wonderful thing . . .'

'Why strange?'

'Well . . .'

'Aren't I too young?'

'Yes, you are. You're far too young, and yet you're old too. You see things with an old soul and you're so serious and so well read, I love to hear what you think of everything. And that's why it's the most unlikely thing and yet sometimes the most unlikely things are the best, don't you think?'

'Yes, yes!' she said, longing suddenly to kiss him. She didn't care that he was married or whatever he was. Actually she did want to ask about this too but what was the etiquette for that? She tried to remember in the nineteenth-century novels she had read: how did they discuss such things? She looked at Lev's broad cheekbones, his thick head of hair, his wide, wide mouth — and they were still holding hands across the table.

Klimov was beginning to panic. What if his boss General Vlasik learned about this? What if Stalin heard? An angry Georgian father is a fearsome thing even when he isn't the Man of Steel, the Father of Peoples, the Leader of the World's Proletariat, the Supreme Commander, Chairman of the State Defence Committee, General Secretary and . . . but Stalin was all these things! He stood up, pacing. He had to call a halt to this right away. His dear little Svetlana deserved some love but this flashy scribbler, this Jew, was forty and married! This was a terrible mistake. He had to stop it at once.

He coughed, and then coughed again, more loudly.

'Svetlana, I am coming in,' he called out, 'in a couple of minutes.'

They were running out of time. They stood up, and he leaned over and pressed his lips to Svetlana's – just for a second; a hesitation, then all of a sudden they were kissing wildly. He seemed to devour her – like a lion of course. The feelings raced through her and she was dizzy with it. She could not make love to him – that was out of the question! Her father would never allow sex before marriage but oh my God.

Klimov was listening outside. He had to do something, right now. He had to! If the girl lost her virginity – he would be finished, he would die in the Gulags, ground to Camp dust. He'd get the Eight Grammes!

He knocked at the door. 'Svetlana! We must go!'

But Lev had seized her for another kiss and she was devouring him back just as fiercely. There was something so heavenly about the feelings of two people so in love, so perfectly attuned – Svetlana had never experienced such delight. Finally, staggering as if she was drunk, she stepped back.

Lev smiled at her. 'God, I loved that! I loved kissing you!' he whispered. Then, still whispering, he said, 'Read every one of my articles and I will send my little Lioness special messages! I will call you and if you can't talk, say "I've got too much homework"; if you're thinking of me, say "The flowers in the Alexandrovsky are blossoming" and—'

'And if I want to tell you I love you and want you every second, what then?'

'Say "The little Lioness is hungry".'

'Oh my God,' Svetlana whispered, steadying herself on the table. 'The Lioness *is* hungry.'

IV

The Red Cross tent was empty; Il Primo was gone. For a moment, Fabiana panicked. It was too soon for him to get up. He had been delirious for much of the morning, shouting about death sentences and the shoeing of a man and shovels and sabres. He was not fit to be up. Had he wandered off? Had someone taken him? She had an idea of who or what he was, and the thought that he might have been arrested stole her breath like a punch to the stomach. She ran out of the tent, looking one way and then the other.

'I adore this countryside,' he had said when he had woken properly earlier in the afternoon. The patient was certainly a chatterbox. *Madonna!* He never stopped, but he seemed interested in every detail of her life: her parents, what books she read, what were her dreams, her first loves, why did she speak Russian, and then how she felt about her marriage . . . No one had ever been interested in how she felt – certainly not her husband, who had scarcely asked her about herself in their four years together. In fact Patient Number One was more like her favourite girlfriends back home, but cleverer, and he was so funny as he switched between Russian and Italian, the very

212

antithesis of Malamore who ground out his words as if conversation was a stone pressed within a vice. When Il Primo talked about himself, it was about his taste in beauty, in books, in horses, in Italy, in writing . . .

'How can you love these grasslands?' she replied. 'So endless! So flat! A horizon that steals your soul. There's nothing for mile after mile . . . How can you love it? I think of the hills of Tuscany, the cliffs of Amalfi, the lagoon of Venice, anything but this wilderness.'

'What I adore is the sunflowers,' he'd replied. 'We rode through them, frosted by dust. The sun beat down, and their faces seemed to smile at me, the only smiling faces in a land devoted to gunpowder and murder.'

She absorbed this.

'There's a huge field of sunflowers right outside the village.'

'Really?'

That's where he would be, she decided. He'd gone to see the sunflowers.

She ran out of the village, cursing her white, frilly nurse's uniform, which being Italian was more elaborately feminine and less practical than that of any other nation, out on to the steppe, across a field of unharvested rye – and there he was: a frail figure wearing the fresh khakis she'd dressed him in, holding her bottle of Crimean wine, looking out at the sea of sunflowers.

'*Maledetto bastardo! Che il diavolo ti porti!* What the hell are you doing out here? Who said you could move? How dare you?' she shouted at him, furious that he'd put himself at risk like this. She grabbed the wine bottle out of his hand.

'Well, you found me,' Benya said. Awakened from his last sleep, he felt superlatively clear-headed and alive, almost reborn.

'You frightened me,' she said, feeling calmer.

'Did I?' he said. 'And you noticed I'd gone? You cared?'

'Haven't you noticed, *maledetto bastardo*, you're my only patient? Of course I noticed!'

'So you can swear too?' He beamed at her. She realized he was used to being loved, admired, and she fought the urge to admire him in her turn. He was a patient with no name. Soon he would go. But where? She handed him the peaked cap he'd been wearing when they found him.

'It's for the sun. You'll get burnt. I'm used to this heat but you're pale . . .'

He looked at the cap. 'It's Italian,' he said.

'It is. It's why they didn't shoot you.'

Benya put it back on, thinking, Dr Kapto must have put this on me, to give me a better chance of getting away. Again, as with Ganakovich, he was confounded by the actions of men.

'Come inside. We need to go back to the tent. It's not safe out here . . .'

'I don't know if it's safe inside,' he replied.

She stood beside him. 'I hadn't thought of that. You mean, for you?'

'Yes, for me.'

She thought of Malamore and his Blackshirted friends, of Dirlewanger and the SS. 'That depends on who you are.'

Benya sighed. 'I've got to go. Now. Today.'

'You're not better. You might haemorrhage. The fever could return. Your shoulder could open up again.'

'I doubt that. Not after your beautiful work.'

'Who are you? I know you're a Russian and you speak some Italian. Are you . . . ?'

Benya caught his breath. This was it, the moment when she could turn him in, end his life. 'Are you asking as a woman, a nurse – or as an Italian soldier?'

She blinked, and he could see her thinking this through. 'Can't you tell?'

'The crocodile Malamore is a Fascist, isn't he, a real believer?'

'Do I seem like one myself?'

'I just don't know.' Benya thought of Kapto and Tonya. He didn't know anything any more. Human nature never ceased to surprise him in its whiplash cruelties and haphazard kindnesses.

He stared at Fabiana, into her eyes – they were a dark brown, and then the sunbeam fell on her face and the brownness turned to the lightness of honey, and he suddenly realized what he already knew, that he was going to trust her. Even amidst these quicksands. In reality, he had no choice.

'My name is Benya Golden.'

'Benya Golden.' Fabiana savoured the name, said it twice.

'*Oh Dio*, it sounds lovely in Italian,' he said. 'But then everything sounds better in Italian.'

'So you are Red Army lost behind our lines? *Madonna santa!*'

She looked back into the village. Soon someone would notice they were out here talking or Malamore might ride up with his SS comrades.

'Can we walk a little into the field of sunflowers? Please accompany me.'

She shook her head but she walked beside him.

215

'Tell me about your childhood in Venice . . . Fabiana, if may?'

She started to answer but then she stopped. 'I haven't asked you a thing about yourself. I've been wondering, trying to guess, what you did in peacetime.'

'I want a sip of wine before I get into that,' he said, and he took back the bottle from her and pulled out the cork.

'Wait,' she said. 'You can't drink. The anaesthetic, the painkillers.'

'Really?' He looked anxious, and for a moment this made her beam.

'I bet in real life you're a hypochondriac,' she teased him.

'Of course I am, but not today. I am unlikely to make it anyway. Allow me this,' and he took a swig from the bottle. 'I love Massandra wine and one day I'll tell you about the Crimea. Now your turn.'

She looked around. Nothing. Just the sky of eggshell blue, the sun, and the tall sunflowers dusted by chaff, on every side of them. 'I can't. I'm on duty . . .'

'Are you? I think you're in the Secret Kingdom of Sunflowers where you can do anything. We're in a dimension outside the real world, and here we're free for the first and only time in this war. You're free of the army and your dead husband and Malamore, and I'm not a soldier, a prisoner, or even a patient. I have no past in the Secret Kingdom of Sunflowers. There are only two inhabitants of the kingdom, and one is often angry, and sticks out her chin, and waves her finger – and one is just grateful to see her angry as often as possible because it makes her look magnificent. Besides, Fabiana, if you don't drink, I won't tell you anything. Deal?'

'An Italian regards it as sacrilege to drink from a bottle . . .'

'Like cutting pasta?'

'Exactly. Or eating it with a spoon.'

'Dammit,' said Benya, 'we're lucky to be alive. I think Bacchus will forgive you. Go on, sit down.'

'This stupid white uniform, I'll get grass stains on it and—'

'Just drink then.'

She took the wine and drank from the bottle. Benya sank down, his strength ebbing, sapping his sight, which had started to blur; he sighed and recovered, the wine recharging him.

'I was arrested, sentenced to death, reprieved and sent to the Gulags. But I got this fresh chance of life.'

'And *this* torture and getting shot is your wonderful new start?' Fabiana asked, kneeling down beside him.

'They let me join the penal battalions so I might live again, and I'm not sure I'll get another opportunity.'

Fabiana smiled at him, her face very close to his. 'Well, wasn't it luck that your horse stood over you on the ground, waiting for you to be picked up? And then finding me to sew you up?'

'And give me wine. But then that horse is my dearest friend, and perhaps you are the only other friend I have in the world at this moment. So I want to enjoy this. It's as simple as that. I have no plan beyond this field of sunflowers, this stale wine, and my conversation with my Venetian nurse.'

'What were you sentenced to death for?'

'Do I seem like a murderer? Or a bank robber?' He paused. 'No, I was a writer. I fell out of favour – and I still don't know exactly why. But I ended up as a Political prisoner working in – have you heard of Kolyma?'

She shook her head.

'Well, the prison gold mines of the far east.'

'I didn't think of you as a miner.'

'It wasn't my chosen vocation.'

'I know that — but of course you're a writer. It's obvious.' Above them in the shimmering sky with a few white contrails, a flight of German planes flew in formation towards Stalingrad. She got up. 'We have to go back,' she said, staggering a little, and as she did so, the atoms between them rearranged themselves: she saw that clearly. Something altered inside them too. But that can mean nothing, she told herself quickly. A beautiful view did that too — one remembered it but the moment passed quickly.

She brushed herself down and glared at him: 'After all you've been through, you have the energy to waste on trying to flirt with a nurse, *stupido*?'

'If it was the last iota of life I possessed,' he replied. 'How could I use it better?' He took a breath and his voice changed tone. 'You know, Fabiana, I'll remember this, somehow forever.'

'Me too,' she said. 'Somehow forever.' And as she said this, she held up her right hand, fingers open towards the sky, and he laughed, imitating her.

'You're laughing at me again?' she said gravely.

'No, celebrating you. Somehow forever!' and they both made the gesture.

Then he turned and started to walk back.

'Benya,' she said.

He looked back. He wanted to kiss her, but he felt suddenly depleted, suddenly hopeless, and red sparks whirlpooled behind his eyes. He almost fell, and she put her arms around him, and held him up.

'You must go to your bed. I'll say I don't know who you are.'

'Better to say . . .'

'. . . that you wore Italian uniform, because you're one of our Russian auxiliaries?'

'If you could say that, it would win me time.'

'Benya Golden, it's a Jewish name, isn't it?'

Benya nodded, leaning on her strong shoulders. 'I have nothing left to tell you. My life is yours now.'

When he awoke, night had fallen. He was back in the tent, and Fabiana sat beside the bed. 'I was dreaming of our conversation in . . .' he whispered.

'. . . the Secret Kingdom of Sunflowers.'

'It did happen, didn't it?'

She nodded, gazing at him, her finger touching her lips. He wondered what she was thinking about.

'I doubt we'll see each other again,' he said. 'Probably not. But I just wanted to say that for me those were truly the happiest hours of this war – no, of the last few years of my life.'

Oh, these words, she thought, she who had learned poetry. She wanted to hear them again, and ran them around her mouth greedily, savouring them, devouring them.

'For me too,' she said, raising one hand, fingers open. 'Somehow forever!'

He nodded; yes, she did remember.

'Listen, I don't want you to take any risks on my behalf,' he said. 'Promise me you won't.'

'I promise. But I want to help you . . . if I can.'

'Just tell me. Where are the horses?'

'The stables are right beside this tent. But watch out for the camels.'

'Is my horse still here? She's a chestnut Budyonny mare with a white blaze on her forehead and white socks.'

'I don't know.'

'Are they guarded?'

'Not at night.'

'I need a weapon before I can go.'

'A gun?' She looked worried. 'Montefalcone keeps all captured weapons in our arsenal, in the cottage next to the stables, but . . .'

'I'm sorry. I shouldn't have asked. Forget about the guns, please . . . But I must go in a few hours' time.'

'Can't you stay one more day?'

'I can't risk that. I go tonight.' He put his hand in hers. 'Somehow forever.'

V

Darling Lioness,

I just want to kiss you again. On your lips, your neck, your shoulders. I want to smell your hair. You delight me . . .

Your very own Lion

Day Seven

I

True darkness in high summer does not come until very late, and Benya waited until it was well after midnight. He listened to his own heart ticking like a fuse and to the sounds of the village. Cats fighting, the camels nuzzling, scattered shots, planes overhead, Italians singing, horses whinnying – then just a hiss outside the tent. 'Benya!'

He opened the flap and there was the white blaze of Silver Socks with Fabiana leading him. Socks searched for him, and Benya stroked her muzzle and kissed her neck.

'*Grazie mille,*' he said to Fabiana, '*grazie mille.*' And Fabiana, now wearing light green Italian uniform with a *bustina* at a raffish angle on the back of her head, said the same thing to him and then he kissed her cheeks, three times Russian-style, and he could feel her, so warm and close to him, and he kissed her mouth, and she kissed him back and whispered:

'Benya, you must strike me so . . .'

'That's not easy for me.'

'Just hurry.'

He slapped her hard across the face and she flinched, and touched her lip.

'OK.' There was blood on her fingertip. 'There's food in the saddlebags. Go then. Go!'

223

Silver Socks skittered as he mounted, and he calmed her with a touch on the withers. He meant to say poetical things to Fabiana, to say 'Somehow forever', but he was too afraid to think of such things. Instead, without looking back, he kicked Socks into a canter and rode away, knowing that she would wait a while and then cry out: 'Help!' They'd agreed that she would say 'the prisoner' had knocked her over and escaped into the night. And would the Italians bother chasing one wounded Russian prisoner on the run? Unlikely.

He rode out across the rye fields, staying close to the hedges. In the dark, he could see the heads of a thousand sunflowers, lowered to the dark ground, waiting for the sun to rouse them, and beyond them, the steppes all the way to the Don. As he rode, he realized he had no weapon, not even a penknife to defend himself – just my fingernails, he thought, smiling grimly. He pulled Socks to a halt. Should he go back and steal a weapon – at least a sidearm so he could shoot himself rather than fall into the hands of Mandryka's men? Indecision over-came him and he rubbed his forehead. He was not very good at this, not good at all. He had no idea where to go, or what to do.

He heard the thud of hooves coming across the fields. His heart scudded – they were chasing him already. He dismounted and stood in the shadows, listening, shaking. It sounded as though just one rider was following him. Was it Malamore? Or one of Mandryka's Hiwis?

Then he heard the soft voice: 'Benya, it's me. Are you there?'

'Here!'

Fabiana rode towards him on her palomino. 'You took no weapons. I forgot to give you these.' She handed over a Parabellum, a couple of grenades, a Papasha with the ammunition, and she had a rifle in her scabbard on the horse's flank. 'I didn't know which to take.'

'Thank you, but you stole too many. They'll notice. Take the rest of these back, and hurry!'

'OK,' she said but she did not move.

'I must ride on. I meant to say – I'll never forget you, or what you've done for me, everything—'

'*Va bene*,' she whispered. 'Somehow forever.' And she made the extravagant gesture he was familiar with. Briskly he put the Parabellum in his belt, the PPSh over his shoulder, and the 'zincs' that held the ammunition for its drum-like magazine in his saddlebags, passing the rifle back to her. She slipped the rifle into her scabbard. He mounted Silver Socks and looked back at her.

Fabiana hadn't moved. He turned Socks around. She was still there.

'Right! Thank you. I must go, Fabiana, and you must go back right now. *Vai subito! Arrivederci.*'

She turned the palomino but in a circle and ended up closer to him. 'You know, Il Primo, I can't go back. Not now. You have your horse and your guns and you are gone. They will know and they will shoot me for treason.'

Benya absorbed this in a second: the Italians would presume he was taking a hostage; they would hunt them down; and probably they would die together. It was not what he had planned, but he knew she was right. In bringing him the weapons, she'd put herself in supreme danger. 'So we ride together. But we must go now!'

The horses were nervous; Socks stamped; there were shouts

from the village; lights were going on; and then the first shot rang out.

Benya leaned over and smacked the rump of her horse with his quirt. Violante almost bucked Fabiana off but she stayed on and then they were galloping. A volley of machine-gun fire thwanged over them and Benya could see muzzle flashes from the village and the pirts of dust on the ground rising from the impacts. A bullet chinged right off his stirrup. A searchlight cast a beam into the dark, seeking them. At this rate, they would shoot him like a dog. He seized her horse's bridle and pulled Fabiana closer: 'Stay next to me.' The searchlight found them and suddenly Benya could see her clearly in boots and britches and khaki, the *bustina* on her tied-up hair – he thanked God she wasn't wearing her snow-white nurse's outfit – and he levelled the Papasha right at her, knowing the Italians could see her too, and sure enough, the voices cried out, 'Fabiana!' and then to him: 'Let Fabiana go!' But the shooting had stopped. They wouldn't kill her, he knew this, when it was he they wanted.

Using Fabiana as a shield, he waged both horses on until they were out of range and the moon was high on that silvery summer night, lighting up the high grasses and the sunflowers and the rye. And, all the time, there she was beside him, concentrating on the riding, spurring her palomino, dressed for this, and he realized that sometime that evening she had made a reckless decision and now they would both live with the consequences. There was a glint of something he hadn't seen in her before, and sometimes, when he looked back at her, she smiled as she rode, her white teeth bright in the moonlight.

II

It was morning in the Kremlin, and Svetlana was wide awake, and thinking about Lev Shapiro. Waking up early was a symptom of being in love, she decided, but love is the only illness everyone wants to catch.

In a few days, she had gone from the ideal Soviet schoolgirl, the diligent student, to a lover, a dreamer, and now she did not care about her homework at all. She kept looking at the phone. She had given Shapiro the number of her private line to her apartment, the one used by herself, Klimov and the housekeeper. She waited, then waited some more; then it started to ring. She was about to answer on the first ring but would that seem desperate, too keen. She held her breath, counting four rings, five, six, and then she picked it up.

'*Ya sluzhoo,*' she said. 'I'm listening.'

The phone line echoed and pranged, a sonar echo fathoms away, and she imagined telegraph poles and wires across steppes, rivers, farms stretching away, a fragile line of communication between herself and her lover.

'It's me, Sveta,' he said at last. 'Can you hear me?'

'Yes, yes. Wait a moment.' She jumped up and closed the door so the housekeeper and her nanny would not hear. 'Now I'm here. The flowers are blossoming in the Alexandrovsky Gardens! How are you?'

'I'm at the front in the headquarters bunker.'

'And where is that?'

The throatiness of his voice echoed down the rough, reverberating line. 'My location is top secret except I can tell you it's a town with your name.'

She laughed too. 'You're talking in such deep code that no one could possibly break it.'

'I know.' There was a pause. 'Are you on your own?'

'Yes.'

'I just have to tell you, darling Sveta, that I want to kiss you again, passionately, deeply.'

'Oh my God,' she answered, her heart syncopating, almost melting into the mouthpiece.

'No, really, I can still smell your skin. Taste your lips.'

Svetlana took a deep breath. 'I want to kiss you too. I wish you were here. I can't work. I am bored by my studies.'

Shapiro groaned. 'If we'd only been alone . . .'

'If we had been?'

'If your detective hadn't been waiting for you.'

'Oh, he was listening to everything, but we managed to kiss,' she crowed. 'And what a kiss!'

'Was it your first kiss?'

She nodded. 'Is it bad if it was my first? Am I too much of a novice for you? Will you be bored of me?'

'No, it's charming, it's delightful. It makes it so special for me. And we had so much to talk about as well. I want to know what you're reading, what you're thinking – but we don't have time now. Now I must tell you the essential things, which are that I am thinking of you in the bunker in the city with the famous name on the Volga, and that I want to kiss you again now. Immediately.'

'I burn for you too,' she whispered.

There was a gap in the conversation. She heard voices like ghosts ricocheting down the line. And then Shapiro was back again, his voice sounding more urgent. 'I have to go. All the correspondents have to use this phone. Grossman is waiting and he's getting impatient. He wants to know who my girl-friend is . . .'

'Will you tell him?'

'God no. You're a secret. For so many reasons.'

'Will you be safe?'

'For you, sweetheart, yes. The fighting is desperate here. But this city won't fall. Sveta, we will win.'

'Kisses, Lev, darling Lion. Call me again. Soon.'

'I'll call you every spare hour I have, I promise, darling Lioness. I'm sending you a kiss down the phone. Here! Can you feel it? It's travelling from this bunker on the Volga all the way to you. It's a sacred vibration. Love sends it. Can you feel it?'

'Yes, I can feel it. Here's one from the Kremlin. Across great rivers and steppes and bridges.'

A pause: 'I've got it. Till tomorrow. I kiss you, darling.'

Svetlana put the phone down. The blush ran up her body, emanating from her middle, her thighs, to her feet and up to her neck and lips, to every spot of her body. She closed her eyes. In a few days she had changed completely. She was no longer merely Stalin's daughter. A beautiful brave man in a bunker faraway in Stalingrad was thinking of her, and she – she was someone's darling, someone's secret.

III

Consul Malamore was furious: Fabiana was gone, and the village was in utter chaos. Accompanied by his adjutant and some of his scouts, he had ridden into Radzillovo at dawn, looking forward to calling on her in the Red Cross tent.

He felt he was making progress. She was shocked by the death of the milksop husband – a terrible soldier and not much better as a man – but war always sorted the strong from the weak; and so it had been with Ippolito Bacigalupe, removed so easily in his first skirmish. That was war and Fabiana would soon recover. She was tough and self-reliant, the sort of beautiful Italian woman he wanted to retire with; he would sire her children and those children would rule a new Aryan empire in the sun. He had been at war for a long time and he was weary; this would be his last fight. He was not short of girls. He had an apple-cheeked Russian girl back in Kharkov. But Fabiana of course was different. Hitler's victory was now so close, just weeks away. If we secure the Don and Stalingrad, he told himself, the Russians will collapse and retreat behind the Urals, and then I can hang up my boots.

As he rode into the village, he was dreaming of buying a vast farm in the rich black earth of southern Russia, like a soldier-settler of the Roman Empire. The Russian peasants would work like slaves on the soil; and he would ride across the golden acres of corn on his black stallion with Fabiana on her palomino, and sometimes he would rest his hand on the amber-coloured skin of her arm . . .

Instead, as he and his men came to a halt, horsemen were galloping in with reports from east and west and God knew where, and Italian soldiers were running back and forth, some were even weeping, shots were being fired out into the steppe, horses were being saddled, Kalmyks were unpacking ammo boxes from their camels – and when they saw Malamore, they all froze. And here was Major di Montefalcone with his flabby oval face sobbing like a girl – yes, like a girl, for Christ's sake!

'She's gone, consul, she's gone. The prisoner took her!' Montefalcone patted his eyes with his handkerchief.

'I see that,' said Malamore, dismounting. 'But who is *he*?'

'A Russian. We thought he was Schuma but he wasn't. He must have been one of the partisans.'

A flash of murderous fury electrified Malamore but he ground it between his teeth. 'Get on the phone to the Schuma and find out. Then we hunt them and we catch them. And when we do, she belongs to me.'

'*Si, si, signore.*'

Malamore scowled at him. These aristocrats lacked Fascist passion; the day would come when he and his fellow Fascists would have to line them up against a wall – but there was more to it than that. He did not like the way Montefalcone was look- ing at him and he knew why the major was doing it. If the person who'd been kidnapped had not been a girl, if it had not been Fabiana, would they be going to all this trouble, taking this risk?

'Just obey your orders, Montefalcone. Are you riding out with us?'

'Me? If you wish it,' said Montefalcone.

231

'The prisoner's escape was on your watch, major. It's your responsibility.'

'Understood, consul.' He turned to his batman. 'Jacopo, bring out Caruso.'

Malamore swung up on to his stallion, Borgia, motioning to his squadron of Cossacks and Kalmyk scouts to follow. He took out a thin cigar and one of the Kalmyks lit it for him.

'He forced her?' he asked Montefalcone, running the scenario through in his mind.

'Surely he forced her.'

'Surely? *Madonna santa*, Montefalcone, give me firm answers.'

'Yes. At gunpoint. What Italian girl would ride off with an Ivan? Yes, at gunpoint.'

'But the horse? How did he get that?'

'He must have threatened her with a knife?'

'Who gave him a knife?'

'Maybe it was one of the surgical instruments.'

'Guns?'

'He just grabbed what he could.'

'How?'

'I'm not sure, sir.'

'Isn't your arsenal guarded according to regulations?'

'Well, yes. But not every minute . . .'

'You bungler,' growled Malamore. Christ, these aristocrats were no good for anything.

Now that he was sure that Fabiana was his woman, he had to know if she was a traitor. If she'd crossed the line, he'd have to deal with it . . . There'd been a girl in Abyssinia, a long-limbed, dark-skinned gazelle, who'd betrayed the Italians and he hadn't hesitated – he'd dealt with her himself. But then she was a native, an African, while Fabiana was Italian. But still . . . He raised his bushy eyebrows and ran his hands over his face.

'Jacopo saw them, he saw the prisoner hit her.' Montefalcone was still babbling.

'*Grazie a Dio*,' said Malamore, breathing a sigh of relief. 'Thank God.' She was still his girl, a good Italian, his future wife.

'When the men spotted them and opened fire, the Ivan grabbed her reins and pointed his gun at her. She had no choice.'

'Then all is clear,' said Malamore. When he rescued her, she would belong to him, Fabiana would know that, and there'd be no more stupid mistakes. He turned Borgia. 'Let's go,' he shouted to his posse of men.

'*Si, signore!* What vehicles do you require?' asked Montefalcone.

'This is horse country. We ride out now. Catch us up, Montefalcone,' and he spurred Borgia towards the east and clattered out of the village, with his Italian men in their black shirts, the Kalmyks on their bony ponies, followed by the Cossacks in their German uniforms, the steel of their spurs catching the morning rays.

Montefalcone mounted Caruso and followed Malamore's men through the dust, his eyes burning. He too was thinking about Fabiana. She was forced, of course she was. He wiped his forehead, his head pounding. And yet he did wonder why she had her horse with her, why she had changed out of her white nurse's uniform, and why so many weapons had gone missing.

He sighed. There was nothing as unpredictable as women — whatever Malamore said.

IV

Martha Peshkova wore her favourite lilac scent and the dress copied from American *Vogue* magazine by Cleopatra Fishman for her first date with the handsomest young man in Moscow. He was Sergo Beria, who could not have been more different in looks from his father. If anything, Martha thought, he resembled the swashbuckling film star Errol Flynn with his slim figure, his thick black hair, his elegant pencil-thin moustache and his well-cut uniform. He was eighteen; she was sixteen, and too young to go out to the Aragvi Restaurant so he had invited her to a lunchtime feast at his house.

Beria was the only Soviet leader to live in a mansion right in the middle of Moscow; most of the leaders, such as Molotov and Satinov, lived in the grand apartment block on Granovsky. But Beria was special. Sergo's father worked so hard that he barely returned to eat or sleep, so it was his mother, Nino, a pretty blonde woman, and also a Georgian, who served Martha and Sergo a Georgian *supra* in the kitchen of the heavily guarded house.

Martha watched Sergo carefully. She knew that his father was in charge of the dark realm of power, the Organs and the

Camps. She was acquainted with this world because an earlier secret police chief, Yagoda, had been in love with her mother Timosha and had openly pursued his passion under the nose of her father, in front of her father-in-law Gorky, right there in his famous mansion. But Yagoda had been tried and shot before the war; and his successor Yezhov had also been sacked and had vanished, almost certainly shot too. Then Beria had been appointed, and it was clear that he was a much more impressive leader, intimately trusted by Stalin himself. Still, Martha had grown up in this carnivorous milieu and even though she was so young, she knew its dangers. Her friend Svetlana was kind but she was still a princess who liked to get her own way in all things, while Vasily Stalin was a vicious goblin, a budding Caligula, a future Nero. Martha's mother, Timosha, had told her again and again: 'Marthochka, don't marry into the Berias. That man Beria is . . . Don't ask but I know things. Just don't!' But Martha had argued with her: 'Mama, Sergo isn't like his father. Really he's a sweet and decent person.'

But there was already one fly in the ointment. Someone else was also in love with Sergo Beria: her friend Svetlana Stalina. Martha knew that, when she was a little girl visiting the seaside in Georgia, where they had been guarded by Beria, Svetlana had fallen for Sergo. But now Sveta was infatuated with her screenwriter Lev Shapiro and she had quite forgotten about Sergo. So, surely, the coast was clear . . .

After the Georgian feast, cooked by Nino herself, of *khachapuri*, a sort of pizza, *lobio* bean soup, *mtsvadi* and spicy *pkhali*, Sergo said, 'Mama, I'm going to take Martha for a walk. Marthochka, shall we stroll?'

'I'd love that . . .' said Martha.

It was a hot afternoon in Moscow as they walked through the battered streets. They came from similar worlds, attended the same schools, knew the same people – the Stalins, the Mikoyans, the Satinovs. They had to be careful but they could speak with some honesty to each other. So naturally as they strolled around Moscow, through the Alexandrovsky Gardens beside the Kremlin, around the Patriarchy Pond, up Tverskaya (now renamed Gorky Street, for Martha's grandfather), they chatted in a way that was possible only for the tiniest coterie of young people. Sergo knew everything – how the Germans were about to burst across the Don and push for Stalingrad, how it was even possible that they might reach Stalin's city and how the Red Army would fight to the death there, street by street, factory by factory – so when he asked after Svetlana, Martha hesitated and then told him all about her passion for Lev Shapiro.

'I'm so glad for her,' said Sergo, lighting up a Herzegovina Flor for himself and for Martha. 'She must be so lonely in the Kremlin. So lonely. How lovely that she has someone. We all need someone.'

'We do,' agreed Martha. 'But promise me, don't tell a soul about Sveta. She told me in strictest confidence, no one else must know . . .'

V

Benya and Fabiana had ridden their horses through a stream and were now headed back the way they had come. Benya was no tracker but, remembering *The Last of the Mohicans* he wondered if there had ever been a mounted Jewish scout before! He remembered that Prince Potemkin, Catherine the Great's lover, had created a regiment of Jewish cavalry, the Israelovsky, but the Prince de Ligne had written that Jews couldn't ride – they looked like 'monkeys on horseback'. Well, it's true Jews aren't born horsemen; we are scholars not soldiers, and now I am trying to be both – just to live another day, he thought.

Benya knew nothing about the countryside he was riding through except the books he'd read – *And Quiet Flows the Don* by Sholokhov and Babel's *Red Cavalry* – and what the Cossacks had taught him. Where were his friends now? Were they even alive? Had they joined the Hitlerites? Not Panka, perhaps, but Prishchepa, light-footed and thoughtless as a wolf cub, could change his path like the flick of his whip. Knowing the Kalmyks would be tracking them, Benya assessed their position. It was not good. As the adrenalin thinned in his veins, he started to become more and more afraid. And Fabiana's presence just made things worse. Then he remembered Panka telling him, 'This is a big country, you've got to stretch yourself just to keep up with it, you've got to hear its voice,' and he understood that he had to expand his plans to match its cunning, its expanse. He guessed their pursuers would presume he would head eastwards towards the Russian lines, so decided to take a more roundabout way to safety.

After an hour of riding, they heard horsemen. They stopped, dismounted, and Benya unhitched his Papasha and pulled the horses into the high grass. A group of men, silhouetted over the marsh grass, were riding towards Shepilovka, the Schuma headquarters. Of course, he calculated, the Italians from Fabiana's command had guessed he would be heading east and had decided to ride into Shepilovka to try and find out who he really was. This was good and bad; good because it gave him more time, but bad because if they recruited any of the auxiliaries or Germans there, the end – if they got him – would be a terrible one.

Malamore and Montefalcone were riding towards the Schuma headquarters at Shepilovka as Montefalcone started to sing a love song in a strong tenor.

'Shut up,' said Malamore, and they rode on in silence.

As they rode into Shepilovka, they heard the clucking of poultry, the nuzzing of camels, and the yelling of soused men – even though it was mid-afternoon.

The Schuma and Cossacks, many glassy-eyed, shirtless and reeking of alcohol, brandishing sabres and Schmeissers, came out into the street when they heard the horsemen clatter in.

Two long gallows of swaying bodies with placards saying 'Partisan' had been placed on the green; one of them a woman. Not all of the men wore Red Army green, Malamore noticed. A couple were Cossacks in German uniforms with placards that read: 'Double agent'. The Schuma were hanging their own people too.

The Italians halted and stared. The gallows creaked like the rigging of an old sailing ship. 'Take a look at that!' said Malamore. There was nothing he loathed more than an unruly unit and these people were dangerous clowns.

Montefalcone peered around him as if he was in the last circle of Dante's *Inferno*.

The new commander, Bron Kaminsky, now apparently calling himself an *SS-Brigadeführer*, was drinking with his crew of renegades. His shirt was wide open, chest like his face, a sunburned puce. Malamore could tell that he wasn't too impressed with the Italians as he showed them to a chair.

'Brigadeführer, was the partisan one of your prisoners?' Malamore asked Kaminsky through his interpreter after he had recounted the bare essentials of how the wounded prisoner had escaped. They were in the handsome single-storey house commandeered by Kaminsky. Once owned by a well-off farmer, it had been converted into a mess room, and cheese and bread and tomatoes were spread on one table, half eaten. Bottles of vodka and local moonshine and boxes of Pervitin tablets were on another. A rack of weapons, mainly German but some Russian, had been stacked nearby.

Kaminsky was half cut and high. 'I don't know,' he drawled. 'We just held a trial. We found two traitors in my outfit, and we hanged them. Over there.'

'I'm more interested in the prisoner we lost.' Malamore's nostrils flared with distaste. Kaminsky called in a short garishly over-made-up girl in a German tunic and jodhpurs that did nothing for her sturdy legs.

'Do we know anything about an escaped Russian prisoner?'

'Yes, Brigadeführer,' said the girl, who had a Schmeisser over her shoulder, 'one of our prisoners got away after the ambush that killed Colonel Mandryka.'

'How did he get away? And who was he?' demanded Malamore.

'Our doctor knows all about him.'

'Get the doctor,' ordered Kaminsky.

239

A man was brought in, a sober and sensible professional; Malamore was somewhat relieved to find a sane person in this madhouse. Dapper in his German tunic with Red Cross armbands and riding boots, his handsome intelligence radiated from his lineless face.

'Dr Kapto knew Colonel Mandryka at school,' the woman explained in her nasal drone. She told the doctor the story of the escaped Russian partisan who had taken an Italian nurse as a hostage or human shield.

'Yes, it's probably him,' Dr Kapto agreed. 'After Mandryka's funeral, one prisoner got out and I saw him ride off. I raised the alarm, got off a couple of shots but . . . it was dark.'

'Who is he?'

'His name is Golden. He was a prisoner in the Gulags, a Shtrafnik who took part in the Mandryka ambush.' It was only now that Malamore noticed the little girl who stood close beside the doctor's legs, almost hiding in the skirts of his tunic, watching them all with the big, deep haunted eyes of a child who had seen the rottenness of the world in all its intricacies. She had a bandage on her leg and a ripped dress.

He was about to ask who she was and what the hell she was doing here when Montefalcone, patting the sweat from his face and his upper lip, said, 'Sir, let's get out of here.'

For once, Malamore agreed with him. 'Thanks for your help,' he said to Kaminsky. 'Will you let me know if they come this way?'

'He's a Jew,' said the woman with the stout legs.

'Who is?' asked Malamore.

'Golden, the Soviet partisan who's taken your nurse,' said the woman. 'A Jew has taken your nurse.'

VI

Fabiana was swaying in the saddle. It was early evening, and the sky was a turquoise blue strewn with crimson-lit clouds. As the sun set, they looked at each other, eyes like sleepwalkers, surprised to be alive. The horses were labouring; Socks had been unhappy for a while, fretting, ears back. She tripped in a marmot hole and lost her footing, and Benya had got down to check her fetlock, but they were lucky, nothing broken. Yet he knew if they went on much further, they would destroy the horses.

'We must stop. Here.' They'd arrived at a farmer's cottage that seemed abandoned.

Fabiana dismounted first, stiffly, staggering a little as she hit the ground. 'I'll water the horses if you check the house.'

Papasha levelled, Benya walked through the cottage. It was empty. There was running water from a well in the copse, and Fabiana tried to lead Silver Socks but the horse stiffened and wouldn't go with her.

'Leave her, I'll take her,' Benya said. Together they poured water over their horses who snorted and threw back their heads. Silver Socks stamped her hooves impatiently.

'Eh! Damned horse,' muttered Benya. 'Don't I look after you all right? Don't I spoil you?'

Fabiana got the food out of the saddlebags and the two of them sat beside the horses and silently ate the Italian rations of smoked meat, black bread, army biscuit, dried cherries and sunflower seeds. There were two beehives by the well and they scraped out the honey with pieces of wood to get to the wads of honeycomb.

241

'Ouch!' Benya winced as he was stung but they scooped out the honey, excited at this amazing find, he eating with his knife and she with her hands like a little bear.

Fabiana stood, rinsed her hands and drank water straight from the bucket, her brown throat straining as she gulped, and then she poured the rest of the bucket over her head. She glanced at Benya and went to the well, bringing out a full bucket for him. As he drank, he wondered whether he could really trust her: she was an Italian on the Fascist side, an enemy, and he was a Russian Jew. Yet she had placed herself in peril for him, and if he sent her back, she could well be tortured and shot. It was true she had served as a human shield during his escape – some Italians were still romantics – but now they were hunting him because she was with him. He was intensely aware that having her by his side would probably hinder his own chances of escaping to safety. And then there was his own side: if any Soviet soldiers saw him with a Fascist woman, he would be the one before the firing squad as a traitor.

He looked at her. Her dark wet hair was slicked back, and he knew she knew he was sizing her up. The way she had ridden out after him, bringing the guns – that took reckless courage, he thought. She was an astonishing character, that was for sure. He exhaled, making up his mind. They should stay together for now. If they survived the night and the next day, they could go their separate ways then. She could tell Malamore that he had forced her, as a hostage perhaps, and recount his cruelties and his violence. This might even squeeze a few tears out of that old crocodile.

'You're worrying,' she said, looking at him.

'Is it so obvious?'

'I know you. How's your shoulder?'

'Sore.'

'It will be. I'll re-dress it. Check it hasn't opened up again.' A pause. 'You're thinking I should go back to Malamore, aren't you?'

He could see her suntanned skin. Every pore was engrained with dust yet shining from the water. Her bravery briefly overwhelmed him: she had lost her husband, and now had to cope with this. He thought of her, the massacred Jews in the woods, the child on Kapto's knee, his own hopelessness – and he wanted to cry.

'Thank you for bringing the guns and food. For everything.' He yawned suddenly, shaking himself to stay awake. 'I'm exhausted.'

'Me too.' She peered at him. 'You're very pale.'

'We must sleep a bit. We'll be safer outside, I think. Let's move the horses.'

The cottage was in a clump of poplars which in turn was guarded by a gilded escort of sunflowers that stood as high as a man. They hobbled the horses just on the edge of the wood so they could eat the grass but not stray, and they spread their horse blankets and lay down in the shade, almost surrounded by the sunflowers, and pulled their boots off. He was so stiff from the saddle that he wondered if he would be able to ride again later. His lower back, thighs and buttocks were in agony, as if the saddle had grated his bones.

Keeping his pistol right beside him, a grenade on his belt, the Papasha within reach, he closed his eyes.

Fabiana Bacigalupe, he said to himself, a name out of a Benya Golden novel.

243

He felt her lie down, then move over, now almost against him. He sensed her breath on his neck. She was asleep.

VII

It was evening in the special family mansion, and Sergo Beria had just got home from his office, where he worked in foreign intelligence while finishing his scientific studies. Only a highly educated person could work in foreign intelligence and Stalin himself had suggested this job for Sergo, who was one of his favourite youngsters.

'Lavrenti,' Stalin had said to his father, 'let me read his reports. I think I'll be impressed . . .'

Sergo spoke perfect English and had read the classics of French and English literature. In the office today he had read the American and British newspapers, analysing the statements of President Roosevelt and Prime Minister Churchill. He was also allowed to see the transcripts of the devices that listened to the Western diplomats in Moscow. As he came into the house, he heard the skid of brakes outside. A Packard limousine followed by a Willys jeep full of guards had pulled in and officers with sub-machine guns stood in the courtyard. His father was home.

Balding and wearing rimless spectacles, Lavrenti Beria, overweight and ashen with exhaustion, yet seethingly alert, dressed in a flowery Georgian blouse and baggy linen trousers, burst into the kitchen and hugged his wife Nino, and then Sergo.

'Darling Lavrenti,' cried Nino. 'You look terrible! You must sleep. How are you?'

'I haven't slept for twenty-four hours,' he said. 'But I'm not the only one. *He* hasn't slept for seventeen hours and he's a lot older than me, twenty years older.' They all knew who '*He*' was. Dictatorship had the power to turn day into night and night into day. Stalin was nocturnal and worked at night so the entire government did too.

'What's the news?' asked Nino.

'Nothing good. We've made idiotic mistakes and now we're paying the price.' Beria was the only man in Russia who could say such a thing and he revelled in his ability to do so. No one was bugging his house; he did the bugging. He radiated the energy of a man at the height of his powers during the greatest crisis of his nation. 'We're surrounded by too many cowards, too many fools.' He stopped and looked at his wife: 'Darling! What a joy to see your face. Kiss me again.' Then he turned to Sergo: 'How's my clever son? How did you get so handsome with an ugly father like me? I'm so proud of my Sergo!' He took Sergo in his arms and kissed him three times on his cheeks. 'Come and talk to me while I rest . . .'

Upstairs in his study-cum-office, Sergo pulled down the blinds, Beria kicked off his shoes and fell back on the wide sofa where he often napped when he got the chance.

'*Mamiko*' – Sergo used the Georgian for 'Daddy' – 'is it really so bad in the south?'

'Worse, *bicho*, my boy,' replied his father. 'We could lose the war there. Not just our war, but if the Germans break through, the British and Americans would lose too. It's desperate. Now tell me about your life. Tell me what the war drums are saying?' All the leaders had read *The Last of the Mohicans* and every one of them talked about war drums and white chiefs. Sergo told him that he had been on a date with Martha Peshkova.

'That girl is adorable,' said Beria. 'And what news of Sveta? *He* never lets her out. Poor child! She's a prisoner in that gloomy apartment. Still so lonely?'

'Well, yes and no . . .'

'Still in love with you? I'd never let you marry into *that* family. Stay away!'

'Don't worry, *Mamiko*, she's over me.'

Beria sat up. 'She's got someone else?'

Sergo took a breath, remembering what he'd promised Martha. 'I didn't say that.'

'You know something, *bicho*. Tell me.'

'I shouldn't say. It's a secret.'

When he was alone, Beria closed his eyes. He saw the face of Stalin earlier that morning hearing that the Russians were losing the battle of the Don Bend; remembered the cowardly panic of the headless-chicken generals at Budyonny's headquarters in the North Caucasus; reminded himself that he had to recheck the plane, tank, rifle production figures and the mines of the Gulag Camps; and noted that today's death roster of 124 eminent prisoners signed by Stalin would, by now, have been executed in Lefortovo Prison; some of their names meant nothing but he had tortured a couple himself back in '38. Finally he indulged himself with the vision of the young woman with her Veronica Lake figure, golden hair and wanton thighs who'd been brought to him by his adjutant Colonel Sarkisian, how she'd ridden him naked in his office and then asked for an apartment for her mother. One day he'd find a girl who loved him for himself, he mused.

And out of all this murkiness and toil, only one thing was bright: Sergo his son, his sun, his hope for the cruel realm in which he was himself the cruellest. I will never let him work in my filthy world, he promised himself. He is too good for that. How I love him.

And Beria slept.

VIII

'A Jew?' asked SS-Obersturmführer Dirlewanger from the doorway of the house in Shepilovka. Malamore, who had been about to leave, looked up. The commander of the *Sonderkommando*, Oskar Dirlewanger, was just forty-seven but wizened by booze, pills, opium and the years in prison for petty thefts and raping children. His needled head was so shrunken and his body, so thin that his patron Himmler nicknamed him 'Gandhi'. 'A Jew has taken an Aryan nurse? Shameless.' He pulled on his shirt and started to button it up.

'He simply used her as a human shield to escape,' said Malamore, aware that he was sounding almost apologetic.

'Fuck that.' Dirlewanger absentmindedly fingered his necklace of what appeared to be yellow beans, wrinkled and shapeless. 'Can't you see the Communist Jew has taken her for sexual gratification? Look, gentlemen, I know all about sexual congress with our enemies. You should see the Polish girls, the little Jewesses I've had along the way. But we can't allow it the other way round.' He strapped on his gunbelt.

'Nonsense, Obersturmführer, and besides we didn't ask for your help,' replied Malamore in German.

'What is this girl to you?' Dirlewanger asked, alert suddenly.

'Careful, Obersturmführer,' said Malamore. 'She is the respectable widow of an officer of the Tridentine killed in action this week, an Italian nurse.'

'But you know her, don't you?'

'I do.'

'Biblically? Inside and out?'

'I warn you—' Malamore seethed inside with a disquieting mixture of anger and nerves.

'Fine.' Dirlewanger waved a hand. 'Let's leave it at that.' He turned to Kaminsky. 'We're responsible for this, Kaminsky. I shall join your detachment, Consul Malamore, with a few of my chosen poachers.'

This was not turning out as Malamore planned. This Dirlewanger was not a real soldier at all. More like a rat-catcher or someone who belonged in a straitjacket in an asylum. He would make a complaint to the High Command of the Armarta Italiana, General Gariboldi himself if necessary. If these cutthroats were with him, how was he to keep Fabiana safe?

'I insist,' replied Dirlewanger. 'Our mission to Russia is to wipe out the very possibility of *Blutschande* – blood-shame – yet you let a Jew, yes a fucking Bolshevik Jew, right here in Russia where we're annihilating the Jewish bacteria forever, steal your own whore from under your nose—'

No one had spoken to Malamore like this, ever. He wheeled

around towards Dirlewanger, his hand on his Beretta. 'She's not anyone's whore.'

'Pardon me, Malamore. Apologies. No need to take offence. None was meant.' Dirlewanger smiled, revealing yellow teeth, little and sharp like a ferret. A point scored. 'But, esteemed consul,' he went on. 'She is something to you or I'll be damned. This is the most reaction I've got from you in six months. Forgive me for speaking directly to a comrade but I can have a whore and cut her throat five minutes later. You can see one of mine hanging outside right here. Duty's everything to me, and we all know you Italians are notorious for letting romance interfere with our mission.'

A vein started to throb on Malamore's forehead.

'Don't do anything,' whispered Montefalcone, who suddenly recognized that the necklace Dirlewanger wore was made of human earlobes. 'Let's get out of here. She's getting further away all the time.'

'He's right,' said Dirlewanger. 'Pardon me but I am known for my frankness. I get the job done and if I upset the prudish bourgeois, I am proud of that. My patron the Reichsführer-SS himself regards it as an admirable quality. Lucky you have us Germans behind you, Consul Malamore.' He turned to the doctor. 'Dr Kapto, we need to get you to the Sixth Army today, but let's also be clear. The Jew escaped under your watch, and I call that a strange occurrence. If you don't want that investigated, I suggest you join us.'

'But the child—'

'Bring your little "lady friend" if you must. Everyone should see this beautiful countryside at least once. I've called the Sixth Army headquarters for you and they know about your map

249

and they are keen to get it urgently. Wehrmacht units will ensure your map reaches Colonel von Schwerin.'

'Thank you. It will be my pleasure to ride out with you, Obersturmführer,' said Dr Kapto, ruffling the girl's hair. He glanced brightly around the room with his colourless eyes.

'All is agreed then,' said Dirlewanger. 'Brigadeführer Kaminsky, report this anti-partisan *Aktion* to the Wehrmacht and Luftwaffe as well as our Italian, Romanian and Hungarian allies in case we pass through their sectors. Grishaka! Mironka!' he shouted. 'Saddle the horses!'

Two Cossack grooms, teenaged boys with topknots and unbuttoned German tunics, appeared at the doorway and then skedaddled towards the stables. There was no time to be lost.

IX

When Fabiana awoke, she imagined herself as a girl during the school holidays lazing in a field in the countryside. All she could smell was the sweet dust that she associated with harvest and the masculine leather of saddles. She was on the ground, on a blanket, her head on a saddlebag. A crackle of shots somewhere, then the familiar boom of the big guns, and the smell of burning and diesel. Though the evening light was beginning to fade, it was still hot. Her blouse was open; fingers of sweat ran down her chest and her back. She opened her eyes. There was someone else with her. She heard a horse whinny and the reality struck her: she was in the war, her husband was dead, Malamore was out there looking for her; and she, a nurse of the Armata Italiana, was with a Russian man – a Jew and probably a Communist, a convict who'd served in the Camps – a stranger whom she hardly knew.

She felt sick. She couldn't see how she could return to her own side now. Her people would surely execute her. She imagined her own end, the massive blow of a bullet smashing into her; she could see herself lying on the grasslands, her mouth a little open, her eyes staring. Could she lie about what had happened? Would they believe her? Or court-martial her? If so, better to perish out here. The shame for her darling parents if she was shot for treason . . . Everyone would hear of it on the Campo San Stin, the archive, the school . . . She would ruin them all.

Fabiana lay still and cursed her own impulsive stupidity. In normal life, there's always a way to reverse even the silliest of decisions but not in war and she wanted to weep. She was going to die very soon and with this knowledge came a bracing surge of freedom. She could be anything now, do anything. She could say what she wished. She belonged to no country, no city, no man. She was living breath to breath. She had seen many men die, she had been beaten by her husband Ippolito, she was in a wild, hostile land and she was surprised to find that she was not so afraid of dying any more. She had seen so many young men step across that threshold, just a breath one side, and no breath the other. Instead, a sudden joy rushed through her. This field of sunflowers was her own private kingdom and here things couldn't be simpler. A cottage, two horses, two beehives, a well – and this man.

She turned over and Benya Golden was looking back at her, lying on his side. Blue eyes speckled with yellow. She had spent hours watching him in the tent but then he had been weak, unconscious, like a sick child. Now he gave her a look of greeting and she returned it. He too, she sensed, was as much himself as he could be out here on the steppe, on the run. They said nothing for a while. He was very thin, she noticed again, his nose hawkish, and he had a certain sort of Jewish face and very long black eyelashes. The thinness made him seem older than his early forties; his fair skin was tanned by riding on the steppe; his shorn hair and his beard were sown with grey.

He sat up and shook off the dust and hay, and the ashes, that seemed to float in the air all the time.

'You've been awake long?' she asked.

'I've been up for a while. I must ride on soon,' he said. She reached into her saddlebag and handed him bread and some fruit. Then they fell upon the honey and this time he watched her as she scooped chunks of honeycomb and ate it off her cupped fingers and he did the same, which made them both laugh as the honey revived them. Then she brought out a flask, a man's regimental flask engraved IB, which he knew had belonged to her husband Ippolito Bacigalupe.

'Armenian cognac.' She handed it to him. He took a mouthful; then she did the same.

'We mustn't take too much,' he said.

'Why not?' she answered. 'We deserve it and' – she shrugged – 'this is a beautiful place and we're alive . . .' She took another swig and he accepted it too. 'There's nothing more decadent and delicious than drinking at breakfast,' he said, the sort of urbane line he'd used to say in his old life. Now it seemed absurd.

Beside them their horses whickered as they drank water from the bucket Benya had brought them. Standing guard on every side, the sunflowers whispered and swayed, raising their faces towards the last rays of the setting sun.

'You said, "I must ride on . . ."' she started.

Benya nodded. 'You have to go back. The longer you're with me, the harder it will be for you. It won't just be Italians looking for us now. Germans and Hiwis will be too. The Kalmyks scouts will track us, and will work out we didn't take the direct route back to the Russian lines. Please, ride to the nearest village . . . You can blame me, say I held you at gunpoint, that I kidnapped you, I committed untold cruelties, appalling liberties, ravished you savagely . . .'

'Am I a danger to you too?' she asked, understanding suddenly what was bothering him.

He sighed. 'If they have you back, no one will bother to chase a Russian prisoner. It's you they want. I'm unlikely to make it but I have a better chance alone. And you don't need to die too . . . Please, Fabiana. You must live.'

'That's a generous offer,' she said, looking at him deeply. 'Traditionally only the gods could make such an offer but you, a fugitive, a convict on the run, make it too . . . That's magnificent.'

'We have a word for that. *Chutzpah.*'

She knew he was right. 'OK, I'll go.' She pulled on her boots and stood up, rolling up the blanket, carrying her saddlebags towards her palomino.

Their two saddles sat side by side, between the two hobbled horses, the leather warmed by the sun. He came to help her with the saddle and, without a thought, she dropped the blankets and bags.

'*Arrivederci*. Somehow forever,' she said, turning towards him. 'No, maybe just goodbye. Forever.'

X

'*Alt!*' Malamore held up his hand and raised his binoculars in the gathering dusk. 'The scouts are coming back.'

Dirlewanger rode on one side of him, Montefalcone on the other. Behind them followed a circus of men in uniforms: a band of Dirlewanger's 'poachers' wearing German army grey with SS runes and those trophy necklaces of human earlobes, a few Italian Savoy Celere with their feathered caps, some Blackshirts, Hiwi Cossacks and Schuma militiamen. The Baby Doctor brought up the rear, his satchel of papers around his neck. The girl sat on his saddle in front of him, his hand on her belly. Wearing tank commander's goggles against the dust, Malamore was scouring the long horizon.

Night was falling but the steppes – so empty in the early morning – were buzzing with activity. They encountered lines of German tanks, hatches open with their drivers wearing goggles. Wehrmacht soldiers were riding on them, dusty boys waving through the haze. Montefalcone noticed that they smirked at the motley exoticism of their squadron, unimpressed by these apparent freaks conducting 'anti-partisan *aktions*'. Occasionally they saw Soviet tanks; a T-34 with a broken track now on the back of a truck was being repaired by some of Kaminsky's engineers, and a burnt-out heavy KV was surrounded by charred wizened figurines the size of children. And everywhere there were dazed families riding in horse-drawn carts piled high with mattresses and pans and household icons, or heaving wheelbarrows, or just walking, walking and pleading for water: 'Water for the children . . .'

In the distance, Malamore saw the Kalmyk scouts, wiry men with Mongol faces, drooping moustaches and scarlet blouses, curved swords on their backs, riding on quick, scrawny ponies. They were approaching fast.

The Kalmyk scouts, Altan and Gushi, saw Malamore's squadron awaiting them and looked at each other. They had only joined the Italians a month earlier. As the German panzers had raced across the steppes towards their villages in Kalmykia, the elders had gathered in the open teahouse in the middle of the village to discuss what to do. The elders warned against acting too quickly, but all agreed that if the Germans reached Kalmykia, they would at last be liberated from the evil Bolsheviks who had destroyed their farms, forced collectivization upon them and banned their Buddhist rites that had endured since Mongol times. But Altan, who was a superb rider and the father of two children, had decided not to wait but to ride across the lines to join the Fascists. Gushi, who was just sixteen and as slim as a reed, joined him as did his cousin Ubashi. Instead of working on the collective farm, drying the grain in the dryer, they could go back to riding their horses, the proper pursuit of a Kalmyk man since the days of Genghis and before. But Ubashi had been wounded in the fight against the Shtrafbat and captured by Communists, and they knew he was dead.

'Not just Italians,' said Altan, the older one, spotting the different uniforms in Malamore's posse.

'Germans, Cossacks and Schuma,' Gushi said, clicking his tongue.

They didn't have the information Malamore wanted. 'He won't be happy,' Altan said, spurring on his pony.

'Well?' asked Malamore as they pulled to a halt in front of him.

'We don't think they've come this way,' said Altan.

Malamore shook his head and ground his teeth in frustration.

'We rode almost as far as the front. Close to the Don.'

'Is it possible they got through?'

'Possible,' said Altan. 'But not likely. They're not experienced riders.'

'So where are they?'

The scouts conferred in their own language then Gushi suggested, 'If they were clever, they wouldn't have come this way at all but ridden around the village, waited out in some barn during the daylight hours, then they will come this way from the other direction.'

Malamore wiped the dust from his eyes and opened his map. The Kalmyks leaned forward and pointed to the route, nodding and chatting in their impenetrable tongue.

'We split up into two squadrons and we'll trap them,' barked Malamore, coughing hoarsely. 'The scouts are right. Even if they looped back, they must come this way in the end – and we'll be waiting.'

XI

Fabiana leaned against Benya and took his face in her hands and kissed him on the lips, once, twice. She could taste honey and the brandy they'd just been drinking, savour the strong smell of his skin, pure and unscented by soap or cologne. Then there was the hay, the horses, the leather of the saddles, and to her this blend smelled of the happiest moments in her life, the freest.

He never lifted the saddle. Instead she unbuttoned his shirt and ran her hands over his shoulders, the hair on his slight chest, then his trousers. He undressed her too and she could feel him hesitate when he found the Browning pistol in the belt of her britches. He seemed to come to a decision. She'd been armed all the time yet hadn't tried to shoot him, hadn't tried to return to her people. He dropped the Browning on the discarded britches and they fell on to the blankets. She felt him kissing the sweat on her neck, her forehead, then, as her legs came up, behind her knees. They were so close that the laws of sound were reversed: hers resounded out of his throat; his came out of her lips.

She had never wanted anyone like this, nor known this urgency nor ever considered her new Goldness. She was shy for a moment, but in the Secret Kingdom of Sunflowers these things seemed natural. He talked to her, told her what he was doing, how delicious she was stroking her with great delicacy, making her skin fizz where he touched her. She felt herself melting with pleasure where she had been untouched, and

257

treasured the words and the nameless feelings that now had names. This was the poetry she hoped to be able to recite in her old age, and she felt her body now held the meaning for what one day might only be memories.

When the red wave came, she found herself thrilling, exulting, and it came out as ringing laughter, her head right back, her hair wild as snakes and her mouth open, teeth gleaming. Imagine myself: Fabiana Pellegrini, doing these things, feeling like this, making someone else feel this. There had only been Ippolito before Benya. But her husband, who had never looked at her in this way, who had become frustrated and angry that she didn't excite him enough, had blamed her for his own shortcomings, slapping her hard in the face till her nose bled and she'd tasted blood. If he saw me now, what would he think? she asked herself, smiling – and then didn't care any more as another wave overtook her.

They lay still, the sweat running down them in rivulets. The unbearable tenderness passed and soon she found herself weltering once more. This time she did not feel as shy as she had before. Now she thought she would do anything she wished, anything he asked, almost with ease without feeling guilty or salacious. It was something quite different she felt now and she wiped her face, using the back of her sunburnt arm, with a new sense of freedom.

Afterwards they lay naked under the tree in the moonlight, guarded by the horses and by the sunflowers, their faces closed and downcast now in the darkness. In the distance, the clatter of gunfire was closer though it now sounded as familiar as the bees that droned home to their hives, as the hooting of the owls.

'Do you really want me to go?' she asked quietly.

'You must. I want you to live even more now. Go back.'

'What if I don't *want* to go back?'

'Then you're mad.'

'What if I am mad?'

'Are you?'

She considered this gravely. 'Yes, yes, I think you've made me so.'

'It will pass. And then you must return. You must do whatever you need to survive.'

She sighed. 'I don't want to go back. I don't want to be Malamore's trophy. I don't want him to think he owns me, and I don't want my old life.'

'Wouldn't that be a small price for being alive?' Benya paused and took a breath. 'Has it occurred to you that Malamore killed your husband?'

'Why would he do that?'

'To get you, of course.'

A long silence.

'It would explain a lot,' Fabiana said slowly. 'Though oddly that never occurred to me.'

'He was right there when it happened, wasn't he?'

'Just after,' she said quietly. It made sense, and what she was going to do now also made sense. She was suddenly clearer about this than she had ever been. 'I'm no longer Fabiana Bacigalupe or Fabiana Pellegrini. I've always wanted to be this woman, the way we are now. Isn't this what all those poems are about, the ones I have read ever since I was a young girl? And I can't go back to a creature like Malamore. I just want to tell you something, Benya Golden: I will not return to the Italian lines. If you ride I must ride with you.'

259

He nodded, seemingly relieved.

'Can we just be bandits in love? That's what I call us,' she said. 'Bandits in love. Nothing more than that. Just for once, for one last time, in our own world.'

They ate together. 'When did you know this might happen?' she asked him.

'I never knew. I am always amazed. Are you studying history now?'

'Every woman knows love is about history,' she said. 'Our history. So, did I choose you or you choose me?'

'I could hardly choose you when I was unconscious,' he joked, and a lazy drowsiness overcame them. Benya, usually so alert, became careless and languid, longing to enjoy the harvest night, the dense, treacley air, the lilac blackening in the mixed palette of the wide-slashed sky. They lay together, still naked, the air was so warm, and the horses settled, swishing their tails, their chests twitching to drive off flies – and she felt new muscles jumping in newly discovered sinews and chambers of her body. She had never understood why people fussed about sex – it had seemed as awkward as it was futile, like a language she couldn't understand. But now, when time was so short, she had learned the language instantly.

Each time they awoke, they sipped brandy and feasted on the spread of stars in the vast depth of that velvet sky. She could taste the liquid pleasure on her lips, like melting toffee. They made love between bouts of almost deliriously deep sleep. Around them they could feel the trees and sunflowers, the very earth itself, moving and buzzing as they were – as if they were resting on the back of a giant, stirring, breathing beast.

But soon the howitzers were building up once more. She

260

saw the black-crossed bombers flying like giant stencils across the sky heading to demolish Stalingrad. The distant roaring was perhaps columns of tanks. Suddenly, over the Don Bend in the east, the sky was ripped wide open, turning a rage of red, as if it had been skinned to reveal the flesh beneath.

It was then that she knew what the intensity of the battle meant for them. Benya was risking his own life for her happiness, sacrificing it for something that could only be horribly short-lived. She should return to her people; she knew she could persuade Malamore she was innocent, to call off his pursuit, and she would make it home to Venice. But every day Benya lingered with her, there would be fewer Russians on this side of the Don. Soon there would be none and it would be nearly impossible for Benya to get back to the Soviet side. Malamore was chasing Benya because of her and if they caught him, a Jew, they would kill him. If he was ever seen with her by his own side, she would be the death sentence of the man who had shown her the secret of passion, of life itself. The threads of their dilemma were unravellable except by her leaving.

'Darling Benya,' she whispered. 'I've decided. You were right: I must go back. Don't try to dissuade me now. It is decided.'

He did not reply for a long time; then he sighed, knowing now how sometimes men perished because they were too weary to go on.

'It's too dark now to do anything. I think we bandits in love must stay together. Somehow forever. And for us forever means now. No one will find us here. Let's decide what to do in the morning.'

XII

The Kalmyks saw the clump of poplars and within it the roof of a peasant cottage. They stilled their horses and their own bodies and listened. They thought they heard the whinny of a horse but couldn't be sure. Altan signalled at Gushi and they slipped their Schmeissers off their shoulders and dismounted deftly with barely a sound, peering through the granular lilac of the falling night.

This place was set perfectly on the route the Russian and the nurse would take if, as they suspected, they had chosen the indirect way back to the Don and the Russian lines. When the scouts had left Malamore, they had ridden hard back over the steppe around the other side of the village in a giant half-circle, starting again at the Italian headquarters, Radzillovo. When they saw the stream they let their mounts drink and then rode them into the water and along it, searching the banks for the tracks of two horses. And, sure enough, they had found the marks of hooves entering the water and they knew what the prisoner had done.

'Not bad for a greenhorn,' said Altan to Gushi as they tracked the place where the two horses came out of the stream and loped up to the cottage.

They listened; then they tied up their ponies, slipped off their soft boots and, clamping a *djindal* between their teeth, they crept on all fours closer to the cottage until they could just make out its gate, wattle fence, white windows. They were looking for horses but nothing moved. No smoke was rising from the house.

They looked at one another and Altan shrugged, gestured backwards and they rose to their feet and returned to the ponies. By now it was pitch dark. Even with the moonlight they would be unable to see properly and there were only two of them. So much could go wrong.

'Why are we stopping?' asked Gushi. 'I sense they are here.'

'Based on what, boy?' asked Altan.

'On the tracks on the ground – and the pulse in my throat,' said the younger one. 'We can cut his throat and take his ears back to the Italians and win promotion.'

'And what if by mistake, shooting in the darkness, we harm her? The colonel's mare! What promotion will we get then, puppy? We will be promoted to the noose, that's what.' Altan drew some dried camel meat from under his saddle and offered Gushi some distilled mare's milk from his canteen. 'Here's the plan,' he said. 'We sleep here, and before it's dawn we will catch them like rats in a trap.'

Day Eight

I

Lying against Fabiana, Benya was dreaming with the near-drugged abandon of one who has ridden all day, made love for hours and, finally feeling safe and inflamed and slaked, has fallen asleep in the copious, floating heat. He was back in Kolyma and it was a month after the start of war, in the summer of 1941.

At dawn, the guards burst into Benya's barracks. 'Get your belongings, Prisoner Golden. *Davay! Davay!* Work brigades leaving now! Back to the gold mines with you, fucking dog's prick!'

Panic jittered through him. He remembered Jaba's warning. He had lost his protection – that meant losing his cushy job in the clinic, and this was his punishment: back to the mines! This was his deepest fear. In nightmares, in daydreams, he saw himself marched back to the mines on the dark side of the moon. He would die out there, he knew it. Every day he expected it and now it had come.

The truck was waiting, engine gunning, and with terrible foreboding he climbed into the back.

'Surprise!' cried Smiley. 'Haha! Look at that face, Boss!'

Deathless sneered, 'You fell for it, didn't you?'

'All right, boys,' said Jaba. 'Join us, Benya. Good news. We're being transferred to the hospital at Magadan – and you're with us.'

'Oh my God, I thought—'

'I know what you thought. But you see, life is a plate of *lobio* beans,' said Jaba and, banging the top of the truck, he called to the guards: 'All right, let's go!'

On the way, they talked about the war with the guards, hungry for the slightest titbit. Comrade Molotov had announced the war to the Soviet people with the words: 'Our war is just. Victory will be ours.' Then Stalin gave a speech addressing his people as 'brothers and sisters' and even 'my friends' – he must be worried, thought Benya, to call any of us 'friends'! The radio reported triumphant counter-attacks but the guard whispered stories of defeat and collapse . . .

Jaba's new headquarters was the Magadan Hospital, where all his boys now got jobs: Benya was still a *feldsher*, a medical assistant, and one of his jobs was to keep the key for the medical supplies room, a key with a leather label reading: 'Only special personnel. Magadan Hospital. KOLYMA.'

When he left Kolyma, it was the only thing he took with him, to remember the luck that had saved his life. But the job had its worries too: sometimes Smiley or Fats Strizkaz demanded morphine and Benya had to give them some – but not too much. If he was discovered handing out drugs, he would be transferred back to the gold mines; if he refused the Criminals, Jaba would destroy him, and as long as Jaba was happy, he felt he would be safe.

The news from the war was dire. Minsk and Smolensk fell. By September, Belorussia lost, the Baltics gone! Leningrad – besieged! The Zeks, patients and doctors talked of nothing else . . . Several dying men even regained a hollow-eyed life-fire to discuss Russia's fate. Ukraine and Kiev had fallen, a million Russian soldiers taken prisoner. Odessa fell to the Romanians – and Benya prayed for his parents. Then suddenly the Nazis were approaching Moscow! The reverberations of panic reached even distant Kolyma.

The moment he had finished that day on the ward for the dying, Benya, still wearing his white medical coat, rushed to see Jaba in his 'clubroom' where he held court. A card game was in progress with the Camp Trusty, Fats Strizkaz; and Prishchepa was singing the brigand song, and the others were joining in like a crew of crooning pirates: '*They've buried the gold, the gold, the gold . . .*'

'What is it?' asked Smiley.

'I want to ask the Boss something.'

'All right. It's the professor, Boss, he wants to talk.'

Jaba waved him in. 'What is it?'

Benya gathered himself: 'Boss, you own me and I would do nothing without your blessing but Moscow is in danger and the time has come for me to ask permission to join the Shtraf battalions,' he said.

'I told you never to ask me this again. On pain of death! Yet still you want to fight for the Bastard?' The Bastard was always Stalin.

Benya looked around him. Prishchepa had stopped singing; Fats put down his cards; Deathless was playing with a switchblade.

'You know what my answer could be?' Jaba said softly.

Benya nodded.

'Boss, there's something I've got to tell you.' It was Prishchepa, still young somehow, glossy as the dawn.

269

'And this is also to do with the war?' Jaba did not glance at him. 'Speak, boy.'

'Boss, I am a Don Cossack, a free man, a fighting man.'

A vein started to beat at Jaba's temple. 'Anyone else?'

'I am going too,' said Fats Strizkaz. 'Otherwise it's death, inch by inch.'

Then Smiley raised his hand: 'Me too. There's spoils in wars. You can get rich.'

'And I heard there's more girls than a man can handle,' squealed Little Mametka.

Jaba started to snigger at that. 'Oh, Bette Davis! What do you know of girls?'

They were all laughing but when they went quiet, Deathless was flicking the dagger back and forth. No one had ever defied Jaba like this.

'Die for the Bastard if you wish, boys,' Jaba said finally. 'But, Golden, you have a problem. You're a Political.'

'I know the rules but things that were impossible a week ago are possible today. Winter will come at any minute and this is my last chance to get the boat to the mainland. Only you can do this, Boss. You've saved my life. Please let me live it.'

Jaba caressed his grey plumage of hair. 'You must bless the Atamansha. Remember the information I won from her about the Commandant? I knew I'd need it one day and now is that moment. Smiley, go to the Commandant's assistant and make an appointment for me to see General Shpigelglas today. Tell them it is to discuss the production delay at Madyak-8. Go now!'

Jaba looked at Benya. 'You see, Golden' – he shrugged in his debonair way – 'isn't life just a bowl of *lobio* beans?'

* * *

In the clump of poplar trees amidst the Don plains, the uproar of the planes flying low over the steppe awoke Benya abruptly. The sun was not quite up yet; it was still dark but there was the spread of turquoise on the horizon. He had slept better than he could remember; and he turned to look at Fabiana, who was stretching. Sometime during the night they had pulled on their britches but she was shirtless and he was overcome with her beauty, her honey-coloured eyes, and his luck at being brought back to life like this. But Socks was stamping the ground, her ears back and eyes rolling white, and he understood instantly something was not right. Fabiana's palomino too was standing rigid, skittering nervously.

'Darling,' Fabiana said very coolly.

'Move quickly,' he whispered. 'Someone's close.' They worked together as if they had always been a team, saddling the horses, their hands shaking as they tightened the girths, checked the stirrups, attached the saddlebags and, pulling on their shirts, mounted the horses, who needed no encouragement. As they loped out, Socks reared, almost throwing Benya, and they saw the two fresh, scrawny ponies pulling at the ropes that tied them to a tree.

'Kalmyks,' Fabiana said. 'Malamore's scouts.'

Leaning down, she cut the ponies free; a burst of gunfire rang out at almost point-blank range, spanged into the earth close to them and Benya, sensing the two shadows lying in the grass, glimpsed the black snouts of their weapons. The two ponies bucked and then bolted with Socks and Violante breaking into a terrified gallop. Pouring sweat, silver hammers beating in his temples, Benya held on to Socks's mane and found himself riding with Fabiana and the two bolting ponies

271

down into the long steppe grass just as the sun came up. When they slowed down, he realized how lucky they had been. The Kalmyk scouts had staked them out, sleeping almost beside them, but no Kalmyk would risk shooting their own ponies and the animals had bolted, leaving them, temporarily, mountless. Nonetheless, Malamore and his horsemen must be close.

II

At 7 a.m., Svetlana Stalina, wearing school uniform and her red Pioneers' scarf, climbed into a Packard limousine outside the triangular yellow palace in the Kremlin where she lived. Klimov sat in the front with the driver as they headed out of the Troitsky Gate across town towards the Josef Stalin Commune School 801.

At the school gates, the director – as the headmistress was known – Comrade Kapitolina Medvedeva greeted her, virtually bowing.

'Well?' whispered Martha as they went into their tedious Communist Morality class. Martha understood what it was like to be in love, to be a member of Moscow's 'golden youth', but even she couldn't conceive how it felt to be Stalin's daughter. There was her father's portrait in this very class – the man she saw every evening. At assembly every morning, they sang 'May Comrade Stalin Live Many, Many Years'; at every dinner or lunch, everyone drank a toast 'To Comrade Stalin'. But as her father had recently explained to her, 'You're not "Stalin" and I'm not "Stalin". Stalin is something bigger. Stalin is Soviet power!'

Martha poked her in the side: 'Have you seen him?'

'Just twice,' whispered Svetlana as the lesson began.

'Letters?'

'Several!'

'Like the one you showed me?'

Sveta nodded. ' "I want to kiss you, I want to smell you, I want to taste you",' she said, quoting what Lev had written to her.

'He actually wrote that? Oh my God! What does that mean, Sveta?'

'I don't know, Marthochka. But I love everything he says, every word.'

'How was the kissing?'

'Amazing. Heaven!' Svetlana suppressed her giggles. 'I'm blushing! Yesterday he sent me a book as a present. In English.'

'What? Something naughty?'

'Yes. The new Hemingway. *For Whom the Bell Tolls.*'

'Oh my God. Have you started it? I can't wait to read it.'

'I've been reading it all night. My father came in and I had it hidden in his *Short Course* and he didn't notice. It's so romantic, brilliant. The American Communist, named Jordan, fights in Spain and falls in love with this Spanish girl who's much younger than him, and damaged by her tragic and difficult life. She's called Maria.'

'Sounds familiar!'

'Yes of course, Lev is Jordan and I'm Maria. Oh, Lev's so clever, so interested in everything . . .'

'Is there anything in the newspaper?'

Sveta had *Red Star* in her satchel; she slipped it out

273

and scanned the front page and there was Lev's article, telling of a terrible battle on the Don Bend to stop the German advance, and then she felt herself almost gasping for air. She read:

Is the sun shining in Moscow, on the roses in the Alexandrovsky Gardens? Standing here as the cannons fire, as your heroic Red Army struggles against the Nazi hydra, I think of our capital and I believe the flowers there are blossoming. You can see the Kremlin's crenellated battlements from your window . . .

The flush swept up Svetlana's body like a scarlet tide and she fanned herself so energetically with the *Short Course* that several of the other pupils looked around. She passed the paper under the desk to Martha who read it avidly.

'Mother of God, Sveta! He's crazy! What would your father say? He might read it!'

But Svetlana was exhilarated. 'He LOVES me! Anyway, it could be anyone looking at the flowers in the gardens. Only *we* know it's addressed to someone inside the Kremlin.'

'True. But your father wouldn't believe that, would he?'

'No, but I don't care! I can't wait to kiss my Lion again.'

The entire class was now looking at the two girls, who always sat at the back. The teacher, the loathsome and pedantic time-server, Dr Innokenty Rimm, hesitated. He was afraid of Svetlana and she enjoyed that. He couldn't tell Stalina to be quiet. He wouldn't dare. Instead he picked on Martha.

'Peshkova! Are you with us today?'

'Yes, sorry, Dr Rimm, I am listening.'

'Good! So tell us about Marx's view of the class struggle and the role of the bourgeois during the 1848 Revolution?'

Martha gave her gorgeous smile. 'Well, that's easy . . .'

III

'Where the hell have the scouts got to?' murmured Consul Malamore. The scouts would have bivouacked somewhere but the sun was up now. He and his posse had spent the night in a village and risen before dawn. Malamore lit a cigarette and he rode ahead with a silhouette like a statue of equine bronze. He had no wish to talk obscenities with Dirlewanger or listen to the whinings of Montefalcone; and no one wished to ride with Kapto and the little girl.

Over the Don the teal-coloured sky was stained jet with burning fuel dumps and illuminated with orange flashes of big guns; Malamore could almost feel the blasts now. The Germans were destroying the last Russian bridgeheads on the bend of the river. When that was done, the Germans would charge across the steppe from the Don to Stalingrad – and perhaps put the last nail in the coffin of Russia. But Malamore knew that the closer to the battle, the more likely that Fabiana and the Russian prisoner would be killed in the crossfire – or, perhaps worse, make it to the Russian lines, and be lost forever. What would Fabiana's life be in Soviet hands? And he would never know what had become of her.

They passed reinforcements of Romanian and Hungarian troops and then a column of panzers, waiting for their fuel tankers. 'To Stalingrad!' was painted on to one tank. 'From the Don to the Volga!' read another. 'Stalin kaput!' the third. The boys sat smoking on the turrets, shirts off, shoulders sunburnt, writing letters: the roar of the fighting at the Don Bend focused their minds on home, sweethearts, the tranquil past.

Dirlewanger asked a sergeant where the Sixth Army staff headquarters was, pointing his whip at Kapto. 'This man needs to deliver something important to Colonel von Schwerin, Intelligence, Sixth Army.'

'That way,' said the sergeant, who had a Bavarian accent. 'Towards the Don.' He paused and looked at Dirlewanger and Kapto properly. 'What unit are you?'

'Commander, Sonderkommando Dirlewanger, attached to Einsatzgruppe D. Anti-partisan *Aktion*.'

The sergeant raised his eyebrows. 'Anti-partisan, eh? Who's the girl? She's just a kid.' His boys laughed rudely at Kapto and the child. 'Is she your daughter or just a friend?'

Dirlewanger swished his quirt and rode on, ears red.

'You make us a laughing stock,' he hissed at Kapto. 'Pull yourself together.' The little girl was fast asleep in the saddle, her head lolling against Kapto's shoulder, held there by his arm.

'Come on,' called Malamore, spurring Borgia out into the grasslands. Soon they were almost alone again on the steppes. 'They have to come this way. Stop wasting time.'

'You're the one who's let a Jew run off with his lady friend,' said Dirlewanger.

'Don't mention her again, Dirlewanger.' He glanced back at Kapto. 'When can we hand our doctor friend over to the Sixth Army?'

'We should be meeting outlying units of the Sixth Army

any time now,' said Kapto, catching up with them. 'She sleeps as we ride,' he said breezily, gesturing to the child.

There was a pause.

'I'm no prude,' said Dirlewanger, and Malamore noticed he was swaying as he rode, half-cut as usual, 'but do you think noble Prussian officers such as General Paulus or Colonel von Schwerin of the Sixth Army will be impressed with a man that rides around with a child of the *Untermenschen* on his saddle?'

'I am taking care of the child,' said Kapto. 'Those we heal we must also cherish.'

'The Kalmyks are back,' called out one of the Hiwis, Bap.

Altan and Gushi rode up and saluted.

Malamore pushed up his tank goggles, his eyes just slits in that sun-gorged face. 'You're hours late,' he snarled. 'Well, where are they?'

The Kalmyks were excited, pointing, their ponies caracoling.

'Very close. We should be able to see them,' said Altan.

'We've tracked them.' Gushi indicated ahead. 'See that dust?'

Malamore pulled up his horse and raised his binoculars. Yes, there was something out there. Across the naked steppe, in the high grass in blurred golden light, he could make out the little pirts of dust: two riders. 'It's them,' was all he said. 'Montefalcone, take the second squadron and come at them from the rear. The rest of you follow me. No one is to shoot or charge without my orders. Obersturmführer, ride with me.' He wanted Dirlewanger close to him so that no harm would come to Fabiana.

Dirlewanger did not protest. His men would deal with the

Jew as they saw fit, collect his earlobes on a necklace if they wished it (and sometimes they did just that) – but the old Italian owned the girl; this was his show.

Throwing up dust, Malamore and his horsemen galloped across the fields, hoping to steal up on the riders before they realized how close they were.

IV

The bandits in love were riding with a giddy recklessness towards the Don. Fabiana had even let her hair down, and was galloping so fast that Benya feared she might be thrown. He sensed she was enjoying their last time together, and relished the sheer stun of his good fortune – that somehow he knew must end, and end soon.

'There!' He pointed ahead. Right before them rose the Donside hills with their woods, and beyond them and down in its valley swept the majestic river. Benya knew he was almost home and his heart was racing – but the closer he came to the Donside hills, the nearer the battle of the Don Bend – and the sooner he must part with Fabiana. And she knew it too. She smiled when he saw the rise in the terrain but then her face fell and he could tell she was brooding. They rode on, almost dizzy with a last-chance joy in a headlong charge of happiness.

The shot spanged into the grass right beside him, sending up a pirt of dust. Benya looked back. A dark swarm of horsemen was gathering in the corrugated, wavy heat of the late morning. He recognized the hunched figure of Malamore at the front, his sabre drawn. Fabiana turned Violante and stared at them, breathless, cursing '*Stronzo!*' – until Benya seized her bridle: 'Come on!'

Volleys of bullets ripped into the ground around them, and Silver Socks reared to one side but Benya managed to steady her. Ahead Fabiana was riding Violante up the hill towards the trees. '*Pronti a fare fuoco!* Prepare to fire!' Benya could hear Malamore (he guessed it was him) yelling at his men to wait a moment, not to shoot until his order, what if they hit the girl – but on they came anyway, twenty, thirty horsemen, hooves clopping on the dry grassland. As he reached the cool of the trees, Benya saw more horses and men ahead of them, another Italian squadron coming around the back of the woods . . . Now they had no hope.

Screwing his eyes closed in a moment of freefalling panic, Benya gripped Silver Socks with his knees, but he couldn't decide what to do – to dismount, to fire, just to give up and die. He was shuddering, already wincing at the agony to come.

He checked the grenades at his belt. If he had to, he would finish this himself.

Two circles of a pair of binoculars range over the Donside hills. The observer stops and focuses the lenses.

He watches two riders galloping across the open steppe, a man and woman. The man is in khaki fatigues with an Italian forage cap, a Papasha on his arm and grenades on his belt. He is riding a Budyonny with white feet. She is in Italian green with Red Cross markings on an armband, her dark hair not tied up, flowing behind her, and she is spurring on her palomino. There is something desperate about them. The man – who's older and not a great rider – keeps looking back, jerkily. There's a sense of fear in the way the woman is lurching in her saddle, shaking and unsure. They are both losing speed.

The observer, who is lying in the grass close to the local collective farm office a little further, and higher, up the same ridge, scans back over the high grass. Behind the fugitives ride two Kalmyks on their scratchy ponies; and then a posse of riders, twenty, thirty, forty horsemen in some disorder: an Italian Blackshirt colonel on a black stallion, Germans with SS runes on their tunics, Russian traitors in Wehrmacht field grey. Amidst them a man carries a female child on his saddle: a refugee rescued? A rare kindness in these flint-hearted times? Amongst these barbarians? Well, that would be a surprise.

He sees the shots spanging into the grass around the two riders. The pursuers are closing in and now he spots a second squadron of Italians appearing around the copse at the top of the hill, firing down at them. This odd couple have his full attention. They are being attacked by the enemy, and his Stavka orders from Comrade Ponomarenko, Chief of Partisan Operations in Moscow, are clear: 'Harass and destroy all enemy forces, communications and weapons in rear of the Sixth Army.'

He turns to the men beside him. He always speaks softly in a tone that commands obedience. 'Fire all four Dashkas now. And mortars. Quickly or we'll be too late!'

'Done, Comrade Elmor!' says Smiley as the heavy Degtiarev–Shpagin machine guns, known as Dashkas, open up with their metallic chug-chug to pump lead into the squadron of Italian horsemen.

V

Fabiana saw the church tower and onion dome of a little Cossack village of colourfully painted cottages, yards and stables. A signpost read: Shebinkino. A foaming riderless horse caught up with them, dragging its German rider, his shirt forming a bundle over his head. She could still hear the machine guns and the whistle of mortars close behind them. Such was their panic that she and Benya had galloped headlong into the main lane of the village without checking what was ahead.

It was noon but the village seemed deserted. A dead dog lay in the road; cats shrieked somewhere. It was sweltering, and Fabiana could smell rotting hops, sweet vines, wormword and dank water. She looked up and now she could see the shells exploding over the Don Bend where the battle raged just a few miles away. She was still out of breath and when she glanced at Benya, he was white, almost slipping off his horse, his hands shivering uncontrollably.

The horses suddenly balked and tried to turn. A mangy wolf stood in the middle of the street. Fabiana looked into its hungry and astonishingly white eyes. Once the wolf had been a symbol of wild ferocity; now it was just another hunted creature in a world where man had outdone the wolf in savagery. 'Ciao, bello,' she said to it, remembering how Natasha had seen the wolf in *War and Peace*. It trotted away – and the horses, sweating yellow foam, staggered to a halt.

Fabiana scissored off Violante in time to catch Benya as he slipped off Socks into her arms, relieving him of the

281

sub-machine gun – she hung it on her shoulder – and leading the horses away. She heard the rattle of traces and the clip of hooves. Benya was lying on the ground in the space between two cottages while she looked around.

A waxy old woman dressed in bright red was approaching them. Halting her tarantass and getting down off its box, she hobbled into a nearby cottage without tying up the horse.

Fabiana tied up their horses and followed the woman through the open front door. How fast we brigands learn, she thought, unhooking her gun, we bandits in love.

In the main room, the crone was putting dried cherries into a bowl and Fabiana also spotted some *salo* and buckwheat gruel.

'You steal from Afonka and you'll die in agony,' said the crone without looking up. Fabiana peered at the shelves around the room, packed with jars of seeds and bottles of cloudy liquids. 'A Jew and a foreigner come into the home of a woman abandoned by all and steal from her at gunpoint. You'll bring the curse of the water spirit of the Don on yourselves. Who's this now?'

Fabiana looked round and Benya was behind her, shakily levelling his pistol. Fabiana wanted to get out quickly but Benya did not look good and the woman had the food.

'The Jew thinks of killing me. But the Immaculate Virgin will decide when I go. You'll be struck down by lightning or steel or poison.' She sucked her bare gums.

'Tell us then, *Matushka*, what should we do?' asked Benya, lowering his Parabellum.

'Let me cleanse you unbelievers with holy Don water, and I shall give you something.'

'We have no Don water.'

'I have it in the bucket. Bring it.'

Benya brought the bucket and the crone glared right at him. Fabiana could see that her eyes were a veined blue-whiteness with no irises.

'I see well for a blind one?' the crone said, making the Cross with a yellowed nail on his forehead. 'The enemy of Christ is forgiven by the Immaculate Virgin, who drives out the beast in the heart. Amen!' Then she repeated it on Fabiana. 'I see a field of sunflowers, faces raised to the sun and in the middle of them a couple are kissing, oblivious to the world. I see a kind doctor and a happy little girl, a Jew child who walks away into the distance. Eat your food – here – and water.'

'Thank you, *Matushka*,' said Benya, gulping down some bread and gruel with his fingers. Fabiana poured water for both of them.

'Leave me something. I don't need much,' the woman said as Fabiana gathered the food, longing to get away.

'Go out the back,' the crone continued. 'That way' – she pushed them through the back door – 'and you'll learn how I never threaten lightly. Go!'

Holding the food, Fabiana stepped into the back yard and recoiled. The body of a soldier, a German, lay on the sandy ground, his mouth wide open, with greenish vomit streaked down his cheek and flies buzzing out of his agape mouth.

VI

'How many dead do we have?' Malamore asked, holding a lit Africa cigarette, goggles on his forehead, patting a sweat-soaked Borgia on the withers. Under heavy fire, they had made their escape over the hill and into a Cossack village but not all his men were with him.

'Six dead,' replied Montefalcone.

'And seven wounded,' added Malamore's young adjutant, Brambilla. 'Two missing.'

'*Figli di puttana!* Motherfuckers!' said Malamore.

The Kalmyks rode up. 'Village is empty,' they said. 'And there's food.'

Malamore noticed Dirlewanger was fritzing and twitching, like the drug addict he was. Malamore himself had survived many ambushes and he showed no nerves even now. 'All right, place careful pickets all around. The partisans aren't far away. Collect grapes and apples from those orchards. Bury the dead and dress the wounded.'

Wiping his brow, he led his squadron down into the village, riding slowly, even majestically, hunched craggily in his saddle. When he reached the priest's house, he dismounted and sat on the verandah in an old basket chair brooding while Dirlewanger popped another Pervitin tablet, then paced up and down, his temples pulsating, and Montefalcone watched him, sipping from a flask – both awaiting further orders as the windows shook from the big guns.

Malamore was chain-smoking and took a swig of cognac.

The partisans had ambushed them from their flank on the adjacent hill, and he knew it was his fault. Fabiana had distracted him and he had watched her carefully when they were close to them. She had looked as if she was waiting for an opportunity to escape. The Russian had the weapons. Still it nagged at him. Could she be collaborating with the Russian Jew? Could they even be . . . no, that was impossible.

Dirlewanger started fiddling with his necklace of trophies, his eyes glittering like red-rimmed pins. 'Let us shoot every Russian we can find.'

'It's lucky these villages are already deserted,' answered Montefalcone. 'Perhaps they knew you were coming.'

'Consul, sir,' said Brambilla from the doorway. 'A Wehrmacht captain is here to see you.'

VII

Fabiana chose a house far from the crone's, in the midst of the village, hoping this would make them less easy to find. They took the horses into the barn with them and closed the door. It was full of hay – and a single old nag, probably a family favourite, abandoned there, looked very pleased to see them. Benya lay on the ground.

'You must eat more,' Fabiana told him, and she fed him the crone's bread and gruel, cherries and the last of the honeycomb. After they had both eaten, they felt better but they were exhausted. It was late afternoon but they agreed not to light a lantern or a cooking fire lest it be the only light in the village, visible from miles away. Benya felt they were a whisper from sudden death, and nothing could be postponed any more.

For a long time they said nothing, both aware they had been run to earth. The hunters were close, yet the horses could go no further, and they themselves were too tired even to put their boots in their stirrups yet alone ride. They might have this night together, or Malamore and his men could burst in at any moment. Benya listened for the whinny of a horse, the creaking of a gate, the clacket of spurs. A wolf started to howl somewhere on the steppe. What had alarmed it? He half expected to hear the voices calling: 'Send out the nurse. She at least can live!'

Finally he sighed and said, 'We both know what must happen now.' He knew that if he survived, he could never admit to ever having known her. She was one of the Fascist invaders fighting on the Nazi side and their very acquaintance, yet alone a physical relationship, would be regarded by the Russian side as treason: both would be shot instantly. To her own side, she had abetted and slept with a Jew, a Russian, a Communist. If they remained together, they would die together. Their only hope was to part and for him to wipe every relic of her existence out of his life.

She nodded. 'How long have the bandits in love known each other?' she asked.

'Studying history again?' He smiled sadly. 'I don't know.'

'You don't know, Il Primo? It's exactly eighty-six hours. Is that need to measure love in every way, the difference between a man and a woman? I think so.'

Night was falling and it was dark in the barn. '*Mia adorata*,' he said, 'don't you think sometimes you can live for years and they can count for nothing and then there are special times when every second is so rich, so priceless, so deep that we live with such intensity that every minute counts fivefold, tenfold, a thousandfold. And we call that time "Love". Sometimes one night is a lifetime.'

'Yes,' she said. 'Yes. That's what this is.'

A dog barked in the village, and Benya caught his breath. Were the Fascists already surrounding the house? He could just see the glaze of her eyes, dark now, catching the very last light. The air changed between them and suddenly he was overcome and he knew she was too. They had been linked from the moment they had first seen each other after she had removed the bullet. Now the space between them seemed to be criss-crossed with golden threads – like the dew at dawn. How often does this happen in a lifetime?

Benya reached out for her in the darkness and her hand was there, waiting for him, and he put her fingers against his mouth and kissed them. She started to cry out loud like a child. For a moment he wanted to quieten her – their pursuers would find them – but then he didn't care any more. Her cries were, he thought, the sound of a life lived intensely and sensitively amidst the cruellest times. Then she was on her knees, holding his face, kissing him, their lovemaking like the final spasm of a dying body, flotsam on a wave, dust lost in dust.

'There's something I've got to tell you,' she said when they were both still, on the edge of a spiky, fluttering mockery of sleep. 'Something about my past.'

Was she already Malamore's mistress? Benya wondered.

'It's about my husband.'

'Malamore killed him during that skirmish. I know.'

287

He could feel her tension in the darkness.

'You think too well of me,' she whispered.

'What are you saying, *mia cara*?'

'Don't you see?'

'It was *you*?'

'Yes,' she said. 'During the fighting in the village, Ippolito was panicking; and somehow I annoyed him and he slapped me, knocked me down. When I fell, his holster was right in front of me and I grabbed his Beretta, and I shot him right there. In the heart. He said nothing, just stared at me with such surprise and a sort of awe, and then . . . and then he died in front of me. The shooting was getting closer and I sprinted behind the cottages through the gardens and made it to where our troops were.' She took a deep breath, shivering as she remembered. 'I had to tell you. So you knew who I was.'

A pause.

'I shouldn't have told you,' she said. '*Che stupida.*'

Benya's mind was thrumming. What did this mean? Had she lied to him? What else was she hiding? Was she a murderess? He saw beneath her mantle of civilized velvet, a seam of the fiercest animal spirit. She had loved him and saved his life; and her impulsive deeds of kindness and courage filled him with wonder at her, and that was all that mattered to him. 'It changes nothing,' he said after a moment.

He felt her relax.

'There's one more thing, Benya,' she said. 'I would like you to give me something, a keepsake, that will always remind me of you. So I know you were real, and this really happened.'

He hesitated; then he reached into his pocket and handed

her the only thing he had – a small key with a leather label that read 'Only special personnel. Magadan Hospital. KOLYMA.'

She took it and he thought he heard her kiss it.

'Somehow forever,' he said.

'Somehow forever,' she replied.

VIII

Malamore walked out of the house and there, tying up their horses, were a German captain and a burly lieutenant. When the captain saluted, Malamore saw he was missing his other arm and that he had an Iron Cross at his throat.

'Colonel Malamore, may I present myself. Von Manteuffel, Gerhard.' He saluted with a click of the heels. 'Captain. Intelligence Corps. Sixth Army. Lieutenant Kreutzer will remain outside.'

'Come in,' replied Malamore in perfect German. 'We were waiting for you. I'll get Dirlewanger.'

'Actually, if I may be so bold, Herr Colonel,' replied von Manteuffel. 'I have orders from General Paulus himself to talk to you alone. Without Dirlewanger.'

Malamore was not surprised. This Captain von Manteuffel, who couldn't have been more than twenty-seven, was one of those Prussian aristocrats who still filled the higher echelons of the Wehrmacht, and his answers were given in a cut-glass accent. He would, Malamore surmised, have a military pedigree; his forefathers had probably fought for Frederick the Great.

'Cigarette, captain?' asked Malamore when they were seated inside on the rough chairs of the peasant cottage. 'An Africa?'

'Grateful, Herr Colonel,' said Manteuffel. 'I've come to take possession of the Soviet defector Kapto and his intelligence materials. Colonel von Schwerin is in the field but will be here tomorrow to collect him and his maps. He's ordered me to interview Kapto and take a preliminary look at the materials.'

'I'll get Kapto now.'

Kapto came in a few minutes later and saluted with theatrical confidence as if he had been auditioning all his life to play this part.

Manteuffel nodded back, and then said in perfect Russian: 'You are now my responsibility. Colonel von Schwerin has asked me to make an initial evaluation. Are you ready to depart?'

The four men walked two houses down where Kapto's horse was tied up.

'Good,' said Manteuffel. 'The lieutenant will help you saddle the horse. Is there anything else?'

'Yes,' replied the doctor. 'I must wake the child who's sleeping inside this house.'

'The child?' Manteuffel sounded startled.

Peeping through the doorway, he saw a little girl sleeping on a couch and exchanged looks with Malamore. 'Who is this girl? Is she your daughter, doctor?'

'No, but she's under my protection. She travels with me.'

'I don't understand—' started Manteuffel.

'She's a patient.' Kapto smiled, his lips turning up at the ends like a dogbone.

'A patient?'

'I found her wounded and, as a paediatrician, I say: Those we heal we must also cherish.' He knelt beside the couch and

Calmed the good man, the stranger and the sat out, the
soldier had gathered at them with his age gesture.

"Take Carrizal and Montezuma," I am safe to go and resolve to
Chihuahua. I have many riches to attended to ... and how to ...
did all I could do," he said.

They waited anxious; and Villa soon reached their side;
away, the swords to which side ... of the defeat." And from
the still left, his boot ...

Mexican troops and Pershing the troops were back for him to the
loads that they had taken away; landed here.

"We will accept," I said then. "and ... but ... his office. We
then ... we dared our to say we would ... let our these seat ...
along as I promise be the freedom and ... came to take charge ...

Villa knew ... challenging the partisans ... I will wipe away the
bold to govern so long as ... not in a ... I determine. I represent the
authorities of ... Mexico. Delivering ... welcome, to this that
... Maximilian left command here ...

"General you came," said the ... said Maximilian ... as distinct
they ... be a ... called everyone." I had you ... and the situation
too ...

He angered, asked Villa's wages. "I to the compassion, I was
not here to kill persons, the other of persons. Whatever I had died ...
pursuit.

The same man was ... a fierce interest as while on the
expedition I continuing to the size, and happened at the battle
... there any losses, and every point. I think it my neighbor ...
retain from a friend.

shook her gently on the shoulder and she sat up, ver
and looked around at them with her moon eyes.

'Herr Captain,' said Malamore, 'I am glad Kapto is sa
your care. I have many matters to attend to . . . and I n
sleep. Goodbye, captain.'

They walked outside, and Malamore watched them
away, the Germans on either side of the defector Kapto
the child on his knee.

Montefalcone and Dirlewanger were waiting for him in
house that they had made their headquarters.

'We still haven't found them,' said Montefalcone. 'We
lost many dead and more are wounded – all for the sake of
nurse. I propose we let them go and return to our duties.'

'I'm here to annihilate the partisans. That was why th
Reichsführer-SS brought me from Belorussia. I've sent fo
reinforcements,' slurred Dirlewanger, swigging from a flask.
'Meanwhile let's hunt the Jew.'

'This is not a task for us,' said Montefalcone to Malamore.
'They've shown some courage. The girl yes – and the Russian
too.'

'Courage?' chided Dirlewanger. 'It's the courageous Jews
we have to kill before the others. *Christus! Oberarschloch!* Super
arsehole!'

'The hunt goes on,' Malamore ordered, standing on the
verandah, looking up at the stars and listening to the battle.
'Search every house, and every barn. I think they might be
closer than we think.'

Day Nine

I

Benya awoke with a start. A safety catch had been clicked off, and the pistol was now so close to his forehead that he could feel the cold metal and smell the oil and the presence of strangers. He had expected this all along, seen it in his mind, and now here it was. But he was so weary that he did not care any more. Let them shoot me, he thought; a man can only run for so long. He feared to open his eyes, expecting to see Malamore's scaly face. He waited for the impact, flinching. But nothing happened and then he heard another sound. God, it was laughter.

'Morning, *dedushka*! It's me, Granpa, wake up!'

Benya sat up and looked into the bright blue eyes of Prishchepa, who was beaming at him, fresh as a chaffinch, his blond hair standing up like a haystack.

'Why so sad?' Prishchepa said. 'You're alive, Benya, and that's quite something. And look who's with me?'

Benya peered behind Prishchepa and there was Spider Garanzha – and the old teak-skinned sergeant, Panka.

'Are you unhurt, lad?' asked Panka, his small eyes scanning Benya and his dressing curiously.

'My shoulder – now its fine. I am just tired.'

'Tired? This is no time to be tired,' said Panka. 'Don't give in to it. Don't even use the word. You were fast asleep. Cheer up! We're close to our beloved mother river and it's always sunny on the Don. We can't boil water here, we can't risk a fire, but eat some bread and have a sip of this' – and he handed Benya some Borodino bread and a flask of cognac. 'Then we must move.'

'Where to?' asked Benya, looking around for Fabiana.

Garanzha just observed him coldly. Prishchepa smiled. 'Home of course.'

'Where might that be?' asked Benya, without thinking.

'I told you,' said Spider Garanzha, those deceptive goo-goo eyes looping in his two companions.

Benya refocused quickly. If and when they got back to safety, they would all be questioned, and if Benya said he didn't know where the Cossacks had been, they'd be shot as traitors. The Spider was watching him, very still, and Benya knew what that stillness meant. The crouch of the hunter before the spring of the kill.

Benya understood that the calculations required of any soldier on the steppes that summer were laden with agonizing twists, but for the Shtrafniki, who had already crossed to the other side of the river, in every sense, the choices were bleak. His three Cossack companions were there not just to rescue him but to save themselves, either by joining up with him – or liquidating a dangerous witness. If circumstances required it, Garanzha, the man who unsettled the horses, would cut his throat with pleasure, and Benya recalled how his leaden tread had quickened into an almost feminine dance step as he killed the Kalmyk traitor. Prishchepa, the thoughtless golden boy with the light lope and appetites of a carefree wolf, would finish him with even less thought. Only Panka would hesitate.

Benya was aware that troops lost behind the lines were deemed to be traitors unless they could prove otherwise; it was how decent men like Captain Zhurko had ended up in the penal battalions. If these Shtrafniki were suspected of the slightest sin, they would simply get the Eight Grammes – without even facing the tribunal. But here was the difficulty: Benya did not know where these men had been for the last few days. Had they defected temporarily to the Fascists? Had they waited to see how quickly the Germans smashed through to Stalingrad and the oil fields? Or had they decided that the Soviet Union was not collapsing as fast as it seemed when Rostov fell and changed their minds, seeking a way to cover their tracks? And if they had, did they know about *his* secret, Fabiana?

'Wait,' he said, holding up his hands. 'I ask no questions. We fought, we were cut off and found our way back to the Don.'

'We killed Mandryka. We've earned our freedom – it's simple!' It was always simple for Prishchepa.

'The partisans will remember we were there,' said Benya. 'Unless . . . we could do something more to earn our redemption . . .'

Prishchepa waved his hand. 'The Zhid's always worrying.'

Garanzha started to scratch his back, always a sign that he was beginning to relax.

'So all is well,' Prishchepa said. 'I'm happy our brother Benya is still alive – but then you learned from the best riders on the Don. This Zhid can certainly ride, eh, Panka?' He embraced Benya. 'Let's eat and sleep and then maybe swim in the Don. Have you ever swum in the Don, Benya?'

'No time for that, brother,' said Panka, spitting. 'Prishchepa, you've forgotten where we are. The Don is a cauldron. The Fritzes are searching this village for us right now.'

'Let me go scout,' said Prishchepa, always keen to volunteer for the most dangerous jobs. They went outside, and Panka saddled Silver Socks. There was no sign of Violante, Fabiana's palomino.

'Just this once, I'm doing it for you, brother,' said the old Cossack – and Benya noted the compliment.

Garanzha scratched, picking lice out of his clothes, and sharpened his dagger until Prishchepa returned.

'They're getting near,' he said breathlessly. 'Let's go.'

As Benya rode out with his three companions, heading towards the Don and the Russian lines, he knew what he had known even as Prishchepa pointed the gun at his head. That he had awoken alone, quite alone. It was as if she had never even been there.

II

Svetlana never saw her father in the morning – except on Black Sea holidays. But now he was right here, standing over her. She was getting ready for school when her father burst into her bedroom, something he had never done before in her entire life.

She looked into his face and she knew she was in terrible trouble. He was blazingly furious and the nanny, who was standing behind him, was so terrified that she couldn't move. Svetlana had never witnessed her father like this. He had almost never lost his temper with her but now he was white-faced and nearly speechless with rage. He was waving some rolled-up papers.

'I've punished Vasily for his antics,' he said. 'I've had him thrown in the guardhouse for behaving like a fucking disgusting baron's son! But your behaviour is as repulsive as his. When our men are dying in their thousands, this is what you do?'

'Father, what do you mean?' Svetlana knew exactly but was stalling for time.

'Don't play the idiot, girl!' he said. 'Where are they then? Your filthy letters from your "writer"? Your so-called writer! Where are those letters?'

'I don't know, Papa . . .'

'Of course, you know – don't take me for a fool. Well, I've read them too!' He tapped the pocket of his tunic. 'I've got them all right here. What filth! I know everything. You don't believe me? What's all this then?' He threw a wad of typed papers at Svetlana's feet and she jumped. 'Go on. Take a look! See all your filthy words right here! Pick them up. Read them. Go on, read them!'

III

Lieutenant Brambilla brought Malamore a cup of ersatz coffee as Dirlewanger joined him. He was, noticed Malamore, already reeking of schnapps, sweating, blinking, fritzing as the meths surged.

'Is Montefalcone up?' Malamore asked Brambilla.

'Yes, sir. I woke him.'

Then they heard a shot. He and Dirlewanger caught eyes and they hurried to the next-door hut. Fully dressed, his feathered cap and his papers laid out, Montefalcone sat at the table with his head in his arms. The pistol was in his hand, and a finger of blood ran down his temple.

'Fuck!' said Dirlewanger. 'This war . . .'

Malamore shook his head. 'He was no soldier.' He lit a cigarette. Brambilla stood behind him.

'What shall we do, sir? What shall we say?'

'The major died in battle on an anti-partisan mission. I'll write up the report on our return. Bury him here in the yard. Quietly. Fast.' He paused. 'And, Brambilla?'

'Sir?'

'We ride out in one hour.'

The single shot rang out over the village, echoing back off the hills, but the four riders paid no attention.

'I saw an old friend of ours,' said Prishchepa. 'Right here. Riding over this very hill.'

They halted in the trees on the hill outside the village. Below them, in the limpid light of dawn, they could see Malamore's men amongst the houses, the horses all tied up outside the church. Behind them smoke rose from the rising uproar of the battle of the Don Bend: the shells bursting over the river, now so near they felt the earth shake. Benya could smell the Don itself, the salt and the rotting reeds, and the water close to them: the border they had to cross.

'Garanzha, ride ahead and take a look,' said Panka. 'Let's

rest here a moment while I have a chew.' As Spider Garanzha
trotted off through the poplars, Panka swung off Almaz and
absentmindedly stroked the animal's withers as he chewed
some *makhorka*. Benya knew this meant he was deliberating.
An observer might think Panka was having a rest but his decision would settle their fate. Benya let Silver Socks graze and
Panka came over and stroked her neck.

'You chose well with that one, brother,' he said. 'I always
loved her too. She's got firm feet, that girl.'

Benya kissed Socks's white muzzle. He was sorry he had
ridden her into this war. She deserved to be free on the grasslands, serene and happy.

'Sergeant, what do we do now?'

'Well, my boy . . . it's simple really.' Panka chuckled, meaning it wasn't simple at all. 'Either we cross the Don here or we
join our soldiers at the bridgehead,' he said. 'Here we'd have
to swim the river and it's wide and, if I recall this place where
I once caught a pike this long, the currents are strong. They
can shoot us in the water and we might lose the horses. But if
we approach the lines further up, it'll be like going hunting with
my Uncle Prokofei, who once shot my cousin Grishaka in the
behind when he was aiming at a bear beside the Vieshenska
stream. What I mean is there'll be crossfire and our own people
might well shoot us by mistake.'

'I once had a girl beside that stream,' said Prishchepa. 'And
that friend I saw last night – it was Dr Kapto.'

'Where?' asked Benya sharply.

'He was riding out of the village with two Fritzes. Wehrmacht
officers.'

'And the little girl?'

'Yes, the child was on his saddle.' Prishchepa turned to Benya. 'You care for that child?'

'I fear for her,' Benya said, but then he remembered the crone's prophecy of the child and the doctor riding happily into the steppes.

'They were riding through these woods.'

Panka chewed hard, his small eyes twinkling like jewels in his wise face. 'They must be going to the Sixth Army head-quarters. But why?'

Benya pictured the doctor, and remembered the satchel around his neck. Now he realized it surely didn't contain medicines but some sort of papers. But before he could say anything, Garanzha was back. 'The two Germans are waiting at the office of the collective farm. And Dr Kapto is back with them.'

'Back with them? Where was he?'

'How should I know? He was in the woods and he came back,' Garanzha replied. 'We could take the three of them if we wished.'

'Brothers,' warned Panka, 'we don't stop for anyone, and we take no unnecessary risks. Mount your horses.'

'Three?' Benya asked. 'You mean four? With the child.'

Garanzha shook his head. 'The child's not with them.'

'You're sure? The two officers. The doctor. And the little girl?'

'I told you, silly scribbler,' said Garanzha, swinging his leg across the saddle of his horse. 'The little girl isn't there.'

Benya flinched and a jet of anger coursed through him. Of course the girl was gone. Kapto had saved her, kept her and then discarded her. She was out there, somewhere, lying on the ground, and it was over. He began to sob in spasms of

302

despair, resting his face on Socks's neck. The horse turned her head and nuzzled him, her whiskers tickling his face.

'Now look what you've done,' Prishchepa teased Garanzha.

Panka shook Benya. 'Come on, Golden. We've all had to harden our hearts, dear boy. We're almost there.' He offered the flask and Benya took it and drank too deeply. He coughed but the cognac steadied him.

'Listen,' he said to the three Cossacks. 'We have nothing to show for our time behind enemy lines. We need a prize.'

IV

'Lieutenant Kreutzer, the horses are restless. Check they're watered or maybe there's an animal out there,' said Captain von Manteuffel of Intelligence, Sixth Army, as he sat on the bench in the office of the collective farm granary. He was reading the Soviet General Staff maps in front of him with a rising excitement. 'Schwerin will be here later tonight. Kreutzer, get some cigarettes and the schnapps from the saddlebags.'

'*Jawohl*, Herr Captain! On my way.'

The office of the manager of the Sergei Kirov Collective Farm 23 was spartan and messy. The walls were plywood, the floor was made of old planks and the room was decorated with a faded print of Stalin and a map of the huge farm that lay alongside the Don. There was a rough bench, wooden chairs, a couch where the managers must have napped after vodka-fuelled lunches with other local apparatchiks, and a gas-ring for heating *chai*.

Manteuffel was waiting for Colonel von Schwerin, who had selected this place for their meeting. 'You'll find it serviceable,' he'd said. 'I will rendezvous with you by twenty-four hundred hours at the latest. Prepare your report.'

Dr Kapto lay on the only couch, smoking a Belomorkanal cigarette. 'Are you impressed, captain?' he asked in his precise, velvety voice. 'Are they useful?' Then, after an interval: 'Will I get a little pat on the head from the general? I better think of a reward, eh? I can think of a thing or two . . .'

Manteuffel was still horrified by the events of the morning, the way the doctor had come back, with his glib smile and his pride in his facility in fixing things neatly. He realized that intelligence was a dirty game in which one had to deal with all manner of freaks and mountebanks. He understood that this was a filthy war against a repellent enemy, that the Führer was waging a savage campaign of annihilation against the Jews – men, women and children – and that this had to be conducted by Himmler's 'specialists' like Dirlewanger who were not much better than beasts and certainly not men whom he would ever entertain at home at Schloss Manteuffel. But that child . . .

After an initial interview with Kapto to ascertain his credentials and how he had procured the materials, taking meticulous notes in his oilskin notebook, Manteuffel had concentrated on the maps, the importance of which dawned on him gradually. He was aware of the danger of Soviet disinformation, and of course he recalled the recent case of Major Reichel whose plane had crashed behind Soviet lines with the full operational plans for the Führer's Case Blue offensive. That paranoid peasant Stalin had believed this was German disinformation and ignored it. Fortunately so, because the plans were genuine and they were currently winning this offensive that would probably secure victory. Such a prize was not always a trick.

If Dr Kapto's maps were genuine (and several factors, which could not have been fabricated, made Manteuffel lean towards this view), they must be flown directly to the Führer's head-quarters as soon as possible. If he was lucky, Schwerin would take him along on the trip. The maps he was now holding could change the Führer's plans for Stalingrad and the Caucasus oil fields.

'Captain von Manteuffel!' It was that fool Kreutzer.

'What?'

'One of the horses is missing.'

'How can that be? *Hornochse!* You ox with horns! Weren't they hobbled? Weren't you watching them?'

'Yes, captain, yes. I can't understand it . . .'

Manteuffel followed the plump lieutenant out of the hut. He looked around. The hills, the woods: all was still.

'You didn't tie it up properly, *Vollidiot!* Total idiot! Your work is shoddy. Be more precise. Now go and find it! I'll be right there . . .' He watched Kreutzer's flabby arse bouncing down the steps to the horses, then went inside to fold up the maps. 'The fool has lost a horse,' he told Kapto, who sat up, about to speak, but Manteuffel didn't wait for him.

He ran out of the office again, swearing at the lieutenant, 'Kreutzer, you *Höllenhund!* Hellhound!' He was still cursing when he found the lieutenant lying full length between the two remaining horses.

'Jesus Christ!' Manteuffel said, and when he looked up, he found himself looking right into the Nagant barrel of a very blond youngster in Soviet uniform and boots who was singing to himself.

But I am flying to the Führerhauptquartier tomorrow so nothing can happen to me today, thought Manteuffel, when something shiny and almost blue flashed so fast in front of his chin that it almost hissed. Reaching up to touch his throat, he was surprised to find it was soaking wet. And then he was falling back into the arms of another man who caught him and laid him on the ground. He was sure that this could not be happening to him because he had been so full of life just moments earlier and because he was so alert even now. He had been looking forward to a cigarette and a shot of schnapps, and there was the appointment with Colonel von Schwerin later, not to speak of the flight to the Führer's headquarters. He was looking up into the face of a man with an oversized jaw and a wide slit of a very scarlet mouth with scarcely any lips. Above was a bleakly cloudless sky. He should have suspected something when the horse disappeared, that was obvious. A shot rang out close by but Manteuffel was not alarmed; it came from another realm.

Garanzha knew Manteuffel was dead. He could see the cornflower-blue sky in the glaze of his open eyes. Brandishing his Papasha, he walked round to the door of the foreman's office, but then he relaxed. Panka was coming out. 'Time to ride on,' he said. Inside, Prishchepa was laughing: 'You can't leave our writer for a moment,' he said. 'He's become a menace. I think he's spent too much time with you, Spider.'

Benya was still holding his Parabellum over Dr Kapto, who had been shot cleanly in the forehead. Now Kapto was dead, he was afraid to touch him. Garanzha searched the doctor for his papers. He found Kapto's new ID as an officer of the Schuma, in German. Benya gathered up the maps that lay on the table, along with Manteuffel's notebook, and put them all in the original satchel which he hung over his shoulder.

When they came out of the building, Panka was helping himself to tinned meat, chocolate and ammunition from the Germans' saddlebags. The four mounted their horses. Benya's hands were shaking: he couldn't believe what he had done. He'd shot a man. Without a word. That ferocity had possesed him suddenly, wantonly. And now he rode on, untarnished. And yet the child – a little Jewish girl – was gone; she lay nearby somewhere on the rough ground, and he ached with sadness, for her, for his family, for Fabiana, and for all the others.

'Only a Cossack could sweet-talk a horse like I did with that German horse,' boasted Prishchepa, 'and only a Cossack of the Don could steal it right under their noses.'

'Shut up, magpie,' said Garanzha.

'Brothers, now we have to decide what to do,' said Panka. 'Decisions are like the carp in the Don!'

'Slippery and full of bones,' explained Prishchepa.

'You decide, Sergeant Panka,' suggested Benya.

'I shall, with pleasure,' said Panka. 'It will be good to see the Don. I can smell it. Our mother river, our darling gentle Don.'

'Even if we might drown in it,' said Benya.

'Well, yes,' agreed Panka affably. 'But it's always sunny on the Don.'

V

They were riding towards the front line. Panka was in the lead followed by Benya with Prishchepa and Spider Garanzha bringing up the rear. The cannons fired relentlessly and each blast shook the air and made their eyes ache; the roar of tank engines ground forward, planes flew low overhead and, around them, black smoke was blanketing the blue sky. In Benya's nostrils, on his clothes even, hung the reek of cordite and burning diesel.

They rode down a hillock and across a plain and down its banks, and there it was. The Don. It seemed an age since they had crossed the great river seven days earlier, and Benya felt he had lived a lifetime since then. As they rode towards it, the water, fringed with foam, seemed to steam as smoke rolled over the sheening shallows, and the grass of the chalky cliff on the far bank gleamed an emerald green. They rode along the beach where old nets and a Cossack fisherman's rowboat lay abandoned. Further up, a dead Russian soldier was being picked at by greedy seagulls, his brainpan open, empty, bone-white. In the river, a half-submerged ferry lay empty, a direct hit. The seagulls, grown fat and truculent on the decay of war, swooped over them with a shrieking keow, sometimes so close Benya felt the wind of their wings.

They said little, knowing that if they were unlucky, they would simply be hit by a blast of shrapnel and know nothing more. If they even located the Russian front lines, they might well be shot down by trigger-happy outposts. They just had to be lucky – but Panka had decided the beach of the Don was the best way to approach, partly because the pickets would be able to see them clearly. There would be less chance of mistakes.

As they rode, the horses became increasingly tense, skittering, fretting and dancing, or champing and refusing to go forward. Benya held Socks on a tight rein, and talked to her: 'I'm here with you, girl,' he said. A volley of artillery, apparently fired by the Russians though it was hard to tell, made him jump and Socks reared. Benya gripped her with his legs and leaned over her mane and soothed her. She went on.

'Who goes there? Identify yourself or we shoot!' There it was, a voice from a position right ahead, a concrete bunker overlooking the beach.

'Sergeant Pantaleimon Churelko and three men, Second Cavalry Shtrafbat.'

'Never heard of you,' said the voice. 'Which Shtrafbat?'

'Second Cavalry Shtrafbat,' said Panka. 'We have intelligence materials for the general.'

'We still haven't heard of you!' said the voice.

'Are you crazy riding along the beach? We might have shot you!' said another.

'We still might shoot you, motherfuckers!' said the first, harsher voice. 'Take off your weapons and throw them down! Tether your horses! And walk up the bank towards us with your hands up!'

They dismounted and, as they set off, Benya looked back at Silver Socks. He wondered if he would see her again.

'Walk slowly! No tricks! No fast moves or we'll shoot!'

Moments later, they were in a small blockhouse overlooking

309

the river. Four soldiers, teenagers in uniform, were searching them.

'Welcome back, friends,' said the gentler one. 'Are you hungry?'

'Volodya, keep your bread till we know who they are,' the harsher soldier said. 'We've called the Organs, and the Special Unit's waiting for you. I'll take you there now. Keep low.'

'What about our horses and weapons?' said Prishchepa.

'Just worry about keeping your head with the Chekists,' said the harsh boy. 'That's my advice to you.' He levelled his rifle at them. 'You go first. Head down and run!' They crouched down and ran to the next stronghold and then on to the next. Finally they reached a larger bunker dug into the side of the hill. Outside the bunker there was an officer waiting for them with four of his men, Chekists from the Special Unit, all wielding Papashas. 'You're back,' said Senior Lieutenant Mogilchuk.

'Oh thank God, you know us! You know who we are!' cried Benya. He had once been interrogated by Mogilchuk, but now the sight of him was as reassuring as that of a parent claiming a lost child.

The Cossacks hugged each other. 'We made it, brothers,' they said. Prishchepa was weeping.

'Enough now, men!' said Mogilchuk. 'Yes, I know who you are, Shtrafniki. We didn't think we'd see you Dead Ones again. We don't know where you've been. We have to check you out. How long have you been out of sight? A week? More than enough time to become German agents.' He gestured towards a nearby cottage. 'You're under arrest. Take a seat in there,' he said. 'We'll question you separately. Answer our questions frankly and all will be well. And don't even think about lying.

Lie and it will be worse for you, understand? The Camps will be the least of it. Proceed!'

It was not a warm welcome but it was what they'd expected, Benya told himself.

Mogilchuk took him into a small room. 'Let's start with names and units and then we'll find out if you're collaborators and traitors. Shtrafniki, eh? We've hardly had any of you Smertniki back. All dead, we thought.' He wrote some notes, which he handed to an assistant. 'A single hole in your stories and you'll all be shorter by a head!'

'Permission to speak, senior lieutenant?' Benya said. Mogilchuk nodded. 'I have here intelligence materials taken from a traitor we assassinated, as stated in the orders of our original mission. I believe these top-secret maps need to be seen urgently by the general at once. They were stolen and handed over to the Germans by this traitor. We also took part in the assassination of the traitor Mandryka five days ago. We hope that these will earn us our redemption.'

'Give me these materials,' said Mogilchuk.

'I wish it to be stated in my notes that these were handed to you by the Shtrafniki Golden, Churelko, Prishchepa and Garanzha.'

'Don't get above yourself, prisoner,' replied Mogilchuk. 'I'll decide what goes into your service record. Hand over these papers or I'll beat them out of you.'

Twenty minutes later, a more senior Chekist with a squint, a Colonel Spassky, was perusing the maps and the notebook, and listening to Benya's story. He seemed more impressed. 'All right.' He nodded, sighing loudly, clicking his tongue. 'I think

311

you've done well. We need to check up on you but your part in the Mandryka operation is confirmed by Comrade Elmor. We've already reported this incident to our superiors.'

Benya was returned to his small room, before being called back again for a third time to see an army general named Chernyshev who received him with the divisional commissar and Spassky.

'Well, Shtrafnik,' said Spassky briskly but with a kind blink of his eye, 'you might just have earned your redemption. We know you've been through a lot. Good work. We're just waiting to hear from our superiors. There's a general based in Stalingrad who knows about the traitors Mandryka and Kapto and it happens he's in this sector. He's coming across to sign off on you.' He called in Mogilchuk: 'Their stories check out. I think they're clean.'

General Chernyshev stood up and shook Benya's hand. 'I would be happy to recommend them for redemption. Draw up the documents, comrades, and I'll sign it. Give them a proper meal, a hundred grammes of vodka and a wash. And for God's sake, get the lice off them!'

Benya was so relieved and overjoyed he could hardly speak. Smiling to himself, he followed Mogilchuk back to the cottage where he found the others. After bolting down *kasha* and black bread and goat's cheese, and even some fresh tomatoes, as much as they could, and a hundred grammes of vodka, they looked at one another, feeling human.

'Will we be signed off as Shtrafniki so we can join a regular unit?' asked Prishchepa.

'I think so,' said Benya. They had said it: *Happy to recommend them for redemption.* 'Yes, yes, we will.'

There were mattresses on the floor, and Garanzha and Panka were both fast asleep. Benya lay down and savoured the way sleep was creeping up on him. They had been through a great deal, and now it was over, all over.

VI

Feeling sick, Svetlana picked up the wad of papers that her father had thrown down.

'You see what these are? They're telephone transcripts of your conversations with your so-called lover!' Stalin grabbed the papers out of her hands and started to read, his hands actually shaking: ' "Svetlana Stalina: Hello, Lion, I long to kiss you, I can smell you, I can feel your lips on me, Lev, and I want more . . ." How can you say such things? You disgust me,' he shouted. ' "Shapiro: Darling Lioness, is it you? I can only just hear your voice. I can feel you in my arms. We're going to meet again in that apartment. I am not going to waste time just talking, I am going to kiss your hair and your sweet freckles and hold your hand and . . ." '

Stalin threw down the papers again as Svetlana started to sob.

'Do you recognize these words? *Lioness?* What is this? Don't you know who you are? Filth! Where did you learn such things? Oh, I know! From your idiotic brother! He's spending a week in the guardhouse. Now give me all *his* letters. Hand them over! No doubt you have them hidden away somewhere in here. Your Shapiro's not even a writer. He's a hack! He's not what you think he is, I can tell you that! We're checking him out.'

'But I love him,' cried Svetlana.

'Love!? LOVE?' yelled Stalin, spitting the word with hatred.

Svetlana tilted her chin at him defiantly. 'Yes. Love! I love him!'

Stalin's lips turned white and he slapped her twice across the face. He spun around to the nanny. 'Just think how low she's sunk. Don't you think I've got enough to worry about? There's a war going on – oh yes, we're fighting for our existence, and she's busy fucking!'

'No, no, no, it's not like that!' the nanny tried to explain, wringing her hands.

'It's not?' said Stalin, sounding slightly calmer. He turned back to his daughter. 'You fool! Don't you know who Lev Shapiro is? He's forty years old and he's got women all around him, and he's fucking all of them. You're nothing to him. Take a look at yourself! You're plain as a plank! Who'd want you?'

VII

'Get up, Golden!' Mogilchuk was back. The Cossacks stirred from their mattresses.

'Do we come?' asked Garanzha.

'You wait here, Cossack,' said Mogilchuk. 'Golden, you come with me. Look at you! A week's beard and food all over you. First wash your face.'

Benya did as he was told; then he walked with Mogilchuk back to the command post.

'You're lucky,' Mogilchuk continued. 'General Petrov is senior enough to sign off on your entire case for all four of you.'

Benya swallowed hard, experiencing the panic of happiness. Could he really be safe? Fabiana came to him suddenly, quite real, right there. He prayed she was alive and safe. He owed her so much, and now she was a secret, so deep, so incriminating, that he warned himself never to think of her – until he was clear. He had slept with the enemy; no one must ever know.

He was shown into an empty room and sat at a table and rested his face in his hands. *Happy to recommend them for redemption. Happy to recommend them for redemption.* These joyful words were echoing in his ears.

'General Petrov!' said Mogilchuk, saluting.

Benya stood up, his heart beating. He had survived Kolyma and the Shtrafbat and seven days behind enemy lines. Now he would be rewarded.

'Remember me, Benya Golden?'

He'd recognize that voice anywhere, the bulk and the laminated skin like glossy chocolate, and the sausagey fingers aglint with rings, all enveloped in his eau de cologne that was based on cloves. This was no front-line general, no 'Petrov' either; 'General Petrov' was Bogdan 'the Bull' Kobylov, Deputy People's Commissar for the Interior and Commissar-General of State Security (Second Degree), who had interrogated him once in Lubianka Prison three years earlier. You don't forget anyone you meet in hell, and a man never forgets his torturer: it is an intimate relationship.

'A lot can happen in three years, eh, Golden?' said Kobylov as soon as they were alone. 'I remember you well.'

'Thank you,' said Benya, not knowing what to say.

'I don't often get thanked by the men I beat with my truncheons, but that's kind of you,' Kobylov boomed jovially and mellifluously. 'But time is short so let's get down to business.'

Benya prayed that Kobylov would sign off on the redemptions. He had the power; he was Beria's special henchman. When Beria had been summoned to Moscow in 1938, he'd brought his own men from Georgia, led by Kobylov.

'I've examined your materials,' said Kobylov in his clotted accent. 'I'm impressed that you have recovered these top-secret documents and even more astonished that you personally claim to have liquidated the traitor Kapto.'

'We, my fellow Shtrafniki and I, also played a key role in the liquidation of the traitor Mandryka,' Benya pointed out.

'A key role? Don't over-egg the pudding, Golden. But I am only concerned with Kapto. Let me ask, firstly, what time precisely did you shoot Kapto and take these documents?'

Benya blinked. He wasn't at all sure.

'Think, Golden.'

'Maybe . . . ten a.m.'

Kobylov looked at his watch: it was now 5 p.m.

'Why are you asking—'

'Don't rile me today, Golden. Unless you want a smack? I thought not. How long did it take you to ride from there to our front line here?'

Benya tried to think: 'Not long. We came slowly. We didn't know where our lines were. Maybe a couple of hours.'

'Did you speak to Kapto before you shot him?'

'No.'

'You just killed him?'

'Yes.'

'Where did you pick up such ruthlessness? From the brigands in the Camps? From Jaba? You didn't know how to kill a fly when we last met. You could join us in the Cheka!' A joke. Kobylov switched off the smile. 'The materials were to be collected by officers of the Intelligence Section of the German Sixth Army. Did you know that?'

'Yes.'

'How?'

'Kapto was accompanied by two officers.'

'Ah yes, you were efficient enough to bring their papers. Captain von Manteuffel and Lieutenant Kreutzer. You killed them too, right?'

'Yes, the Cossack Garanzha killed them.'

'Very good, Golden. Did either of them speak before they were killed?'

'I wasn't there. I was with Kapto . . .'

'Do you have any idea who's coming to collect them? From the Sixth Army?'

Now Benya was worried. Where were all these questions going? He thought quickly. 'Could it be Schwarzer? No, Schwerin? That's it.'

'Colonel Gerhard von Schwerin. Very good. When was Schwerin due to collect the maps and Kapto? Think hard, Golden. Did any of them say anything?'

'No, I don't think so. Hang on, yes, whilst Prishchepa was stealing the horse, the German captain called out that Schwerin would come . . . sometime later – perhaps in the night.'

Kobylov gave him his hairdresser's smile and he sat back, lit a Belomorkanal cigarette and gave it to Benya before lighting his own. Benya watched the Bull inhale his slowly, closing his eyes under black eyebrows, thick as grubs, and blowing the blue smoke into Benya's face. A long silence. Then suddenly he banged his fist on the table. Benya jumped.

'You have fucked up an intelligence operation sanctioned at the highest fucking level by the Instantsiya. Yes, the Instantsiya! The highest! You're not in line for redemption, Prisoner Golden. Your recruitment into the Shtrafbat was against regulations. We're investigating this and if you survive this conversation, you'll be returned to the gold mines of Madyak-7.'

Benya felt cold suddenly. Cold and sick. 'Oh God,' he groaned.

'But you won't even get that far. Your death penalty is hereby reinstated owing to your treasonable actions on the Don steppe. Prepare yourself, Prisoner Golden, for the Eight Grammes, you and your three donkey-fucking villagers!'

Benya bent double, sure he was going to vomit. How could this have happened? He was going to die!

But Kobylov was still speaking. 'Wait! Pinch yourself! You're still alive and I'm still talking to you. What does that signify?'

'I don't know. I don't understand.' Benya was shivering, red specks whirling behind his eyes.

Kobylov spoke very quietly now: 'Every word I tell you is secret, you understand. You were not meant to kill Kapto. He was one of our agents, trained for months for this task. You were not meant to reclaim the maps. They are the creation of our counter-intelligence services.'

'But Kapto was a traitor,' Benya protested. 'He was in the Camps with me. He looked after me but I learned later he was an invert. There was a little girl . . .'

318

'A child? No surprise there. He was in the Gulags for child rape and murder.'

'But he was a paediatrician . . .'

'A doctor?' Kobylov grinned. 'No, no, he was never a doctor. He studied to be a vet, but he didn't even qualify to treat dogs. The doctoring was all lies. But he had connections to Mandryka and nationalist White elements which made him perfect.'

'Perfect? You used scum like that to work for you?'

'Scum like Kapto? Yes, and scum like you too, Golden. He was ours. Ours! And you wiped him out! I've been down here for ten days waiting for news of this and then you turn up thinking you've done us a favour and we're going to pat you on the head. Do you understand, prisoner?'

'I am beginning to . . .' Now Benya thought about it, what were the chances of Kapto turning up with his maps in the same sector as Mandryka? It was not a coincidence. Perhaps the entire Shtrafbat charge had been devised just to get him there; eight hundred Shtrafniki sacrificed for this mission. And he had ruined it. 'Oh God!' he groaned again.

'Do you know what Lavrenti Pavlovich said? He said: "If you find the man who fucked up this operation, beat him to a pulp until his eyes pop from his head. Punch him so hard he swallows his own teeth."'

Benya was shaking.

Kobylov paused. 'But here's the thing. It's now five oh five p.m. You left Kapto and Manteuffel dead at around ten thirty. Schwerin is not expected until, shall we say, around midnight. Do you see what I am getting at?'

'I am not sure I do.'

319

'You and your horse-riding clods. Don't you remember, Golden, who you are?'

'I'm a writer, that's all. And we fought the Fascists, we did our best, but I'm no soldier. Just a writer . . .'

'A writer? No, no, prisoner. You are a convicted terrorist and British–Japanese spy, found guilty of the gravest and most shameful crimes, including planning to murder Comrade Stalin and our leaders, in conspiracy with your mistress, the spy Sashenka. Yes, I remember her all right! Quite a beauty.'

Is she alive? wondered Benya.

'You are a terrorist sentenced to death, and you already have Eight Grammes lodged in your head. It's just unfired. You have helped our enemies. If you resist me in any way, you and your Cossacks will be nothing more than smears on a wall within a few minutes. I'll do it myself' – and Kobylov slapped his pistol on to the plywood table like a gambler throwing down his money.

Benya flinched.

'Ah yes,' said Kobylov. 'But there's another way. Do you want to hear it?'

Benya tried to speak.

'Do you know what we believe in? Watch me say it. Re-demp-tion, Golden, re-demp-tion! Do you know what that means for you?'

Benya shook his head.

'If you correct your mistake, you may be redeemed. Not just sent back to the Camps but truly redeemed! I can't promise anything for your donkey-humping bumpkins. They need to be checked out. But for you, that's a promise! Golden?'

'You want me to . . .' Benya was overcome by a new panic.

as the others approached the door, Mogilchuk creeping up as if playing grandmother's footsteps. Garanzha winked at them.

As they scaled the steps into the office, Benya tentatively looked round the corner to the couch and Kapto was there, untouched, paler and chalkier as if made of plaster. He already looked deader than he had appeared before. As if he had subsided a little.

'There's our friend,' said Garanzha.

'Right,' said Mogilchuk, trying to assume the gravity of command. 'Shtrafnik Golden, proceed to replace the documents.'

Benya hesitated, still unwilling to touch the body.

'Get on with it, Golden,' said Garanzha. 'He won't bite. Or maybe he will – ha!'

Benya unstrapped the satchel around his neck and put it on the table, taking out the maps, the notebooks. He opened the maps, laid out the pencils, positioned the notebook open at Manteuffel's neat notes. Then he took out the ID papers of the dead men.

'Put them back in their pockets,' ordered Mogilchuk, wiping his forehead.

Benya moved closer to Kapto's body. 'I can't,' he said.

'Mother of God!' Garanzha took the papers.

'Make sure you put the right papers in the right pockets,' said Mogilchuk.

'Mother of God!' Garanzha said again. He slipped them into Kapto's pockets and then, to shock the others, kissed him on the forehead and rolled his eyes like a clown as the body slipped slowly sideways.

'Done,' said Benya thankfully.

'Shtrafnik Garanzha, how dare you fool around with official business!' said Mogilchuk.

'Who's going to believe these maps are real when there are three dead bodies here?' asked Garanzha, going outside to replace the papers in the pockets of the two Germans.

'Don't ask, Spider, don't think,' said Benya. 'We're just screws in the big machine. They must have thought of that . . .'

'Shtrafnik Garanzha, this is your second and last warning!' blathered Mogilchuk from behind them. 'You are prohibited from speculating on this top-secret mission. And, Shtrafnik Golden, that applies to you too.'

'Are we finished here, senior lieutenant?' asked Panka. 'The shooting has increased over at the Don and I really think we should try to get home . . .'

'Yes, yes, let us proceed, Sergeant Churelko.'

'Let us proceed up my arse,' leered Spider Garanzha to Prishchepa behind Mogilchuk's back. Prishchepa grinned.

The sun was almost gone now but the sky was cloudy for the first time Benya could recall. The air wafting over the Don was burning and dusty. Ahead of them, the artillery was thundering. Benya was relieved. Tiredness was making his vision blur and he swayed in the saddle. Twice, Prishchepa nudged him. 'Wake up, Granpa.' But he drifted off again and then he froze.

The men around him in the greyness were no longer Garanzha and Prishchepa but other horsemen, one or two, then more, phalanxes of them, ghostly squadrons in the grainy red twilight. The Italian cavalry were moving up to the front line. Benya could hear swear words in Italian and the sounds of hundreds of horses on the move, snaffles clinking, the creak of leather. Men whispered to their horses, and all around Benya was the smell of horse shit. Silver Socks nuzzled an Italian horse, and Benya caught his right spur on an Italian spur and he heard the clacketing of the steel. His body stiffened and poured sweat as he looked straight ahead. A single word and it would all be over but he kept riding through them, Socks making her way towards the horses she knew who were standing, waiting under the trees ahead.

'Thank God!' said Panka.

'Thank Silver Socks!' They turned silently and glanced back. The air around them was the colour of good coffee, the sky a gaudy, blood-spattered crimson with new terraces of backlit clouds through which shone stairways of sun-gold, the Day of Creation one minute, Apocalypse the next. The countryside itself was alive with the grit of a thousand hooves, the chink of spurs; and on another, aural level, the gunning of engines, tanks on the move, the crump of howitzers.

Panka raised his hands: Don't move; they can't see us here; wait. Then he pointed. On the hill a few hundred yards behind, illuminated by one of the day's last sunbeams, they could see the Italian command in a heartbreakingly beautiful square of golden light. A few horses stood towards the front, commanders watching their squadrons coming up. Benya took Panka's binoculars, knowing what he would see: and there he was, the hunched shoulders, and that way of leaning in the saddle like a fearsome but half-collapsed castle. It was Malamore, and behind, one hand on Violante's mane, right there where he knew she would be, was Fabiana.

IX

Svetlana climbed the steps to her Kremlin apartment fearfully. At least her father would be in his office, she told herself. It was late evening, and he'd still be working in the Little Corner. But she halted at the top of the steps. Four uniformed Chekists — she knew their names of course — stood outside with their Papashas on their arms.

'It's going to be OK, Svetlana Josefovna,' General Vlasik whispered, breath fishy and spicy. Unmistakably *ukha* soup.

'How long has he been here, Uncle Kolya?'

'All day. He hasn't even been to the Little Corner yet.'

'All day? Is he still furious, Uncle Kolya?'

'A little, yes, but it will pass. Daughters fall in love, fathers are angry! It's the order of things. But, Sveta, you've been a bad girl! If it was my daughter, well, I'd give her more than a slap . . . He's a Georgian and Georgian fathers reach for the shotgun even before Russian ones. And he's under unspeakable pressure. Don't make it worse, Sveta. Be calm. Go in.' And he took her by the shoulders and guided her through the front door.

Inside the sound of papers being torn, the smell of pipe smoke. In the sitting room stood her father ripping up Shapiro's love letters while Svetlana's nanny watched miserably.

Stalin looked up at her. 'Calls himself a writer, does he? I found his letters. I've read them.' He was speaking calmly, tearing Lev's letters into little pieces and sprinkling them around the table, barely looking at her. 'There's the war on.

326

Every family has lost someone. Have you any idea what I am going through? In the south? And this hack is sending messages to a schoolgirl in his newspaper reports! Oh, that playboy played you all right, didn't he? You fell for it, you fool! What kind of writing is this? It's repulsive claptrap. And what does he want you for, did you ask yourself that? Only one reason. To get close to me. Yes, to worm his way to me! And if you wanted a filthy writer, couldn't you have chosen a proper Russian? This one's a Jew. Out of all the filth in Moscow, and the scum around Vasily, you had to choose a Jew. Yes, a Jew!'

With this, Stalin walked out of the room, leaving Svetlana standing there looking at the shreds of her love letters from the Lion all over the carpet.

The moment he was gone, she threw herself into the arms of her nanny, who kissed her hair.

'There there, bright one, it's going to be OK,' said her nanny.

'Is it over now?' Svetlana sobbed.

'I think so.'

'Will he . . . will he punish Lev?'

'Of course he won't,' answered her nanny. 'Your father would never do such a thing. But, Svetlana Josefovna?'

'Yes?'

'Promise me you will never contact him again. You can't. It's over. Your father is calmer because I've promised him that. Promise me!'

'Of course! I promise,' said Svetlana through her tears. 'Never again!'

X

Panka tapped Benya on the shoulder and they rode on towards the Don. Another field and they looked back again. Malamore was still on his hill with Fabiana behind him.

A bolt of pain coursed through Benya as he thought about Malamore and Fabiana together. In the shrouding darkness, the countryside, the grasses, the trees, the sibilant wheatfields all seemed alive with men and machines. By now they were close to the river, and Benya could see the muzzle flashes of big guns and the tracers of small ones zinging through the dusk as the Germans, Italians, Romanians and Hungarians threw their forces against the last, beleaguered Russian positions on the west bank of the Don. In front of them, the Russians were lobbing shells over the river, each one sending waves of vibrations pulsating through them. Flashes lit up hillsides, and explosions rendered cottages and vehicles and running men as light as day before darkness washed back over them. How would they ever get back now? Benya thought.

A shell whistled right over them. Panka turned back – and so did Benya – and suddenly they were all looking at the Italian group on the hill as the shell hit its mark. In a halo of orange brilliance, a doll-like figure was tossed in the air, and then nothing, nothing but horses running, dead animals scattered and people on fire. Garanzha and Prishchepa were cheering, and Mogilchuk was staring wide-eyed at the scene. There was no sign of Fabiana.

Benya knew she was gone. In that moment, he felt a little

piece of him wither and die. They had loved each other 'somehow forever' but his 'somehow forever' never once envisaged that it would be her who was gone. He had always assumed it would be him. He saw her quite clearly at her most beautiful, her eyes honey-coloured in the sunlight and burning with indignation, her chin raised and hands open – until her fury was breaking into the widest laugh, and she was raising her eyes to him, and he was kissing those soft lips with the slight twist, smelling her amber skin.

Now he stared at the hillside, almost reclaimed by darkness except for small fires burning on the grass where Fabiana had been just a few minutes earlier, and he was glassed off, feeling and hearing nothing, nothing at all. She was no longer amongst the living and he was utterly blank.

Panka grabbed him by the collar, telling him to ride on – now was their moment. Benya didn't care what happened now. That was his last investment in the world and he was nearly fearless, careless, heedless. Panka was explaining what lay ahead to Mogilchuk, who managed, even now that things were dire, to rustle up a last reserve of pomposity. 'Let us proceed, sergeant.'

They couldn't get back along the beach, Panka was saying, and German armour was crushing the last Russian positions on the bend. The stronghold they had been in that morning had been abandoned, and the advance of the Italian cavalry could only mean a charge against Russian lines was imminent. What was left? There was only one course of action.

'We must embrace our darling mother,' said Panka, spurring Almaz forward.

'What's he talking about?' asked Mogilchuk.

'Follow me,' said Panka. Up the bluffs they galloped and down the chalky escarpment of the high bank, down a thin snaking path that led to the River Don. Here they could see the battle, a multi-faceted panorama across the mirror-like expanse of the great river, reflected in the water and in the sky above it, as were the muzzle flashes of the Russian guns fired from the other bank. Suddenly the sky went dark, and now the clouds were right above them, rolling over the riverbanks, and they too were jet black. It was, Benya thought, as if they were riding inside a black drum.

'Perfect timing,' said Panka as forks of lightning hit the water. 'A Don fury.'

The horses were stamping and pacing and snorting. 'I hate the rain, I hate the rain,' said Garanzha, whipping his rearing horse. Panka rode down to the water, Benya following as foamy waves lapped Silver Socks's hooves.

'What now?' shouted Mogilchuk.

Prishchepa threw his head back and started to sing, '*I fell in love on the night of a Don storm . . .*' A red wall of fire illuminated the bank for a moment as a fuel tank exploded; then glimmers of orange flickered behind the clouds as the rain started, dense pails of rain, slanting in to burn and lash their faces and necks, blinding them. Benya was soaked instantly. The world was ending, and he was so tired that he might as well slip off his horse and die right here. But he was brought to by a sting of pain: Panka's whip on his hand.

'Come on, Granpa! This storm is a fierce bitch and every Cossack knows the bitches are fiercest on the Don. It's our chance. We cross the Don here!' shouted Panka. 'Ride right in, look neither right nor left. Tighten your reins and say your prayers!'

'But the horses . . .' cried Mogilchuk, trying to hold the reins.

'Reins tight! They'll be fine, dear boy,' replied Panka.

'I can't swim,' said Mogilchuk.

'This is the Don,' Panka shouted. 'The sun shines yonder on the far bank!' And he spurred Almaz straight into the river. A shell landed ahead of them, and Almaz balked but Panka whipped him on.

Benya knew he was going to die in the waters. He and Mogilchuk peered at one another, petrified, wiping their eyes, fellow Muscovites now, townies, sharing the same fear.

'I can't!' cried Mogilchuk.

'Me neither!'

But Speedy Prishchepa had galloped in with an escort of foamy spray, one hand raised as if riding a bronco in some Western rodeo, and he was singing right into the storm.

Benya leaned over Silver Socks's neck, throwing his arms around her, burying his face in her mane, talking to her and Fabiana all in a seamless stream of love and fear and fury. Socks snorted and backed, trying to avoid the water, but she went deeper with each leap. Spider Garanzha leaned over and whipped her so hard that she bled and she rode into the frothing water, now up to her knees and then her shoulders.

An explosion rocked them forwards, and Silver Socks stepped deeper into the river. By now Benya's boots, and then his britches were in the water, its coldness soaking up his legs. Prishchepa was ahead, the water around his waist and then his chest as his horse started to swim, her head thrashing, her eyes frantic. Mogilchuk was beside him, shaking with fear.

Benya pivoted and seeing a riderless horse, he turned Socks around, riding back up the bank. Spider Garanzha was on the ground and Benya jumped down beside him. Spider looked up at him with those surprisingly goo-goo eyes first pleadingly then defiantly, his bulging face mushroomed with sweat and pale as paper. Benya saw his belly was open, a mass of blue and red guts smoking, and stirring on the stones of the beach. He raised his eyes to Spider's, eye to eye as if quite alone, two wolves on a wide steppe. He knew that if Spider had ridden straight in with Prishchepa, leaving him and Mogilchuk to die on the bank, he'd be halfway across now, and living. Poor Spider, Benya thought, he must be cursing his one kindness: staying behind to whip them in, a Zhid and a secret police bastard!

Benya pulled the saddle off Spider's horse and put the shabraque under his head. Garanzha gave him his hand, squeezing it like a child. He peered up at Benya and his eyes – one minute they looked back at him and the next they didn't. That was all it was, a slither of a second and Garanzha seemed part of the bank, of the mud, the hulk of an old wreck half sunk in the sand.

Benya took a breath, remounted Silver Socks and spurred her forwards, whipping her once with Garanzha's quirt. She was up to her girth again, higher, as the black water enveloped him amid the sheeting rain that was so thick it seemed as if the river itself was raining upwards into the clouds. Socks was in the river up to her point of shoulder, and then she was swimming, her head high, her legs pumping under the water, thick veins pulsating in her neck.

'Go on, Silver Socks, go on, good girl . . .' Benya was

saying close to her ears. Something heavy touched him and he flinched. Socks was thrashing beneath him, and he was gulping water, about to flounder – was it a snake, a crocodile? Then he saw the arm and the blue face of a Russian soldier floating downriver, swollen like an overstuffed sofa. They were in the middle of the Don, the banks as far behind as ahead, and a shell flashed whining over their heads, the banks whorling and erupting in yellow and orange. Machine-gun fire raked the water, and a dancing line of serpentine splashes spanged around him.

'You fools, we're Russians!' Benya shouted but no one could hear him; he couldn't hear himself. Then Socks's hooves found the solid riverbank, and they were out of the water on the stones of the Don beach. Alone. Machine-gun fire chugged across the stones, so close he felt it punch him. Benya leaned forwards and hugged Silver Socks. Panka and Prishchepa were calling him up the bank. Silver Socks fell to her knees suddenly, Benya collapsing beside her.

It was pitch dark now, almost midnight, and Socks was holding her head up high, rocking back and forth, and Benya was beside her on the stones of the riverbank, stroking her neck, her mane, her satiny muzzle.

'Silver Socks, I love you, dear friend' he sobbed. 'Thank you for all you've done for me, for saving me a hundred times. No man ever had a better friend than you and I didn't think . . . I just didn't think . . .' He remembered the glow of her four silver legs at the stud farm, and the starflash on her face. 'You chose well with that one, brother,' Panka had said. 'Tend her like a wife. Respect her like a mother. Feed her like a daughter.' But she'd been more than all those things to him. He remembered the charge against the Italians, the way she'd watched as he made love to Fabiana . . . Then her head was down, and a shudder ran through her, and Prishchepa and Panka were pulling him up the bank until all three were lying at the top, panting, their horses standing nearby.

'Mogilchuk?' asked Benya.

'Down the bank somewhere. He's OK. I saw him ride out.'

'Silver Socks?'

'Gone, my brother,' replied Panka.

'Shot?'

Panka nodded. 'One in the neck. She was quite a girl. Not many born like that. Even on the Don.' He handed Benya the flask. They stood up, swaying. Benya was half mad with grief. He felt his midriff and saw the blood on his finger.

'I'm hit,' he said, remembering the punch.

Hands gripped him.

'Hold it,' said Prishchepa, his eyes cold, his dagger in his other hand. 'Mogilchuk's coming for us now. We'll be checked out by the Cheka. You need to vouch for us. Say that this week we were with you every minute. Or they'll shoot us. Swear it, Zhid, or I'll cut your throat now and we'll say what we need to say about you. Say it right now!'

Benya shook him off. He didn't care where they'd been for those days; he guessed they had played some double game out there with the Nazis, but right now he was too tired and angry to be spoken to like this. He'd lost Fabiana; Silver Socks had died in his arms; now these goons were threatening him, and they had no idea that he was way past rock bottom. 'I can do better than that . . . Drop the knife. Step back!' he said.

'We know where you were too,' said Prishchepa. 'You weren't alone. We know things too . . .'

Benya sank to his knees, weakness creeping up on him in flickerings of dizziness, but a hopeless and doom-laden fury made him fearless. How dare they threaten him with Fabiana? He pointed his pistol at them, keeping them covered, feeling the power within him.

Prishchepa switched on his happy-go-lucky bandit's charm. 'Wait a moment, dear brother Golden—'

Suddenly Benya could not tolerate any more.

'I'm not your brother,' he said, raising his pistol and firing twice.

Day Ten

I

Unshaven and weary but bursting with the images and p[...]
he wanted to use in his articles, Lev Shapiro was in the h[...]
train heading back to Moscow, his typewriter in its cas[...]
his shoulder. He was walking up through the wagons: [...]
were old ones from Tsarist passenger trains with soft seats[...]
smooth by generations; some were from cattle cars – all[...]
full of wounded. The walking wounded sat on the seat[...]
every inch of the floor was crammed with broken men, s[...]
lying on bare wooden planks; others were lucky enough t[...]
on stretchers. Some smiled at him as he stepped over th[...]
and he noticed a couple who were so still, they were prob[...]
already dead. And all around him came the sound of groani[...]
of men crying for the doctor, or their mothers or for G[...]
Shapiro was accustomed to such things but it was still hard[...]
hear. Always the reporter and observer, his notebook was o[...]

'What sector were you in?' he asked a man with bandag[...]
over one eye who was well enough to sit up on a wooden sea[...]
'I want to tell your story.' To a Tartar boy from Kazan, wh[...]
had lost his arm: 'What section were you in, what happened?[...]
He crouched beside the men, taking notes, and they could se[...]
that he had been with the troops and suffered with them and[...]
they were happy to talk to him. They wanted their stories to[...]

be known. He walked on, thinking about the battle and then his secret, Svetlana . . . If they knew who his sweetheart was, would they believe it?

He looked around him at the wounded from the battle of the Don Bend which had ended so badly. Now the Germans could advance – they were already crossing the Don on great pontoons and pushing on to the outskirts of Stalingrad.

Lev had been ordered to report to his editor in Moscow and had hitched a lift back on the train. He was excited because he would get the chance to see Svetlana – his little Lioness! Lev was fascinated by her. As a man, he found her so fresh, so youthful; and as a writer, well, what writer would not want to know all about her? She was at the centre of history.

He shrugged. Women liked him for some reason, and he knew she did too, with all the solemn passion of her age. Hell, the women in Moscow liked him at least partly because they loved movies; every young actress wanted a part and he was the scriptwriter – 'Lyovka sweetie, Lev darling, won't you write me a beautiful part in your new project, *Stalin at Finland Station*. Or how about the empress in your *Peter the Great, Part Two*?'

'Of course,' he would answer, 'shall we meet at the Aragvi for dinner – I'll book a private room – or a cocktail at the bar in the Metropole Hotel?' Well, of course he was married and he'd been married a long time – but any stray bullet at the front could kill him tomorrow. Who could blame him for enjoying himself?

But Svetlana was different. She brought out his best qualities – he was the finest man he could be with her. He was her teacher: she wanted to learn about writing and literature.

340

And though she was so young, she didn't bore him like most teenagers he'd met. She was an old soul, and no wonder. He wanted to protect her, to make her feel cherished, to boost her confidence. In some ways this was a crazy, quixotic affair, a reckless adventure that gave him a thrill, but the war had opened society up and afterwards there would be more freedom. He mocked himself as a knight, a loving friend for the loneliest girl in Russia, and Svetlana truly was a damsel in distress, a sensitive girl living in a wilderness of fear, neglect and boredom. It is my mission, he thought, to rescue her. Oh, he loved their calls, and her letters were so romantic. And when they had kissed and held each other, her touch was so sparky, so forthright . . . How she had blossomed in just these few days. He would see her tonight if he could. Then he had to get his editor to send him back to Stalingrad to report on the coming struggle. If Stalingrad fell to the Germans, where would the Russian retreat end?

Then he heard a voice he recognized.

'Lev! Is it you?' He looked around at the damaged men in the wooden seats and on the floor as the train steamed northwards. 'Lev, what are you doing here?' He was stepping over the wounded, careful where he put his boots. 'Shapiro! It's me!'

'Christ! Can it be—?' And it was – it was Benya Golden, lying in a filthy uniform on the floor, pale and older, so much older. He and Benya had been members of the same worldly, rather privileged milieu of writers, actors and jazzmen. The novelists Babel and Ehrenburg, the actor Mikhoels, the jazz singers Utesov and Rosner, the film actresses Valentina Serova and Sophia Zeitlin – these were the friends they had in

341

common. But they also shared the jealousies all writers can't resist – he had called Golden's book 'overrated, a bit childish', while Golden had sneered at Shapiro's script: 'stiff, formal, I could do better'. But then Golden had been arrested, vanished off the face of the earth, and Lev had presumed he had been shot.

Lev stretched over the two boys lying between them, one of them unconscious, the other with no legs, and crouched on the planks next to him. The men shook hands, and Lev leaned down and kissed his cheeks thrice, all ancient jealousies forgotten in the familiarity of a long-lost friend, newly found. He glanced down at Benya's dressings.

'Hit in the leg and hip,' said Benya. 'I won't be able to walk for a while. But I think I'll live.'

He was a shrunken sunburnt shell of a man; only his blue eyes were the same, Lev thought. When he offered cheese and bread, Benya wolfed it down with a swig of vodka and some water from his canteen.

'Do you know where you're going?'

'Gospitalnaya Ploshad.' Hospital Square. The main military hospital in the centre of Moscow.

Lev whistled. 'You were lucky,' he said.

'More than you know.'

Lev did know but everyone was listening in the carriage and they had to be careful. 'You were . . . out of Moscow for a while?'

'Innocents abroad,' said Benya and, used to talking in riddles with his friends, Lev got it immediately: *The Innocents Abroad* was by Mark Twain who had said: 'Reports of my death are greatly exaggerated.' So he had been in the Gulags; Lev had heard all the stories of that netherworld. But how had Benya got out? He was a Political yet somehow he had joined a Shtrafbat.

'You were there, weren't you, in that mad cavalry charge? I was covering it. The commander was a heroic guy . . . let me see . . . Melishko?'

Benya nodded but Lev saw the sadness in his face.

'He didn't make it?'

'Not many of us did but . . . we broke through the Italian lines.'

'And you were on horseback? I never had you down as a Cossack athlete.'

Benya smiled weakly. 'I was better than I expected.'

'Did you . . . ?' Shapiro raised his eyebrows and Benya guessed what he was asking. Had he been redeemed or was he still a Smertnik?

'Don't you despise religion?' replied Benya. 'How can those fools believe *extra Christum nulla salus*.' Shapiro got it: 'outside Christ, no salvation'. Benya meant that he had found salvation in the redemption of his own Soviet Christ; in Stalin. He had redeemed himself by shedding blood. He was free.

'Do you know what you're going to do?' Lev could see Benya was struggling to stay awake.

'I haven't thought . . .' Then he whispered, 'Teacher. I want to teach . . . Yes . . .' And his eyes closed.

'That cavalry charge seems an age ago, but it was only eight days,' said Lev. 'So you had a pretty easy war, eh? Eight days and you're invalided out.'

But Benya was already sleeping as Lev, his eyes full of tears, leaned over and embraced him.

II

It was a short flight, just fifteen minutes.

The Junker 52 landed on the heavily guarded airfield amidst the dark pine woods, and the officer who'd climbed out on his own, carrying a leather briefcase, jumped straight into the open-topped staff car that drove up to the plane. He didn't talk en route but rehearsed his arguments, over and over again. This was not the first time he had reported but he felt it was the most important and he wanted to get every detail right. As the car drove into the woods, he noticed the anti-aircraft guns, tank traps, concrete fortifications. They approached the first checkpoint, then the second and third. Each time his papers were inspected carefully. Security was tight; they drove swiftly along the road past twenty or so single-storey log huts, over-shadowed by the hulking concrete ramparts which were the visible parts of the bunker complex, towards a large wooden hut, heavily guarded. He had been here once before, and enjoyed having his hair cut at the barber's and soaking in the sauna. But this time his attendance was different and all the more urgent.

Entering the adjoining hut, he showed his papers for the fourth time and surrendered his handgun. He could see there were other officers from different fronts and a minister waiting, and he sat down with them in the anteroom, twice getting up to check his appearance in the mirror. Finally he was called and he walked into the low-roofed wooden hut where he could just see the backs of the men leaning over the maps on the table and hear the famous husky, guttural voice.

'They're falling apart,' he was saying in a jovial tone. 'Faster than last year. Like a house of cards. They're close to collapse. The big decision is what resources to assign to Army Group B and Stalingrad. Army Group A is sweeping all before it. You know, gentlemen, what my instinct tells me, but this new intelligence may help us decide. Let's hear what he has to say. Is he here?'

'Colonel von Schwerin?' said the Chief of Staff Generaloberst Halder. Schwerin noticed the two Iron Crosses won in the Great War.

Schwerin coughed a little self-consciously. 'I'm here.' The air was sweltering in the hut.

'Welcome to Führerhauptquartier Werwolf, Colonel von Schwerin,' said Halder. 'Step forward next to Generaloberst von Weichs . . .'

The wall of backs in field grey opened up for him. Keitel and Jodl gave him a brisk nod, and the bespectacled Weichs, commander of Army Group B, his ultimate superior, shook his hand and made space on his right around the map table.

The new arrival saluted. 'Mein Führer, Colonel von Schwerin, Intelligence, Sixth Army, reporting.'

Across the table, Hitler was leaning forwards on his elbows. He was wearing a sandy-coloured double-breasted jacket with a dark tie, his Iron Cross was on his chest, a scarlet swastika band on his right arm.

'Welcome, colonel,' said Hitler. 'Your flight to Vinnitsa was easy, I hope?'

'Very quick, mein Führer. General Paulus sends his regards.'

Hitler nodded. 'What have you got for us?'

'Tactical plans for this sector from Soviet headquarters that I believe may impact on Operation Fischreiher. Hence I've rushed them here as soon as I had analysed them.'

There was a beat of silence.

'First of all, how reliable is the provenance?' asked Halder, who was next to Hitler. 'Have they been missed?'

'The documents belonged to a Soviet staff officer killed when our planes strafed his car. Kapto, a medical officer in a penal battalion, attended the scene and procured the documents which the Soviet General Staff believed were destroyed in the fire. Kapto, a long-standing anti-Soviet agitator, then defected to our side. He was a childhood friend of another defector and anti-Soviet agitator Mandryka, who set up a Schuma auxiliary police unit. This Kapto had been serving a sentence for anti-Soviet agitation in the Kolyma Camps. This is the first factor that encourages us to treat this material as legitimate. Kapto was interviewed by my colleague Captain von Manteuffel, who made the first inspection of the materials and was convinced of their importance and authenticity. Sadly, yesterday partisans attacked and killed them.'

'But they left the maps?' asked Halder.

'Yes, Generaloberst.'

'Why didn't they take them?'

'Doesn't that suggest that they *wanted* us to have them?' asked Weichs.

'I have considered this at length,' said Schwerin. 'First the provenance: the anti-Soviet credentials of Mandryka and Kapto are flawless and long-standing, confirmed by other assets. If this *was* a Soviet intelligence operation, they would never have sent partisans to kill Kapto and my fellow officers as that would have undermined the credibility of the documents. So in my opinion, the attack strengthens the case for believing this is genuine. I also believe personally that the partisan attack was not by Soviet partisans but by Ukrainian nationalist elements at large in the sector who were unaware of the documents and circumstances.'

Hitler was fidgeting, his fingers tapping on the green baize table. Halder held up his hand to signal that this was too much information: could Schwerin hurry up and give his judgement?

'Yes . . . yes, my conclusion!' answered Schwerin. 'I have consulted with Abwehr colleagues. We conclude these battle plans are authentic and significant.'

Hitler, smiling, impatient, even excited, tapped both forefingers on the table again: 'Well, colonel, cut to the quick. What do they say?'

Schwerin opened his briefcase and drew out a package of maps, selecting one, which he unfolded. Hitler rested his chin in his right hand as he looked at its arrows and Cryllic lettering.

'This is a complex series of plans by Soviet headquarters for different scenarios created by the advance of Army Group A in Operation Edelweiss and Army Group B towards Stalingrad in Operation Fischreiher—' Schwerin continued.

'Yes, yes,' interrupted Halder. 'And you regarded this as of such importance that you wished to tell the Führer yourself.'

'Yes.'

'So what's so important about it?'

'I am all ears,' said Hitler, smirking, and the generals laughed.

347

'The maps suggest that it is unlikely Stalin ever considered Stalingrad to be in peril—'

'Well, he's in for a big surprise then!' said Hitler. More laughter.

'If I may continue, mein Führer? These plans suggest that, if we advance on Stalingrad, Stalin will resist vigorously. But only up to a point. He's learned the lessons of our blitzkrieg. One of these scenarios is for an orderly withdrawal from the city. Rather than bleed his forces and risk encirclement, he may defend a new line that we believe is being prepared to the east. After the encirclements of Kiev and Kharkov, he cannot afford to lose more of his diminishing reserves.'

'Just one of several scenarios?' asked Hitler.

'Yes, mein Führer.'

'Do any of these plans envisage defending Stalingrad at any cost?'

'Not specifically. This is the most detailed plan and—'

Halder interrupted him again: 'That makes no sense, no sense at all. They're fighting for every inch and I've been read- ing about Stalin's command of Stalingrad, then called Tsaritsyn, during the Civil War in 1918. Then, as now, he built up vast reserves to throw at our flanks where we are over-committed. The city is the symbol of his name, of his prestige. He will never let it fall! It is *we* who will be bled, *we* who risk encircle- ment. Mein Führer—'

Hitler cut him off hoarsely with a slicing gesture of his hand. 'As usual, Generaloberst Halder is frightened of ghosts. You vastly overestimate Stalin's reserves and capabilities. He's scarcely managed any such complex operations so far. All along I've expected the Russians to withdraw behind the Volga and ultimately the Urals. It's the Russian way: fight with the insane, bestial bravery of the *Untermenschen*, then headlong retreat and mass surrender. Here you have it, gentlemen. Here's the proof provided by Colonel von Schwerin and the maps of this man, Kapto. Wasn't I right in Poland, in France? My instincts were right to divide Army Group South into A and B, and correct now to take Stalingrad at once, whatever the cost. Here are my orders. Move the Fourth Panzer Army, and more air cover and bombers, directly to Army Group B. Generaloberst von Weichs: you are to advance on Stalingrad. It will be ours within four weeks.'

'I must protest, mein Führer,' said Halder, face flushed and anxious. 'I wish to register my view that this is a mistake. A fatal mistake.'

Hitler ignored him. 'Fine report, Colonel von Schwerin, and while you're here, enjoy a good meal, a sauna and, if you wish before you fly back to the Sixth Army, a dip in my swimming pool – although I must admit I haven't had a swim yet myself.'

Smiling, Hitler offered his hand across the table and von Schwerin shook it.

III

It was just before three o'clock, and Svetlana Stalina and Martha Peshkova were walking out of the Josef Stalin Commune School 801. On the street outside, Moscow was faded in its glories: battered, grey, with shrapnel scars on the building opposite.

The eyes of all the parents and teachers were on the two girls, School Director Kapitolina Medvedeva almost bowing as they passed, but Svetlana was used to being the emperor's daughter. Nannies, bodyguards and mothers were picking up the children outside the gates. There were no fathers; all the leaders were at the war. There was Hercules Satinov's wife, Tamara, the English teacher at the school, walking out with her little daughter. Svetlana waved: she knew them well from family holidays on the Black Sea.

'My father knows!' whispered Svetlana.

'Oh my God, what did he say?' replied Martha.

'You didn't tell anyone, did you?'

'Of course not. What did he say?'

Svetlana just shook her head: 'I've never seen my father like that. He slapped me. He tore up the letters.'

'What did Lev say?'

'He doesn't know.'

'But he must be coming back soon?'

'Maybe,' said Svetlana.

'Are you going to see him again?'

Svetlana remembered her promise to Nanny. 'No, never again.'

Maybe that's for the best, thought Martha. 'Your father . . . Be careful, Svetochka.'

They had reached the street corner where her bodyguard, Klimov, was waiting with the Packard.

As the girls kissed each other goodbye, Svetlana glanced at her watch and enjoyed the sensation of power, the fact that she had control of her life. Amid this perpetual surveillance and her father's relentless supervision, she was still her compact self, her own kingdom. Only she ruled her heart.

'Svetlana!' Klimov was holding open the car door.

'I'd like to walk a bit . . . I'd like to wander around the House of the Book.'

'I'd prefer you in the car,' said Klimov.

'Drive behind, if you like?'

The black Packard purred slowly behind her as she set off along Ostozhenka, then past the university and the Kremlin and up Gorky Street towards her favourite bookshop. Waving at Klimov, dear Klimov the kind Chekist who wanted to help her, who wanted her to know love, she skipped inside where she found herself surrounded by the familiar ramparts of shelves, and the sweet smell of book leather and yellow paper and glue. Her eyes scanned the shelves for something to take home, a new American novel perhaps? Books were so romantic, she thought, book-lovers all over the world – London, New York and Moscow – were linked in a web of sensibility.

She only hesitated for a moment then she walked straight through the shop to the back where the metal lift brought up the books from the storeroom downstairs, and where there were piles of books in their boxes, not yet unpacked. She pressed the button for the lift, which shook and groaned but nothing happened. Swearing to herself a little, Svetlana ran down the steps. It was cooler down there. The tang of book glue and new paper made her nose twitch. In the basement, a young man with big ears was unpacking a box of her father's speeches and this amused her.

'Excuse me,' he said in a southern accent, Stavropol maybe, 'but you're not allowed down here.'

She smiled at him winningly.

'No, really, I'll get sacked.'

'No you won't,' she said. 'Not if I tell them not to . . .'

'Who are you? Hey, you! Please go back upstairs.'

But she could see the light now from the loading door. 'It will be quicker to get out this way!' she called and ran down the ramp and out into the brightness. Then she turned up the side street, peeking into Gorky Street where she could see Klimov leaning on the car, smoking a cigarette, and jumped on a tram.

She was free. Not for long. But free.

IV

Benya opened his eyes. The bandages and the cast around his hip and right thigh were reassuringly tight. He enjoyed the float of the morphine, its timeless haze. He was propped up so he could see the entire room.

Everything was drab and washed-out in the ward. All around him were steel beds, brown sheets, soiled blankets and the smells of carbolic acid, disinfectant, the hot fug of strange bodies, the fruity sugariness of putrefaction and the acrid urine of the living. The boy two beds down had died; they hadn't got round to removing him yet. Then the morphine bore Benya away again: here he was visiting his parents, and grooming Silver Socks, next he was swooping through roiling skies on to the steppes where he saw Tonya and Kapto and the little girl. He woke up, sickened, with the rust of blood in his mouth.

He heard the hiss of whispering down the ward, and noticed a retinue of nurses and doctors and a general close by, three beds away. High and buzzed, nothing could dent the rapture of being free and redeemed – but things had gone wrong before. And now? Now he was alive.

The general was getting closer, speaking to each patient, the doctor commenting and the anaemic voices of flimsy men responding. Sharp questions to project urgency and care. 'How are you feeling? What unit? Where did you serve? Stalingrad Front?' Then another note, the moving-on-we-have-ten-wards-to-get-through tone: 'Your service to the Motherland is appreciated. Good luck in your recovery. Long live Stalin!'

They were at the next-door bed and then it was Benya's turn. He already knew the questions by heart and was tempted to call out the answers in one insolent blurt to save time when he heard the general speak. 'Leave us a moment, comrades, I know this one. Yes, thanks, nurse, I'll pull up a chair.' The accent was so Georgian. Benya was suddenly very much awake.

'Benya Golden,' said Colonel General Hercules Satinov, older but still lean and trim, a man to whom power seemed as natural as angst to a Jewish writer. Once, in another almost forgotten life, at a beautiful woman's house, Benya had seen Satinov dance the *lezginka*, the waist in his Stalinka tunic tight and wasp-like, the footwork in his boots impressively fleet. A vanished life.

Benya, so exuberant one second earlier, shrank in the icy

presence of Stalin's comrade-in-arms. What had they in store for him this time?

'How are you feeling?'

'I was feeling good . . .' Benya said. The past tense, too honest.

'Until you saw me?' replied Satinov. 'Again.'

The last time Benya had seen Satinov was when he presided over his sentencing to death, then the reprieve – to twenty-five years in Gehenna.

'A coincidence, I am sure.'

'You still believe in those, Golden?'

'I want to.'

Satinov looked searchingly at Benya. 'I am the Stavka representative on the Stalingrad Front,' he said. 'My front. When possible, I visit the wounded.' A pause. 'Your case came straight to me. I had your wounds checked; when you were asleep, I arranged for the Kremlin Clinic to send a doctor to examine you. Signing your redemption, in this particular case, I had to be certain.' Benya knew Satinov was referring to the Sashenka Case, because he too had known Sashenka.

'Understood,' said Benya. 'Thank you.'

'You were nominated for the only medal available to Shtrafniki: Order of Glory Third Class.'

Benya shook himself. 'Really?' He'd never won a prize, even at school.

'Of course it's impossible for a Political.'

Benya had seen Satinov's hawkish face on countless banners and newspapers; he had even passed through a town named Satinovgrad on his way to the Don. Now, in the flesh, this presence took him back: Satinov had been the close friend of

Sashenka, the love of Benya's life, and yet Stalin had assigned
Satinov to 'curate' the case and oversee her destruction. A test;
a very Stalinist one. Family, sentiment, friendship were the
trappings of bourgeois sentimentality, and Stalin liked to say
'A Bolshevik has no family but the Party'. Satinov had presided
coolly over the trials and the sentences. Had he played a murky
part in the whole case, had he denounced his friends, even
Sashenka? Had he been particularly severe in order to save his
own skin? If Sashenka was alive, Satinov would know. What
things he must know . . .

An adjutant was whispering something in the great man's ear.

'Golden, you're drifting away. Listen to me. If you are
allowed to reside in Moscow, what would you like to do?'

'Teach literature.'

'At a school?'

'Yes. And if it isn't possible, I'll do anything, sweep floors,
build tanks, or become a barman or . . .'

'Your chatter gets you into trouble. Stop talking, Golden.'

Satinov stood up. He didn't say goodbye, just a slight dip
of the head. But this was extraordinary: no one helped returning Zeks and yet here was Satinov doing exactly that. Benya
felt hopeful again. Satinov's entourage of doctors, adjutants
and bodyguards reassembled and escorted him into the next
ward.

A shadow fell over him and Benya looked up.

'Granpa!'

Benya jumped. Two men, tamed by their standard-issue
hospital blouses and fraying long johns, were standing next to
the bed.

'You should go back to your ward,' said the nursing sister,

a battleaxe with the face of a puff adder. 'Go on, I say! Or I'll report you to the Party committee.'

'Right, sister, one minute . . . please!'

Benya could see there was something about the way Prishchepa said it, the pirate's smile he gave, the tousle of his flaxen thatch, that made her melt.

'One minute, then, Speedy, and not a minute more!'

'You see? She even knows my name,' said Prishchepa, who had a dressing on his shoulder.

'Behave yourself, Speedy,' she said sternly as she waddled out.

Prishchepa sat himself on the edge of the bed. 'Who was that bigshot?' he asked.

'Some apparatchik.'

'What's he want? Appointing you Inspector of Cavalry?' Panka had appeared, his face and chest sunburnt, his grey hair longer, the whiskers shaggier. He leant on crutches, a cast on his shattered leg.

'Nothing. Maybe less than nothing.'

'I think Granpa Golden would be better as Inspector of Marksmen,' said Prishchepa with a wink.

Benya sighed. 'I was never much of a rider and I wasn't much better as a shot.'

'Don't do yourself down,' replied Panka, his tiny foxy eyes bright. 'You turned out to be a better shot than you thought. God bless you, boy.'

What kind of topsy-turvy world was it where you could only save the lives of your friends by shooting them? Benya thought. But Stalin's decree was specific: Shtrafniki could only be redeemed by sacrificing their own blood and so

Benya had given his friends the wounds they needed to win redemption.

Perhaps it was the relief of knowing that Satinov had secured his redemption or perhaps it was just the morphine wearing off a little – he needed some more; where was that nurse? – but quite suddenly he felt a jolt of stunning grief and he was choking. The sadness rocked him, the sense of loss pounding through him: Fabiana was dead. He pictured her dipping her hand into the honeycomb, scooping it out and eating it like a bear. Love, he thought, is all about the details – a dictionary of visions, moments, sounds that have no names, no words necessary. Love is always selfishness at its most delicious – but with Fabiana, there was no time for selfishness. Sometimes the very shortness of an affair, he decided, grants it an immaculate purity that passes directly into legend – and nothing afterwards can ever equal it. But their mere hours together were lived in a rougher, higher realm; they never said 'I love you' to each other; they were just the 'bandits in love', and that said it all. From the start, they were fighting to escape death and, ultimately, to survive each other – and the miracle was that they had managed that, at least for a while. Should he have told her that he loved her? Would that have comforted her? Such trifles would have been somehow futile and irrelevant beside the immensity of the courageous sacrifices she made for him. 'Are you out there somewhere, darling ally, brave, brave friend?' he called to her quietly. 'Are you there, secret dreamer of the lagoon, *mia adorata*? I kiss you! I kiss you!'

I knew her somehow forever. But for us, forever was too short.

V

Poskrebyshev, a drear gnome in a general's uniform, stood at the door of the Little Corner. 'Satinov's here,' he announced.

Stalin beckoned, and Poskrebyshev stepped aside and Satinov entered.

Satinov's Packard had raced from the hospital to the Kremlin and then round to the Little Corner in the triangular yellow Senate. He did try to visit the wounded from the Stalingrad Front when he could but he acknowledged to himself that this visit had been connected to Benya Golden. He had played a role in the Sashenka Case against Benya Golden and now he wanted to ensure he was treated justly. But he had not had the heart to tell him a terrible truth: his redemption was not final. There were millions of prisoners in the Camps whose names Stalin had never seen – but they were not Politicals; nor were they Politicals convicted in cases known personally to Stalin. If he, Satinov, concealed the pardoning of a Political, a writer known to Stalin, the Leader could destroy him with it. He had seen comrades shot for just such a legerdemain. No, he must ask Stalin directly, although it was likely Beria would advise against it. Beria was not just the master of the security forces and the Gulags but he was also jealous and wary of Stalin's affection for Satinov, which was why he had not wasted much time on poor Benya Golden who would probably be heading straight back to Kolyma.

Satinov entered the room and saluted. Little seemed to have changed. Beria was back at the table. Further down, Vasilevsky had been joined by General Georgi Zhukov, with his prehensile jaw and tauric shoulders.

'Permission to report from the Stalingrad Front,' said Satinov.

Stalin raised his hand in approval.

'We are fortifying Stalingrad. The Germans are reinforcing Army Group B and the Sixth Army specifically. We hear from the Southern Front that they are even now, as of this morning, moving panzer units out of the front line, probably for transfer to our sector. They're already racing across the steppe.'

'How close are they to the city?'

'Units have already reached the outskirts,' replied Vasilevsky.

'How are the generals on your front?'

'Chuikov's bunker is right by the river and he will fight to the last. He's a tough one. I commend his harshness, Comrade Stalin,' Satinov continued.

'But will Stalingrad hold? Will we be able to cling on to the Volga no matter what?' asked Stalin. 'Tell me honestly as one Bolshevik to another.'

Everyone looked at him and waited. Satinov did not rush to answer but considered the honest answer which an old Bolshevik expected from a comrade.

'Yes,' said Satinov finally. 'I know we will hold Stalingrad.'

'Good, *bicho*,' said Stalin standing up and walking towards the generals, who were leaning over the maps.

Vasilevsky and Zhukov stiffened as Stalin approached.

'We have ourselves the battle we wanted,' he said. 'Hitler has taken the bait but it will cost us much blood to hold the city. We must draw in the Germans without destroying ourselves. The only people in Russia who know of this are in this room. After many reverses, the golden hour is here. Good luck,' and he offered his hand first to Vasilevsky and then Zhukov. Satinov and Beria glanced at each other, unsure what exactly the Leader had cooked up with the two generals. Stalin had never shaken hands with anyone like this. 'Make your preparations, comrades,' he said as the two generals saluted and left.

'Stalingrad will be a great struggle,' said Satinov. 'Permission to return there as permanent front commissar.'

Stalin thought for a moment, and then nodded. 'Agreed.' He swivelled towards Beria. 'Hitler's moving more units to the Sixth Army. Is this the result of that little trick with the Shtrafbat defector? Did that go according to plan?'

'It did,' replied Beria. 'The maps were flown to Sixth Army headquarters. We have no idea if they reached Weichs or Hitler himself but the preparations for these troop movements started at once.'

'It worked?' Stalin mused, almost to himself. 'Melishko's bandits served their Motherland.'

'Comrade Stalin?' It was Satinov. 'A small matter. One of the few Shtrafniki who redeemed themselves in that operation was Benya Golden, the writer and—'

'He's a Political,' interjected Beria. 'Politicals can't redeem themselves.'

'Convicted of?'

'Planning to assassinate you, Comrade Stalin.'

'Send the bastard back to the Gulags,' Stalin said wearily. 'Anything else?'

'Golden fought hard and was even nominated for the Order of Glory,' persisted Satinov.

'Politicals can't receive medals,' said Beria.

'Agreed,' replied Satinov, 'but he redeemed himself with deeds of bravery and shed blood.'

Stalin wiped his face with both hands and took a pack of cigarettes out of his pocket.

'Lavrenti?' Stalin asked Beria.

Beria threw a triumphant glance at his rival, then winked. 'This case seems clear,' he stated, 'doesn't it?'

VI

The tram took Svetlana rumbling right past her bodyguard and her chauffeur, both of whom were leaning on the car and smoking outside the House of the Book. Svetlana was exhilarated. I will show them, I will show my father, she thought. I am free of them all! Stepping down from the tram, she walked across the bridge to the House on the Embankment and caught the lift to the seventh floor and let herself into the empty apartment of her cousins, the Alliluyevs.

And there sitting at the kitchen table was Lev Shapiro.

'My new article will be in tomorrow's paper,' he told her, getting up. 'My editor's pleased with me. I am his favourite. Stalingrad is going to be the greatest battle of the war, and tomorrow I'm going back there, with papers allowing me access to headquarters with General Chuikov and Satinov.'

'So you're leaving in the morning?' Svetlana felt a little breathless suddenly.

'Yes. I've got to go home and see my children, but also I

have an old friend who served in a Shtrafbat, who's earned his freedom, and I want to visit him in the hospital.'

'How long have we got here?'

He walked to her and took both her hands. 'It's only six,' he said. 'At least an hour.'

She sighed. 'It's lovely to be with you. I am so relieved you're OK. I thought maybe my father . . .' But he'd taken her in his arms and was kissing her.

'He just wanted to give you a fright,' said Lev eventually, 'and he did. But he has more important things to do.'

'He's a Georgian, my Lion, and you're a married man of forty.'

'That's why we're going to be very careful and maybe not see each other for a while.'

'Really?'

'Yes.'

'You're probably right,' Svetlana said reluctantly. 'But can we keep kissing now?'

After much kissing, Lev smiled at her: 'After the war, everything's going to be easier. There'll be a thaw — that's what everyone says. But don't worry, little Lioness.' He stroked her hair and looked into her eyes. 'Nothing is going to happen to me.'

VII

'On reflection,' Beria announced to Stalin and Satinov in the Little Corner, 'this case isn't so simple. Comrade Stalin, may

I advise that, in my view, this prisoner deserves your reprieve. I recommend letting Golden work in Moscow.'

Satinov was surprised and had a hard time concealing it, but recovered enough to push his advantage. 'Comrade Stalin, he wants to teach literature. There is a vacancy at a Moscow school.'

'Pah.' Stalin waved his hand and sat back behind his desk. 'You two agree too much. Is this a conspiracy against the Central Committee?' A dangerous moment. Beria and Satinov were about to deny this when Poskrebyshev appeared at the door.

'Comrade Molotov here to report on the visit of Churchill.'

'Comrade Churchill.' Stalin grinned. 'He's our greatest enemy. I wouldn't trust that diehard imperialist. Roosevelt plays for high stakes but Churchill, he'd pick my pocket for a kopek, yes a kopek. Now he's coming to see us.' He paused, recalling the previous conversation. 'Give that bastard-writer a job in one of our best schools, Satinov.'

Satinov realized that Stalin did not believe Golden was a terrorist. Perhaps he didn't believe many of the cases against the thousands, even millions, he had sentenced to Vishka and Gulag. But they had been sentenced because that was what was necessary to keep the Soviet Union safe. A chilling thought – but this was the Bolshevik way: better to kill ten thousand innocents than spare one enemy.

'We need good teachers. We can always shoot him later, eh?' Stalin smiled his tigerish smile, and his yellow eyes glinted. 'Later? A movie tonight? *Jolly Fellows* again? At my place? Good.'

Beria and Satinov walked out through the antechamber into the corridor.

'You supported me?' said Satinov in Georgian. 'That's a first. What's come over you, Lavrenti Pavlovich?'

'I wasn't going to admit any mistakes in there but your friend Golden almost ruined that operation. I was a minute from having him shot like a partridge. But he surprised us: he corrected his mistake and saved my arse.' Beria smirked. 'Exceptional case.'

'Yes,' said Satinov, 'it must have been.'

Shortly before midnight, at his home, the Nearby Dacha at Kuntsevo, a plain two-storey mansion painted khaki-green, Stalin was piling his plate with Georgian meat stew. The spices curled through the high-ceiled room as Satinov, Molotov and Mikoyan helped themselves. Seeing that Stalin wanted a word with Beria they stood back and kept their distance. They still had to sit through that damn ridiculous film *Jolly Fellows*, which they had seen about twenty times here and which they knew by heart. Stalin even hummed through some of the songs. Satinov would sit behind Stalin if he could; this way he might be able to sleep.

'Josef Vissarionich,' said Beria, 'Svetlana played a trick on Klimov this afternoon and vanished for a while. She's home again now.'

'She's seeing the Jew again?'

'Possibly.'

'Love has as much to do with boredom as anything else,' said Stalin softly but inside he was fuming. He thought of the ways he and Beria had removed people, how they relished the ingenuity of the 'black work' they did together. One man, one problem, Stalin used to say, no man, no problem. A shot in the back of the head was sometimes too obvious. An injection from a doctor occasionally did the job. Or a faked car crash. Or a home burglary that ended in a massacre. He considered all these options for Shapiro. But he had to be careful. His daughter was involved. Nonetheless, his pride as a Georgian father had been affected, and this insolent hack had disrespected him. Most people feared him but not this Shapiro. What a bungling clumsy fool Svetlana was. He would have to marry her off soon – to a respectable Soviet youngster, Beria's son Sergo maybe or Yuri Zhdanov or one of Satinov's boys. But what to do now? 'Did you check out Shapiro?'

'We did.'

'A British secret agent?'

'Quite possibly. American, more likely. He has a taste for American literature. What would you like me to arrange?'

VIII

The clocks on each ward of the hospital chimed midnight, the end of the tenth day of Benya's war, and he had a visitor.

'You're my only friend who knows I am even here,' said Benya.

'Or even alive!' added Lev Shapiro. 'What are you going to do? Any idea?'

'I've had a visit tonight from a schoolmistress who offered me a job.'

'So you are becoming a teacher? That was quick.'

'I had big help.'

'Impressive, my dear. But tell me, how did you survive out there, in the Camps?'

Benya sighed. 'I lived each minute and each day as it came. I sought joy in the smallest things. I looked at the stars and the moon and thought that those I love might be looking at them too. Moon magic.' He looked at Shapiro searchingly: 'You're in love, Lev. With someone you shouldn't be.'

'You know all that? Just by looking at me?'

'We Galitzianers can see through each other and I know how dangerous it is. Believe me, I know.'

'How did you guess now?' asked Shapiro. 'I just met her this afternoon, secretly of course. Oh, she's so sweet, but very clever.'

'Who is it? Let's think. Who's the most unsuitable wife in Moscow for you to choose? Molotov's wife?'

'Oh, she's no one's wife. She's someone's daughter.' Lev leaned forward to whisper.

Benya held up both hands. 'Don't tell me her name. I don't want to know. No names! That's what we learned in the Zone. My name is Nothing, my surname is Nobody. Just tell me the story! Oh, I love an intrigue. How did it start?'

'Well,' said Shapiro, 'one day I got a letter from a fan . . .'

As he came down the steps of the Central Military Hospital, still chuckling to himself about his conversation with Benya, who so understood the excitement of a love affair, Lev Shapiro stopped.

In the foyer a general and some men, with NKVD tabs, were waiting. Lev knew immediately they were there for him, and what was going to happen. He was either going away, far away, for a long time, or he would die that night in a cell under the Lubianka. He would probably never see Svetlana or his wife or his children again. He had miscalculated everything.

Patting the pockets of his jacket, he acted as if he had left something behind. 'Oh no, hell, I left my case upstairs . . .' he said, turning back up the steps, trying to move calmly, not to run, to sprint, to scream.

As soon as he was on the next landing, he asked a nurse, 'Is there another staircase?'

'Yes, straight down the corridor.'

He walked fast, faster; now he was running to the other staircase, down the steps and before he reached the bottom, he crouched down and . . . there they were, more NKVD uniforms. He turned and raced up the steps. Now he was pouring sweat, his heart was throbbing, and he was feeling nauseous. Oh my God, how could I have been so foolish? he shouted to himself. But what could he do? There was nowhere to run. He could try to get back to his home to see his wife and children and say goodbye, but they would be waiting for him there. Running would just make this worse. Besides, they had covered both staircases and lifts.

He found himself walking up the stairs towards Benya's ward with a feeling of freefalling through a void. He felt guilty about his family. If he was shot, his wife might be told 'Prisoner Shapiro has been sentenced to twenty-five years — *without right of correspondence*', which usually meant someone had received the Eight Grammes. Or they might be told 'Article 158. Twenty years' and they would guess he was just about alive, if he survived the journey to Kolyma, if he didn't die of exhaustion. Either way, he might be gone forever.

If only he could get a letter to Svetlana . . . but there was so little time . . .

He peered down the long corridor and there they were: the Chekists were walking right towards him, looking into each ward. He spun round and it was too late: they held his arms.

'Lev Shapiro?' asked the general.

'Yes.'

'Come with me. We've got a car outside. Do you know who I am?'

'No,' said Shapiro.

'I am General Vlasik, Chief of Security for the Head of the Soviet Government. You understand what this means?'

Shapiro nodded. 'It might mean any number of terrible things.'

'Prepare for all of them,' said Vlasik.

Epilogue

I

'Dear friends, beloved romantics, wistful dreamers!' said the new teacher of literature, Benya Golden, to his class at the Josef Stalin Commune School 801. Limping into the classroom with the help of his flamboyant walking-stick, he jumped on to the wooden platform at the front.

He had their attention immediately.

After the arrogant bombast of Dr Rimm, the senile babblings of Dr Noodelman, the droning sincerity of Director Medvedeva, they could see this one was a different species altogether. There were rumours about his past, his sins, his war – but no one knew anything and they never would. And conversely, Benya was enjoying a new life, teaching Pushkin, Tolstoy, Gorky, the classics.

It was winter in Moscow, December '42, and at Stalingrad in the south, now clad in snow, fettered in ice, Stalin had sprung his giant trap and the Russians were strangling the German Sixth Army. Benya had found a little apartment so he could walk to work, and although on his first day in the school common room he had experienced the hostility of Dr Rimm, who smelled his flawed past, he had the support of Director Medvedeva, who was proud to recruit such a distinguished teacher of literature. Of course she had made enquiries with the Central Committee, Education Department, which was curated by Comrade Satinov, and with the Organs, and all had signed off on her appointment of Benya Golden.

He looked out over his class. 'Open your books. *Eugene Onegin* by Alexander Pushkin. I hope you will always remember what we're going to read today. We are about to go on a wonderful journey of discovery.'

On that first day, Benya noticed that there was a girl named Stalina who sat next to one called Peshkova at the back of his class. He could only wonder at the vagaries of this world where a man could travel from a death sentence for planning to assassinate Stalin one day to teaching his daughter about *Onegin* the next. He paid no attention to her but when he handed back their first essays, he saw each child in turn for a tutoring session after class. After all, he had nothing better to do. He was living quietly, and had no wish to become the flâneur of the 1930s — that had cost him dear. He was just happy to breathe the free air.

When he talked to Peshkova, he told her that he had known her grandfather Gorky, who had corrected his first articles. 'I was a writer once,' he said.

Then it was the turn of Stalina. He saw no resemblance to her father. Perhaps she was more like her mother? Her essay showed her intelligence, her culture. He talked to her frankly, as if she was anyone else. And he wondered about her. He agonized. Just when he was free again, he faced this dilemma that could entangle him in her family. But also he knew about Love, its agony and its necessity for living, and tried to keep the memories of his own loves – of which there were really only two – fresh in his mind. There had been his first mature love, the fatal liaison with Sashenka; and those hurried days, hours really, with Fabiana. He saw their ride across the Don, and the moment she died. What an exceptional person she had been, how I let her down by failing to protect her, he thought. Whether my home is a small apartment or a prison cell, loving is what keeps the stars in my sky. You give up one truth after another, you compromise every day, but you always hold something back – you keep the jewels in the secret casket locked with the golden key in the final alcove within the unbreakable strongroom of the last tower of the fortress of your self – and *that* you *never* give up.

'Teacher Golden?'

He looked into the hazel eyes of the freckly and rather imperious redhead before him in her school uniform and Pioneers' scarf. What a curse it was to be the child of great men, especially this one. Was she reliable? Would she betray him? He wavered, holding back the essay.

'Is there anything else, Teacher Golden?' she asked.

What the hell! He handed back the essay written in her curved girlish hand. 'You write well,' he said. 'A plus. And, Stalina?'

'Yes?'

'Go somewhere on your own and look carefully at my comments.'

Svetlana went into the ladies' room at the school and opened her essay carefully, page by page, until she found a piece of paper, folded over, and held on to the last page with a paper clip. Hungrily she seized it and opened it. It was a piece of prescription pad headed 'Central Military Hospital'. Hospital? But when she opened it and recognized the writing she found herself breathing fast. She deciphered the scrawled words, understanding they were written in the hieroglyphics of desperation . . .

Beloved Lioness,

I write this in haste. 'Our friends' wait for me downstairs. I don't know my fate but I do know I am going away. You will not hear from me. But know that I love you, that you have made my life beautiful, that I shall think of you every day. I shall search the horizon for a vision of you, for the playful brightness of your golden eyes in the rising sun, the thoughtful sensitivity of your soft mouth in the sunset, the kindness of your brow in the silver moon, and your infinite qualities of delight in the luminosity of the stars. Look at them and you will feel me looking back at you.

Love others, marry a decent man, have children, read great literature, choose stimulating friends, be kind. Live your life as if I will <u>never</u> return but <u>not</u> as if you never knew me. Live in my spirit at least, and that way, if I never return, our time together will have meant something very dear to me. And if I do return, you will be as worthy of our love as you are today.

One day, if the world still turns, my love, if the Fates are kind, I <u>will</u> come back for you.

Your Lion.

Destroy this note. Never betray its bearer, promise me this above all else!

II

More than two years had passed. The war was won, and Hitler had killed himself in the ruins of Berlin. Benya had never found his parents. He had to presume that they had perished during the war, in the streets of Odessa or in some Ukrainian ravine. He could not forget them but he often felt them close to him as he relived the blessing of an early life with loving parents. He still loved Sashenka and believed she was alive in a Camp somewhere in the vastness of Russia. And the wounds of the war were still raw to him in both senses. At night, he dreamed of Fabiana – and Silver Socks. Fabiana was already a ghost, lost in the haze over the steppes, the distance between them ever more unbridgeable, time and circumstance burning away the memory of her as the sun does with mist. He had known her such a short time.

At the Josef Stalin Commune School 801, he'd become a respected member of the staff. In his free time, he collected books that he bought in flea markets; in the evenings and some-times even during his lunch hour, he made love to a teaching assistant, marvelling at her beauty and youth and astonishing wantonness. But mostly he lived for his teaching, and had become the favourite of many of the children. Svetlana Stalina and her class had left the school but his classes were still filled with the children of the Politburo and the government. His days were ruled by the ups and downs of the school, frequently rewarding, mostly tedious and occasionally dramatic. Like everyone, he had presumed, or at least hoped, that the freedoms of the war would endure. The children had become confident and playful, so different from before the war — but there were signs those easy times were over; Benya prayed they would last . . .

Then, one morning that summer 1945, he received an envelope in his pigeonhole. Inside was just a simple note that read: 'Tomorrow 6 p.m. to midnight. Yaroslavsky Station.'

For a second, he wondered if it was Sashenka coming back. Could it be? Yaroslavsky Station was the terminus for trains from the Kolyma Zone in the far east but surely he would have somehow known if she had been there too? He had always believed Sashenka might be in the Camps to the north but Vorkuta trains arrived at a different station. He feared this could be some kind of trick by the Organs to compromise him with a *provokatsia*. But then he absentmindedly turned over the scrap of paper and saw the devil's trident, and he knew he had to be there.

I live, he thought, in the realm of stations, of leaving and returning and leaving again. Stations were surely one of the essences of Russian life.

He waited out the next day, and around 6 p.m., after school, he arrived at Yaroslavsky Station under the Russian Revival tower that looks like a bishop's hat. It was a drowsy summer's night. He walked along the line of platforms but it was easy to find the right one. MVD guards in their blue epaulettes were already guarding the terminus. He took his place in that very Russian gathering of those who await the return of loved ones who have fallen into the abyss. No real Russian novel, Benya thought, would be complete without a station scene — every book should have one. Looking around him, he saw people who had learned to become almost invisible during the years of their eclipse appear out of the shadows of the station: the wan wife with her young children, never seen by their father; the old woman who had waited decades for the return of the ruin of a man who would arrive on the next train.

'If their relatives look like carcasses, imagine what the passengers are going to look like.' Benya turned and there was Smiley, still in uniform, visored cap pulled low, and Little Mametka, still elfishly callow – but both now decorated Soviet officers tempered by war, Smiley a captain, Mametka a lieutenant. Both were wearing the new Stalin-imperial uniforms, golden buttons, chunky gilded shoulderboards, red stars.

'Just as well you came,' said Smiley.

'We've missed you,' added Mametka malevolently, the threat implicit though Benya had no idea what they had on him. He had wondered whom exactly he was waiting for. The devil's trident was a signal from the underworld, one unwise to ignore: surely from Jaba the Brigand-in-Power? He was just about to ask but Smiley held up his hand: 'Don't ask. Duties and rewards, that's what Jaba always said, remember?'

'We can say we're welcoming back a friend,' Mametka promised.

'Well, this is a dreary party,' said Smiley. They leaned on the railings chain-smoking, waiting for the train. The hours passed. Smiley bought a bottle of vodka; the three of them drank shots while nibbling greasy *pirozhki* and tepid *pelmeni*, station-food.

'I helped capture Vienna,' said Mametka. He had neither grown nor had his voice deepened despite all the battles he said he had fought. But his face had thinned out, and now he looked more shrivelled and fiendish than before, the lips too red, fat enough to burst.

Smiley had stormed Berlin in Marshal Zhukov's armies. 'You wouldn't believe the girls we had. As many as we wanted,' he told Benya. 'Girls and watches! See?' He pulled up his sleeves and cackled: three Swiss watches on each wrist. 'And I saw exactly where they burned Hitler's body.'

They talked about girls, fights and crimes, but never Kolyma, nor the Shtrafbat. Former Zeks did not talk about such things, certainly not in a bar. And besides, Benya was wary of the two Criminals, and getting more nervous by the minute about what Jaba would want.

The clocks struck 1 a.m., 2 a.m., and they ordered more bottles. Then the guards started to take up positions again, and just after 3 a.m., a train emerged out of its own cloud of steam, the doors opening and figures stepping out from the mist.

Benya, Smiley and Little Mametka moved closer, in a crowd of others. The returnees, haggard men and ancient women with sunken faces, appeared slowly, holding their belongings in bundles of string, bags of canvas, burlap or carpet, their watery eyes searching through the crowd. Showing their papers at the gates, they received their stamps – and then fell into the arms of weary relatives.

A powerful man, blue tattoos lapping up his neck, strode up the platform, quite unlike his meagre fellow travellers, and embraced Smiley and Mametka: it was Deathless. Uneasily, Benya observed their lugubrious bonhomie, their almost incomprehensible Criminal patois, fearing what monster would rear up out of his past to ruin his present.

'You have it?' Smiley was asking.

'Oh yeah, I have it!' said Deathless.

'Well, let's see it then. The writer's here!'

'Is Jaba not coming?' Benya asked.

'Maybe he is,' said Deathless. 'Or maybe you just get me.'

'What are you looking at us for?' Smiley was pointing at the train. 'Keep watching.' Through the steam, like a cavaderous foreign army emerging out of a fog-draped battlefield, came a host of men in foreign uniforms. Benya spotted some Romanians in brown. A few Hungarians. Each nationality sticking close to their own people, forming a capsule of their homeland around with them wherever they ended up.

'Prisoners going home,' explained Smiley.

'We taught them who was master in the Zone,' said Deathless, smoking.

Going home. Benya glanced at the brigands who were smirking beside him.

'They're not free yet,' added Smiley. 'Still being guarded. They have to cross Moscow to Kievskaya Station.'

'And where do they change for . . . ?'

'Bucharest, I suppose,' said Benya. He didn't like this game at all.

'No, Rome. Or maybe Venice,' said Smiley.

'What do you mean?'

'Look.' Mametka was pointing. 'Look at those uniforms, there! They're *Italians*.'

Smiley gave his metallic grin, and Benya winced in pain at the very thought of his own private Italy, his Venice lost.

Some of the prisoners were close now to the gates and of course they were Italian: even the Zone couldn't quite grind all the gloss out of them. The thought of Fabiana stung Benya with unbearable sadness. He wanted to tell these broken Italians, 'I once knew one of you. Very well, for a short time. A nurse from Venice? Yes, that's her! Fabiana who died back in '42 – did you know her?' But he would immediately be denounced as a Fascist fraternizer, a collaborator with the invaders who had almost destroyed Russia. Yet the Criminals knew something and he feared what was coming. And then it occurred to him – perhaps someone had talked? Sensing that the times were getting dangerous again, the possibilities for disaster started to eat at him.

At the gate, the Italians showed their papers for another check; and then they were surrounded by MVD troops with blue shoulderboards and guns on their arms, who started to march them slowly through the station, watched by a few morose Russians.

One older Italian, a swarthy one with a grey beard, almost tripped, and an MVD guard gave him a shove: still prisoners. Benya wanted to look into their eyes, wanted them to know that he wished them luck, that he didn't want to join in their humiliation.

And then he noticed that one of the Italians was staring right at him, and he turned, and there under a peaked cap was a woman with brown eyes. It couldn't be. She was dead – but there she was, and she was smiling at him, right at him, just a few feet away. She was much older, drawn and pale, but still so much herself. She had just a filigree of grey frost at her temples. She had recognized him, and her extraordinary honeyed eyes shone with such a radiant delight that he wanted to shout out, 'Fabiana! I never forgot you – I still think of you every day, I still dream of you!' He pushed himself

378

forward – but Smiley and Mametka gripped him so hard that it hurt. 'Careful, you fool!' said one.

'Say a word and I'll cut your tongue out,' said the other.

'Can it really be her?' Benya whispered.

But it was, and she was waving her right hand, fingers together, in the gesture that he had not seen since that last day – the bear gathering honey! Tears were running down his face, and he was mouthing the words to her, two important words, and she was mouthing them back.

She turned, reached behind her, and lifted something up. For a second he thought she had dropped her bag. Then he saw she was holding a little person, a small girl whose bright blue eyes looked right into his. She looked like a photograph of him as a baby, one that had stood in pride of place on the mantelpiece at the family home in Lvov and then in Odessa.

But the guards were pushing them on. 'Hey, prisoner, no stopping! Hurry up!'

Fabiana stayed still, holding up the child, and she was pointing at Benya and he heard her, that unforgettable voice saying clearly and loudly in her singsong Italian, 'Aurelia, *guarda quell'uomo*! Look at that man! Aurelia, *mia dolce amata bambina*, see that man!'

Spotting a delay, the guards were shoving them and she was passing, her face still turned towards him. He had to say something, he had to follow, but Smiley's hands, those claws accustomed to break and hold, were clamped on him and he couldn't move – yet he felt the wings of the angel of the past fluttering over him, taking to the sky, coming back to life.

Now they were disappearing, the little girl waving, and Fabiana still repeating those two words, over and over,

'Somehow forever, somehow forever,' and Benya was making their silly honey sign and she saw it and she smiled, tears pouring down her face too, half covered by her little Aurelia, who was still waving – with that smile that was entirely his.

Only once they were gone, warded into the buses waiting outside, did the Criminals release him slowly.

'See, Deathless, he almost ruined everything,' said Smiley.

'Look at him now – sobbing like a girl!'

'Lucky we had that shot of vodka!'

'Did you see her?' cried Benya. 'Did you see the child?'

'Quieter!' Smiley ordered. 'What do you have to say to us?'

'Thank you! Thank you!' He hugged them, Smiley, then Mametka, then Deathless.

'Oy, get down, bitch,' said Deathless, pushing him away.

Smiley waved a finger at him: 'Don't get queer on us now.'

Benya remembered himself and understood the danger. They had given him this gift but it was more than enough to get him the Eight Grammes or sent back to Kolyma.

'How did you know?'

'I was with Elmor's partisans when we ambushed an Italian cavalry squadron chasing a Russian man and an Italian woman on horseback,' said Smiley. 'Comrade Elmor ordered "Fire the Dashkas!" and I fired one and Mametka here fired the other. Blew some holes out of them. And you got away.'

'But how did you discover she was alive?'

'I was the one that captured her,' said Little Mametka. 'The Italian officers received a direct hit. Blown to pieces most of them but she was right there – scratched and cut up, but nothing serious. We would have finished her off like we did with the Germans – she was beyond having any fun with – but

Elmor said she might have useful intelligence. So we sent her back, and off she went to Magadan for two years. She was a nurse, so guess where she ended up? The hospital. That's where she had the baby. It was Jaba who put it all together.'

'Jaba has an old-fashioned idea of right and wrong, of loyalty,' said Deathless.

'The devil's trident?'

'We're all his,' said Smiley. 'Sworn for life. If you obeyed the summons, you'd get this reward.'

'So what does Jaba want in return?'

'Here.' Deathless reached into his canvas bag and pulled out the file. Benya opened it and there was the manuscript, typed by the secretaries in the Commandant's office. 'It's draft seven of Jaba's play. He wants your comments, says he's been waiting for them for years and he's got a bit stuck. He says he's got something called writer's block and that you were always the best teacher.'

'That's it?'

'That's it. For now. Goodbye, Golden. We've got an apartment of watches and jewels from mansions and museums across Europe. In other words, we've got work to do,' said Smiley.

'But how do I give my comments to Jaba?'

'Send a letter,' replied Deathless. 'He gets his mail. Goodbye, writer-in-residence.'

As the three Criminals walked away, Benya remembered something else. As Fabiana had passed, he'd heard a metallic ching, the sound of a small object dropped in a crowded station. He got down on his haunches, groaning a bit from his old wound, and then on all fours and searched the filthy floor.

And he saw it: a key with a label. He stood up and turned it over in his hands. The label was light leather now much aged and worn but the words were still visible: 'Only special personnel. Magadan Hospital. KOLYMA.'

Smiling that he had just seen the most 'special personnel' on earth, Benya staggered through the archways of the station out into the deserted streets of Moscow, dazzled and drunk with happiness and yearning. So *this* was the meaning of the crone's prophecy – *this* was the child she foresaw, saved by the kind doctors of Magadan.

Would it be better if he had never known that Fabiana was alive and that his daughter Aurelia was in the world? He would never be able to kiss her, and that pain scorched him. And yet he was grateful that he did know. In a distant city, in Venice perhaps, Aurelia would look at the same sky as him, the same stars. Moon magic.

As he walked, he stopped with a horrible thought. Would Fabiana give Aurelia her husband's name? He realized that this would be the best idea because she would not have the stigma of being illegitimate. Then it suddenly occurred to him that Fabiana, who thought of everything, had thought of this too: Aurelia *did* have his name. 'Aurelia' meant 'Golden' – and this touched him to the depths of his heart.

'Oy, you walked right into me, you fucking dog's prick,' said Deathless. 'Are you disrespecting me?'

'Leave him alone,' said Smiley. 'He's talking to himself like a madman and sobbing like a bitch.'

Benya had bumped into the three of them outside the station.

'He's lost his mind, the motherfucker!' said Little Mametka.

Smiley poked Benya in the side. 'Pull yourself together,

cocksucker! Bye then!' As they walked off, he heard Mametka asking what was wrong with him.

'It's the Italian girl, you idiot, and he's found out he's got a brat.'

'What of it?' said Mametka. 'I've got brats all over the place.'

Smiley smacked him on the back. 'Of course you have.' He turned back and called out: 'What was the brat's name?'

'Nothing,' said Benya.

'Did you catch your daughter's name?'

'Yes. It was Nobody.'

'That's the way to survive! Anything is possible but everything is a secret. You'll read Jaba's play?'

'Yes, I will,' said Benya, smiling through his tears. And he found he was fiddling with the key and its label. Under a streetlamp, he saw that on the raw leather of the disintegrating little label were some words that he could barely decipher. The ink had smudged on the soft leather but he turned it back and forth in the light until he could read what Fabiana had written:

You gave me this key to remember you.

Now I give it back because you gave me something better.

This is to help you remember us.

Somehow forever.

Author's Note

FICTION AND FACT

This is a work of fiction. The main characters, Benya, Fabiana, Jaba, Panka, Melishko, Kapto and many others, are entirely imagined and so is the story and the plot – and it should be enjoyed as a novel, no more no less.

Some of these characters, especially Benya and Satinov, appear in the other two novels in my series, *Sashenka* and *One Night in Winter*. This now completes my Moscow Trilogy, but this novel – like the others – stands alone. There is a special pleasure in writing about characters and families that one has come to know well – like old friends. This is a novel about love, survival, courage, life and death at a time and place of astonishing horror in what was perhaps the most atrocious moment in the human experience. It is also about a short, desperate relationship between a soldier and a nurse; all these novels are really about the agony and the magic of love – in any circumstances. And of course it is a novel of action, of horsemen on the steppes of Russia – and one of my favourite characters is not a human at all but a horse, Silver Socks.

Anyone interested in the novel's plot, in my inspirations and in great books on these subjects should read on. The background of the penal battalions, Cossacks, Italians and Russian defectors are lesser-known parts of World War II history but many of the characters are instantly recognizable: Stalin, his daughter Svetlana and son Vasily, his henchmen Beria and Molotov, and his marshals Vasilevsky and Zhukov are accurate portraits, as is Budyonny, Cossack and breeder of the Budyonny horses. Many of the things Stalin says are based on his own words: for example sometimes he did telephone quite junior officers to encourage and threaten them in the heat of battle. The bizarre but fearsome idiosyncrasies of Stalin's system of terror and favour are accurate too. As is the case with my character Melishko, some of Russia's greatest generals were prisoners in Camps or prisons, having been arrested and tortured by Beria, but when the Nazis invaded on 22 June 1941 they were suddenly restored to their rank and welcomed by Stalin as if nothing had happened.

My Cossacks, their lore and songs and behaviour, are based on three masterpieces, first *Red Cavalry* and *1920 Diary* by Isaac Babel, which tell how a Jewish writer rode with the Red Cossacks during the Civil War, and then Mikhail Sholokhov's novel *And Quiet Flows the Don*, set amongst Don Cossacks during World War I. I have used these as sources for my Soviet horsemen. For the Italians in Russia, I have used as my source *The Sergeant in the Snow* by Mario Rigoni Stern, a novel/memoir that deserves to be read more.

Svetlana did have a love affair with an older Jewish screenwriter but actually it took place a year later than it does in the novel and his name was Alexei Kapler, not Lev Shapiro. He really did have the chutzpah to address her in a newspaper article and some of the story is based on Svetlana's memoirs *Twenty Letters to a Friend*. As research for my histories I interviewed Martha Peshkova Beria, who appears in the novel: she was the granddaughter of the novelist Maxim Gorky and she married Beria's son Sergo, who also features. When I interviewed her she was still a beautiful woman. To learn more on Stalin and these other characters, see my *Stalin: The Court of the Red Tsar*.

In the novel, Hitler appears at his Ukrainian headquarters at Vinnitsa (code name: Werwolf). On 28 June 1942, he launched his southern offensive, Case Blue, to knock the Soviet Union out of the war. During the fighting on the plains, the villages are invented and so is the entire plot that takes place there but the battles of the Don Bend are real; the crisis was dire. Stalin, faced with this relentless German advance, created the penal battalions in his *Not One Step Back* decree 227 – and Benya's experiences reflect how they worked, based on *Penalty Strike: The Memoirs of a Red Army Penal Company Commander* by A. V. Pulcyn. I have also used the classic books – Antony Beevor's *Stalingrad* and *Absolute War* by Chris Bellamy. To create a realistic Soviet war journalist in Lev Shapiro I read *A Writer at War* by Vasily Grossman (edited by Antony Beevor and Luba Vinogradova).

The peculiar but horrifying hell of the gold mines and Gulag Camps of Kolyma is based on many books but particularly *Man is Wolf to Man* by Janusz Bardach who survived them; *Gulag Boss* by F. V. Mochulsky, an unusual account by a Gulag guard; and the classic history *Gulag* by Anne Applebaum. For those intrigued by Jaba's tattoos, read *Russian Criminal Tattoos* by D. Daldaev and S. Valiev.

My espionage plot of Stalin's effort to misinform Hitler is totally invented. In my fictional conceit he deploys an agent to lure *more* German forces into the Stalingrad trap. In fact, Stalin only realized the potential to trap and surround German forces later during the battle. But Soviet intelligence specialized in just this sort of operation: later in the year, when Stalin launched Operation Uranus to encircle the German Sixth Army in Stalingrad, he used a double agent, Heine, to warn the Germans that he was about to launch a huge offensive, Operation Mars, around Rzhev further north – in order to dissuade the Germans from sending reinforcements to aid their beleaguered forces in Stalingrad. In effect Stalin was betraying one group of armies in order to help another; his ruthlessness cost hundreds of thousands of Soviet lives; Rzhev became known as the Slaughterhouse. But Stalingrad was won.

The summer campaign of 1942 was the last use of cavalry in warfare on a large scale.

Both the Soviets and the Germans used millions of horses at the front, not only to pull artillery and supplies but also for their speed on the steppes: in 1940, the Red Army had around twenty million cavalry horses of which around ten million were lost in the initial campaign so Stalin had a reserve of around ten million. The Red Army started the war with around four cavalry divisions – about 115,000 cavalrymen – but the destruction of tanks during 1941 led Stalin to create another eighty-seven cavalry divisions in early 1942 so that at the time of this novel there were over 500,000 sabres of cavalry including many Cossack units. Meanwhile the Germans had six cavalry divisions on the Eastern Front as well as SS cavalry units. They also deployed four regiments of Cossacks who had defected from the Soviet side and Kalmyk cavalry corps too. The Italians,

Romanians and Hungarians, who were less mechanized than their German masters, fielded even more cavalry.

By the summer of 1942, the Italian army in Russia numbered 235,000 men, reinforced by Mussolini, who did not want to miss out on a German victory. Few Italians supported this mission – except his special Fascist troops, the Blackshirts, led in the novel by Malamore. Absurdly Mussolini did invent Roman ranks for his Blackshirts, such as 'consul', and their units were named 'legions' because he was hoping to create his own Roman empire. The Italians fielded the 3rd Cavalry Division Amedeo Duca d'Aosta with a total of 25,000 horses. They were extremely proud of their famed cavalry regiments such as the Savoia Cavalleria and they did win a few successes: on 24 August 1942, the Savoy Cavalry launched a spectacular headlong charge, one of the last in history, against Soviet infantry and routed them at Izbushensky near the Don River. Albino, one of the Italian horses, was blinded in the charge but lived on as an equine hero until 1960. But ultimately the Italian adventure in Russia was a catastrophe that shook the Fascist regime. They were destroyed in the Battle of Stalingrad where 25,000 Italians were killed and 60,000 captured and they had to fight their way out. Altogether it is believed around 90,000 Italians were killed in Russia. The return of the cadaverous survivors speeded the fall of Mussolini, who was deposed in 1943.

In the novel, defectors from the Soviet side such as Mandryka and Kaminsky, Tonya and the doctor, are based in fact. Like Mandryka, the founder of a pro-Nazi militia of Russians named Konstantin Voskovoinik was assassinated by partisans in January 1942. But he was succeeded by Bronislav Kaminsky, who built up his security unit into his Russian National Liberation Army, later transformed into a Waffen-SS unit, more usually known as the Kaminsky Brigade, which assisted in the murder of civilians and Jews and the suppression of partisans. He was allowed to rule a small area of Belorussia, the so-called Lokot Republic. Soviet partisans repeatedly tried to assassinate him. He served alongside various murderous SS units including that of degenerate German SS officer Oskar Dirlewanger, who also appears in the novel with his penal brigade of German criminals and psychopaths who murdered and tortured hundreds of thousands of Jews, Russians and Poles. Kaminsky was decorated with the Iron Cross by Himmler. In 1944 the Kaminsky and Dirlewanger Brigades helped crush the Warsaw Uprising, during which Kaminsky and his deputy Shavykin killed tens of thousands of Polish civilians, looted brazenly and were so out of control that in August they were executed by the order of Himmler himself. The Dirlewanger Brigade helped murder tens of thousands in Warsaw. In June 1945, Dirlewanger was arrested by the French and died in custody, possibly beaten to death by his Polish guards. Even by the grotesque standards of the SS, Kaminsky, Dirlewanger and their men were extreme monstrosities. For more, see Mark Mazower's excellent *Hitler's Empire*; and a personal story, Rita Gabis's powerful quest for her grandfather's role in the Holocaust, *A Guest at the Shooter's Banquet*.

Tonya is based on one of Kaminsky's executioners, a girl named Antonina Makarova, nineteen years old, who joined his unit and, while drinking heavily and having sexual liaisons with German officers, specialized in mass executions which she called 'cutting the nettles' – killing 1,500 civilians. At the end of the war, the Soviet secret police searched for her, never giving up the hunt – but she had vanished, marrying (possibly a Jewish husband, named Ginzburg) and having two children. She was only exposed over thirty years later in 1978 by a coincidence. In maybe the last execution for World War II atrocities, she was shot in 1979.

Hundreds of thousands of Soviet citizens defected to the Germans or volunteered to serve them, as many as 600,000 or even a million: these Hiwis – *Hilfswillige*, meaning 'voluntary assistants' – performed a variety of tasks, from guarding Nazi death camps to fighting at the front. It was estimated that during the Battle of Stalingrad, 20 per cent of German manpower were ex-Soviet citizens. Some 250,000 served as auxiliary security police, known in German as the Schuma, who appear in the novel; and around 50,000 served in regular German units. Hitler resisted the creation of any Russian forces because he regarded Slavs as subhuman *Untermenschen* and feared they would try to create a strong nationalist Russia after the war. But, later, a captured Soviet general Andrei Vlasov was allowed to form a Russian Liberation Army that fought the allies in the last year of the war.

Around 5,000 Kalmyks fought for the Germans and Italians, often serving as scouts. As for the Cossacks, many had fought against the Soviets during the Civil War and loathed the Communists. The Germans formed their first unit of defecting Don Cossacks in December 1941 and ultimately there were around 25,000 Cossacks fighting for Hitler: they were used for anti-partisan actions in Russia and later in the Balkans. To be fair, far more Cossacks served with the Red Army – seventeen corps on the southern fronts as opposed to just two corps of German collaborators. After the war, the Cossack and Russian collaborators captured by Britain were handed over to the Soviet secret police who either executed them or despatched them to the Gulags.

Finally the Germans issued their troops with Pervitin, a methamphetamine that allowed them to overcome fatigue and fight more viciously; the pills were addictive and often abused by units involved in the Nazi genocidal mass murders. They were nicknamed Stuka-tablets since their extreme ups and downs resembled the flight of the Stuka dive-bombers.

In many ways this is meant to be a homage to some of my favourite writers: I have mentioned Isaac Babel and Mikhail Sholokhov. But even though this is a very Russian, very Soviet and very Second World War novel, it is impossible to write about horsemen riding across sunbaked grasslands in times of unrelenting cruelty without recalling the brilliant Western masterpieces of Larry McMurtry, Cormac McCarthy and Elmore Leonard. This is also a homage to them.

Acknowledgements

I am hugely grateful to my superb editor and publisher Selina Walker for her delicate, energetic, tireless and sensitive editing, but also her sense of fun and comradeship on this and the other two novels – and to her assistant Cassandra Di Bello. Thank you to Mel Four, who designed this glorious cover; and to my American publishers, Jessica Case and Claiborne Hancock. Thanks to my outstanding and irrepressible super-agent Georgina Capel and her team: Rachel Conway and Romily Withington (who have now sold these novels into twenty-seven languages) and her dynamic film/TV maestro Simon Shaps. Thanks to Lorenza Smith for the Venetian and Italian details; to Jonathan Foreman for his excellent editorial advice; and to my nephew Major Johnny Hathaway-White for his invaluable expertise on cavalry lore and horsemanship.

I want to thank my dear mother April Sebag-Montefiore, once a novelist herself, who came up with the name Silver Socks – and manages to be witty, wise and acute at the age of ninety.

Thanks above all to Santa who is wife, mother, novelist, friend, partner and *consigliere* on all matters – and to my children, daughter Lily and son Sasha, who make me laugh so much, and who, together, make up our 'musketeers'.

This book is dedicated to Sasha.

Main Characters

Historical characters are marked with an asterisk

KOLYMA: 'THE ZONE'

The Prisoners of Madyak-7

Benya Golden, writer, sentenced to 25 years
Jaba Leonadze, the Brigand-in-Power, *Vor v Zakone*,
the Boss, a Georgian
Ramzan Ulibnush, 'Smiley', Chechen Criminal
'Deathless', Russian Criminal
Kuzma Prishchepa, 'Speedy', young Criminal, Don Cossack
Little Mametka, 'Bette Davis', Georgian Criminal
Dr Kapto, the 'Baby Doctor'
Tonya (Antonina) Makarova, his nurse and assistant
Nyushka, 'Bunny', nurse

SHTRAFNIKI

Yevgeny Melishko, 'the General', ex-prisoner
Senior Lieutenant Pavel Mogilchuk, NKVD officer,
Head of the Special Unit

Captain Vladimir Ganakovich, *Politruk*, Political Officer
Captain Leonid Zhurko, officer
Sergeant Pantaleimon Churelko, 'Panka', Don Cossack,
veteran of World War 1
Garanzha, 'Spider', Zaparozhian Cossack
Ismail Karimov, 'Koshka', 'the Cat', Uzbek

THE ITALIANS

Major Ippolito Bacigalupe
Fabiana Bacigalupe, nurse, his wife
Cesare Malamore, Consul (Colonel) of Blackshirts
(Voluntary Militia for National Security)
Major Count Scipione di Montefalcone,
Savoy cavalry officer

RUSSIAN COLLABORATORS/'HIWIS'

Konstantin Mandryka, Chief of Schuma auxiliary police
(Schutzmannschaft: 'protection team')
Bronislav Kaminsky,* deputy to Mandryka, Chief of
Schuma, later commander of the SS Sturmbrigade Kaminsky
(Russian National Liberation Army), Waffen-SS
Brigadeführer, Iron Cross

THE GERMANS

SS Obersturmführer Oskar Dirlewanger,* convicted rapist/
murderer, commander of the Nazi penal battalion known as
the 'Poachers' Brigade' and the Sonderkommando
Dirlewanger, later Oberführer, Iron Cross

THE KREMLIN

Josef Stalin,* Supreme Commander, Chairman of
the State Defence Committee, Chairman of the Council
of People's Commissars, People's Commissar of
Defence, General Secretary of the Communist Party,
'the Supremo', 'the Instantsiya'
Hercules Satinov, Soviet leader, member of the
State Defence Committee, colonel general
Lavrenti Beria,* head of NKVD Security Organs,
member of the State Defence Committee, Commissar-
General of State Security
Svetlana Stalina,* daughter of the Leader, schoolgirl
Vasily Stalin,* son of the Leader, colonel in
the air force, later general

Lev Shapiro, 'the Lion', journalist, screenwriter, war
correspondent for *Krasnaya Zvezda* (*Red Star*) newspaper